W9-BDN-853

SPIRIT IN THE FLESH

Other books by Joel Gross

THE BOOKS OF RACHEL
MAURA'S DREAM
HOME OF THE BRAVE
THIS YEAR IN JERUSALEM
THE LIVES OF RACHEL

SPIRIT IN THE FLESH

Joel Gross

E. P. DUTTON
NEW YORK

PUBLISHER'S NOTE

This novel is a work of fiction. Names, characters, places, and inci-
dents are either the product of the author's imagination or are used
fictitiously, and any resemblance to actual persons, living or dead,
events, or locales is entirely coincidental.

Copyright © 1986 by Joel Gross

All rights reserved. Printed in the U.S.A.

No part of this publication may be reproduced or transmitted in any
form or by any means, electronic or mechanical, including photocopy,
recording, or any information storage and retrieval system now
known or to be invented, without permission in writing from the
publisher, except by a reviewer who wishes to quote brief passages in
connection with a review written for inclusion in a magazine, newspaper, or broadcast.

Published in the United States by E. P. Dutton,
a division of New American Library,
2 Park Avenue, New York, New York 10016

Library of Congress Cataloging-in-Publication Data

Gross, Joel.
    Spirit in the flesh.

    I. Title.
PS3557.R58S65   1986   813'.54   85-29367
ISBN: 0-525-24418-2

Published simultaneously in Canada by Fitzhenry & Whiteside
Limited, Toronto

COBE

Designed by Fritz Metsch

10 9 8 7 6 5 4 3 2 1

First Edition

This book is for my brother Marc,
a man in touch with his spirit.

Acknowledgments

Many people helped me with this book, not only in directing my research into areas that would have otherwise remained unexplored, but into an awakening of personal feelings about the nature of medicine and the healing process. Special thanks go to Susan Forney and Lynn Goodwin for their historical research and bright dispositions. And for guidance in the literature and experience of spiritualism, my thanks to Brian Hurley and Roberta Tager. And to Linda—who once again proved herself a noble spirit by never once throwing me out of the house during the past two difficult years.

There be three things which are too wonderful for me, yea, four which I know not: The way of an eagle in the air; the way of a serpent on a rock; the way of a ship in the midst of the sea; and the way of a man with a maid.

Proverbs

There is only one disease, and one cure.
—Franz Anton Mesmer

SPIRIT IN THE FLESH

New York City, 1983

D<small>R.</small> E<small>LIZABETH</small> G<small>RANT</small> stepped into the white-walled loft, dazzled by the summer sun. Light poured through huge windows arranged along three sides of a rectangle, hushed and cool after teeming, sweltering streets. Men and women clutching cocktail glasses padded about Richard's pale metal figures, so much more at home in this rich and powerful place than in his own small apartment.

Once this space had contained a hundred immigrant girls, hunched over clattering machines, dreaming of quiet meadows and streams and lives outside the great city. As factories went, it must have been a relatively healthy place: There were the great benefits of natural light and cross ventilation. Still, Elizabeth knew well the stressful consequences of overlong workdays, of trying to accomplish too much without proper equipment or supervision, of being bombarded by a dozen alien languages. The girls who had worked in this sewing factory had been better off than others who had labored in noxious glue factories or in steaming laundries, but their lives had not been healthful, had never been allowed the possibility of joy.

"Lizzy!" said Richard, calling from across fifty feet of oak floorboards. He left a chattering group of gallery-goers so suddenly that it seemed for a minute as if they might all fall down, deprived of a center and a focus. As he walked toward her, tan and tall, dressed in linen slacks and silk T-shirt, the sunlight seemed to wrap about him, like a whirling current of bright air. But of course there was no breeze in the loft. A powerful central air-conditioning system managed to cool the space, in spite of the curtainless windows and the heat and humidity of an August day in New York.

She wished that he was as happy as he looked. But she knew that he disliked the sculpture that had been created by his own hands, as he disliked the people who had come to look at and judge this fashionable-looking work. He had wanted an exhibit in this gallery, and the gallery owner had explained very carefully the direction Richard must take with his sculpture in order to reach his goal. Elizabeth hadn't completely understood Richard's quarrel with this agreement. To her nonprofessional eye, the work on exhibition didn't seem like such a radical departure from his unsold sculpture. Besides, no one had held a gun to his head during the months he had labored putting together the pieces for this day. He had tried to rationalize that the quality of the work was good, the execution competent, even if the thematic content was clichéd. But she had little empathy over what he agonized. Exposed on a daily basis to matters of life and death, she found dramatic complaints about compromising one's artwork difficult to fathom.

"Thank God," he said, pausing for a half moment before taking her in his arms, and kissing her as if they had no audience, as if they were in the privacy of his bedroom, and had all the time in the world.

"Congratulations, darling," she said, the first words she'd said to him in person for a very long month.

"Lizzy, Lizzy," he said, "I need a doctor."

"You have a doctor," she said.

"Do I?" He looked at her in his characteristic way, his eyes concentrated with an intensity that could only be flattering. It was one of the reasons she had fallen in love with him. He listened so carefully, that she always felt called upon to tell the truth. Frequently, this meant discovering it for herself.

"You have me, darling," she said. "House calls, blood transfusions, anything you want, as long as it's not too kinky."

"Do you hate everything?"

"I've only just walked in."

"But your first impression is that it's uninteresting, panders to crass commercial tastes, and is totally without artistic merit."

Searching frantically about the room, Elizabeth tried to remember if she had seen any of the pieces before, so that he might have already told her what they "meant." But though everything looked similar to the sculptures cluttering his small apartment, these were larger, produced in the studio she never had time to visit. "My first impression," said Elizabeth, trying to recall the few catch-phrases of the art world that she had in her repertoire, "is that you haven't even asked about my vacation."

"Vacation? What vacation? You go to Texas to cut through living persons' skin and bones and take out all the bad stuff without killing them, and I'm supposed to think that's a vacation?"

"It was a vacation. I had lots of sleep, and I was only there to observe—"

"A vacation is Martha's Vineyard, okay? You want to know what a vacation is? Sardinia, Sicily, Fire Island—that's a vacation."

She paused for a moment, taking in the vehement tone of his easy remark. Suddenly she felt warmed by the fact of his desire. He had needed her, had missed her, and not as a patient needs a doctor, but as a man needs a woman. "You're right," she said.

"I'm right?" said Richard. "I'm right about something?"

"Not for the first time, and maybe not for the last time," said Elizabeth. Richard found her guilty of various crimes he believed endemic among physicians: She was unsentimental to the point of cold-bloodedness, overreliant on the intellect instead of the heart, unable to admit to having erred. In turn, Elizabeth found him oversentimental, frequently misled by emotional—instead of logical—judgments, and pigheaded. When she had decided to spend her vacation observing new surgical techniques instead of going off with Richard to a rented beach house, he had accused her of being a career-mad technocrat, while she had accused him of being insensitive to the time constraints of a fledgling surgeon. But this had been nothing more than the squabbling of lovers; they were familiar enough with each other to voice displeasure, to shout and scream when one or the other wanted to be heard.

"Do you mean that you were wrong, and that I was right?" said Richard. "That I should have taken off a month, and you should have taken off a month, and together, like normal people, we could have actually gone to a white beach and walked for miles along the sand?"

"I was wrong," said Elizabeth.

"You're sure you're a doctor?" said Richard. "You're sure you're not really some incredibly clever little nurse who forged a medical degree?"

"I'm sure," said Elizabeth.

Richard beamed. "Well then, Doctor. Please give me your diagnosis. Is it this exhibit that's making me sick, or is my illness completely psychosomatic?"

"What illness?"

Richard squeezed her smooth white hands, the nails filed down to a surgically appropriate neatness. "That's what we creative artists call a metaphor. I am not the least bit ill, unless you call fatigue illness."

"You look a little tired, darling."

"I am tired. I'm sick and tired of this whole New York thing."

The vague alarm bells that had already sounded in response to his anxious tone were suddenly growing louder and more distinct. Richard was broad-shouldered, with well-cut long hair. He was vigorous in a way that had been developed not in athletic clubs, but in wielding hammers and mallets; still, there was something about him that suggested the cross-cultivation of Soho galleries and Ivy League graduate schools. Usually, when he looked at Elizabeth, when he put his arm about her shoulders, she felt not just strength, but well-being. But today, there was little strength. It was disturbing to find him so unnerved, so unhappy.

"For the first time in years," Richard continued, "I've got my foot in the door of a decent gallery, and it's all because I've produced made-to-order garbage."

"I don't think it's garbage," said Elizabeth, knowing a beat after she had said it that her choice of words was regrettably faint praise. But then her expertise as a doctor had never centered on bedside manner. She had spent too many years assimilating facts, learning painstaking, difficult techniques to have developed what she thought of as "professional compassion."

Besides, Richard was certainly not himself. She was used to his speaking with easygoing humor, with wit, attention, and intelligence. She liked to think of him as a man satisfied with his work, his health, his present, and his future. In all these things he was completely different from any man she had ever known.

She used to wait for the true Richard to step out from behind this splendid facade; but she had learned to quit steeling herself for disappointment. It was her life that was surrounded by the dead and the dying, by cynicism and despair, not his; it was she who had better learn the secret of his beaming face rather than teach him her own thin-lipped smile.

"Finally," said Richard. "You finally gave me your first impression!" He brought his head close to hers and whispered: "The love of my life has seen my work, and does not think that it's garbage!"

"Richard, I did not say—" she began, then stopped herself short. The last thing she wanted was to get caught in an argument about his sculpture or her "superior" attitude toward his career. "Richard, I think we should leave," she said.

"Leave now?"

"Right now."

"In the midst of all this glory? At the moment of my absolutely greatest triumph?"

"Doctor's orders," said Elizabeth.

"Really? What does the doctor have in mind?"

"I'm prescribing immediate bed rest," said Elizabeth.

"God, I've missed you, Dr. Grant," he said, laughing out loud at the outrageous notion of leaving his own exhibition before it had hardly gotten under way. "Hey!" he said, picking up his personality and putting it back on as if he had only just dropped it on the floor. Turning about with exuberance and confidence, he found and grabbed hold of the gallery owner, a rail-thin young man dressed in gauzy clothing suggestive of some desert of the imagination. "I want you to meet my doctor. Isn't she gorgeous?"

"Yes, Richard," said the gallery owner. "Your doctor is gorgeous."

A minute later, they were making their escape, leaving the flabbergasted gallery owner to embellish on his artist's attack of nerves. Elizabeth wondered if she would have so whimsically escaped from an obligation of her own—a lecture, an autopsy—to be alone with the man she loved. It was upsetting to return to the city, filled with a new sense of purpose for her career—the "vacation" at the Texas clinic had done wonders for her appreciation of what surgeons can do with the proper time, facilities, and commitment—to find her lover so forlorn. She had become used to Richard's state of happiness, a happiness she liked to imagine as a continuous stream from golden childhood to glory days on the athletic field to satisfaction with artistic growth and maturation.

She knew she hadn't been paying enough attention to his signs of distress. But in spite of her love for Richard, it was difficult to take seriously the creative problems of a sculptor of scrap metal when she herself was learning surgery on four hours of nightly sleep.

"You actually do seem a little under the weather," said Elizabeth when they were out in the street, walking briskly through hot and humid air. "Are you really not feeling well?"

"Not so well," said Richard. "I'm actually fading if you want to know the truth. I'm actually on the verge of a total collapse. I think I need medical care. Intensive."

"You didn't tell me anyting about a cold on the phone."

"Who said I had a cold? You know I don't believe in colds. And if you don't believe in colds, you don't get colds. Ask Doctor Hippocrates."

"I would if I could, Richard," she said. "But since he's been dead for twenty-five hundred years or so—if he ever lived in the first place—I'll settle for the evidence of my own eyes."

"You think I have a cold, Doctor?"

"Yes."

"Well, get that fantasy out of your mind, or you might catch one."

"You don't catch a cold with your brain—" she began, but Richard interrupted her.

"You catch it with your spirit," he said, partially because he was intrigued by this newly fashionable theory, but mostly because he knew how voicing it irritated her empirical heart.

"Even if it was your *spirit* which caught cold, you could have told me about it."

"You're cutting up hearts, and I'm going to talk long-distance about a cold?"

"Not about a cold, darling," she said. "About everything. How you're feeling about the work, the exhibit. I want to hear."

Richard looked at her, as if he was once again about to jump off a tightly secured boat into wild water. "Maybe you do, Lizzie."

"There's no 'maybe,' Richard."

"I don't like to take up time that I know is very precious to you at this point in your life—no, let me finish—with matters that are not all that important in the scheme of things."

"What are you talking about?" she said. "Anything and everything that is of concern to you is of concern to me."

"Sweetheart," said Richard, "surgery is of concern to you, not sculpture, and there's nothing wrong with that. Nothing."

All she had wanted after a month's absence was to fall into a taxi, waft up the three flights of stairs to his apartment, eat five or six cholesterol-packed scrambled eggs, drink a quart of double-strength Melior coffee, and make love as long as the air conditioner held out. That he would be busy with the gallery opening the morning of her return was unfortunate; but that he would want to be reassured that his work and life were worthwhile when placed on the balance with her own would have been impossible to imagine. Richard was nothing if not confident, self-assured. His charm was the charm of one who liked to win, and didn't have to ask what would happen if he lost. She would have preferred one of his regular diatribes on the mercenary nature of contemporary physicians, or the mechanical medical training which had spawned them—full of facts and bereft of compassion.

"Richard," she said, picking up their pace through the half-deserted streets, "is this talk going to be conducive to lovemaking?"

Finally he laughed, and the laugh built and built until it was big enough to wipe away his foul mood, wild enough to return to his face and figure the spirit of the man she loved.

"Sorry," he said. "That's enough introspection and narcissism for today. Too much time talking to artists. You know what artists talk about? Money. That's how they measure their art these days. Naturally, I got a headache. Naturally, I'm falling apart waiting for you to come home. I gotta start hanging out with the interns again."

"Residents," she corrected.

"Bourgeois tax-paying members of the medical establishment," he added. "Drivers of large-engined Mercedes with M.D. plates."

When they had walked the few blocks to his Sullivan Street apartment, she almost began to apologize for not coming back sooner. "I guess I tend to rely on you too much," she said. "Don't think you could have any problems, because you're so good at everything you do. The idea that you might need my opinion about your sculpture . . ." Elizabeth let the sentence trail, waiting for him to interrupt her. But once again his handsome face was expectant and vulnerable, waiting for her reassurance.

"I do need your opinion," he said.

"Richard," she said. "What do I know about art? I haven't worked with any kind of art since I fingerpainted in kindergarten."

For a moment, she thought her words had made him a shade more serious. But then the familiar boyish smile returned to his face, and as he urged her quickly into his apartment building, he spoke in flat, conspiring tones:

"Take off all your clothes," he said.

"We're not in your apartment yet."

"It's ninety-five degrees and I haven't seen that famous body in a month." As they made it up to the fourth floor and walked to the scarred metal door of his apartment, one of half a dozen on the floor, Richard stripped off his silk T-shirt.

"This is more like the Richard I know," she said.

Smiling, he turned his back to her and put his key in the door lock to let them in. "I left the air conditioner on. Sinfully extravagant waste of kilowatt hours, but I too am desperately in need of love in the afternoon. Doctor, are you coming in?"

"Yes," said Elizabeth, her heart pounding, but not in any kind of sexual anticipation.

"What's wrong?"

"Richard, did something happen to you?"

"What?"

"To your back."

"My back?"

"Did you fall or get into a fight?"

"Lizzy, what are you talking about my back for?" He had pulled her into the apartment, frigid and dark, and closed the door behind her. Now she noticed something else: The three flights of stairs had winded him. And Richard was a man who regularly ran six miles.

"Richard, there are bruises on your back," she said, remembering to speak calmly and deliberately. She knew she was smiling her thin-lipped smile, the muscles of her face locked into yet another rigid lie. "I want to know if you have any idea how you got them."

Naturally, he hurried to the bathroom mirror, twisting his head over his shoulder in the harsh light. They were big bruises, flat and purplish, like the black-and-blue marks that could have been raised by a pounding fist. But there had been no fight, there had been no fall.

Richard, golden-skinned and clear-eyed, was smiling affably through his fear. "Hey, I *knew* God would punish me for sleeping with that gorilla last night."

Elizabeth moved closer, touched her fingers to the surface of the bruises.

"Feels better already, Doctor," he said.

"Does it hurt?"

"No. It must have been all that tossing and turning, missing you at night." Richard's smile grew a shade brighter. "Now, you're the doctor. Just tell me that it's going to be all right. Just touch me all over and tell me that everything is going to be all right."

But Elizabeth told him nothing. It was not her style as a doctor to tell patients what they or she wanted to hear. Automatically, she observed, she remembered facts, she compared symptoms.

The last man she'd seen with such enormous black-and-blue marks had been a patient. His bruises had covered not just his back, but his abdomen, hips, and thighs. He was twenty years old and had made his living in Yankee Stadium, hawking hot dogs in the stands. His mother had brought him into the emergency room. Tests had diagnosed his illness as acute leukemia.

Two weeks after being admitted to the hospital, he had died in his sleep.

PART ONE

Greece, 448 B.C.

The spirit is smothered by ignorance;
but as soon as ignorance is destroyed,
spirit shines forth,
like the sun released from clouds.

—Sankaracharya,
Atma Bodha

Chapter 1

CORINNA BELIEVED that illness was an unnatural state, certain
to pass. There were few who had traveled the long valley
trail to the Sanctuary, up the narrow, windswept ravine to the
sacred place of healing, who had returned with their illnesses
unchanged. Most diseases reached a crisis, a climax, at which
point the body's heat would either overcome what was foreign
and repugnant, or would itself be overcome in the struggle to
discharge morbid matter. At the Sanctuary of Asclepios many
who had come to be cured grew strong, corrected the imbalances
in their bodies and spirits, and lived; many others worsened,
their souls embracing death as surely as other souls reached for
life.

But blindness was unlike most illnesses. Blindness didn't
weaken the body. Neither was it destroyed by the natural heat of
the body, nor did it itself bring the body to crisis. Its baleful effect,
once done, didn't progress to threaten destruction to the life
force. Indeed, the gods favored some of the blind with the
strength of prophecy; other blind men and women had powerful
senses of hearing, taste, touch, smell; many among the blind
were strong-limbed, graceful, quick. Still, this did not mean that
blindness was natural, and not an ailment. Cataracts that clouded
the vision of the old might be a natural process, a way in which
the gods turned the thoughts of men inward before their souls
departed their earthly frames; blindness received from a wound
must be the work of gods, marking a mortal with the sign of their
displeasure. But blindness came about from many more causes
than old age or the wounds of war. Whether these were natural

causes or divine intervention in the lives of men made little difference to Corinna. In either case, one could only appeal to Asclepios.

As she moved quietly along the columned portico to where Diagoras rested on a couch in the shade, she felt the spirit of the god rise from belly to heart to throat. Corinna opened her mouth and let her lips shape the muted syllables of an ancient prayer.

"Asclepios," said the young man, the accent of nearby Athens foreign, derisive, and decadent to her ears. The athlete, beautiful as smoothly chiseled stone, lay with his head tilted toward the morning sun, eyes open and unblinking, his tunic thrown back from the single jeweled clasp at his left shoulder. "Do not pray too loudly to Asclepios, girl, or you will risk the wrath of the priests of Epidaurus."

"I am sorry if I have disturbed you," said Corinna, so softly that her words barely interrupted his own stream of sarcasm.

"It would be a pity if the god heals me before I agree to pay the priests for the cure. I understand that blindness cures are especially dear. Some say as high as twenty thousand *staters*. With so much money, we could build our own temple to Asclepios in Athens, and all we poor sick Athenians wouldn't have to brave the waters to this miserable piece of Greece."

"I am sorry if you do not like it here, Diagoras."

"Is it beautiful?"

"Yes."

"In what way is it beautiful? Do not keep me in suspense, girl. It is not hospitable."

"Well, sir, there are high walls, and we are up high, on a promontory looking down to the sea."

"What color?"

"What?"

"What color is the sea?"

"Well, it's blue," she said, as Diagoras contemptuously shifted his position on the thick cushions of the couch, turning his back to the sun's life-giving strength.

The young Athenian had come to the house of her father the night before, led by a servant at least seventy years old. Though wealthy enough to hire litters and guards and dozens of slaves, Diagoras had wanted to travel alone, walking the twisting rocky path from the port with a speed that led to frequent stumbling.

Twice he had fallen to his knees, and though a silent crowd lined the way, no one, not even the slave who accompanied him, offered him a hand.

Corinna was not the only one in the crowd who had seen him, three years before, race the last leg of the relay from Piraeus to Athens. Diagoras, son and grandson of famous warriors, had been the greatest runner among the young men of that city. Long before his military training was completed, he had competed in festivals to which Athens sent athletes. At the age of twenty-one, his participation in the traditional footrace from the port of Piraeus to Athens had attracted crowds from as far west as Sardinia, as far east as Phrygia. But most of the crowd were Athenians, citizens as well as resident aliens, all of them inordinately proud of this evidence of their city's superiority. The men who raced were the best of Athens' young soldiers, trained not simply in military drill, but in music, geometry, literature. They were chosen not just for their speed, but for the beauty of their naked bodies as they carried blazing torches through the crowds. Corinna had been a child of fourteen then, and had found a place next to her father among the foreigners watching the race.

"He is as beautiful as a god," her father had said, and Corinna had agreed. Though no other fires burned than the torches carried by the runners, Diagoras was so much talked about in the city that when his head of golden hair appeared, shining in the dancing light of his torch, a great shout went up from all those about her. He was gone in a moment, but that was long enough to remember the savage planes of his face, the wildness in his eyes, the easy lifting of his lips in a self-mocking smile, sure of his victory, and of its unimportance in the scheme of the world.

"Are you a child?" said Diagoras, suddenly.

"No. I am the wife of Coreus, priest of Asclepios."

"Are you young?" insisted Diagoras, turning about once more, bringing his dead eyes to bear on Corinna.

"I am seventeen."

"Are you pretty?"

"That is not for me to say, sir," said Corinna, embarrassed before the blind man.

"You are not very much help, woman. If great Homer had you for a helpmate, he would have left the world nothing but dull lists of names. There would have been no color, no beauty.

Imagine Homer describing the sea as blue. Is it blue at midnight, midday, at daybreak? Is it never green, never black, never boiling with white foam, never breaking into a hundred colors among the rocks of the shoreline? No, here I am in this despicable, superstitious haven, where the sea is blue, where the young wife of the priest of Asclepios is too tongue-tied to tell me whether she is at all pretty—"

"I am."

"What?"

"I am considered pretty," said Corinna.

"Are you dark or light?"

"Light. Not very light, not light like you."

"No. Of course not. I am most unusually light. One drunken poet has gone so far as to say I am blind because of the blond dye I put in my hair."

"But your hair is not dyed."

"Of course not. I am not some pretty boy who smells of perfume. I was given my blond hair by the gods, so that I could stand out at the festivals—so that my name would be cheered in every race that I ran."

"I saw you run."

"Naturally you saw me. Everyone saw me. The gods gave me my beautiful hair. Every whore in Athens paints her hair the same color. Why do I keep mentioning the gods? I do not believe in them."

" 'Whoever obeys the gods, to him they will listen,' " said Corinna.

"That is not the correct quote from the poet," said Diagoras.

"I am sorry, sir, but those are Homer's words. I have them by heart, as do all the children of my father, girls as well as boys."

"How remarkably modern of you Epidaurians. Not only to force their girls to memorize Homer's words, but to give them the audacity to contradict a citizen of Athens. If you were my wife, I would have my hands full teaching you to forget everything you have already learned."

"I am not your wife. In fact, I am your guide, and your escort to the Sanctuary."

"I do not need a guide anywhere. I have my slave."

"I do not think your slave would find his way very easily. It is two and one half hours from the city, through very rough trails.

Besides, it will be useful to you to be accompanied by a priestess. It is a great courtesy that my husband extends to you, though you are an Athenian and have already shown such disrespect for your hosts."

For the first time, Diagoras smiled. He sat up from the couch and slapped his long-fingered hands onto his bare, sun-browned knees. "Yes, you are pretty," he said. With a swift show of dexterity, he fastened the twin belts of his tunic. "Not very tall, I guess, but very pretty. You come up to here, I think." The athlete brought his hand to his mouth, large and pink in the neatly trimmed blond beard, and stood up, stepping close to Corinna, so close that his measuring hand nearly touched her forehead.

"I am taller than you imagine, Diagoras."

"Black-eyed and shapely, insolent and married to a quack and a fool." He pulled his tunic sharply down from the jeweled clasp at his left shoulder; his right arm, as tautly muscled as a discus thrower's, was free of any constricting cloth or clasp, as if he were still a man of action. The fine linen was unadorned with any foppish colored hems; pure white, its only show of wealth were the gold buckles of the tunic belts. He fastened these tightly now, blousing the bit of fabric between the belts so that he looked like a marble Ares, needing only sword or javelin to complete the warlike image.

"Please, sir. Your words are offensive to me and my household."

"Come here. I want to hold you," he said.

If he could see her, she wondered if he'd be this forward, this overweening. Perhaps all Athenians felt they could act with impunity in city-states less potent than theirs. But she was not truly offended. No matter what he said, what move he made, he was helpless.

"No," she said, stepping out of his grasping reach.

"Yes," he answered, moving deftly her way, almost as if she were a vision before his eyes, and not a shifting sound in the blackness.

"Diagoras, please. This is dangerous."

She moved more quickly now, hurrying about the carved-wood couch, taking hold of a soft cushion against her chest.

"It is never safe to love an athlete." He moved so impulsively toward her that she thought it impossible he would not trip over the hard frame of the couch; but at the last moment, he turned his body, as if some unseen god had whispered to him where to move, what to avoid, what danger blocked his way.

"Please be careful, sir."

"It is not manly to be careful."

The portico was partially in shade, partially dazzled by thick bands of morning sun. Trying to keep him away, she was afraid to move too far. There were columns, steps, urns, even pots of hyacinth and narcissus bought from a flower girl an hour before. But she found herself quickly out of breath, trying to stay within a small area about the couch. He was too fast, too sure.

"I am going to go," she insisted.

"I will follow," he said, careless about where her noisy steps would lead him.

"Please stay. Please, sir. It is not safe."

"Then kiss me," he said, lunging at her gamely. This time he missed her by a hairbreadth and as he turned wildly about, he slammed the side of his body into a portico column.

"Are you all right?" she asked in a small voice, already off the portico and onto the smooth stones of the house's interior courtyard. She watched in horror as Diagoras stepped rapidly off the portico, his powerful knees nearly buckling from the shock of the unexpected step. "Wait. Please."

"Then stay!" He hurried toward her, oblivious of danger: the uneven stones paving the sun-bright courtyard, the rough columns about the cistern, the steps leading up to Hestia's altar, where a fire burned during every festival in the year, the broken waterpots about the abandoned corner vegetable garden, victim of the dry Greek summer. Golden-haired, eyes wide open, he tripped on a stone, he fell against a column about the cistern, he banged his toes into the stone steps of the familial altar, he fell and cut his hands and knees on the fragments of the broken waterpots. Corinna hurried to him, but when she touched his elbow he pulled away.

"Don't touch me," he said. He was humiliated, and to hide his shame, he turned from passion to bitterness.

"But sir, that is what you wanted. Now you have your chance."

"I do not think you are funny, thank you," he said, ignoring the pain in his bloody palms as he pushed himself off the ground, letting the sharp bits of earthenware cut into his skin.

"Well, I did not think it was funny that you were trying to catch hold of me like some Athenian courtesan."

"In Athens our courtesans stand still."

This was too much even for her sympathy. "I am going inside, sir," she said. "You can have your pity all to yourself in the open air. May Zeus take pity on your insolence."

"Wait," he said, and though she stopped, she was very quiet about it. She would let him wonder whether or not she was giving him another chance at civility. "You. Where are you?"

"I am here," she said, wanting very badly to call the slave for fresh water and cloths to wash his cuts and bruises.

"I don't know your name."

"Corinna."

"I am sorry, Corinna. There is no excuse for my behavior. You are quite right. I deserve shame for the way I bear this burden. It is not your fault nor is it your responsibility. I am in your father's house, and I shame him and your husband, looking for a chance to shame myself."

"I would like to call the slave for some water for your hands."

"Wait. In a minute. Is the sun high overhead?"

"Yes."

"I can feel it. Not just the heat. I feel the brilliance. In my eyes." Diagoras paused, as if to carefully measure his words. "Do you think that means something?"

"Yes," said Corinna, willing the word to be truly spoken.

"You've said you've seen me run," said Diagoras.

"Yes."

"Where?"

"At Athens. The night race from Piraeus. You overtook the other runner. Everyone was shouting."

There were tears in his eyes, and she felt as if this, coupled with the heat of the open courtyard, would make her faint. But she forced herself to be still, letting the sun beat down on her uncovered head, letting his words run through her spirit like bits of fire against blackness.

"I still run," he said. "A circle is cleared for me in a field of stones. I run until my toes bang into the stones. My eyes are open, and the wind reddens my cheeks. I run at dawn and I run at dusk. Only with one slave, too old to follow me. He watches. He said that it is impossible to tell that I am blind."

"Diagoras, you have come here to ask the help of the god. You must believe that you may be helped, if the god wills it."

"Stop it," said Diagoras. "I do not believe in the god, not in Apollo, not in Imhotep, not in Asclepios."

He no longer tried to hold back the tears, and the sobs tore out of him like from a child not yet begun his schooling.

"I cannot be helped, and I cannot believe, and I am blind now and forever. Now and forever."

He let her hold him now, not like the supporter of someone blind and infirm, nor yet like a lover, but like the priestess of Asclepios that she was: Corinna held his beautiful face in her hands, letting the healing strength of her gaze soothe his troubled brow. She had heard his words, but she knew that he, like all men, was a believer.

Without gods there would be no generations, no past or present, no future. And in spite of his words, Diagoras wanted a future, and believed in the chance of a reprieve from some unknown god's stern decree. No matter what he claimed, he had come of his own will to Epidaurus. Here he would visit the Sanctuary, and with her help he would place his broken spirit in the hands of the god.

Chapter 2

A N HOUR LATER, she led him out of the city, toward the Sanctuary.

The way was steep, running along a dry, rocky valley, along
an ever-narrowing track. There was a small clustering of huts past
the walls of Epidaurus, but after this the only sign of man was
the clearly beaten ground beneath their feet. It was a climb usually made in silence, the hopeful worshippers subdued by the
austere terrain. Moment by moment the wind grew wilder as the
valley became a dry ravine, cluttered with sharp stones. But Diagoras wanted to talk, as if afraid to let the atmosphere of the
Sanctuary take possession of his heart, and he made himself
heard over the rushing wind.

"Corinna is the name of a poetess," he said.

"A Boetian. Famous for having taught Pindar to accept the
religion of his people." The wind suddenly stilled, coloring her
shouted words with an unintended pride.

"You know a great deal for such a young woman. In Athens
our girls are taught to read and write, but we do not encourage
them to read and write too much." Corinna would have answered this with a sharp comment on the shameful way women
were treated in Athens. In spite of that great city-state's power
and prestige the government turned its back on half the population, denying women political and civil rights, allowing them no
recourse against tyrannical husbands and fathers. But she was
forced into sudden action, shutting her thoughts to anything but
the blind man's safety as he nearly lost his footing. With strength,
she took hold of his elbow, pulling him back from the edge of a
great crack in the dry ground.

21

But this did not endear her to the athlete.

She watched his face redden, his lips twist as if in pain. "I do not need help in walking," he said.

"There is a break in the ground," she answered, but the wind had risen, suddenly scattering her words. Corinna repeated herself, so that he could hear.

"I have been this way for nearly a year. There have been many breaks in the ground, in many places. I am still alive."

"Diagoras," she said, the syllables harsh and insistent. "If I give you help, you had better take it. That is the way here. If you come to the Sanctuary with nothing but anger in your heart, you will leave the way you come."

"Thank you for your advice, priestess," he said, his words more harshly spoken than hers. "I am sure without your advice and without your help I would have long since fallen to my death. But as you are so concerned with my welfare, let me explain why I am going to your Sanctuary. I have already sacrificed at the altar of Athena, goddess of my city. Athena, who does not exist except in our dreams, chose to leave me without sight. I ignored the fact that my own brother had followed the dictates of Apollo from his oracle at Delphi and was thereby murdered before my eyes in a useless battle. Put more plainly, I could say that it was that great god's advice that killed him. But when my blindness came, I prayed to Apollo anyway, to my shame, begging the god of medicine and light and youth for the return of my sight. When Apollo, who does not exist, chose to ignore my pleas, I traveled to Cos and Cnidus across the Aegean, and was examined by a hundred physicians. They told me what I already knew: I am blind. I will never see."

"You are wrong."

"What? I am wrong that I will never see? You think there is some reason why this has happened to me, the greatest runner among the Greeks? What sin against the gods did I commit that they must punish me? Do you know that I would have come here, anyway, to Epidaurus? Nine days after the festival at the Isthmus of Corinth, you people hold games. I would have run here. I brought glory to a dozen festivals, glory to the gods in whose names they are held. I would have been more famous than any boxer, archer, discus thrower. Everyone in Greece would have seen me run."

He was getting close to another narrow ledge of dry ground,

but before she could warn him, he stopped of his own accord. "I will tell you why I am here. One young doctor of Cos, a boy really, his name was Hippocrates. He and his father examined me. But it was Hippocrates who spoke with me. We were together for a long time. He wanted to know about my family, about the death of my brother, about my studies, about my hopes and dreams as a runner and warrior. When we were finished he put his arm about me, a strong arm, the arm of an athlete. And he begged me, he made me swear an oath that I would come to this place. He, the son and grandson of physicians, on that island of nonbelievers, men of knowledge, outspoken enemies of superstition. He begged me to come here and beseech the god for help."

She had never heard of Hippocrates, but of course knew all about the great school at Cos. Many of the physicians who passed through Epidaurus had studied there, learning how to set complex fractures, how to dissect animals, how to heal the body with proper diet and exercise, with special ointments and massage, with enemas and bloodletting and pain-killing drugs. But these therapies dealt with the body, which was but the frame for the spirit; and the physicians of the school at Cos knew that a sick man possessed a sick spirit.

"I am grateful to the physician Hippocrates," she said, into a sudden silence. For once, the wind had stilled at the moment she had spoken. Diagoras turned blind eyes her way, as if about to express gentle words of thanks for her concern. But the gentleness couldn't set in the angry planes of his face.

"Yes, you should be grateful. You will have another buyer of prayers and charms and oracles for your husband."

Corinna resolved to let Diagoras' angry words pour over her without effect. She would understand them as pleas for help, as anger at the state of his spirit. If the loss of his brother in battle was a fresh sore in his spirit, it was no wonder he was so angry at being in Epidaurus. Athens had lost many men in the last few years enforcing its claim to empire among the Greek city-states. Epidaurus and Aegina had both refused to pay the tribute Athens had demanded until useless battles had been fought at sea. Meanwhile Colophon, Miletus, and Erythrae had all dared to engage in skirmishes with their former ally, fruitlessly trying to break the growing Athenian power.

"I am sorry that you lost your brother," she said, trying to

extend her sympathy like a balm over his anger. But her words
had the opposite effect. He stopped and nearly sat down in the
path, so overcome was he with inarticulate rage.

"I have lost everybody," he said. "I can't see you any better
than I can see him. He's dead, but so is everyone to me."

"That's not true," she said, trying to undo what damage
she'd done by mentioning the dead brother. She explained how,
in spite of his blindness, he was part of the world, and not a
shade of the underworld.

"When I'm dead, at least I'll see what everyone else sees.
Don't talk to me about my brother: He is the one who led me to
battle. He died, but I lost my sight. The gods struck him dead,
but they left me blind."

Corinna would have spoken again, but decided there would
be no good in antagonizing him shortly before he must meet with
the sober priests of the Sanctuary. She remembered the way her
husband dealt with nonbelievers who came to the Sanctuary:
Without deigning to answer blasphemies, regardless of the state
of their health, impious supplicants were forcefully expelled by
the guards.

They walked steadily, talking only of the ground and the
weather, until they reached the last part of their journey. Here
the track began to widen, the wind began to calm. The climb
eased to a nearly flat angle. An awkwardness had grown between
them, as if they had become antagonists forced to share a meal or
a bed or a vessel at sea.

"Your husband," said Diagoras. "Is he as ferocious as his
reputation?"

"He is a priest of Asclepios, and a worthy man."

"In Athens, he is famous for his cures. Also his prices. But
they say he has made the difference between life and death for
many. Blindness should be an easy trick for him."

It pained her to see how much he wanted to believe, but how
essential it was for him to mock the very gods he wanted to
embrace. Corinna had witnessed this before: the bizarre need to
hold on to what was ill and dying in one's soul. She tried
to explain that Coreus didn't have or claim to have the power of
life and death. Life and death were not the work of the priests,
who only served to mediate between gods and men. Only the
gods decided who would live and who would die. Even if it were

true that disease was not sent by the gods, but arose from natural causes, it was still the gods who chose the moment when one's soul vanished from the earth.

Asclepios himself, the god of healing for all mankind, had been born a mortal. Many centuries before, in the age of heroes, he had walked the earth as a man, a physician with great skill. But Asclepios never doubted that his power came from the gods above, even when men began to worship his power. When his feats of healing had grown too prodigious for the taste of Pluto, lord of the underworld, Zeus tore the earthly physician apart with a thunderbolt. In the same instant that he was made immortal, Asclepios' fate served as a humbling to all earthly healers. No mortal could avert the will of the gods.

"Please do not tell me that Coreus has no power," said Diagoras, making every word sarcastic, even as his pace slowed, as if he wanted to delay his entrance to what was his last hope of happiness in the world. "If he has no power, like the doctors of Cos have no power, like Apollo and Athena have no power, then I shall have to ask your help to lead me to the top of the precipice. If Zeus doesn't tear me apart with a thunderbolt, I shall tear myself apart by crashing down the mountainside."

"Coreus does have power," said Corinna. "My husband is a great man. But you must understand that he can do nothing without your faith."

Now Diagoras stopped altogether, turning his head as if to rest his eyes on her image. She tried to help him understand that priests were physicians, men who could help heal the spirit. Some could intercede with the gods, beg their indulgence for a few more years of life for a supplicant. It was no wonder that so many foreigners came to Epidaurus. Athenians were not uncommon here, though they were frequently at war with neighboring Aegina and were detested by the average resident of Epidaurus.

But far stranger and more hated people risked the voyage to the Sanctuary: Egyptians who had come to identify their own healing god Imhotep with Asclepios' power, Lydians temporarily abandoning a thousand superstitions to offer their hearts to Asclepios and beg for his cure. Even detested Persian soldiers cut their hair and trimmed their beards in the fashion of their Greek enemies so that they might approach the healing Sanctuary.

Corinna was convinced that her husband was one who was

favored by the gods, for she had seen him assist in the cures of many. She had seen him bring back to health a man so colorless and still that the other priests had refused him a place of rest within the Sanctuary. The sick man had been forced to lie among the women giving birth and the warriors dying of their wounds in the guest house at the outskirts of the sacred ground, as birth and death were both forbidden within sight of the Sanctuary.

"How young were you when you were married?"

"Fifteen."

"How old is your husband?"

"Forty years," she said. "He did my family great honor to take me as his wife."

The questions made her uncomfortable, though there was nothing but truth in her answers. It was common for a man to wait until his late thirties to marry, and when he did, a young girl, with her years of child-bearing ahead of her, was what he expected. Coreus was far too august to fall in love with her, but this didn't disappoint her, because she had never expected to find love from her husband. All her life she had been ruled by her father. Now Coreus was her master. Indeed, when Coreus had sent her to the city to bring the Athenian to the Sanctuary, she was honored by the status it gave her in the eyes of the world. Though she had not been welcome at the dinner given for the blind athlete on the night of his arrival—for of course she was confined to the women's quarters with her mother and sisters— she was no longer treated as her father's property. She was a wife, and a part of another household, and one of great importance in the community. Moreover, she was herself a priestess, a lofty position granted her by Coreus' grace.

"So you have never loved your husband," said Diagoras, turning his sightless eyes back to the path, picking up the pace quickly, so that Corinna had to hurry to stay alongside.

"It is not proper to make such statements," said Corinna, hurrying to his side, to push him away from an outcropping of jagged stone.

"He has never loved you, and you have never loved him," said Diagoras. "I am familiar with such marital relationships, believe me, as I am an Athenian, and a member of a good family. It is only among the lowest classes that love is allowed as a reason to marry. But of course, such marriages are unhappy, as the babies of the poor are almost never allowed to live."

"I have not said that I don't love my husband."

"Where are your babies then?"

"Diagoras, I must remind you that my husband is capable of helping you, and you must do what you can to make him like you."

"That will not be a problem. People always like me. My brother's wife, for example, she liked me. Before my brother died, she liked me so much, she wanted to marry me."

"I do not understand," said Corinna, though she paid close attention. Once again he had mentioned his brother, not with love, but with a violent resentment. She would tell all this to Coreus, who could lead men deep into their pasts, send them visions from their future and ghosts from the land of the dead. Perhaps what the god needed to cure was not his blindness, but his angry heart.

"That is how we are in Athens. Very civilized. One of our women could fall in love with almost anyone. That is because no one believes in the old gods, even though Pericles finds the money to rebuild every temple. No one marries for love but everywhere there are men killing each other over a pretty face."

"I do not know anything of Athens," she said. "But in Epidaurus, men and women who marry learn to love and respect each other."

"And if not, the husband brings in a concubine, then a second wife, then establishes a home for his mistress, frequents brothels, visits courtesans, and remembers to tell his wife not to go out in public unless he has given her special permission to do so."

Corinna wondered whether he was talking about his brother and his brother's wife, or about some failed marriage that was to have taken place for the athlete himself. But her thoughts were shattered by the sudden movement of a patch of red and brown in the rocks flanking the trail.

"Be careful," she shouted, but he had already moved back, far more quickly than she could have pushed him, from the hissing passage of an adder nearly two feet in length.

She was certain that it wouldn't strike. In her mind's eye she could already see it retreating along the sun-swept rocks, its redbrown body disappearing into the dry terrain.

But this vision wasn't prophecy but a wish that was to be unfullfilled. Diagoras moved back, taking rapid steps about the curving path, as if he had eyes in the back of his head. But of course he could see nothing, not from behind, not from any-where.

"No!" she shouted again, but Diagoras couldn't see the snake twist off the rock that hung at the level of his outstretched arm, and as he moved back yet further at her shout, the snake's head moved with a swiftness that no sighted man could have avoided. The snake bit, and Diagoras felt a brief stab of pain. If not for Corinna, he wouldn't have known what the pain repre-sented; it could have been from any of a hundred sources in the blackness about him.

"We must hurry," she said. The snake was gone, and Dia-goras turned about to face her, touching his fingers to the place where the fangs had broken the skin of his forearm.

"What sort of snake was it?" he said, hoping that she would tell him it wasn't a snake at all, but an insect, or a vine, or a pinch from a nymph with sharp fingernails.

"I must tear a bit of your tunic," she said, getting to her knees before him. She began to tear at the hem of his garment, but Diagoras took the fabric from her and tore it himself.

"So you are a doctor as well as a priestess," he said.

"Yes."

"We do not allow female physicians in Athens," he said, still waiting to hear what had bitten into his arm. "What color was the snake?"

"It was an adder."

"Then I shall probably not die," he said. Corinna quickly tied the fine linen of his tunic very tightly about his forearm, higher than the neat bite marks by the breadth of her fingers.

"Now you must sit," she said.

"Make sure you don't push me into a nest of vipers," he joked, but already his head was feeling light, and he bit into his tongue to bring clarity to his thoughts.

"What are you doing?" he said, but now his voice felt strange to him, whether from fear or from the effects of the snakebite, he couldn't know. He listened carefully as she told him to keep still, explaining that she had to cut into his skin for a moment and that all he need do was remain calm.

She had no proper knife, but used a sharp blade she was bringing Coreus for use in the animal sacrifices. With a single decisive motion she connected the points where the adder had punctured the forearm, sending its venom into Diagoras' body.

Silently invoking Asclepios' name, Corinna shut her eyes and sucked up blood and venom from the incision; she waited a long moment before spitting it out. She knew that she would taste nothing, and that the venom would have no effect, because she had placed the name of the god in her mouth. When she opened her eyes, she saw the dry ground draw up the spittle with a preternatural speed. Diagoras continued to sit very still, as a new pallor struggled to get to the surface of his sun-browned skin.

"Please stand up, Diagoras," she said, and he did so too quickly, so that a light flashed behind his sightless eyes, and he shook his head to clear away the dizziness.

"This is very funny," he said. "I come to the Sanctuary of Asclepios to get cured, and on the way I am murdered by a snake."

"Take my arm," she said, and not waiting for him to do this, she wrapped his hand in the crook of an elbow and began to walk quickly. "We must hurry, so that you shall have no ill effects. The adders don't usually bite, but you must have scared this one, moving so quickly. At least it wasn't one of the African snakes. They could kill you in an hour." Corinna explained how all snakes were sacred to Asclepios, and how a variety of snakes, from many lands, of many colors and sizes, were used in the Asclepian rituals. Unfortunately, some of these trained snakes had escaped over the last half century, and their descendants were wild. Most of these snakes were nonpoisonous. The few poisonous varieties rarely attacked pilgrims traveling to the healer's shrine.

It made sense that the god would protect his supplicants. There was a reason why the snakes left most people alone, as there was a reason why the adder had left Diagoras dizzy and weak, hanging on to her arm as they entered the Sanctuary. Corrina had worked among the sick and the wounded too long to believe that accidents were freaks of nature, twists of fate that no god had forseen.

But the gods were unfathomable.

Young men in their prime drowned in the same shipwreck that spared old widows; children died before their parents; evildoers survived war and rebellion, flourishing while the saintly were singled out for slavery and destruction. With wild beasts, volcanoes, thunderbolts, earthquakes, with runaway chariots, plagues, violent storms, and falling rocks all about them, Corinna believed that the gods chose where and when and whom to strike. If the gods didn't show restraint, surely the natural terrors of the world would devour everyone, indiscriminately. When the plague struck a city, sometimes half its inhabitants perished. It was beyond human comprehension to understand how the gods chose victims and survivors; but it was within the comprehension of humanity to believe that the gods did *choose*.

Sometimes she had seen the sick with nothing to live for fight back and conquer illness, putting their faith into the cure of their spirit; but she had seen other sick people—with everything to live for—simply give up and die. Perhaps in this was a hint of how the gods chose; the gods might reward those whose desire for life was greatest. But Corinna knew that it was difficult to know what man desired. Surely there were reasons for this, even if they were unknowable to man. Often outward appearances of happiness or despair were deceiving. The miser might be free with his money in secret, as the loud proclaimer of his misery might be a man who loved life. Men famous for their bravery on the battlefield were often cowards, parading their ferocity only to hide the chance of humiliation at the world's discovering their fear; these cowards, mildly wounded, sucked in the strength of their ills, embracing death eagerly to avoid the chance of pain.

Looking at proud Diagoras, momentarily subdued as they approached the crowded marble path that led from the wild trail to the Sanctuary's entrance, Corinna thought the answer might be simpler. Perhaps the gods singled out warriors in battle for death, wounds, sickness, as retribution for evil deeds. Perhaps accidents befell those whom the gods deemed too full of pride, perhaps snakes bit those pilgrims who were without piety.

"We have arrived?" he asked, his useless eyes turned to the gateway, the silent guards, and the first of many tents that housed the sick.

"Yes, Diagoras," she said, knowing that the youthful priest who approached them now would find in the athlete's demeanor only awe and piety. Corinna asked Diagoras to remove his sandals and replace his tunic with the simple unbelted robe of the supplicant, handed to her by the priest. Diagoras answered this gatekeeper's questions without arrogance, his sightless head raised up toward the sloping path to the olive trees and the low stone buildings which housed the priests, the temple attendants, and their families.

"Are we approaching the temple?" he asked, when the priest had finished with him, the usual demands for contributions cut short because of Corinna's intervention.

"There are temples all along this way," she said. "But first we must visit my husband." Diagoras' pallor was no better, and she wanted her husband to look over the incision she had made. A group of young boys passed them, members of the temple choir, hurrying from their chores of incense bearing and altar lighting before the solemn assemblies of the sick to a game of knucklebones or a run up and down the rocky hills. The path still rose gradually, as various buildings came into view: the water reservoir, an old bathhouse, a modest temple devoted to the worship of Apollo and badly in need of repair to its facade of soft, Corinthian limestone.

"Where is the well?"

"We are close to it now," she said, and he smiled, as if he had known this was the case. "The sacred well of Asclepios."

"I would drink from the well," he said, his words slurred, his head inclining forward, as if his neck had lost its rigidity. "The doctors of Cos thought that a drink from the sacred well . . ."

"Yes, of course," she said, holding on to his thickly muscled forearm, as if this would somehow prevent him from falling. She looked up the path for help, but there were only other sick men and women, dressed in the white gowns of supplicants, leaning on staffs and the shoulders of slaves. An Egyptian family came up behind them, chattering in a clumsy dialect of Greek she could barely understand. But the youngest among them, a girl of ten, was not sick, and she ran up the path at Corinna's bidding. "Soon you will drink from the sacred well," Corinna said, feeling the strength ease from his body.

"My brother's wife is very beautiful," he said, his words beginning to slur together. "But the marriage was an alliance, as it should be, enriching two families with allies. Families are stronger than the state, no matter what tyrants attempt. You will see that someday. Nothing is stronger than the ties of family."

He had lost any awareness by the time the slaves came,

lifting him into the litter. Corinna tried to keep up with them, but these slaves were from Numidia, swift and tall and strong. The athlete was laid out on a pallet in the courtyard of the house of her husband by the time she arrived, breathless and fearful. Coreus, trained at Cnidus and Cos as a physician, had his fingers at Diagoras' neck, feeling the pulse as he looked into the man's open, sightless eyes.

"Snakebite," said Corinna unnecessarily, for she had already so informed the slaves. Coreus had ordered them to bring the aromatic mixture of plant extracts that he used in such cases. But he was not concerned with the snakebite. The mild venom was already losing its strength in the powerful body laid out before him.

"They are not the eyes of a blind man," said Coreus.

"He does not see, my husband."

"Neither do you, when you shut your eyes."

"His eyes are open," said Corinna.

"There are those who sleep with their eyes open. They see nothing," said Coreus. "This man is asleep. He has sinned against the gods, and when he has paid for his sins, he will see again."

"He is very angry," ventured Corinna. She would have told him more about their talk on the way to the Sanctuary, about his dead brother, and about the brother's beautiful wife. But the slave came with the plant decoctions and the physician's tools. Coreus cut open the freshly clotted wound made by Corinna's incision and let the blood flow into his own open palm. Diagoras woke out of his stupor and grimaced slightly before he stilled himself.

"What are you doing?"

"Silence," said Coreus. "I am bleeding you."

"Where is Corinna?"

"I am here," she said, and her husband took time out from his careful work to turn about and glare at her. He did not want her interference when he spoke with a patient.

"If you open your eyes, you will see her," said Coreus.

"My eyes are open, but they are dead."

Coreus drove his cutting tool a bit further along the surface of the athlete's forearm, so suddenly that Diagoras let out a sharp cry of pain.

"If you open your eyes," repeated Coreus, "you will see her."

"Are you Coreus?"

"You are to speak only to answer," said the priest. He pressed with both thumbs against the center of the forearm, as if to wring every last drop of blood from the man. But Diagoras seemed strangely content. He shut his eyes, as if this afforded him strength to bear the pain. The shadow of a smile insinuated itself around his now pale lips. Coreus' slave had made a plaster out of the plant decoctions and as he placed this over the bloody wound, Diagoras' smile broke forth in all its glory.

"Yes," he said, though no one had asked him a question. "Thank you."

"You are not blind," said Coreus sharply. "Are you blind?"

"I cannot see," said Diagoras, still smiling, flat on his back, his supplicant's gown pulled back so that every part of his body was revealed, as glorious and unselfconscious as a statue.

Coreus took hold of the other forearm, where no snake had bitten. With a single sharp cut, he drew blood, so that Diagoras started once again.

"I still cannot see," said Diagoras, his smile retreating now, so that Corinna wanted to speak, to reassure him that she was there, that she watched over him, and understood that what Coreus did was for his good, and that it would succeed. Bleeding was sometimes helpful in restoring the harmony of the four humors of the body's fluids: Blood, phlegm, black bile, and yellow bile must be present in precise proportions within the body, or imbalance would lead to sickness. The body fought imbalance with fever, with discharge, with turning hot or cold, dry or damp. Bleeding was the physician's way of hastening discharge of an excess humor. Corinna had seen her husband cut into a man's veins and release black bile; other physicians had told her of blood that had carried green phlegm, of blood so hot that it steamed in the air.

"You will see when you want to see," said Coreus, drawing his knife across the athlete's ankles now, one after the other, so that blood ran from four corners of his body. Already the supplicant's gown and the pallet itself were soaked with blood. Corinna tried to quiet her heart with logic. Each of the humors had physical attributes that together unified into a healthful whole. Black bile was cold and dry, yellow bile was warm and dry, phlegm was cold and damp, blood was warm and damp. If no discharge could be seen in the athlete's blood, it might mean that his blood was what was in excess, as shown by the warm, moist sweat that glowed on Diagoras' forehead.

"My husband," said Corinna suddenly. "May I ask if it is good procedure to bleed after the body has already been weakened by the venom of a snake?"

Coreus didn't hear her question, which saved her from a slap. The priest had a rare gift of concentration. For the moment, his world consisted of the body before him, the veins that must be opened, the eyes that must be made to see. The other priests were often in awe of this ability to focus on the task at hand, the intensity with which he approached his divinely appointed tasks. During the nocturnal healing sessions, when many priests and attendants wandered through the sleeping tents, where music played to relax the sick into a state of semisleep, Coreus was neither lulled by the musicians, nor distracted by the panoply of the other priests. No gongs, no incense, no fire flashing in bronze pans could shake his attention when he had a patient, a supplicant, in his hands.

"Listen, Diagoras," said Coreus, bringing his mouth to the athlete's eyes, as if he would talk directly to the spirit which deadened them. "You are no match for the power of the god. Asclepios is the son of Apollo, and therefore of light. Blindness is repugnant to the god, and it will be removed if you will it."

"I do will it," said Diagoras.

"Do you see?"

"No."

Coreus brought his palm across the athlete's face with violence, once, twice, and then a third time. With each blow, Coreus watched the sun dancing in the open, irresponsive eyes.

"I do not see!" said Diagoras, moving his bloodied arms to protect his face. "I do not see!"

Coreus turned suddenly, and smiled at his wife. "You will take this man of Athens to his quarters. See that he is bathed in cold sea water. Give him water to drink from the sacred well. No food. Let him rest for one day and one night. After tomorrow, at midnight, he will sacrifice at the Temple. Then we will begin the cure."

Coreus drew his young wife closer, his smile malevolent in its strength and willfulness. "He sees," he said. "Even if he does not yet know it, he sees. It is only the god that blocks his view."

"Yes, my husband," said Corinna.

She went to Diagoras and spoke to him as soon as Coreus had left, offering words of encouragement for the pain, for the light-headedness after the bleeding. She could have told him more, for the god who blocked the view of her heart had moved and there was much that she could suddenly see.

The athlete had spoken the truth: She had never loved her husband, and now, as she supported Diagoras' body in his bloody gown she had a glimmering of what this might mean. She supposed it was not unlike the way the blind can sometimes react to the presence of light, without getting a clear image of the surroundings. Eyes open, walking to the tented enclosures for the sick, she felt the possibility of passion all about her. It was bright, luminous, reaching into every part of her body, like a fever riding the strength of a dream.

Chapter 3

COREUS AND CORINNA shared a meal at sunset, attended by a single slave. The High Priest's second, final meal of the day was spare: flat bread made edible with a leavening of honey, a cold soup made from beans and onions, a final course of nuts and figs and cheese. The slave brought the food in on three-legged tables, taking care to serve the master reclining on his couch, before the mistress, sitting across the room on a backless bench. Save for an ancient chest, couch and bench were the only furniture kept in the common room.

Unlike most of the priests, who frequently entertained visiting dignitaries in their homes, Coreus preferred to dine alone. Had there been men present, they would have been seated two by two, on the simple, uncomfortable couches that were stored on the second floor. Corinna would have been banished to her room, picking at her food with only a cat for company. But Coreus' very unsociability placed her in constant contact with her husband. She breakfasted and dined with him; she assisted him in the sacrifices at midnight, as well as those at dawn. She was at his side in the examining rooms, at the sacred well of the god, in the sleeping chambers where the priests walked in ceremony between the beds of the sick.

But the daily intercourse did not breed closeness. Coreus remained as aloof and impatient with his wife as he was with pilgrims and supplicants. She learned to be afraid to question him, much less to refute his word. As she picked at her figs and cheese, carefully cleaning her fingers with the flat bread the way Coreus had taught her, she longed to ask him about Diagoras: Did he truly believe the god would cure the athlete's blindness?

As it was, she knew she must be glad he had not yet castigated her for questioning him during Diagoras' examination. Indeed, she had refrained even from asking him why he had told the slave to serve them indoors. The evening was mild enough to eat on the portico, with its view of the mountains, the tiny fires from the altars to Zeus and Hera flashing from distant peaks. A Greek went indoors only under duress. Most of the year was warm enough to treat the courtyard, and not the common room, as the focal point of the home. Here men talked, ate, drank, sang, slept, feeling the health of their bodies dependent on the clean air, the healing rays of the sun, the harmonious arrangement of the canopy of constellations. Corinna wondered if her husband's desire to be served inside was a way of distancing himself from the frustration he'd experienced in the courtyard. Coreus didn't expect the touch of his hands to heal any and all those afflicted by disease; but he did expect piety, reverence, gratitude. Diagoras had shown nothing but defiance.

"Is the athlete at rest?" said Coreus, speaking to her for the first time since they'd sat down to their meal.

Corinna carefully held her tongue, remembering to gather her thoughts before answering Coreus.

"Yes, my husband. I brought him to the tents of the sick. I assigned a keykeeper to provide him with water from the sacred well, to see that he partakes of no food, to bathe him every two hours with water from the sea and see that he remains quietly at rest."

"Did you leave him sleeping?"

"No, my husband," said Corinna.

"Did he speak with you?"

"No, my husband," said Corinna. This was strictly true, because the athlete had not spoken in answer to her words. But *she* had spoken; the words had spilled out of their own accord, asking him if he was in pain, promising him support, begging him to believe in the cure that would come to pass. It had been all she could do to prevent other words, other promises bursting forth from her mouth.

"The Athenians will make much of this," Coreus said. "If he does not open his eyes, they will blame his sin on the Sanctuary.

They will accuse us of practicing false magic. All the philosophers of Athens will laugh at us, even as they dare laugh at the gods themselves. But such laughter will cost us pilgrims. The sick will be afraid to come here, even if their hearts are sincere. They will be told that Asclepios is a false god, and that only fools go to his Sanctuary. Only fools."

As in the home of her father, the diminishing light and rapidly cooling air reached them from the courtyard, where earlier that day Coreus had struck at and bled the blind athlete. Of course, the common room of her father's house was not so simply furnished: Instead of bare plaster floors, Corinna's childhood home was paved with smooth stones and covered with bright carpets; there the couches were intricately carved, outlined in silver and ivory, the walls covered with marble and hung with tapestries imported from across far seas. Coreus frequently reminded her of her father's wealth and the showy magnificence of her father's dinners; he seemed to take pleasure in listing the shark meat, the stuffed eels, the wine-soaked cheesecakes that were brought into the place of feasting, as if each excess was another sin for which she must be held responsible. When he had given her the honor of going to the city to bring the famous athlete to the Sanctuary, it was not without reminding her of the wealthy, prideful display with which her father would be greeting the visitor from great Athens. Coreus, who was himself wealthy from a thousand gifts, from his wife's great dowry, and from the estate of his father, lived as simply as any supplicant at the Sanctuary. He believed ostentation to be an affront to the gods and a cause of disease. Athens influenced all of the city-states of Greece; and the Athenian way of life was a godless pursuit of fame and riches, therefore unhealthy, dangerous to spirit and flesh.

"He must be made to see," said Coreus, "in spite of himself. If I do not succeed, it will be a victory for Athens, for their godless philosophers, for their builders of palaces and empires."

The slave brought in the *krater*, the earthenware bowl in which their wine was mixed with cool mountain water. Coreus shifted his position on the couch, so that he faced his wife. When the slave had finished pouring the mixture of wine and water, Coreus lifted his cup and drained it swiftly.

"Drink," he said, though she already had the cup to her lips, had already taken a swallow of the sweet, cold stuff. Corinna suppressed a shiver of distaste—not for the wine, but for what would follow. Coreus urged her to drink only when he was about to take her into his bed. The slave poured a second cup, and she drank this too, though her belly was full, and then a third cup, and then a fourth.

"Thank you, my husband," said Corinna, when she had finished this last cup, twisting her lips into a smile and getting awkwardly to her feet.

"Drink," said Coreus, his blue eyes unblinking as he raised his fifth cup to his lips.

"I am not accustomed to such quantities," said Corinna, sitting back down even as she spoke, so he would not presume that she was contradicting him. It took no more than three cups to make her head light, so that her husband's tightly strung bed was yielding as a cloud, his rough black beard as soft as silk on her cheeks and neck and breasts. She drank, and the slave hovered over her, prepared to fill the cup yet again. Though Coreus owed her no explanation, he chose to explain.

"Seven cups," he said. "As there are four times seven days till a woman bleeds. As there are forty times seven days until she delivers a child."

"I am sorry, my husband," said Corinna, once again apologizing for the barrenness of her womb. She drank yet more quickly, and was sloppy, as the fifth cup was drained, and the sixth cup begun.

She was thinking of Diagoras, whom her husband must cure. Hours before she had confirmed in her heart what the athlete had taunted her with; she had never loved her husband. When she had left Diagoras on his clean pallet, in his white supplicant's tunic, surrounded by a score of other pilgrims, each with his own complaint against the workings of his body, she had felt a sudden urge to throw herself over him, covering him with her urgent, inchoate feelings. He must be made to see, Coreus had demanded, but Corinna wanted more than this: She wanted to protect, she wanted to comfort, and she was drawn to the anger and loathing in Diagoras' face, as if she alone could provide the forgiveness that would heal him. All day she had worried about the athlete, and about her sudden passion, as hopeless and wild as that of any story of mortal woman and god.

"Drink," said Coreus, lifting the sixth glass, and Corinna squinted at his dark and brooding face, twisting the image before her until her husband's features blurred behind a tear, until the creases along his brow were smoothed by a memory, until the black hairs of the slender wrists holding his cup of wine were transmuted to strands of gold.

"Yes, my husband," said Corinna. She shut her eyes and drank, and thereby saw the blind man's head yet more clearly: blond-bearded, his sightless eyes a gray-blue that might easily lend themselves to a mask of serenity. The slave had to help her to her feet after the seventh cup, but Coreus waved him away.

"Go to the kitchen," he said, his words reaching her as if from a far distance. Diagoras' head remained securely placed on her husband's torso.

"Go to your bed," said Corinna dully, as if she were repeating the words he had said, instead of those she had expected to hear.

"Listen, woman," said Coreus. "Kitchen. Across the courtyard. Pots. Pans. Food. Go to the kitchen."

"Yes, my husband," said Corinna. "The kitchen." She brushed against one of the shaky three-legged tables, laden with the figs so precious to Greece, sending them to the plaster floor. But she paid this no mind. The slave, one of many given to the Sanctuary by grateful masters healed by the god, was already attending to the mess of broken earthenware and fruit. Her only duty was to follow the command of her husband.

"The kitchen," she said again, stumbling across the threshold to the portico. In a moment, the cool air sent a shiver and a smile through her girlish figure. She did not know where she was going, to whose heart she was listening. The kitchen made no sense as a place for her husband to try once more to gift her with his child. But then it made no sense that Coreus' face was suddenly smooth, twenty-four instead of forty years old.

He was as beautiful as a god, her father had said, three years ago, when she had stood in the crowd watching him race through the torch-lit night. But that was Diagoras, the athlete, reluctant supplicant to the Sanctuary, and not its High Priest. She stumbled on some loose stones as she crossed the garden, remembering the athlete on the pallet, under the all-knowing hands of her husband. But what if the hands were not all-knowing, what if

Coreus' slapping of the young man's face was not a sign of healing and love, but of injury and hate?

"Corinna," sang out a deep female voice from across the courtyard, a lovely voice, one both familiar and dear. For a moment she was thrilled, the way only a child can be thrilled, acknowledging a dream as if it were real.

"Mother?" she said, but even as she said this, the word turned to ashes in her mouth, for she was not a little girl, but a young woman, married to a brute who was a holy man. It could not be her mother, for her mother had been dead since she was a little girl. Once more her name was called, and she turned her head to the source of sound, and saw for the first time the kitchen fire burning at the edge of the courtyard. Over it was suspended a large bronze pot, but this made no sense, as nothing that night made sense; they had already had their dinner. Who could be boiling soup at this time of day?

"Corinna," said the deep voice once again, and a tall dark-skinned woman gestured to her from where she stood at the fire, stirring the pot with a long metal stick that flashed in the light of the flames.

It was then that she noticed that the sun had set, and that the stars had risen. Indeed, she had never seen this woman save at night. Corinna understood that she was drunk and thus capable of great feats of the imagination. But this was not a vision. This was the woman she had seen among the priests during the nocturnal rites performed in the sleeping chambers of the sick.

"Doricha," said Corinna, the smile leaving her lips, the fear rising through her light-headedness like a knife. The name was as exotic as her painted lips and eyelids. Doricha spoke to no one at the rites other than the priests who had summoned her; even Coreus approached her with hesitancy. Doricha was rumored to be Persian by birth, Egyptian by training, and to have traveled to distant India in search of greater skills. As Greece was the crossroads of Africa, the East, and Europe, Doricha was crossed by three traditions: medicine, religion, and necromancy. She was a witch.

"Your husband, High Priest of Asclepios, has entrusted me with a sacred task. It is two years since you are married, and still you are without offspring," said the witch, stirring her pot, which was not soup but a roiling heavy liquid, sending puffs of sickly sweet clouds into the still, cool air.

"I have sacrificed to Hera and Demeter, even to Athena—" said Corinna, understanding that the contents of the pot were somehow to be used on her by the witch.

"At dawn?" interrupted Doricha.

"Yes, of course, at dawn," said Corinna, hoping that her words were politely spoken. But when else but at dawn would one sacrifice to a goddess of Olympus?

"Cows, pigs, and heifers," said Doricha, smiling. "Butchering the dumb beasts just as the sun returns to light the earth." She reached her left hand out and touched Corinna's face. "Do not be afraid, child," said the witch. "My hands are not cold, in spite of what you may have heard. My breath does not poison, nor does looking directly into my eyes stun. Look at me."

"Cows," said Corinna, feeling the last effects of the wine slip away, like the coming awake of a sleeping limb. "Cows for Hera, pigs for Demeter, and heifers for wise Athena." The witch's eyes were black, and she remembered that she had never corrected Diagoras when he had imagined that black was the color of her own eyes. But of course he had no idea what she looked like; if he had thought her short and black-eyed, perhaps he imagined her bowlegged and crook-nosed as well. What if the gods restored his sight, and the beautiful athlete found her repulsive, as ugly as a Spartan woman? She wished she could be as beautiful as Doricha; as she drew closer Corinna could see that the paint under and about the witch's eyes was green, but sharp and black lining the lids. Perhaps she would paint her eyes when Diagoras could see; she would adorn herself with fine clothes and bathe in perfumed waters like an Athenian courtesan.

"But what if your problem is not with an Olympian, but with some darker spirit?" said Doricha. "Remove the knot from your hair, girl."

"I have never offended Hecate," said Corinna, removing the gold wire that bound her long hair. As a participant in the Asclepian rites, she knew that hair tied in knots, like rings on fingers or bracelets about wrists, could hamper the effects of an incantation. "Are you going to put me under a spell?"

The witch moved her hands about Corinna's fingers, as if feeling for invisible rings, then up and down each thin arm, then around the young woman's neck and forehead. "Is it possible that you do not want a child?"

"No, Doricha."

"Is it possible that your husband does not please you?"

"No, it is not possible," said Corinna, knowing that this lie would be transparent to the witch, fearing that she would add a love-charm to the spell. Certainly it was within the province of magic to make of her husband's angry probings and thrustings something lovable. She recoiled at this idea. Now that she had felt the stirrings of love for Diagoras, she didn't want to be over-whelmed by a false potion.

"In Egypt, there were women whose husbands had sent for my help to help them conceive, but no dogs sacrificed to Hecate at midnight, no charms inscribed on lead tables, no talismans placed under the bed had any effect. Then I would discover that the women had lied. Bring over those stones, child."

"What stones?" said Corinna fearfully. The witch gestured imperiously to a pile of black stones, lying under what appeared to be a copper saddle, which was itself set up on a raised wooden plank, as high as a woman's waist. Corinna tried to pick up three of them at once, but they were far too heavy for her. She picked up one, the topmost; it was smooth and cool, like the statue of Asclepios made from African stone that never turned hot under the summer sun.

"They use mixtures of dung and honey, stirred up with sharp-smelling salts," said Doricha, taking the stone from Corinna's two hands with one of her own and dropping it noiselessly into the boiling pot. "Before their husbands approach them, they retire to their chambers, and place these mixtures into their womanly parts. No magic can bring the seed of a man past such abominations."

"I have never used any such thing—" said Corinna, but Doricha interrupted her, gesturing once more to the stones. Corinna picked up two this time and, staggering under their weight, brought them to the witch. Doricha once again took the load in one hand and dropped them into the pot as if they weighed no more than a feather.

"Sometimes they use the leaves of the acacia," said Doricha. "A secret learned from whores, who must never conceive." The witch took her stick out of the pot and dropped it to the ground.

She moved quickly, stooping over the pile of stones and picking up a dozen of them, bringing them to the pot and dropping them in as quietly as she had the others. "Take off your clothes," said the witch, as if this was no more or less surprising than any other order she'd given the wife of the High Priest. Corinna, following the woman's order, removed first the white linen band under her breasts, worn outside her *chiton,* a long chaste light woolen gown in the Doric fashion, then unfastened the golden clasps at each shoulder which together with the thin belt at her waist held this gown to her body.

"Hurry, hurry," said Doricha, who was herself moving quickly, placing the last of the stones into the pot and turning about to see that the girl was undressed. "Your husband will come for you as soon as you are prepared."

"My husband," said Corinna, freed of her clothes, turning to the dark spot in the center of the courtyard where she had helped the athlete rise from the pallet, supporting the heavy weight of his muscular frame as she led him from the house of her husband to the tents of the sick. Behind her, the witch had taken another instrument from the kitchen—a large, ominous set of tongs. Corinna watched in wonder as Doricha plunged the tongs into the pot and used it to remove a mass of stones, and then hurried to place this on the makeshift copper saddle. The stones gave off fumes, white and luminous against the dark night. For a moment, the sight was so arresting that Corinna didn't quite hear what the witch ordered.

"Hurry girl," she said again. "Straddle the stones."

Corinna turned to where the witch plunged the tongs yet again into the pot, removing more of the stones, increasing the fury of the steam coming off from the copper saddle. Slowly, she walked toward the stones, swallowing against her fear, wondering if it was her fate to succumb to this assault on her most private parts.

"Take off your sandals," said Doricha exasperatedly. "You must be naked. You are not naked with your shoes on, are you?"

"No," said Corinna, doing as she was told, closing her eyes as she took a step closer to the hot, magical stones.

"I have a question," she said finally.

"Of course you have a question. They always have questions," replied Doricha. "Listen. This is not magic. This is medicine. This is what we do in Egypt to clear the vagina of disease, either of the body or of the spirit. It is not only effective against sterility, it is effective against improper discharges. It is effective against half the special problems that plague women. All right? Does that answer your question?"

"Doricha," said Corinna, looking closely into the black eyes, framed by paint and firelight. "My question is: What will this do, if one loves someone besides one's husband?"

"What will it do?" said Doricha. "It will make you cleaner for receiving his cock."

"Oh," said Corinna, not a bit less fearful as she raised her naked leg high over the gleaming copper saddle, glistening with the sweat from the stones. She stood over the steam on the tips of her toes, though she would have been quite clear of any contact if she had rested squarely on the soles of her bare feet. Doricha's words slowly penetrated her, even as the too-sweet vapor rose into and about her private parts. *The witch did not care if she loved another.*

"It does not hurt," said Corinna.

"Of course not, child," said Doricha. "Why would I hurt you? Do you believe what they say? Do you think I cut up little dogs and feed them to Hecate in the caves on the other side of the mountain? Do you think me a witch?"

"Are you Egyptian?" said Corinna, deflecting the question, and looking directly at the woman, the way her husband had taught her to interview a supplicant, so that he would see you had the power to discern the shape of his soul.

"I am of Egypt, and of other places, child. You have another question for me. I feel it."

"The paint you wear on your eyes," said Corinna. "It was told me by a physician of Cos, that such paint prevents blindness. I would like to know—"

"So it is the blind athlete that you love," said the witch, placing a finger to Corinna's lips before she could offend her with yet another lie. "You wonder how I know, of course. You think it is magical that I should know what everyone at the Sanctuary does, that the famous Diagoras has arrived to be cured of his blindness. And you are not the only young girl that has fallen in love with him. He is beautiful."

"As beautiful as a god," said Corinna softly.

"And the paint I wear on my eyes will cure nothing," said Doricha. "Only the gods will decide whether or not Diagoras will ever see again."

But which gods? Corinna wondered, thinking for a moment that such a question might offend the witch of distant lands. Imhotep, worshipped as a healer in Egypt, was not always welcome by the priests of Asclepios as a helpmate. Isis, earth-mother and healer to generations of Egyptians, healed her own brother, Osiris, after he had been cruelly torn apart by the evil Seth. This healing was a sexual union as well, and this union of siblings produced a son, Horus, whom Seth attacked, destroying one of his eyes. This time it was not Isis, but Thoth, another god of healing, who saved the boy from blindness. Corinna knew that Thoth was worshipped as a physician-god, as was Imhotep, as was Hathor, Bes and Thoeris, Keket and Khnum.

"My husband says that he will see," said Corinna.

"Let us hope that this will come to pass, child," said Doricha. "Coreus is not a god, but a man."

"What will happen then? Can you see the future, Doricha?"

"Everyone sees the future, child. The difficulty is that there are so many futures from which to choose."

"I do not understand—"

"Be quiet, girl. Let the stones do their work. Your husband will be here soon, and it would be best for you to be in a relaxed state, not an excited one."

"But you must tell me," insisted Corinna. "If not all futures, tell me the one you see for the athlete."

The witch smiled faintly, as if taking this insistence as a kind of praise. Then she ceased her attentions to the steaming stones, closed her black eyes, and placed her hands on top of Corinna's thick, unbound hair.

For a time, there was no sound in the courtyard, save the crackling sticks of wood under the bronze pot, the settling of the hot stones as they cooled on the saddle of copper beneath her. She could hear nothing from the path outside the house, nothing from across the courtyard where Coreus waited for the finish of the witch's ministrations to his wife. Corinna gentled under Doricha's touch. She felt the steam rising up her belly, to her neck, rubbing against her shut eyes.

"You have the gift," said Doricha. When she finally spoke,

the words were so softly uttered that Corinna thought she might be listening to an illusion in a drug-induced dream. The wine, the stones steeped in the witch's brew, the nakedness of her body in the starlit courtyard, all left her open to the possibility of phantoms, trances, spectral visions. Just as the priests of Asclepios opened the victims of disease to visitations from the god through sacrifice, meditation, music, Corinna felt herself open to any floating spirit.

"What gift?" answered Corinna, but the witch was not listening to the girl's words, but rather taking the measure of her soul. She could feel the force of love like a great wave, held back by enormous effort; the girl was given a gift that she had terrible need of using. "Will he be healed?" asked Corinna. "Tell me what you see of the future. Tell me."

Doricha suddenly broke the contact of her hands with Corinna's head. She moved away quickly, sidling awkwardly to where the portico extended from the kitchen door. Corinna turned and saw that the witch had seated herself. The woman who had lifted the heavy stones without effort was now exhausted.

"What is wrong? What did you see?" said Corinna.

"Please stay," said Doricha softly. "Do not get off the saddle."

"You said I had a gift. What gift?"

"Your husband has the right to divorce you," said Doricha, not looking at Corinna, no longer disputing her will as she stepped over and away from the hot stones. Her words had the flat tones of a priestess, reciting words given her by the god. "He has not married for your dowry nor for the prestige of your father's house. He wants a son."

Corinna felt a chill, as the wind swept in from the seacoast, scattering its strength against the mountains. She picked up her clothes and dried her wet torso, never taking her eyes from the witch.

"He saw you, and he wanted you," said Doricha. "He asked the god, and the god approved, and he believed that you would give him the son he needs to continue his line. But you have not given him a son. You have instead taken from him. He has lost desire. He has become tired and weak when in your arms. Tired and weak."

"Please, Doricha," said Corinna. "What did you see?"

Doricha looked up slowly at Corinna. "I am not here to prophesy," she said. The witch turned away, looking at the still boiling pot, then across the courtyard to the common room, from where torchlight glimmered onto the raised portico. "The seed of man comes from his brain. If the brain is deadened by a woman's disrespect, a woman's loathing, the seed dries up. No man can have a child if his woman takes away his desire. You will have desire. Listen to me. Your husband will come to you and you will have desire."

"Please," said Corinna. "Even if you are not here to prophesy, you have *seen*. What will happen to the athlete?"

"Come close," said Doricha, suddenly rising, the strength that had left her in the wake of her vision returning in force. Corinna moved into the witch's embrace. "Your husband is approaching. There will be grave trouble if you do not please him."

But Corinna did not want to hear this. She struggled against the powerful arms that held her. She opened her mouth to shout her defiance. There was a vision. There was a gift. There was knowledge of the athlete's fate. There was a future whose lineaments the witch had seen as clearly as a face in polished bronze.

But the witch refused to hear her. There was a substance in Doricha's hand, black and sour-smelling, like hellebore soaked in vinegar, and as she pressed it into Corinna's mouth, the witch's eyes turned inward, twisting in quick, ever-diminishing circles.

"That's good," said Doricha, as if the girl had ceased her complaints. As she spoke, her embrace grew less rigid, for Corinna was no longer struggling.

"You desire your husband, as he desires you. You give him the power of pleasing you, so that his pleasure feeds on your own, renewing his potency."

Corinna felt rebellion drift away, as she leaned more and more on the witch's powerful frame. Black hellebore was used by the priests, as well as the doctors of the flesh, in inducing sleep and visions, but this was more than hellebore acting on her. She was not simply light-headed, but ecstatic. Every moment seemed to contain the possibilities of a lifetime, every twisting of the witch's black eyes seemed to promise another hour of unbridled joy.

"Do you understand, child?" said Doricha. "He is coming to you, and you will be full of desire."

I am full of desire, thought Corinna giddily, swallowing the drug in her mouth, letting it join the fear and solace of the witch's presence in her heart, in the dwelling place of reason.

Full of desire, she thought, turning about at her husband's command, as he came effortlessly to her, as if floating over the stones of the courtyard.

She wondered if this could be a dream, this touch of Coreus' familiar hands, this grasping of her neck and forearm as if she were a slave at the market. But it didn't matter, real or not, it was the same, it was all lived, either in the courtyard or in the dream of the courtyard. He was smiling, and she took this as a good omen, for she knew she must please him.

Somehow, the High Priest took her from the witch's kind embrace, and though she shivered when his hands touched her breasts, when she understood that the courtyard was gone, replaced by the broad expanse of his bed, when his teeth bruised her shoulder, when his penis, thick and hard and dry, entered her peremptorily, moving in and out as if to enlarge her terrified passage, this shiver lasted but a moment, or a series of moments, each replaced by a shock of delight induced by the witch's art.

For nothing was long distasteful that night, nothing was allowed to be heavier than a breeze. Even Coreus' body, usually as stolid and heavy as a boulder pressed to the flat ground when it lay on top of her own, was tonight eager and light and full of grace. Usually so quick to blame her for his lack of potency, Coreus was tonight full of strength. Even if he spoke no word of endearment, even if he penetrated her without a single caress, she was full of the desire inspired by the witch. She was mad, and the madness gave her a wildness, an intensity that might have been self-enclosed; but Corinna let him enter her sphere of joy.

It was as if Doricha was in Coreus' bedchamber with them, holding Corinna in chains of ecstasy. Corinna couldn't think of anything but pleasure, couldn't feel anything but the certainty that every moment was bliss.

It was not till the slow minutes before the rising of the sun when she felt herself free of the witch's spell.

She was alone, in her own narrow bed, on the second story of the house of Coreus. There were questions, and they came back to her, even as the joy spilled out of her, even as the vaguest of memories began to gnaw at her waking heart.

What gift? she asked the god of the coming dawn. *What would be the fate of Diagoras?*

But no god answered.

There was no need for a god to respond to what Corinna already knew.

Doricha had told her, had whispered in her ear. There had been a true vision of the future the night before, and such visions must be shared, lest the prophetess be eaten up by a god's message left untold.

Corinna remembered the whisper, could feel the breath of the witch against her pale face in the starlit night. Either in the moment when she had thrust Corinna into Coreus' hungry arms, or at midnight, when witches are invisible, when Corinna had given her husband such strength and joy, Doricha had been there, had whispered what future she had seen.

"Your gift is the gift of healing," Doricha had said. "Diagoras will be cured of his blindness. He will be healed through the strength of your love."

Chapter 4

CORINNA WALKED to the tents of the sick, careful to keep her
eyes to the ground lest someone engage her in talk; other
than Doricha, who was never to be seen during the day, she
wanted conversation with no one. She was afraid guilt and fear
and love would trip up her tongue, as surely as that of any penitent under the hieratic stare of her husband.

But it is Coreus who will cure him, she told herself, deliberately
exposing the thought to the light of day. This was the encouragement she had offered Diagoras, this was what she herself had
believed. She tried to remind herself of Coreus' great skills, his
many famous cures, his dedication; but all she could think of was
his brutal slapping of the athlete's handsome face. This violence,
and Doricha's words. *She* would cure Diagoras, and not with
violence, but with love. And she would heal with the gift she
knew she possessed, knew it in her heart long before Doricha
had received her vision from the god.

Not without reason did patients reach out for the touch of
her hands, not without reason did physicians seek her to hold
their tools during the cutting away of diseased tissue, not without
reason did Coreus want her at his side in the long nights of
howling nightmares, when men confronted their pasts and
begged to be visited by the god. She had never thought of her
presence as a healing presence, but simply as a comforting one;
though perhaps the providing of comfort was a kind of healing.

Perhaps all people possessed this power, she thought, and
Doricha's whispering of her gift was simply an extravagant compliment.

But no, she remembered the night, the presence of the witch, the voice that spoke, not simply into her ear, but into her heart. She, not Coreus, would heal Diagoras. This was true, she believed, quickening her step, as if her presence was required not only to heal, but to protest.

Lifting her head from the path, she was dazzled by the whiteness of the five large tents, and by a sudden rush of wind that ran through her hair, still unknotted from the night before. A thrill ran through her, no less shocking for its familiarity. This was a holy place.

Most pilgrims felt it when first entering the Sanctuary gates, or even more, when waking on the high ground, after a night's sleep on the sacred earth. It was the great privilege of the dwellers within the Sanctuary to feel the healing presence of Asclepios every day. There was no illness among the priests that Corinna could remember. No one even took cold during the winter months. Newly arrived physicians, employed by Coreus to examine the pilgrims, credited the spare diet and the salubrious air for the healthy permanent population of Epidaurus' great shrine. But after a month or two at the Sanctuary, even the most sacrilegious began to look for the presence of the god.

And Asclepios' presence was not hard to find. Removed from the everyday urgencies of life, only the angriest and the most bitter pilgrims did not feel better just for the wild breeze, the view of the mountains and, most important, the absence of what was familiar. Be it the noise of a city, or the crying of infants from the children's room, or the urgent duties of a morning on the farm, there were none among the Greeks who could not profit from a change.

Before Coreus inherited the position of High Priest from his father, there were few buildings of substance at the Sanctuary. Penitents were scarce in those days of war, and other holy places drew men and women who wanted the promise of greater things than the priests of Asclepios could offer: Visions of the future, expiation of murderous crimes, the surety of victory in battle were not within the province of Asclepios' powers.

Still, the windswept high place had attracted some of the faithful. Pilgrims had labored tents and provisions up the narrow path, the able-bodied aiding the sick. Precious bits of the Sanctuary ground were assigned on which to erect these temporary structures, open to the winds and sun of the gods, and to the songs, paeans, and hymns of the temple chorus. No one but the High Priest had been allowed to erect a permanent dwelling on the high ground, so that the Temple and the awe-inspiring statues of the physician god had stood out in even greater majesty than it did with its present complement of homes for priests and physicians, inns for the relatives of the penitents, bathhouses and a host of smaller temples to lesser gods. Now even the markets, stocked with every sacrificial animal save the goat—which was sacred to Asclepios—were built of stone.

Still, these innovations had made the Sanctuary not only immensely richer and more popular with pilgrims, but also a far more effective place for priests and physicians. It was only under Coreus that learned men of medicine and surgery joined the priests of Asclepios, partners in the healing art. Corinna knew that it was not the comforts of a Greek house that brought the healers to the Sanctuary, but rather its combination of philosophy with religion, in an age when so many men of reason were turning their backs to the gods.

Coreus was himself physician as well as priest, and ensured that all pilgrims were examined for evidence of physical wounds, unnatural pulses, discolorations of the skin. Before men were allowed to approach the sanctity of the god's presence in the *abaton*, the sleeping chamber where the priests beseeched Asclepios to remove pain and sickness from the lives of the sick, they were not simply bathed: The physicians and their attendants took care to dress wounds, to prescribe purgatives and emetics, to set broken bones; even, in some unhappy cases, to perform surgery. It would not be considered a mark of faith for a pilgrim to place himself at the mercy of the god without first consulting a physician of the temple, but rather an affront to the god's dignity. Asclepios was after all a physician himself; it did him no honor to turn one's back to the god's own calling.

If the tents of the sick were now permanent structures, open to the sacred wind only in deference to the old ways, they kept pilgrims to a uniform standard of cleanliness, both of the body and the spirit. The licentious atmosphere that surrounded most Greek festivals, where travelers would pitch their tents in the midst of orgiastic anonymity, was unknown at Epidaurus. The Sanctuary was a permanent place, and if the ebb and flow of pilgrims changed the contents of the population, it never changed the standards of behavior set by its High Priest. When Corinna entered the first of the five large tents reserved for the ill, she was not met by prostitutes or sellers of superstitious charms but by a trio of musicians, dressed in the same simple white as their audience. Everything here was designed to calm the *thymos*, or life force, to allow the patient a chance to return to harmony. *Thymos* was not only sustained by food and drink, but by the quality of the air, by the sun and the wind. Music was sustenance to the life force, particularly in the wake of disease or wounding, when *thymos* could leave the body through a bloody discharge or even through the exhalation of a dispiriting breath.

An attendant accompanied her to Diagoras' pallet, guiding her through the threescore patients who shared the tent. The musicians played a kithara-harp, a lyre, and a double-flute, the last instrument unusual for the tents of the sick, because it tended to a heavy melody, unsuitable for patients. Coreus allowed the music at the Sanctuary its religious function, accompanying the ancient hymns and prayers; but he believed in its efficacy as a healing force, removed from the purely benedictory tasks of hailing the gods with music. Sometimes it seemed as if there were more musicians at the Sanctuary than there were priests. They played in the tents of the sick, along the paths to the Temple, about the sacred well, in and around the bathhouses. Sometimes the music was so joyous that Corinna found her own steady rhythms shifting to the meter of the lyre-player; sometimes in the midst of gloom over a dying patient, a phrase from the kithara-harp would lift the corners of her lips in an unexpected smile.

"Mistress," said a small voice, calling out to Corinna from a pallet set on the low platform shared by the array of white-clothed sick. A young boy's smooth-skinned face smiled up at her, and she started in amazement at the transformation in the child's features since he had arrived at the Sanctuary a week before.

She had forgotten his name, but remembered that he was from Cos itself, where the very able physicians of that island had cut into his body to remove a growth but had not been able to restore the harmony of his *thymos*. Even when the surgical cut had healed without festering, the boy's strength had continued to dwindle.

"Hello, child," said Corinna. "You look very well, may Asclepios be praised."

"Mistress," said the boy. "Please hold my hand."

"Of course, child," said Corinna, surprised at the strength with which the boy took hold of her outstretched fingers. Suddenly she remembered his name, Hippias, and as she asked him whether he had taken a walk that fine morning, the grip on her hand intensified.

"I feel better," said the boy, tears in his large brown eyes. A singer had begun the famous paean to Asclepios, a lengthy joyous song of the rise of the ancient physician to the status of god, and the accompanying rush of music nearly brought Corinna to tears as well. For who could doubt that the god had healed this boy, whose *psyche* had, only days before, been ready to depart his broken body for the underworld. The words of the paean were framed in a Laconian Doric accent and would have been difficult to comprehend just from this handicap; but like most of the prayers recited at the Sanctuary, the words were ancient, half a millenium old and more, and slurred out of shape by the fabric of the music. One knew the paean, of course, knew that it was the story of the god, but one didn't listen for familiar words but rather for the familiar rhythm of the music, as beneficial to the *thymos* as listening to the rush of mountain water to the sea.

"You made me well," said the boy, holding tight to Corinna.

"No, child. The god healed you. I am only the servant of the god, praise Asclepios."

Corinna tried to remove her hand from the boy, but he would not yield. Instead, he whispered for her to come close, as if not wanting the attendant to hear his words. Corinna smiled, and sank to her knees on the platform, so that she could rest her head next to his on his clean and scented pallet.

"When you touched me," said Hippias, "you made me better." Corinna tried to still him, but he would not stop. "If you didn't come to me in the night, when you thought I was asleep, and you touched me and said soft words, I would be dead." The boy looked past Corinna's face to the attendant. "The priests tried to kill me," said the boy.

"Now, Hippias, child," said Corinna. "You must not say that. I serve Asclepios as they do. I am priestess and a healer as they are."

"No, mistress, you are not like them. They hurt me. They hurt me very badly, and all you did was try to help me. They never tried to help me."

"Mistress," interrupted the attendant. "As you know from long experience, disease removes sense from otherwise logical people. And in the case of a child—"

Corinna put her cheek against Hippias', to stem the flow of recalled anguish. "All that is important," she said softly, "is that you are now better. You know that we all serve the god. We all are the same—"

"You don't understand," said the boy. "They hit the soles of my feet. Why did they have to hurt me? They cut me many times. And the worst of all was when they brought fire up to my eyes, so close that I thought I would burn or that my eyes would melt. They tried to kill me."

"Hippias, quiet. Listen to the paean. Listen, let your heart still."

"I will listen if you stay here."

Corinna stroked the child's hair, trying to let the music restore her harmony as much as she hoped it would restore his. The boy's father had not come from Cos with his son, but had sent a trusted slave who had given the family history: The boy's mother had died in giving birth to him, and the father, though pleased with the gift of a son, had been so in love with his wife that he had found it difficult to be a loving father. When the boy had been struck by illness, a philosopher, one of the many itinerant wise-men who ply their trade throughout the Greek city-states, had expressed the belief that the boy's illness was a result of the death of his mother: that he would not be cured until he could wash away the pollution of sin.

When she had quieted the boy sufficiently to be able to release herself from his hand, she addressed the attendant.

"Was this boy bled?"

"Yes, mistress," said the attendant, not reacting to the sharpness of her tone.

"Did someone actually strike his feet?"

"The soles of his feet, mistress. With an olive branch."

Corinna shook her head, as if she were a madwoman attempting to speak the incomprehensible language of logic.

"He said that a fire—?"

"A torch was brought near to his eyes. It is a common practice for removing pollution."

"I know the practice, thank you. But are you aware that he is no more than nine years old?" said Corinna. "What sin could he have—"

"Mistress. Everything that was done for the child has worked to great effect. He has suffered for the guilt of his mother's death in giving birth to him. This sin has been washed away. He has no more guilt. If he clings to you now, it is because you are a woman, and he now feels like reaching out to the mother that is long gone to the underworld."

"I want to know," said Corinna, convinced that the child, and not the attendant, was correct—her hands, her love, had done more to ease his pain than any brutal washing away of a sin committed in the first moments of life. "What priest ordered such treatment?"

"The High Priest, mistress," said the attendant. "Your wise husband."

"Thank you," said Corinna. It took all her strength to walk from the boy's bedside to that of Diagoras without exhibiting her anger. Even if Coreus had healed a thousand men with violence she would no longer believe his way was the only path to a cure. "Shall we wake the athlete?" said the attendant.

"No." Corinna made an effort to turn her eyes from Diagoras' gentle, unlined face to the eager attendant. "Coreus has ordered rest for him, and saltwater baths. If he is sleeping so late in the day, it is best to let him be."

"Your husband said that he is to be waked every two hours for the baths."

"Let him sleep," said Corinna, so harshly that the attendant looked at her in wonder. She was only a young girl, in spite of being the wife of the High Priest.

"Would you like to see the woman who cannot wake?" he said politely. "She is in the seond women's tent—"

"No." She had no desire to see another's pain, no matter how unusual. This was where she must stay, in order to fulfill Doricha's words. This was who she must heal, and in her own fashion.

"Last night she is said to have acted out the events of the earthquake, mistress. Two priests shouted at her, but she could hear nothing. She spoke, but not to them. It is very like the athlete, though he is a man."

"No," she said again. The woman who would not wake had good reason to stay in the world of dreams. She had lost three sons in an earthquake, running from her collapsing home instead of fighting her way to the second story children's chamber. Even if the priests would wake her, they would never cure her misery. She was doomed to regret all the days of her life.

Corinna placed her hands on the athlete's chest, feeling the powerful beating of his heart. Her husband had once used a powerful drug, *ephedra,* imported from the distant east, the land of the yellow people; *ephedra* was used to induce a fever, to release heat and sweat the body of dangerous imbalances. The drug came in a smooth colored vial that seemed to carry the mystery of the unimaginable distances from the land of its origins, across vast deserts, over high mountains, through treacherous seas. Coreus had told her that the physicians of that distant nation believed the liver—and not the heart—to be the home of the soul. Anger resided there, because the liver gathered the blood from all the body's canals. Sorrow lived in the lungs, reason in the spleen, they believed; why this was so was probably best explained in the legends of their heroes. But what made most sense to her, and always lingered as a notion that contained truth, was their belief that the quality of happiness lived in the heart.

"You may leave me," said Corinna to the attendant, pulling aside Diagoras' tunic, so that she could place the heat of her palms over the center of his heart.

The priests and attendants had all noted that he spoke in his sleep, giving clear and unequivocal signs of the pollution of guilt. Because Diagoras was a famous man, they were glad of the chance to cure what they believed was within the powers of their High Priest. Coreus knew well how to remove the agonies of pollution from the soul.

"Shall I call for your husband, mistress?" asked the attendant.

"No," she said, closing her eyes, letting the rhythm of the heartbeat overwhelm the music within the tent, the confusion of ills from the pallets of the other sick men and boys, the anger from the rebuffed attendant. Doricha said Corinna would heal him through the strength of her love; and so she let the passion that was long suppressed, the rising tide of madness never before experienced as the High Priest's bride, twist itself into the rhythm of the athlete's great heart.

Behind her shut eyes she could feel the pounding waves of blood through his body, and she felt her love riding the wild current. She was like a child caught in the surf off Epidaurus, full of the power of the sea, but out of control.

"Very beautiful," said Diagoras, speaking from sleep.

She had expected this, but not so soon, nor so easily. His voice was quiet, his shut eyes twisting at the corners as if he were smiling at someone in his dream. She wondered what dreams men blind from birth had, what manner of visions they conjured with no experience of sight in the real world.

"Hold me," said Diagoras, the smile intact, the voice suddenly authoritative. "There is no sin in holding a brother, or even the brother of a husband. No sin."

His heartbeat was wilder now.

"No sin," said Diagoras again, his upper torso lifting off the pallet. Corinna opened her eyes and stepped back, breaking the contact of her skin to his. The pallets on either side of the athlete were empty, but several attendants approached them hesitantly, and sick men near enough to hear turned to them from where they rested.

He had opened his eyes, but she knew he could not see her. And she was certain that he was no more awake than any prisoner of a nightmare.

"You don't love her," said Diagoras with such plaintive force that Corinna was drawn back to his body, to touch him and give him of her love. His eyes shone, as if looking into a bright light, and Corinna suddenly feared that blindness might never be cured in the *abaton*, in the famous temple sleep of Epidaurus.

Perhaps the gods had nothing to do with Diagoras' blindness. Perhaps no madness, no sin, no crime against his brother had brought on a punishment by a god yet unnamed; perhaps nothing but natural causes had brought catastrophe to the athlete. The organ of sight, she knew, was but a glass residing in a messy gel. One had only to look at a sheep's eyeball, removed from its head, to see what sight was. The old grew blind when their eyes clouded, blocking the penetrating light; the young became blind when wounded in battle, or struck by disease. One could see natural destruction in the gel of their eyes: discolored, running, polluted not by sin but by some physical force of no interest to the gods.

But she knew her thoughts were wild, unfounded. Coreus would tell her that no mortal could know what was and what was not of interest to the gods. And anything manifested on the earth in physical form might have a divine origin. Even a battle wound, even the gouging of a prisoner's eyes by a brutal conqueror could have originated in the anger of a god.

"You don't love her," repeated Diagoras. "It does not matter to you what becomes of her. Let it be my sin, not hers. You don't love her."

He shut his eyes now and lowered himself back onto the pallet. His heart raced faster than before. The physicians of Cos often spoke of the progression of an illness. There was a beginning when the imbalance, such as a racing heart, might be observed. Then, in the second stage, this imbalance would worsen; the heart, for example, would beat faster than before. The third stage would end the imbalance. Either nature would root out the problem by intensifying the patient's pain, fever, or accelerated heartbeat to a point where the imbalance would be thrust from the body's shell, or the patient would die.

"Calm yourself, Diagoras," said Corinna, speaking to the athlete for the first time that day. She was afraid his heart would beat too fast, that nature's violent cure threatened to destroy him. "You have commited no sin. You are at Epidaurus, in the hands of the healing god."

"My brother does not love her," said Diagoras, more slowly than before. Corinna had the sense that his words were emerging from a shell, thrusting aside the protection of sleep and therefore tentative, wary. "He has never loved her. It was an alliance. He is older and was therefore chosen for the marriage. He learned that she loved me, but did not care. He told me as much. He loved me better than anyone. Everyone loves Diagoras."

"Then the gods must love you too," said Corinna, moving her hands from his heart to his cheeks. "Then the gods will cure you out of their love."

His hands grabbed at her wrists and held them. "Who is touching me?"

"Corinna."

"Corinna," he repeated, slowly releasing his grip, easing himself from sleep. He sat up with the fluid confidence found only in athletes. "The wife of the High Priest. The one who thinks herself beautiful."

She kept herself from recoiling at his arrogance. She knew it now for nothing but a mask. "How do you feel, Diagoras?"

The athlete blinked, smiling with an assurance born a thousand footraces ago. "Blind," he said. "I feel absolutely blind. I can't see a thing. All this rest and bathing is doing a great deal of good. Making me very rested and salty-clean. It's funny. In Athens we use fresh water and oil. But I suppose Epidaurus knows better."

"You spoke again of your brother."

"My brother is dead," said Diagoras.

"And your brother's wife. Is she dead?"

"How would I know? Alive or dead I can't very well see her."

"Diagoras," said Corinna. "I am trying to help you. Tonight you will burn cakes and incense on the altar. You will be prepared, in body and spirit for the *abaton*. Please do not talk like that. If you are angry, if your spirit is full of fear, you cannot expect the help of the god."

"My brother's wife is alive. Disgraced, and living in her father's house, but alive."

"Disgraced because of you?"

"Of course, because of me," said the athlete. He got off the pallet, crossly gathering the loosened white tunic about him. Standing, he was a glorious image of health. "She made love to me when I was drunk, and that was my fault. She fell in love with me and that was my doing, of course. I wanted her the way I wanted every woman I saw, and whose fault could that be but mine?" Diagoras turned about, as if scouting through the dark for a servant. "I would like water," he said.

"Bring it from the sacred well," said Corinna to an attendant.

"I am still being starved, I suppose?"

"Fasting purifies more than the body," said Corinna.

"What did I say?" said Diagoras, turning suddenly back to where he supposed Corinna stood. "In my sleep? What did I say about my brother?"

"That he never loved her," said Corinna.

"It is true."

"How did he die?"

"In the battle Apollo sent him to. In the battle in which I was blinded."

"Did you see him die?"

"No, I saw nothing," said Diagoras, turning about like a wild animal in a cage. "Where is that water? Am I a prisoner here? Isn't it enough that I am being charged a king's ransom for the privilege of feeding on nothing without killing me of thirst as well?"

The attendant was already hurrying back, holding an earthenware jar in both hands. "Your water is here, Diagoras," said Corinna. "Please sit, and I shall help you to drink."

"How much more will they charge my family when I leave this place? When I am still blind, and my sister-in-law still disgraced? All the old gods will be pacified, of course, now that the once great athlete has spoken out his sins, but how much more will my family be charged? I simply want to know the price of your magic water."

Corinna turned from the athlete's anger to take the jar of well water into her hands.

And then she nearly dropped the sacred drink.

Coreus was walking their way, the sober face fired by a preternatural brilliance. She expected his words to rock the tent, but they were mild, which was much worse; sometimes the priest saved his hatred, building it block by block so that it could emerge at once, an enormous edifice of resentment and violence.

"There is no price for the water," said Coreus. Gently, even more gently than his speech, he took the jar of well water from his young wife's hands. "Drink," said Coreus, and he brought the jar against the athlete's chest, so that the young man could grasp it and bring it to his lips. Coreus watched silently as the athlete drank, gulping down enormous draughts, as if he had finished a two-hour run under the summer sun.

"And the water is not magic," said Coreus.

"He has only just awakened, my husband," said Corinna.

"And there is no charge for the services of the Temple," continued the High Priest, as if his wife had not only not spoken, but was not even within the confines of the tent. Corinna noticed that the music had stopped, and wondered if the musicians had done so spontaneously, out of respect and wonder for the High Priest's words, or had been ordered to do so. "There is a mandatory offering of wheat or barley cakes, which you may purchase at the market. If these are too dear for you, someone will offer you charity. There are many charitable among the sick at Epidaurus. Would you like more water?"

The athlete had managed to drain the jar. Slowly, he brought the jar down from his lips to the center of his chest and turned his eyes toward where Coreus stood.

"I have had my fill, High Priest," said Diagoras.

"Then give me the jar." Coreus, five paces from the athlete, held out his hands for the blind man's offering. Without hesitation, Diagoras walked toward the priest. But Coreus moved to the side, silently, his face a mask of loathing. Corinna felt her heart leap as Diagoras came up to where Coreus had been.

"Here, High Priest," said Diagoras.

"Look at me," said Coreus, moving to the athlete's rear.

Diagoras turned, showing neither exasperation nor pleasure. He couldn't move quickly, the way he had lunged at Corinna in the garden of her father's house, because his hands held the heavy jar. But he moved, following the sound of the High Priest's voice, even as Coreus shifted about the tent, backing silently between the pallets, sidling about a group of gaping attendants to one of the open flaps, from where the clear Greek air puffed in a scent of the sea.

Corinna wanted to stop it, but knew she dared not question her husband's wisdom. Surely this was not a game to torture a blind man, but a method of healing. Surely this was not cruel, but wise, and beyond her ken.

"Look at me," said Coreus, again and again, never exhibiting any anger, but always staying out of reach. "Come here, I said. Why can't you come when I call? Aren't you the fastest man in Greece? Aren't you the great Diagoras, the champion of Athens? Come, give me the jar. I am right here."

The High Priest continued in this way for what seemed to Corinna like half a day. Diagoras never complained, never answered the High Priest's words. It was almost as if he relished the rough treatment, so different from the coddling concern he was given by most of the world.

"Open your eyes," said Coreus, though Diagoras' eyes were already open. "Open your eyes and you will see."

Slowly, as if exhibiting to children how to trip up an opponent, Coreus raised his foot so that it menaced Diagoras.

The athlete neither heard nor saw the danger. When he tripped, the earthenware jar made it impossible for him to regain his balance. He fell, cradling the heavy jar with his elbows so as to prevent it from shattering.

Corinna, alone among the attendants and priests, rushed to help the athlete to his feet. But Diagoras shook off her hand as if she had the plague. He placed the jar on the ground, a hand's breadth from Coreus' feet.

"Do you want to kill me, High Priest?" asked Diagoras.

"No," said Coreus. "But if you do not tell the god what sins are in your heart tonight, you will wish for death. Believe me, Diagoras of Athens, you will wish for death."

Diagoras, his hands free of the burden of the jar, sprang from his awkward position on the ground to a wrestler's hold of the High Priest's knees. It could have been a blind man's awkward stumbling, but no one who saw the graceful speed with which the athlete moved could believe it anything less than an attack. Diagoras pulled in the backs of the High Priest's knees, as he himself rose, tall and golden and strong. It was all the work of a moment.

Coreus fell hard. The wind was knocked out of him, and the pride. His white tunic was filthied by the sacred ground.

Diagoras, his face as gleeful as a small boy's, stood over him. "I'm sorry," said Diagoras. "I can't see. I just can't see."

Chapter 5

SOMETIMES A CHILD will pray for the return from Hades of a loved one for only an instant. To the child this temporary request seems simpler to grant than one beseeching a permanent return to the land of the living.

Corinna, guiding the athlete with her hand at his elbow, made a silent wish to Hygeia, goddess of health and daughter of Asclepios, as they approached her statue. She didn't wish for the return of Diagoras' sight—she had been wishing for that since the first time she saw him—but for something fleeting: Corinna wished that Diagoras could see the Temple of Asclepios.

At sunset the fading light lent a radiance to the statues and images, to the marble columns, to the adornments of ivory and gold. Up the path beaten by white-clothed, barefoot pilgrims was the three-part Temple structure: The *tholos*, where swine and rams and cocks were sacrificed on one altar, and cakes of barley and wheat on another; the *abaton*, where the words of the priests induced dreams, leaving open the door for a curative visit from the god; and the inner Temple, where the wealth of the Sanctuary, product of the pilgrims' votive offerings, was exhibited.

If only the athlete could see the pictures cut into stone of a hundred cures that had taken place under Asclepios' benevolent gaze! If only he could count the offerings made by a thousand pilgrims: terra-cotta figures of arms and breasts and ears; silver figures cast in the shape of vaginas and uteri; exquisitely formed golden noses and lips and eyes. Each bit of sculpture was donated in gratitude for the god's restoration to health of a part of the body. Each would be a blow to Diagoras' refusal to hope for the aid of the god.

"We are in front of Hygeia," she said, marveling anew at the hard marble's appearance of fleshly tenderness.

"The goddess, a statue, or a priestess dressed up to frighten the pilgrims?" asked Diagoras.

"Please," said Corinna. She hesitated before speaking, to lend import to her words. Though he couldn't see it, she turned him toward a stone shelf at the statue's base. "There is a new offering at her feet. A pair of eyes, Diagoras."

"Perhaps it is an omen," said Diagoras.

"Yes," said Corinna. "I believe—"

"Perhaps," interrupted the athlete, "your husband means to cut out my eyes and offer them up as a sacrifice along with our barley cakes."

"Diagoras," said Corinna, letting go of his elbow, so that she could turn about in frustration.

"If you let go of my arm, I might walk into a god," said Diagoras. "Please." He held out his elbow now, his dead eyes looking strangely penitent.

Corinna took his elbow and began to walk past Hygeia. "We have already begun the cure," she said. "You have fasted, you have rested, you have cleaned your body."

"Yes," said Diagoras. "I have never been so clean, nor so hungry."

"There is a reason for everything we do here at the Sanctuary," said Corinna. "Even for your white robe."

"My white robe?" said Diagoras. His tone was no longer sarcastic, but sympathetic. He could hear the terror in her voice, and for a moment was able to forget his own pain. "Tell me about my white robe."

"If you would only let us help you," said Corinna.

"I am here to be helped. To be cured. Please don't let go of my elbow. I feel much better for the touch of your hand."

Corinna hesitated so long before answering this, that her words confused the athlete. "It is for the dreams," she said.

"What?"

"The white robe," said Corinna. "The color white is worn in the *abaton* because white helps induce the dreaming."

She had been with him at the ritual bathing, as she had been at his side the entire day, following the command of her husband.

Coreus had not shown any anger when the athlete had thrown him to the ground; when the attendants had helped him to rise, he had taken Corinna out of the tent and instructed her to spend every moment of the day with Diagoras. The High Priest would prepare for the mysteries of the *abaton* with solitary meditation.

"Remember," Coreus had told her. "The wise men of Athens are looking forward to our failure tonight."

"I will spend every minute of the day with him," Corinna had said. She was amazed that he could not sense her love for the athlete. Grown to enormous size in her heart, she did not know why it didn't scream its presence to omniscient Coreus. If the gods themselves could be jealous, surely so could the High Priest.

"He must open his eyes tonight," Coreus had said, barely looking at her, though for two years she had been his priestess, his assistant, his companion, though the night before he had made love to her with an ecstasy he had longed for since the first night of their marriage. "It will be better to send back his ashes to Athens than to return him healthy and blind."

"I will stay with him," Corinna had said, and this time she had felt as if she were announcing her fate. She would leave Epidaurus, she would flee the wrath of her husband and her father, she would disappear with the athlete into some distant region where no one knew their names.

But now, standing before the Temple with the athlete, his golden hair and beard still damp from the cold ritual bath, she turned her mind from this impossibility. In some parts of Greece it was possible for a woman, with the support of her family, to dissolve the bonds of marriage. But not in Epidaurus; and certainly not in the case of a seventeen-year-old woman married to the august High Priest of the Sanctuary. Coreus would sooner murder her than divorce her.

"You must hold these, Diagoras," said Corinna, taking from a slave a basket of flat, round barley cakes for the sacrifice. Carefully, she placed the basket handle into the blind man's right hand.

"Aren't you afraid I will eat them myself?" said Diagoras. The cakes were sweetened with wine and honey, and their smell was delectable to a man with an empty stomach. "Do you think the god would mind if I take just one?"

"How can you speak like that?" said Corinna. "You just said

you are here to be helped. To be cured. Don't you have any hope at all?''

"Yes.'' They had entered the *tholos* and joined a dozen others at the altar, part of the three score and more who would enter the adjacent *abaton* in hopes of a visit from the god that night. Diagoras, not responding to the flames or the hymns or the music of the kithara-harp but to the earnestness of her question, dropped his bantering tone.

"I hope,'' he said. "I hope that your husband kills me tonight.''

"I don't believe you,'' said Corinna. All about her was the power of piety and devotion; even the Athenians who visited Epidaurus hoping to find quackery and charlatans were impressed with the passion with which priests and pilgrims experienced their gods in this high place. "You hope to be able to see again. You don't want to die.''

"How does someone not an athlete know whether I want to live or die? How does someone not a man know what I need in order to live? How does a girl of seventeen married to a priest know anything at all about Diagoras of Athens?''

"Get to your knees,'' said Corinna, pushing on his shoulders.

"I cannot go through with this,'' said Diagoras, refusing to partake in the ritual before the altar. The scent of the sea was overwhelmed by that of burning incense. But this was itself not strong enough to obliterate another sense: not an odor or a sound, nothing that could be touched or tasted, but something drifting and sharp, something that cut through the assembled bodies about the altar like an invisible knife. The blind man sensed this as well as anyone with sight.

"They are afraid,'' he said. "This is the last chance. They sacrifice, then they go to sleep. If this doesn't work, they will have nothing more to hope for.''

"Is that why you won't kneel?'' asked Corinna.

"No,'' said Diagoras. "I am not afraid that this will not work. I already know that it will not work. Dreams have nothing to do with sickness. Neither do sacrifices nor statues nor prayers. Neither do priestesses. I am blind. I am tired of it. I want to go where no one can see any more than I can. I want to be rid of this life.''

He had turned slowly toward her as he spoke, and with each

despairing phrase, his powerful body seemed to weaken. Even denying the chance of a miracle is an act of will, requiring strength. Suddenly, he was through denying, finished with hopelessness. It was without thought that Corinna took him into her arms, without reason that she brought her lips to his ear and breathed a breath from her heart into his body.

"Corinna," he said, as if she had called to him from a distant place, and he would answer her, if only he could summon the strength.

"My eyes," she said. "They are not black. You said they were black, and I wanted to tell you."

"I am sorry," he said. He brought his hands slowly to the bridge of her nose, and from there to her green eyes, shining with purpose.

"You must kneel," she said.

"What color are they? Your eyes?"

"Kneel, and I will tell you."

Diagoras lowered his hands from her face and got to his knees in front of the altar.

"I have green eyes." She hesitated. "Very pale green eyes. Paler than your blue eyes. Coreus says it is the best color eyes for a priestess, and even Doricha, who has black eyes, agrees."

"I am sorry," said Diagoras, "that I have been so ungrateful for your kindness."

"Don't turn, please," insisted Corinna, thrilled by the change in the athlete's spirit. "And if you would kneel a bit more deeply, the god will feel your respect." She pushed again on his shoulders; this time he didn't fight her, but sank slowly to the ground. Corinna followed suit, watching the flames devour the offerings, letting go of his shoulders so she could add her prayers to those of the pilgrims with her hands exposed to the sacred altar.

Next to her a young man held up a tablet to the sacrificial flames, as if the spirit in the fire could read as well as burn. Those too sick to travel to the Sanctuary sent representatives with gifts for the Temple and prayers for the god. Sometimes a brother or sister would take the place of an invalid in the *abaton*, hoping the god would visit the sick one's spirit through another's body. Such things were possible, she knew, because she had seen them occur at the *abaton*, seen the votive offerings after the cures, had met with pilgrims who had been healed while lying in their sickbeds on the other side of the Aegean Sea and who afterward insisted on sacrificing at the Sanctuary which had given them renewed health and life.

But even in those cases where the sick were absent from Epidaurus during their cures, she knew that they believed. In the heart of their sickness, when their loved ones departed on a journey of faith, the sick sent their hope with them; otherwise the healing was impossible.

Corinna desperately wanted Diagoras to believe, she wanted him to hope, even if only for that night. No healer, not even one in love with her patient, worked without the aid of the sick.

A gong sounded, and the music of the kithara-harp abruptly ceased. Those among the sick who could walk unaided formed a line behind a very old priest. In his hands was a dog, small and silent, his black fur shot through with gray; at the end of the line was another priest, as young and straight as the other was old and bent. In his hands was not an old dog, but a green snake, its head moving from side to side, its nonpoisonous tongue hissing forth, ready to do its sacred work.

"We must go," said Corinna, and slowly she helped the athlete to his feet.

"I did not mean what I said," said Diagoras. "I want to live and I want to see."

"You must not talk, Diagoras," she said, whispering the words. She placed his hand over her forearm and walked so close to him that their thighs touched. A chorus of incense-bearing boys chanted a paean as Corinna and Diagoras took their place in a second line: Here the sick were accompanied by slaves, spouses, friends—someone who could help them to see, to walk, or to understand. This line was slower than the first, but like the other was preceded by a priest carrying a dog, and followed by another carrying a snake. A few priests recoiled at using these animals in the healing process, even in the ritualized licking of a wound or the part of the body where surgery was to take place; but so long had snakes and dogs been used in the rituals of the Sanctuary that their presence was always expected by the faithful.

Snakes were often brought to the Sanctuary by pilgrims from distant lands; every priest as part of his training learned snake-handling during his essential training. Even if they were useless in calling forth the god in the *abaton*, even if they brought no balance back to the bodily humors, they served another purpose. The snakes provided the same kind of healing as the gongs and the incense and the kithara-harp. They were part of tradition and tradition heals.

The space was brightly lit as the sick entered, but once each pilgrim had taken a drink of the *abaton*'s drug-leavened wine, and found his place on a pallet, every other torch was extinguished. Corinna helped Diagoras find his place, and as he settled stiffly on his back, his dead eyes looking toward the arched marble ceiling, she once more breathed into his ear, holding his hands in her own.

"Live," she said. "Live and be well."

She had to leave him, to take her place behind Coreus as he visited each of the sick. But it was difficult to go. For the first time since she had met the athlete he seemed in that peculiar, childlike state so conducive to the healing process; when the patient's life-force opens like an embrace, expecting nothing but a mother's omnipotent caress.

"Corinna," he said, his voice languid and loving, breathing in the smoking herbs the priests used to relax the pilgrims. But he was not simply weak from the heavy air, from the fasting, and from having been bled. Corinna had seen this too: How when the spirit is finally opened to change, the body is suddenly fatigued, like an athlete at the end of the race—when the ordeal is finished. "Corinna, I hope I will see you."

"You will," she said. "You will live and the god will grant you sight, and you will see everything that I see." And then without thought, she brought her lips not to his ear for a whisper, but to his lips for a kiss. The kiss lingered in the dangerous half-dark for only a moment, but the time was long enough to shut out the world, to exchange a silent vow of passion, to make a mad commitment where none was possible.

Then she felt a touch at her elbow.

"Your husband is watching," said a familiar voice.

It was a woman who had touched her, as this voice was a woman's: Doricha the witch met her eyes with a disquietingly respectful stare.

"The athlete will see," said Corinna. "I can feel him releasing whatever it is that imprisons his sight. He will see."

"Your husband is full of violence," said Doricha.

"Coreus is always angry in the presence of disease," said Corinna.

"But not you," said the witch. "You know that anger is not the way to healing."

The striking of the gong had stopped, and the kithara-harp had begun a slow, ethereal melody, accompanied by a quiet lyre. It was dream music. The priests had long ago learned that dreams could come about before sleep, as long as the sick were receptive to the visions that were always around them.

All about the *abaton*, opened on two sides to the night air, the smoke of incense and herbs danced in the light of the few remaining torches. The priests, many of whom carried vials of medicine, surgical instruments, and bandages, assembled about the figure of Coreus. Most would not use these tools that night; removing a growth, feeding the juice of the opium poppy to deaden pain, binding of loose teeth with gold wire, and a hundred other tasks more physical than spiritual were usually done under the light of day, at a remove from the Temple. This did not mean that the healers of Epidaurus made a separation between the treatment of the body and the spirit; even the simplest cleansing of a wound was meant to be both physical and spiritual. But the rituals of the Sanctuary were divided. Cures obtainable by rest and fasting, by simple surgery, by binding limbs, were attempted before taking the patient to the *abaton*. Not every patient had to conjure the god for a visit to make him whole and in harmony, though every patient must be grateful to Asclepios for any benefit received at the Sanctuary, even if just a drink from the sacred well.

Like the snakes, the medical accoutrements carried by the priests and priestesses were marks of office. Asclepios was a physician before he was a god. His daughters Hygeia and Panacea were the goddesses of health and remedies; his sons Podalirios and Machaon were gods of physicians and surgeons. The priests and priestesses, assuming the roles of Asclepios' divine children as part of the ritual, used the medical tools as props. The High Priest, assuming the leading role as Asclepios himself, wore special sandals, built up on soles so thick that it was difficult for him to walk without leaning on an attendant. But he needed the extra-mortal height to give him the aspect of an immortal.

In the *abaton* the hope of the visit from Asclepios and the attendant healing gods was thought to be helped by the priests' assumption of divine forms. This was not an attempt to trick or delude, as some of the self-appointed wise men of Athens liked to say, but rather to conjure. The priests did not conjure the gods alone, any more than they healed without the aid of the patient. It was a mutual process. The patients wanted to dream; the priests helped the dreaming along.

"Hold the knife, daughter," said Coreus, addressing Corinna for the first time that evening. He spoke as Asclepios, and addressed her as if she had already assumed the role of Hygeia, goddess of health; in these guises they had often visited the supine and faithful patients, who had peered into the smoke and in the dim lights beheld what they had long wished to see.

Coreus' eyes were shadowed by Egyptian kohl, his fingernails painted gold; this was usual for the High Priest in the *abaton*, as was his taut-skinned concentration, his face as white as a cloud. What was not usual was the violence beneath the skin. Doricha had warned her, and Corinna could feel the fury all about her husband, as strong and unharmonious as any imbalance in the bodily fluids. This much frustration and anger was either a sickness or would be the cause of one.

"Yes, Father Asclepios," said Corinna, taking the knife from the High Priest's hands. His tension had extended itself to his retinue. In spite of their attentions, Coreus stumbled in his clumsy sandals and would have fallen had not Doricha grabbed him with her powerful hands.

"Where is your pain?" said Coreus, speaking to the first patient, a woman whose legs would not hold her weight ever since the death of her husband. Unlike the tents of the sick, women and men were not segregated in the *abaton* but lay on their pallets in haphazard fashion, united not by gender but by illness.

"I have no pain," said the woman, shutting her eyes against the sight of the High Priest and his attendants. One priest brought the snake in his arms close to the woman's face, another brought a cup of burning herbs along the length of her body. A third opened a vial of sweet-smelling spices under her nose. "It is just that I cannot walk."

"You will walk," said the High Priest. He spoke in a deep, preternatural voice that always came to him in the *abaton*, without effort or thought, as if the god proclaimed through the mortal lips of the priest.

"Look at me, woman of flesh and blood," said Coreus, taking the knife from Corinna's hands and cutting into the woman's palm. "Can you not feel the blood in your hands?"

"No," whispered the woman, speaking between clenched teeth, her eyes tightly shut.

Coreus brought the woman's palm up against her mouth, so that she tasted the fresh blood of the wound. Then he drove his thumb into her neck, so that her mouth opened wide, without thought. The shock of the blood-taste opened her eyes.

"I can't walk," she insisted, though this had not been demanded of her. Corinna could see that the woman's eyes were wild, but what part of that was from the incense and the drug-leavened wine, what part from the dignities of the sacrifice, what part from the ritual of the snakes and dogs, she could not say. The appearance of Asclepios and his family in the dimly lit *abaton* was but a part of a play that began the moment the pilgrim decided to make the trip to the Sanctuary. The woman, like the other sick at the Sanctuary, knew how they wanted the play to finish. It was up to each of them to fulfill their sacred tasks.

"Can you not feel the blood in your hands?" repeated Coreus, so that the words must have penetrated past the shut eyes and myriad fears of every one in the *abaton*.

"Yes," said the lame woman. "Yes, Asclepios."

"And can you not, woman of flesh and blood, can you not feel the blood in your legs?" said the High Priest, his voice more powerful than that of any mortal man.

"I am sorry," said the woman, retreating from the god's wild-eyed look.

Coreus cut into the woman's leg, so swiftly and effectively that she felt no pain, only the slightest sensation, like a scratch from a thornbush. Not Coreus, but Corinna, in her role as Hygeia, and another priestess, in her role as Panacea, dragged the woman's unprotesting hand along her naked and bloodied thigh, and then brought this hand with its daub of blood against the woman's quivering lips.

"Asclepios," she said. "I cannot walk. Please, you must help me to walk. I want to walk."

"Woman of flesh and blood," said Coreus. "Do you feel the blood in your legs?"

"Yes, great Asclepios."

"Say the words, mortal woman."

"I feel the blood," she said. "I feel the blood in my legs."

Incense was brought closer by the attendants, so that another one of her senses might be overwhelmed.

"Your husband has left this world, mortal woman, but you will walk with him again. You will walk with him again in the underworld when your *psyche* leaves the frame of your body. But until that time you must walk here. You must walk here, in this place. Even while you lie sleeping you must get up and walk here. You must walk in your dream."

But it was no dream for Corinna, nor for any of the attendants as they dragged the woman off the pallet, as they propped her up and marched her between the sick waiting to be visited by the god. The woman walked on legs held up by faith, a faith more powerful than the mourning for her husband that had left them without strength at all.

And when they let go, she walked alone.

Asclepios had cured her lameness.

When she finally fell, it was not due to any weakness in her legs, but only to the tears of thanks, the overwhelming gratitude she felt for the god. Whether she would walk in the morning, without the help of a priest, could not be known. But to the woman, a cure had been effected. Asclepios himself had bled her, had demanded her obedience, had put her on her feet. She had walked in the *abaton*, in her dream, and if she could not walk in the light of day, she would return again and again to the hands of the healing priests and the god they served until she could walk all the time.

There was no special path through the sickbeds in the *abaton*. Coreus turned from the woman who couldn't walk, to a boy with a head wound whose parents hoped a visit from the god would speed the healing process. There was an old man gone deaf, an even older woman whose hands would not stop shaking; there were new brides who couldn't conceive, there were old husbands who had lost their potency; there were men already healthy anxious to be assured by the god that the ache in their heads was not a sign of swift-approaching doom.

"Great Asclepios," said Corinna to her husband, when the succession of cures and visions, the illnesses of the head and heart and spirit, the parade of divinities in the torchlight had

gone on long into the night. The ceaseless music, the fear and
awe and faith and guilt seemed to have risen up from the beds
and mingled with the incense and the drugs in the dream-laden
air. "Great Physician-God. When will you approach the blind
man?"

Coreus had not stopped his labors, but neither had the hours
slowed his pace nor dulled his concentration. Always the knife
flashed in his hand with sure, unhesitating movements; always
he possessed the harsh words to bring forth the sin that needed
to be forgiven, always he had the strength to put each patient
into a state of mind so like a waking dream that each had felt
himself the center of the god's attention, the focus of all the
healer's power and care.

"The athlete is last," said Coreus.

"We have gone to every pallet but his," said Corinna.

Coreus' black eyes reflected the torchlight, and nothing else.
They seemed not to see her at all though they were turned her
way. "You are all dismissed," said the High Priest.

It was very late, an hour before dawn, but there had been
later nights than this in the *abaton*. Never before had Coreus sent
priests and attendants home before the night's work was done.

"I am not tired, Great Asclepios," said the priestess who
acted as Panacea. Doricha spoke up too, eager to be of service to
the athlete, and to Corinna. It suddenly seemed as if all the
priests were speaking, in defiance of Coreus: Everyone wanted
to treat Diagoras, to share in the glory of his cure.

"You are all dismissed," repeated Coreus. "All except Hygeia. My daughter."

No one questioned this order further, not even Doricha, who
briefly clutched Corinna's hands before leaving the *abaton*.

"May the god heal him," said the witch.

She knew that Doricha prayed not for Coreus' cure, but for
that of the true Asclepios; and for the healing through Corinna's
love she had seen in a vision. Before Corinna could thank Doricha, she was gone, as were all the others. She understood that
she was tired, and in a state very much like the sleeping patients;
susceptible to visions and visitations from the god. Still, she could
not remember the moment when she had walked through the
abaton and gotten to her knees before the athlete's pallet. And if
she could not remember this, there might be other things that

had eluded her in this dark and mystical place. Certainly Diagoras had been drugged; perhaps she herself had been drinking
wine laced with herbs from Doricha's garden. She held Diagoras'
hands, but sleep didn't leave him; even when she softly whispered his name, there was no bringing him to awareness.

"You love him," said Coreus' voice.

For a moment, Corinna couldn't see her husband. There
were tears in her eyes, but she hadn't been crying. She looked up
and saw the knife she had been holding as Hygeia, in the hands
of Asclepios. It caught the light, which was itself strangely bright
for the dimness of the *abaton*. And there was Asclepios, black-
eyed and grim, no longer as tall as a god.

"You are my wife and you love him," said Coreus.

"Yes," said Corinna, not knowing where she got the
strength to speak. She wondered if the knife was for her: If he
would lunge at her and slit open her throat or wrists; or perhaps
he would only pluck out her eyes, so that she could go off with
her lover, as blind and helpless as he.

"And you, faithless one," said Coreus, moving about the
pallet with great speed, so that Corinna understood that he had
shed his sandals, the better to be able to strike. "You adulterer,
worthy of death, do you admit to loving my wife?"

It seemed impossible that he would speak. Corinna looked
at the athlete's hand in her own, and it was cold and still, nearly
lifeless with a numbing sleep. This was not the famous temple-
sleep of Epidaurus, but something different, something very like
death.

"Speak, adulterer," said Coreus, slapping the athlete, the
way he had in the courtyard, hitting him with a viciousness that
barely seemed to register except in the reddening of Diagoras'
cheek. The High Priest had placed torches on the ground about
the pallet, torches that had before been scattered about the *abaton*;
only at that moment did Corinna realize why the light had grown
so bright about the three of them, and why all the rest of the
abaton had grown so quiet and dark as to almost disappear.

"Yes, I love her," said Diagoras, his voice steady and deep,
as if he had woken to his full powers.

"You mustn't say—" began Corinna, but her husband
stopped up her words with a backhanded blow.

She moved back, terrified of what he had discovered. Of

course Coreus knew everything. How foolish she'd been to imagine that he might not have recognized her love for the athlete!

"But she is forbidden to you," said the High Priest, returning his attentions to the athlete.

Diagoras' hand was no longer still. He pulled free of Corinna's hand and sat up, his face and chest streaming with sweat.

"I love her," he said. "And I want her, and you must set her free."

If he had sight, he would have been staring at Coreus. The High Priest rested one knee at the foot of the pallet, and held the knife between himself and the athlete.

"Not until I die," said Coreus.

"No," said Diagoras, the steady voice suddenly small and full of regret. "You must not die. I never wanted you to die."

"Not until I die," repeated Coreus, bringing the knife so close to the athlete's blind eyes that Corinna prepared to throw herself at her husband. "You cannot have her until I die, so you let me die. Isn't that right?"

"No," said Diagoras, his dead eyes blinking, as if bothered by the light of the torches. "I did not want you to die."

"You let me die, you didn't stay by my side, you let me die." Coreus held the athlete by the hair of his head, pulling him close to the knife in his other hand. The High Priest whispered the words, and Corinna heard, and understood that thus far she had understood nothing. Diagoras continued to deny what the High Priest accused him of, but seemed unable to speak. He shook his head on its short tether, he tried to retreat to the shut-eyed solace of sleep.

"You let me die, though you are my brother," said Coreus.

Magically, the High Priest had brought the athlete back through time, to that terrible moment when his brother had died in battle, before his eyes.

"I stayed. I fought," said Diagoras, his words a lament, knowing they would never be believed. "I didn't want you to die."

"Look at me," said Coreus.

"I didn't want you to die," repeated the athlete, but now he tried to pull his head back from the grip on his scalp, and the pain was so wild in the space about the pallet, that Corinna could scarcely breathe.

"You wanted to make the journey," said Diagoras. "I warned you it was dangerous. There was little profit in it. It was a deliberate attempt to excite the gods. Even when Apollo's oracle urged you to go, I knew it would mean battle, it would mean death and destruction. But I didn't want you to die."

"Then look at me."

"I can't see."

"Look at me, and you will see. Look at me, and know that you wanted my death, and then I will forgive you."

"I didn't want your death," said Diagoras. But this shouted denial was cut short by Coreus, slashing the knife into the skin of the athlete's neck.

"You wanted my death, as you wanted my wife, and your guilt must be washed away by your own blood." Coreus was shouting now, but he had not lost any concentration or control; in her heart Corinna understood that the High Priest was trying to heal.

"I did not want your death," said Diagoras, the blood running from his neck, mingling with his tears.

Coreus cut again, bringing the blade up the neck to the cheek, shouting his words into the athlete's shut eyes. "Look at me! Confess your crimes! Look at me and you will see!"

"No," said Corinna softly, and then again, much more loudly: "No, that is not the way." She flung herself through space, with a determination and strength she didn't know she possessed. She could not let Coreus torture the athlete a moment longer.

"Let me," said Corinna. "I can heal him."

She found herself grasping her husband's wrist, pulling back the knife-hand and shouting at him, again and again:

"I can heal him!"

Coreus was immensely strong, and he had resisted this sudden wild attack. But the young woman's spirit had gifted her body with a sudden ferocity. The High Priest not only let go his hold on the knife, so that it fell outside the pools of torchlight to the dark ground, but released his hold on the athlete's scalp. "Stay where you are, you idiot," said Coreus.

"That is not the way," repeated Corinna. "I can heal him. I can help him to see."

"Do not contradict," said Coreus, bending low for the knife, and as he looked for it in the dark, Corinna listened to the healing spirit who guided her and she struck the back of the High Priest's neck with both her hands.

"I did not want him to die," said Diagoras. The memories raised in the long night had left him shaking. Corinna took his bloody face against her chest. "I did not want him to die," he said again, but already she could feel a lessening of his pain.

"I forgive you," she said.

"But I wanted you."

"I forgive you for wanting me, Diagoras. I wanted you. I was as guilty."

"But the gods killed my brother. They blinded me. There is a reason for such things."

"A reason that we cannot know," said Corinna. She had been Hygeia, daughter of Asclepios, all night; now she was the beautiful sister-in-law of the athlete. Like Helen of Troy, she was a cause of madness and death. "But listen to me. I forgive you. You must hear me, and believe me. I forgive you, and I believe you. You did what you could to help your brother. But he is dead, a year is past, and Asclepios will heal you now. Now."

She could hear the High Priest begin to rise, but surely, she felt, he would not interfere.

There is a confidence that comes into a healing at a certain point, when one feels in touch with the god and the diseased spirit; Corinna felt herself as much a conduit as any great oracle. She held Diagoras in her arms, and she extended her love to him, but this was paltry compared with the greater powers running through her hands, the powers of harmony sent from Olympus.

Diagoras slowly opened his eyes, but Corinna did not look to see whether life had entered them.

"Do not hate your blindness," she said. "If you believe it was sent by the gods, it must have had a purpose. In some way, your spirit asked for it, needed it, and now you must tell your spirit that it may release what it called down from the heavens. Release the blindness, because you no longer need to be blind."

"I love you," said Diagoras, and Corinna knew that the words were not for her, but for a woman of Athens; or perhaps for that woman and for a goddess as well. Why would he not love Hygeia, in whose shape she now held him in her arms?

"Release what was given you by the gods, because you no

longer require it," said Corinna. "Let it go, let your spirit turn from the past, let your body return to harmony."

"I love you," he said again, and she wondered if he was even listening to her words, if all his response now was to the healing love in her hands and breast. She shut her own eyes, as she often did in a healing, and with all her strength she begged for the release of the blindness from the healthy body. She tried to reach back through space for the healing power that was everywhere; for the world was made from chaos, brought into being in harmony, and harmony was all she requested for the man she loved.

"Let go," said her husband, getting to his feet, his voice no longer that of Asclepios, but his own. "Now that you have had your fill of touching him, leave the Athenian to me."

"No, please," said Corinna, not letting go of Diagoras, but opening her eyes and cringing, expecting a blow.

But no blow came.

Like the slow dawning of a miracle, she saw Diagoras raise his golden head, his eyes wild with anger, looking past her to where Coreus stood, ready to strike.

"No," said Diagoras, because he could see.

But Coreus, long used to the failed powers of the sick, ignored Diagoras' warning. The High Priest reached out toward his young wife's shoulders, but before he could touch the surface of her skin, Diagoras moved, sure and fast, faster than Corinna had ever before seen a man move.

He was gone from her embrace, off the pallet, springing up from one knee and at Coreus' throat in the breadth of a moment. "It's all right, Diagoras," said Corinna. "Let him go."

She was certain he would have strangled the priest if she hadn't gently touched his arm, and repeated his name. "Diagoras," she said. "Diagoras of Athens."

Coreus gasped for air when Diagoras released him. But this did not prevent a smile of triumph from coming to the High Priest's face.

"Who are you?" said Diagoras, looking at Corinna. But then he answered his own question. "Green-eyed Corinna. Wife of Coreus, High Priest of Epidaurus." He turned around now to the man he had nearly strangled. Corinna approached him, and gently brought a clean white cloth to his bloody, tearstained face.

Diagoras was even more beautiful with his eyes responding to every image in the room; like a pauper at a banquet, he wanted to feast on what was so long denied him.

"Praise Asclepios," said Coreus. "Praise the Physician-God."

To his dying day, Coreus maintained that the athlete had been cured by the drawing forth of guilty sins, and their expiation in the letting of the athlete's blood. In the legends of Epidaurus, the cure was remembered as the High Priest's greatest triumph. For hundreds of years, the enormous pair of golden eyes donated by the family of Diagoras of Athens to the Sanctuary was prominently exhibited to new pilgrims.

But Corinna, who never again saw the athlete after that night of wonder in the *abaton*, knew that Coreus had cured nothing. She had learned that love is a greater force than hate and that there was no better way to healing.

Eventually she gave Coreus sons. Perhaps because of this, or because of her fame as a healer, he grew to respect her, even to show her the kind of love that men less sober show their wives.

Regardless, the legends say that Corinna met Diagoras in Hades, and that the Lord of the Underworld married them to each other, and to eternity. Theirs was a bond stronger than any marriage arranged on earth: His spirit had been sick, while her spirit had been wanting; their coming together had been more powerful than any mere physical union of lovers. It was a joining of incomplete spirits who together made themselves whole, who healed not just a blindness, but a lovelessness. For the rest of her life Corina knew passion, and she brought this to every patient under the touch of her healing hands.

New York City, 1983

*E*LIZABETH PUT HERSELF to sleep with three glasses of red wine. She woke with the alarm at half past four, and stumbled three steps to the galley kitchen. There she ran hot water from the tap into a cheerful yellow mug until it steamed over the top.

"Think, Elizabeth," she told herself out loud. Still, she could not remember where she had hidden the instant coffee. Slowly, with great care, she opened, one by one, the three tiny kitchen cabinets that hung over the sink. All were empty and lined with ghastly Con-tact paper: She found herself drifting in contemplation of a bouquet of psychedelic flowers, relic from an earlier generation of medical residents. How could she have lived in this space for the better part of a year without ever having seen the garish colors of flowers, peace symbols, slogans urging mankind to love one another?

The phone rang, and she picked it up after the first ring.

"Good morning, Dr. Grant. Four-forty-five," said the answering service.

"Hi," said Elizabeth into the phone. Out of the corner of her eye, she saw the wayward jar of instant coffee, sitting center stage on the counter, a spoon stuck into its open mouth. The wake-up call was one of Elizabeth's few "luxuries," a backup system for her alarm clock. Even on three hours sleep she couldn't remain oblivious to a phone ringing next to her head. "You wouldn't happen to know if it's still raining?"

But there was no response to Elizabeth's question. The telephone girl was off and running, calling other early risers: movie stars required to be made-up and on the seat at half past six, commodity brokers needing to review prices in a dozen time zones before their clients called, athletes urging themselves to train before first light and the debilitating effects of the August sun.

"Well, thanks just the same," said Elizabeth smartly. She put down the phone and stared out her filthy window into the black air shaft that provided no air. "I don't actually care if it's raining or not. I just wanted a little early-morning chat. Nothing serious. Just to make my mouth move."

She stirred four teaspoonfuls of the coffee powder into the mug of hot water and brought the muddy mixture to her lips. "Delicious," she said to herself. "I am finding nice things to say about everything, and enjoying what is enjoyable about every lovely moment."

Smiling like a madwoman, she went about searching for a change of clothes. As she had insisted on enjoying her morning cup of coffee, she would enjoy wrapping herself in a laundry-fresh shirt. But when she tore open the package of laundry sitting on top of her chest of drawers she saw at once that the blood-stains on her man-tailored white shirt were still there, exactly where she had exhibited them to the laundryman a week before.

"You son of a bitch, you should die in a hospital," she said. For a moment, she thought she was crying, but when she lifted her fingers to her eyes, there was nothing wet there. All she could feel were the crusty leavings of sleep.

Quickly, Elizabeth drank the coffee and dressed. She had given herself enough free time to indulge in hysterics. She put on the bloodstained blouse; it smelled fresh and clean. Her white coat would cover the stains anyway, and by tonight coat and blouse would be ready for the laundry all over again.

She waited for the elevator for thirty seconds, before deciding to run down the seven flights of stairs. Now that she wore track shoes, she often found herself running, as if eager to test the limits of her fatigue. Outside, the rain had indeed stopped, and she smiled at the small victory of not having brought an unnecessary umbrella. The humidity cast a haze about the streetlights and brought a welcome wetness against her face. As she crossed York Avenue, she tried to remember whether she had finished her terrible coffee and whether she had brushed her teeth. A lone taxi, looking for a fare, slowed as she put a foot into the street. Elizabeth caught a glimpse of the driver: a young man with a shock of wiry hair held back by a red headband. She wondered when he would be going home to sleep, whether this was the end or the beginning of his run.

At the nurse's station, she was offered a slice of pizza by an intern. "It was good pizza at midnight," he said, placing it into her hands before hurrying off, trying to put speed into sleepwalking legs. Elizabeth ate it greedily, drinking three cups of lukewarm coffee as she looked over charts.

"Mrs. Brendan died," she said, reading the information aloud as if this might penetrate the shield about her feelings. The woman had been admitted with a multiplicity of problems, chief of which had been liver failure, the result of a lifetime of heavy drinking. Elizabeth had been surprised to find out that she was forty years old. The woman's skin had been yellow from jaundice, lined from a thousand cares; she had looked twenty-five years older. But it had been her heart and not her liver that had given out first; though the cause of death should not have been listed as heart failure, but more directly, life failure. For Mrs. Brendan had failed at everything she had ever done. She had told Elizabeth that she had failed at school, had failed in love, had failed in finding a job to support herself.

"Think of all that wasted blood," said a nurse.

"Public money. Out of your paycheck, honey," said another.

Elizabeth put down her Styrofoam cup and looked at the two nurses as if seeing them for the first time. After minor heart surgery, Mrs. Brendan had needed a great deal of blood. Her blood vessels were weak, and the years of drinking had impaired the ability of her blood to clot. "I'm even no good at bleeding," she had told Elizabeth.

"How dare you!" said Elizabeth.

The nurses looked at her quizzically. As a group, surgeons were notoriously unsentimental, and this particular surgeon, although young and female and attractive, had never seemed to object to any irreverent reference to the newly dead. In fact, if Elizabeth Grant, M.D., had any reputation among the nurses, it was for an honesty that was often too brutal, a manner too mechanical to allow for any feeling to get in the way of diagnosis or cure.

"Something wrong, Dr. Grant?"

"Every patient in this hospital is entitled to first-rate care. We never give up on anybody, we make no distinctions between rich and poor, we don't withhold treatment because some idiot thinks the patient's going to die anyway."

"Sure," said one of the nurses, remembering that surgeons, even third-year residents, were allowed their tempers, their idiosyncrasies, their aloofness.

But the other nurse, older and more experienced, was not as eager to let the insult pass. "Excuse me for living, *Dr.* Grant," she said, accentuating the "Doctor" as if it were a title worthy of her contempt. If a doctor wanted to lash out at her, it had better be a man, and not some nose-in-the-air girl who would have been a nurse like herself, if not for the "liberation" of medical schools in the last generation.

"Mrs. Brendan is dead, and you will show some respect," said Elizabeth, looking straight at her antagonist. She knew well that the older woman's heart was filled with bitterness and envy for being born too early to have been trained as a doctor instead of a nurse; harassment by veteran nurses was a common complaint among female interns. But Elizabeth ignored this. She was a surgeon, and she would demand to be treated like one. No one would complain about her temper.

"I don't like to be called an idiot," insisted the nurse, but Elizabeth's eyes, fueled from a reservoir of anger that rose with each passing day of Richard's illness, gave her pause.

"Then don't talk like an idiot," said Elizabeth. Some of her third cup of coffee had splattered against the chart in her hand, but Elizabeth ignored this. What did a filthy chart or a resentful nurse mean in the greater scheme of things? Richard was asleep in a private room on the fifth floor, awaiting the results of a bone marrow test for acute leukemia, and any time not spent with him was wasted time. But how could time pass more slowly than watching his beautiful face, twisted with fear and pain?

"I'm sorry," said the younger nurse, who had first made the crack about the waste of blood. She offered to get the doctor a fresh roll to go with what was left of the coffee, but Elizabeth was no longer hungry. "You will show some respect," she said again, but this time her words were gentler, no longer a violent reproof but a comment to herself.

She spent the rest of the morning making rounds, but her

usual machinelike efficiency had broken down. Elizabeth had lost her concentration.

Customarily, she thought about nothing but the facts before her: symptoms, test results, responses to treatment. Elizabeth knew that some doctors listened to everything and anything said to them by their patients, as if complaints about hospital food or less-than-perfect mothers would somehow offer insights into the nature of their ailments. She knew too that doctors in other specialties were quick to imagine surgeons as being particularly impatient with any "holistic" data received from patients; surgeons were accused of wanting to cut out defective "parts" without analyzing the patient as a "whole" being, living in a world that had created him and continued to work its influence on every aspect of his health. But Elizabeth believed that if a tumor threatened to grow into the brain, it had better be cut out; that if torn cartilage in the knee caused an athlete to limp, surgery was a better cure than psychiatry; that if a man bled from an open wound, it was best to stop the bleeding with physical measures and not waste precious time talking about the general sickness of the modern world.

Ordinarily, patients sensed that they had best be quick and to the point in talking with Dr. Elizabeth Grant. Few bothered her with queries about the weather or complaints about the demoralizing effect of trying to watch a broken television set when they were too sick to read. But that morning some imagined that the doctor was there to listen patiently and to respond with care. They could not know that this attitude was prompted not by compassion but by fear. Only by filling her mind with everything that came her way on the rounds, reading not only their charts but the covers of their magazines, looking not only for symptoms of disease but for signs and symbols of the way they lived their lives, could she try to avoid thinking about Richard.

She listened to a Mrs. Green talk about her fears of being infected by the germs of the woman coughing in the bed on the other side of the curtain; she sympathized with the old man recovering from heart surgery, talking not only about the pain that was distributed all over his body but the brother who never visited him; she took clear and careful notes from a man newly admitted for stomach pain, listening to his illogical explanation of how his runaway daughter was responsible for every misery in his life. But it was no use. Not for a moment did she stop thinking about Richard, not for a second did the constricting fear let go its hold on her chest. Try as she might to concentrate on the problems of others, she could think only of Richard's fear, and how it was of a piece with her own. He had been tested, and now he waited for the results of his test, and when those results were in, they would find her, and tell her.

In that way she would be prepared to help him when he was told. She would know exactly what to say.

It will be all right, darling. You have leukemia, but you've got nothing to worry about.

Though far from being a cancer specialist, Elizabeth knew enough about leukemia, and yet not quite enough, to have fallen into a state of terror from the moment she had seen the black-and-blue marks on Richard's back.

That had been ten days ago.

It was a week since he had been admitted to the hospital.

It was six days since the results of the first blood test.

She had told him what the oncologist had told her: The tests were inconclusive. She had explained, slowly and repetitiously, why the tests were inconclusive, and why they necessitated more tests. Over and over again, she had explained that although he was anemic, his red blood count might be abnormal for any number of reasons other than leukemia.

But Richard knew, the way sick people often knew, long before the tests were analyzed, appraised, and reappraised. He was angry, he was afraid, and he wanted it all to be over before anyone was even willing to give it a name.

"I don't see the point of a bone marrow test," he had said.

"Richard, we have to know what is happening to you—" she had said, but she stopped, because he had not yet finished. Even as he spoke, she could see the beads of sweat appearing on his smooth forehead. Everything was an effort now. What he had shrugged off for two weeks as a low-grade summer cold, as a vague fatigue resulting from depression over his recent sculpture, was no longer able to be ignored. Any kind of vigorous motion exhausted him.

"What is happening to me is that I am sick, and that I am going to die. The question is when, and what kind of shape am I going to be in until I die. But Lizzie—I'm telling you right now,

I'm not going to tolerate feeling like this. I'm going to take something, or jump off some high place. I don't care what the reason is for feeling like this. I don't care what kind of cancer it is. It's cancer, and I don't want to deal with it. I don't have to, and I don't want to, and so I won't."

Of course this anger had quieted, as it always did.

No one was as eager to die as all that.

There was, even in the heart of fear, a dream of survival. Tests were often wrong, confused, misapplied. Richard was eventually eager to listen once again, to hear that in many cases of leukemia, the first blood test pointed clearly to the disease. Primitive blast cells—insufficiently developed white blood cells —replace normal white blood cells in such high concentration that they are readily visible in a blood sample under magnification. Richard's blood sample provided no such clear results. This did not mean that he was free of the disease; but it was a kind of reprieve.

Sometimes, the abnormal, underdeveloped white blood cells are not present in the sample of a patient with leukemia: Either the blast cells are not being discharged into the bloodstream, or they are so quickly eliminated from the bloodstream that they cannot be identified. A diagnosis of leukemia cannot be made then until a bone marrow sample is taken, because it is the bone marrow that is the source of leukemic cells.

And when Richard could think of his hospitalization as a kind of testing ordeal, where he must pass first one exam, then another, and then be well, he was stoic, he was patient, he was respectful and attentive to the oncologists who examined him. But when he thought of it as an exercise for the doctors, as a chance to write down another statistic in the grim book of death whose pages he had entered, against his will, he rebelled, he grew sullen, he alternated refusing to believe that he was sick at all with believing that his death was inevitable, and that he wanted his life to end at once, without pain.

"We don't know anything, yet," was Elizabeth's constant refrain. But this hardly cheered him. It was not as if the doctors were advising the young man that he was probably fine, and that the bone marrow test was to be a final proof of this; it was precisely the opposite. They believed that he was sick, they named the sickness leukemia, and they were searching for a way to prove that what they believed was true. Richard did not want to be part of this proof. He did not want to look any further into what awful secret had lodged in his body. He wanted to wake up and discover that he had suffered no more than a nightmare. It was no great leap of the imagination for him to picture a grinning oncologist, reporting the glad news that their beliefs were corroborated, that he was just as sick as they had supposed!

But finally he had agreed to the test. Elizabeth had requested permission to be at his side for the procedure, and when she had entered his private room, he had kissed her with a mock romanticism that was somehow still full of feeling.

"My only regret is that I don't have enough organs to give away to everyone in the country," he had said. Richard had then suggested that the local anesthetic being administered to his left lower back was probably unnecessary: He was so in love with Dr. Elizabeth Grant that all he could feel was bliss.

But this joking mood did not last.

Elizabeth had told him that the bone marrow test was quick and, thanks to Novocain, not painful. Indeed, when the doctor cut through the skin to the flat wide posterior iliac crest bone in his left lower back, Richard simply fixed his eyes on hers in an open smile. Even when the doctor cut into the bone itself, exchanging his scalpel for a more menacing instrument and putting his muscle and weight into the operation, Richard continued to be at ease.

"It's no good," he had said. "I won't talk. You can cut me and you can beat me, but I'll never tell on Lizzie. Never."

"This won't last but a moment," said the doctor, his eyes turning to those of his colleague, Elizabeth, for a moment of complicity. He had picked up a syringe, which Richard, lying on his front, could not see, and inserted this into the tool that had cut into the bone. With the syringe in place, the doctor suddenly drew out the bit of marrow.

It was the work of a moment, but in that moment, Richard's eyes ceased smiling.

So great and surprising was his pain, that he had no time to stifle his scream. It came out, hoarse and unformed, a sharp expulsion of breath mixed with an incipient indignation. There were tears in his eyes now, and as he sucked in his breath, he shut them and violently gritted his teeth.

"Are you all right, darling?" she had said, knowing at once that it was the wrong thing to say. Richard had placed his head on the bed, letting his racing breath slow down. The doctor shot the blue substance from the syringe into a dish.

"That was great, pal," said the doctor. "You're a trouper."

Richard laboriously raised his head and turned to where the doctor was holding the dish closer to the light. "I'm not your pal," said Richard hoarsely.

"Okay," said the doctor. "Sorry it hurt. We got a good sample."

"Good for what, you bastard?" said Richard.

Elizabeth softly touched Richard's hand. "No one meant to hurt you, sweetheart."

"Stop it, Lizzie."

"Hey," said the doctor to Elizabeth. "You got to be there to know how much it hurts."

"Just stop it," said Richard, pulling his hand from hers. "I'm not his pal, and I'm not a trouper. And I won't be patronized. Do you hear me? I won't be patronized, locked up in a bed like a prisoner on display."

"Richard," she said. "Darling. I had no idea it would be so painful for you."

"Maybe you did and maybe you didn't."

"I did not have any idea—"

"Yes, you did. You had an idea. Your idea was for me to go through with this bone marrow test. Okay, I'm through. I hurt, and I'm the doctor's pal and a trouper, and it hurt so much—it still hurts—"

"I'm sorry," she said. But he was not through with chastising her, for she was a doctor and therefore the enemy, one of those who would prod and pull, who would stick him with needles and attach him to tubes.

"Look, do me a favor. Don't come back until you know."

"I like to spend time with you—"

"I said do me a favor. I know you think it's a great favor to give me some of your valuable time, but I don't want it. Use it for something else. I want to be alone. I want to be alone, because then when you come back, I'll know that you know for sure, and then I'll know for sure, and then it will all be over. Over. Do you understand what I'm saying?"

"Yes. You need some time to think—"

"No! Stop interpreting for me. I'm telling you what I want. Do it. Don't come see me until you have the results of this god-damned test."

"Okay, Richard."

She couldn't stand to see the hateful look in his eye. It was enough to brave the indignation and fury of strangers, always ambivalent about their desires to be touched by her physician's hands. But this was Richard, whose body was mated to hers, whose heart had beat against her palms, whose lips had gentled every part of her. This was her lover, and she felt his fear like a betrayal, she felt his hurt like a stabbing pain.

"Lizzie, it hurt."

"I'm sorry."

"I'm not mad at you. But it hurt, it hurt more than anything, and I don't want to be hurt anymore." She searched for something to say, but in the momentary silence, he turned about and reached for her hand. He had tried to smile, but had succeeded only in part. "Come back when you know," he had said.

They told her at the end of the morning's rounds.

It was conclusive. Richard had been stricken with acute my-elocytic leukemia. He would need chemotherapy. He could be dead in a month.

"I am going to the park," he said, when she walked into his room a few minutes after she had been told. The minutes had not helped her prepare a speech. They had done nothing but bring her closer to where she imagined he would be—utter despair.

"Has Dr. Berghof come by?" she said.

"No doctors, no nurses," said Richard. "Just you and me, babe." He looked well at that moment, as if fatigue and weakness were as foreign to his nature now as they had always been. She watched in wonder and fear as he stood next to the hospital bed, slipping on a T-shirt over his tanned and muscular body. "I feel great and I want to go to the park."

"Richard, darling. You can't just walk out—"

The sunny mood broke abruptly. He interrupted her with a grim look. "No," he said. "Do not tell me what to do, or not to do." He sat down at the edge of the bed, and began to lace up his sneakers. "I asked you not to come back until you know. So you know, right?"

"Yes."

"You're not shouting and jumping up and down, Lizzie. We creative artists have imagination. It's one of our tools, like you guys have bedside manner. I can *imagine* what you've got to tell me."

He turned to face her, putting up a hand for silence. "I am going to the park, Lizzie. If going to the park kills me, then let it kill me. But I'm going to the park while I still can. You can't guarantee me another August day when I'm going to feel this good, or even another August day when I'm going to feel anything. I'm going to the park, Lizzie."

There were facts she had absorbed in the last ten days, eating them up with the rigorous discipline that had pushed her through medical school with distinction:

In the past fifteen years, the remission rate among children stricken with leukemia had gone from twenty-five to ninety percent. Although the treatment of adults is far less successful, it was improving on a statistical basis with each passing year of innovative treatments. She would tell him about chemotherapy, trying to remove the dread from the word by explaining clearly the purpose of each drug to be used on his body. There was hope, there was a great deal of hope, if only one had courage and the right attitude. She would give him facts, and he would understand, and then he would fight back, beating back the cancer with her knowledge and his will.

"It's hot," said Richard, looking up joyfully at the cloudless sky, falling into his familiar long stride as they walked the short block to the highway overpass. "We ought to be at the beach."

"I would love to go to the beach with you," said Elizabeth. She felt the pressure growing around her temples, conspiring with the tightness about her neck as she tried to believe in a dream of health. Even as they descended from the overpass to the park flanking the river, she could see the pallor behind his brave front, she could hear his breath growing shorter behind his rigid smile. How could he possibly have the right attitude, when her own, based on a knowledge of what he would have to endure, was equally bleak?

"But this is nice, right here," said Richard. Leaning against the railing, he looked out onto the sparse river traffic: two small tugs, a large empty barge, a fireboat, a flotilla of city refuse— soaked bits of decaying matter trying to cling to the surface. The

offshore wind whipped his lovely hair, and brought tears to his
squinting eyes. "I like it here. It would be fine to come here in
the morning, watch the sunrise. I haven't seen enough sunrises.
I never got up so early like you." He turned to look at her, the
antagonism gone completely. "I've been shouting at you for ten
days," he said.

"You can shout all you like," she said.

"I'm just not as tough as I thought."

"Oh, no," she said. "You're tough. You're plenty tough."

Their indirect chatter was framed by familiar city sounds: the
roar of traffic from the FDR Drive to one side, the gentle lapping
of the river to the other, the distant wail of police sirens, the
muffled explosions from a construction site a mile to the north,
and very much closer, the high-pitched, breathless laughter of
young boys.

"Kind of hot for football, guys," said Richard as one of the
boys ran past, neck craned to look for the high pass from his
scrawny friend. The pass went awry, the ball rising so high and
wide of the receiver that it threatened to go off the walk into the
river.

But Richard didn't let this happen.

Elizabeth, standing at his side, felt a surge of vitality lift him
spontaneously into the air. Like a broken-jawed boxer oblivious
to pain until the end of the match, like a delicate woman suddenly able to lift the two-ton car pinning her child to the ground,
the sick young man cast off his fatigue to reach for a moment's
strength and grace. Logically, it made no sense to Elizabeth that
someone so anemic could suddenly twist about in the air, slapping his hands on the flying football, brining it down into the pit
of his stomach as if he were fifteen; some magic had brought him
back to the glorious season when he had been a tight end on his
high school team, prepared to run over the frozen field through
the goalposts to glory.

"Great catch, mister," said the boy who had thrown the
pass, and he smiled in the camaraderie of sportsmanship as he
watched Richard run down the cement walkway with speed,
weaving as if to avoid any attempts at tackling. He ran so far that
Elizabeth didn't even call to him. He couldn't have heard against
the rush of the wind, the roar of the traffic, and the memories
that fueled his body. But even from forty yards she could see the

effort he put into the pass he now threw. Throwing back his head and arm, then snapping his entire upper torso forward, he sent the ball into space. It was a beautiful pass. The ball didn't twist on its own axis the way it had when the young boy had passed it, but flew straight and true, a desperate trajectory that landed in the skinny boy's hands with such force that he cried out in surprised pain.

"Wow, mister," he said as Richard came running back, indefatigable, giving the boys a clenched fist salute and patting Elizabeth on her rear as if he were once again a high school athlete and she his adoring cheerleader.

"You had better take me back, darling," he said, smiling happily.

But the smile was for what had just passed, not for what he faced. The energy that had been his when he had claimed it was gone, no longer called for. She could see him remember that he was sick, and that his sickness had a name that all civilized men fear.

Beyond the smile, his face was ashen, and the sweat poured from his scalp into his eyes.

She knew what he was thinking as surely as if the thoughts were in her own head; she knew too what he was feeling. The catch, the run, the toss were the last ones of his life, and he was glad that he had made them, glad that he had done them so well. He would no longer look back. He would return with her to the hospital because he was tired, but not to be treated. No one would pour drugs into his blood, would blast him with radiation. If he could not live the way he had always lived, he would die.

"Darling, it's curable," she said. "Once you've rested, we're going to have a talk, no jargon, just the two of us. It's important that you understand everything about it, everything."

"Yes," he said, still smiling, leaning on her heavily as they climbed the stairs to the overpass, his eyes looking lovingly at her. Richard did not believe a word she had said, and more than this, did not believe that she did either. What he believed in was her love, a love so strong that it would allow him anything, a love that would not stand in the way of his death. "Yes, baby," he said. "Anything you say."

Elizabeth said no more at that moment. Love had stopped

her tongue as surely as it had twisted her reason. If Richard imagined that she would allow him his death, he saw only one side of her terrified heart. He could not see that the mad confusion worked both ways; that a love strong enough to grant her lover death was also strong enough to insist that he live. As the weight and warmth of his body brought the fact of her love to an unbearable intensity, she felt like a mythological creature torn between two opposing gods—and therefore immobile. One god demanded an end to Richard's fear and pain; another god demanded an unreasoned belief in his survival. One god wanted death; one god insisted that she shut her eyes to mortality.

It was only when she had gotten him back to the hospital, guided him to his room, and helped him into his bed that she let go of him, exhausted by physical exertion and emotional confusion. "I want you to live," she said to him, but Richard could barely hear this as he drifted away to a drug-fueled sleep. "You must please live," she said, but the words held no belief, only childish insistence.

One god wanted death; one wanted life, and she could believe in neither because all the facts were not yet in, the charts not yet written, the sophisticated therapies not yet begun. An understanding clamored for her attention from some distant place, but it could not penetrate her reason, it could not pass through her fear. She needed to know what to do, but all she could think of was her love, all she could dream of was Richard's joy as he threw a football through infinite space.

Sitting over his sleeping form she felt her hands drawn inexorably back to his flesh. She had always loved to touch him, had always wanted his own beautiful hands resting on her body. But this was more than sexual attraction. She wanted to place her hands on his chest, over his heart, not simply to answer desire, but to fulfill a need.

But reason stepped in the way of this fulfillment.

Suddenly Elizabeth understood that when she brought her hands to his body she was attempting nothing less than the soothing of the wild misery that roiled beneath his skin. This attempt was more than a metaphor, more than a figment of imagination, and was therefore mad, as insane as faith-healing, as logical as witchcraft. She imagined—was imagining at that moment—that she could feel his need for her touch. It seemed a clear request from his heart to hers, a need as carefully expressed as a baby's cries for his mother's milk.

Elizabeth believed that giving in to these feelings, these sentimental promptings of her heart, not only made no logical sense, but was destructive to her already friable emotional state. She was a doctor, not a voodoo priest. Because the world did not suit her, she could not suddenly pretend that she didn't understand it; because she understood perfectly well that Richard was sick with cancer, and that placing her hands over his heart would not do anything more than express her love.

But some force kept her hands where her overwrought imagination felt they were wanted.

She would have liked to believe that love was a force, as real as any potent energy manufactured by man for healing or destruction. But she knew that love was less strong than chemotherapy, less powerful than the surgeon's knife. To believe in mystical healing powered by love would be to deny everything she had ever learned about the body or the world. She would not let despair overwhelm the hallmark of her being—her reason.

Still, it could not hurt to let her hands express the love that so crippled her purpose; a love that left her unable to grant his deathly wish, unable to believe in the certainty of his cure. She stroked her lover's body, she let her hands rest on his flesh, she let her love flow unfettered from her body to his: not to heal him, but to love him; not to imagine that she could do any good, but wanting only to be with him through these terrible moments.

All the while she forced herself to ignore the insistent madness of her heart, the wild knowledge that as long as she touched him, she would not give into the god of death; as long as her hands rested on his flesh there was the vague possibility of a dawning of belief.

PART TWO

Francia, 776 A.D.

Many waters cannot quench love,
neither can the floods drown it.
—*Song of Solomon*

Chapter 6

*L*IOBA, WHO WAS a disgraced woman, knew nothing of the glories of Epidaurus.

A man, a prince named Felix, handsome and wild, had betrayed her. Now she could no longer practice the gift granted her by God, the gift of healing, the gift that beat against the walls of her heart, waiting to be used in this world of calamity and destruction.

Banished to the distant Abbey's *scriptorium*, she had been put to work transcribing the works of the ancients, vouchsafing their wisdom and achievements for future generations. Lioba read of glorious physicians as she read of gods and goddesses, philosophers and gladiators, men of war and prophets of peace: All were pagans, living in a time so long past as to be unimaginable except as legend or spiritual lesson.

The great god Asclepios was but one name in a pantheon of forbidden pagan idols, confused with a hundred other cults and rituals from Greece to Egypt to Rome to the endless barbaric northlands, peopled with false gods without number. She had never heard of the physicians of Cos, nor of the famous medical school at Alexandria, nor of Roman physicians who specialized in diseases of the eye or limbs or internal organs. Lioba could scarcely imagine a time when surgeons operated on kidneys, cut into the abdomens of birthing women, excised tumors with scalpels more cunning than any instruments used by doctors of the Frankish courts.

Only three kinds of surgery were still practiced in Francia: bloodletting, tooth-pulling, and amputation. Even though ancient surgical texts survived, they were consulted with awe and trepidation. But this did not leave the sick without resources. Lioba healed not with a knife, but with a knowledge of herbs and the strength of her faith. In spite of her willfulness, her beauty, her pride, no one could doubt the strength of her belief. And everyone knew that the greatest healer of all time was not a doctor to the flesh, but Jesus Christ. Regardless of the vast knowledge possessed by the ancients, only the Grace of God allowed any of the sick to be cured.

Surely the ancient pagans of Greece and Rome knew all that God had ever intended man to be able to comprehend; but those were Godless times. Man no longer had need of so much knowledge, and so men of faith were no longer capable of learning as much as the ancient savants. Lioba remembered many lines and phrases from these great men, whose works she copied with diligence, but their names didn't fire her heart like those of the saints, whose steadiness and piety she wished she could emulate. What difference did it make if the saints knew little of the seven liberal arts, and less still of what some called the eighth—medicine? Their hearts were full of the love of the Lord, their souls were radiant with divine glory.

Because Lioba copied Latin texts, she assumed that Aristotle, Plato, Pythagoras, and Hippocrates, like the entire vanished civilized world, had been Romans. She would have been astonished to learn that even residents of imperial Rome, like Galen—the great codifier of Hippocrates' doctrines, living six centuries after the master physician of antiquity—wrote only in Greek.

Greek was, after all, the language of Byzantium, where men and women wore heavy silks and heavier perfumes, where Christian faith was tainted with pagan luxury. Few Western scribes, even at the great *scriptorium* at St. Martin, could read the Greek language. But in spite of ten centuries of Roman influence, an influence that survived the sacking of the imperial city and the destruction of the empire, the connection of the Roman-speaking peoples of Europe to the ancient Greeks remained in their language, beliefs, memories. As Galen was connected to Hippocrates by his passion for observation and diagnosis, Lioba, living six centuries later than Galen, was connected by bonds as strong to Corinna, ancient healer of Epidaurus.

These were not bonds of intellect but of feeling, not of blood, but of spirit. Each had been placed into a world made and ruled by men; like Corinna's, Liona's faith had been prompted by a god made in man's image. But even in the cold, silent prison of the Abbey, in the beast-filled wilderness six days northeast of St. Maurice, even deprived of food, companionship, light, and music, Lioba's heart was drawn to those in pain. Even if her tongue had been sometimes wild, her actions impulsive, her appetites for food and wine inappropriate for the daughter of a great lord, she had always held on to a belief in her own goodness. Only goodness could heal. Even if demons tempted her, she knew that her gift came from Heaven, and God would not have chosen her to do His work if she were evil. Like healers of every generation, educated and illiterate, rich and poor, flamboyant and reclusive, Lioba's goodness was as inchoate and urgent as a sudden flame—wild and eager, needing to consume all ills.

But Lioba's goodness was not evident to everyone.

Not to her mother, who had brought her lovingly into the world, but now accused her of rebellion. Not to her father, whose battle-wounds she had cleansed twice a day for weeks, refusing the help of any doctor or servant, who now no longer spoke to her because of her refusal to marry the great Prince Felix. Not to her sister Monica, who had followed her devotedly as she went about distributing food and healing herbs to the poor, but harried her from their home when she refused to marry her brutal abductor.

Rather than blame Prince Felix for his lechery, they blamed Lioba for the demons with her. It was as if her entire family had suscribed to the tales of the peasants, that their faithful healer wore two faces, one saintly and one devilish; that she was as capable of lust and witchery as she was of benevolence and healing.

Months after she had been banished to the Abbey, when Brother John, master of the *scriptorium*, told her of Monica's marriage to Felix, Lioba's heart had gone out to her, knowing that her sister had sacrificed her happiness to prevent war between his family and theirs, that Monica had provided the obedience that could never be in Lioba's heart.

But in that same moment, her infernal pride had reddened

her face, brightening her recently acquired nunnish pallor. Monica would not be pleasing to Felix, she thought. He would never lust after her flesh.

Brother John was forever reminding her that she was bad, unworthy. Her lack of obedience and excess of pride would lead to suffering, in this life and in the world to come. Though he pretended to suffer this indiscipline—greatly exacerbated by the fact of her gender—only because he had been ordered to do so by the Abbot, Lioba knew better. Brother John needed her talent. No other scribe, no matter how devout, had so fine a hand. But he concealed the joy which thrilled his starved senses every time he looked at her finished manuscripts.

He was far less adept at concealing his joy at finding her guilty of some fault or sin, as he did at that cold winter's moment, an hour after the mid-morning prayers.

"You are reading," said Brother John. Without hesitation, he brought his ink-stained ruler sharply down on the knuckles of Lioba's left hand. The pain, greatly augmented by the cold, astonished her. "You are not given the sacred task of the scribe so that you may amuse yourself like a lord in his library."

She was not, in fact, simply reading, but committing a sin far greater: using the holy words she copied to send her into another world altogether, not only beyond the confines of the Abbey's walls, but beyond the kingly writer's stately declarations of love. Solomon's words were vital, but they propelled her into a more fleshly sphere, where the poem's "sweet mouth" became one wet with desire, where "sick of love" became sick with lust, where every tenderness became a ravaging. Beyond the words, images sent by demons flew up at her—powerful hands and delicate breasts, tongues so long and large that they threatened to blot out the sun, the open mouth of a blond-bearded giant, each tooth as straight and strong as a castle of stone. Only by concentrating on the innate elegance of each letter, by repeating the words as if each was a talisman against the visions assaulting her, was Lioba able to beat back these images. This time, however, it was the monk's blow which brought her back to earth.

"I am sorry," she said automatically, prepared to apologize for whatever sin had been committed in Brother John's eyes. But a moment later, the rebellion that was as much a part of her being as her need to heal, the defiance and fury and passion that fired her soul, nearly shot a tongue of fire into the monk's stupid face. Of course she read, she wanted to shout at him. If not for the words, she would be burned up by the inhuman passions forced on her by demons jealous of her gifts, knowing them as clear marks of the Lord's favor.

But she held this violence in check, as she had learned to hold back all her passions for the Lord's service. She remembered that Brother John was sick, and she turned her anger to love, even as she lied sweetly to him:

"I am sorry, Brother John," said Lioba, feeling the sickness in his body like a heavy weight on her breast. She kept her eyes on the faint letters of the tattered manuscript, damaged by water and two centuries of use, the marginal notes from the original scribe illegible, the parchment as friable as sun-baked clay. But she didn't need to raise her eyes to be aware of him. The holy monk, following the custom of the most ascetic members of the Abbey, refused to bathe, save at Christmas and Easter. The stench of his body announced his presence at ten paces. "It is difficult for me to copy, without reading the words."

Once again the monk slapped at her frigid fingers, finding insolence in her remark. "No true scribe reads. The true scribe is content to be God's instrument. That is why the true scribe is and has always been a man, and nothing less."

He didn't have to list for her once again the crimes inherent in the state of womanhood. Lioba knew all too well that women did the devil's work, seducing the righteous, turning men from the contemplation of spirit to a lusting after flesh. Had not her own yellow hair and smooth, pale skin nearly brought murder into her family and that of Felix, each of them of the highest Frankish lineage, with bishops and abbots and lay princes among their closest relations?

Perhaps the monks were right: that it was not her physical beauty, but her spiritual ugliness that had drawn Felix to commit his crime. Or rather, in the eyes of the family, that Felix's crime was her crime, that in wanting to rape her, he had done no more than reveal Lioba to the world as a witch.

She was fortunate that no one had accused her of witchcraft in filling Felix with such wild passion. There would have been more than one witness, including her sister Monica, who could have vouched for the artful ways in which Lioba had made herself an object of obsession in Felix's eyes. Monica, at Lioba's insistence, had once spent an hour belting and rebelting Lioba's silk tunic, painting forbidden colors onto her pale cheeks, trying first gold pins, then jeweled headdress, then brightly colored ribbons in her younger sister's yellow hair in the anticipation of the rakish prince's visit. Surely Lioba had flirted with him in public, had dazzled him with her knowledge of the many dialects of Roman speech, had regaled him with tales told her by the peasants she went to heal.

But the prince, on close examination, frightened Lioba.

Not because he was big and strong, or rough with his men, or sharp with horses and dogs. Nothing physical frightened her. She had walked into huts on fire to pull a baby to safety. She had ignored cold and dark and fatigue in order to help heal, to reach for God's blessing and extend it to the sick.

It was his heart that frightened her.

She had imagined herself capable of loving this man, but now all she could see was selfish. Felix didn't want to love her, but to eat her up, to let her fill his entrails, let his power overwhelm her so she would be no longer an obsession, but a conquest.

This was strength, but not any strength that she wanted in a man. His heart was strong, but not kind; his power lay in subjugation, not toleration. Lioba knew that such a man would never let her practice her healing, particularly among the poor. Carefully, she had spoken to her mother, then to her father, and then, after neither proved sympathetic, had written a letter to Felix himself, explaining why she would never agree to marry him.

She neither loved nor admired him, she wrote in artful letters of black; she would never love him nor admire him; she wanted no union with him, no children by him, no future with him in this life.

Such a letter would have angered any man. When the words were read to Felix, he struck the reader with enough force to leave him senseless for half a day. He didn't like the idea that a woman could wield a pen; but that a woman he lusted after not only could write, but would dare inscribe words that would be laughed about in all of Francia for decades drove him into a rage.

All Lioba had wanted was to break Felix's passion, the way her hands could break a fever.

But Felix had not been deterred.

The men of his family knew how to draw love from a reluctant woman: Indeed, violent abduction was thought of as a method of courting among Felix's battle-scarred uncles and cousins.

Taking advantage of the hospitality of Lioba's family, Felix had attacked her person, slapping her face, throwing her to the floor in her own bedchamber. Later she would wonder whether her father's absence on an extended hunting trip had been a coincidence, or rather a deliberate plot between her father and Felix to let her see things their way.

Like brigands preying on the peasantry for fresh slaves to bring to market, Felix and four of his men had bound together her wrists and ankles, gagged her cries with a leather strap, and removed her from her father's house in a trunk stuffed with straw. It was only the power of prayer that saved her from suffocating.

Though long famous for his temper and willfulness, the abduction was surely an act of madness. Lioba's father had concluded the formalities of her betrothal to Felix ten years before, but the Church had made it clear that all nuptials must be public ceremonies. All must be able to witness, within the cathedral's sacred space, that bridge and groom take willingly the holy vows of matrimony.

Lioba's father could do no less than put up a show of anger at the abduction, particularly when the local bishop—who was also his younger brother and therefore Lioba's uncle—condemned the abduction as an outrage. When Felix was forced to surrender Lioba to her father's knights, the young prince was so angry that blood ran freely from his nose. Clearly, he had lost all reason.

Even Lioba had to admit the possibility that she had somehow bewitched him. Being sent off to the distant Abbey was a comparative blessing, regardless of loneliness and drudgery, of inadequate diet and warmth in the harsh climate. Lioba remembered clearly the fate of her cousin Mildred: After a witchcraft trial brought on by a spurned suitor, she had been shut up in a cask and tossed into the Sâone.

"I am sorry that you find me wanting as a scribe," Lioba said to Brother John, fighting back an impulse to tell him that his sickness made him stupid, that his truculence was a simple frustration of his spirit with his body. But even her apology seemed to incense the monk.

"Stand up, woman," he said.

Lioba stood, glad of the chance to stretch her youthful limbs. Before she had been sent to the Abbey, it seemed she spent half the day running through the fields. Though that was but half a year ago, when the summer had just begun, when the world had promised nothing but bounty and warmth, it seemed now like a memory from some ancient text, some pagan rite preserved for future chronicles. Once she had been placed under the austere care of the Abbess Tetta, ruler of the nuns attached to the famous monastery, her world had shrunk to the dimensions of the *scriptorium*.

From first light she would sit on the hard bench, trying to slow the inevitable cramping pain rising from fingers to wrist to shoulders to neck. By the end of the day, the simple turning of her head from the page she copied to the parchment before her gave rise to sharp stabs along her hunching spine. Worse even than the cold—so bad this time of year, that her benumbed fingers would sometimes lose their grip on the quill—was the rule of silence. Though neither novice nor nun, she was surrounded by monks, all of them confirmed in their faith, inflexible in their regimen. Talking was absolutely forbidden. Even the slavish practice of some writing rooms, where a master scribe dictated the text to a group of scribes, forcing a steady, quick pace, would have been preferable to Lioba to the wintry quiet of the *scriptorium*. It was no wonder she caressed every word she copied, no wonder she carried on a dialogue with sages and poets long dead.

Still, as long as she was considered too faithless to work with the sick pilgrims of the infirmary, Lioba understood that she was privileged to be employed in the *scriptorium*. This too was God's work. The cold, badly-lit workroom of hungry scribes was known throughout the civilized world. From here books were sent as far as Hamburg and Pavia and Rome. Princes commissioned copies of favorite manuscripts, bishops sought rare volumes to enrich their cathedral libraries, merchants paid great sums for bibles, Psalters, biographies of the saints; next to holy relics there was no more valuable commodity that took up so small an amount of space.

When Lioba was surrendered to the authority of the Abbess,

it was not with the understanding common between aristocratic castaways and the officers of the Church. Though the location of the Abbey was remote from civilization, it was large, well-appointed, guarded by peasants raised to the specialized status of soldiers. For one whose family was willing to donate lands to add to the Abbey's wealth, the Abbot furnished simple quarters, a plentiful diet, a chance for prayer in the church, for exercise and meditation in the grounds and gardens cared for by monks and novices. Not only women who refused marriage, but widows and widowers, men too weak of mind or body to inherit the responsibility of martial leadership, found refuge here.

But though Lioba's family had extensive estates, and made a donation worthy of their position, they made only simple demands on the Abbey's hospitality. They wanted rebellious Lioba to be treated like any peasant girl throwing herself on the mercy of the Church: Their daughter must work.

Indeed, had Lioba not had more skills than the ordinary aristocrat, she might have spent her days chopping vegetables or digging irrigation ditches.

But Lioba not only could read—a not unusual feat for a young aristocratic woman—she could write. And this was a skill worth employing, especially since her letters were clear and straight, and practice showed her to be accurate at copying. Indeed the prince who had commissioned the copy of the *Song of Solomon* that she was now working on, had specifically demanded the same scribe—Lioba—who had penned the little biography of St. Ambrose he had purchased a month earlier. Even if Brother John found her insolent and stiff-necked, he could not deny the prestige—and silver—she brought the monastery.

"Why do you not stand straight, woman?"

"My back is crooked from too long sitting over—"

"Silence! I do not need an answer in words. Simply stand up straight."

"Yes, Brother John." She did not remind him that she had taken no vow of silence, had taken no vows of any kind. He, and every other monk in authority, had made it clear that she must behave in the same manner as those with whom she spent her days.

"Do not speak! Do not 'yes' me or 'no' me! Stand still, stand straight and say nothing, unless I ask you to speak."

She was not the only one at whom the monk directed his anger. But Lioba, unlike the monks he was forever slapping and pinching, was forgiving. She understood that sickness added fire to his temper. When she had first begun to work in the *scriptorium* she had told him—as she had told the Abbess—of her skill with herbs and medical treatments. She had advised him earnestly to take fennel for his constipation, hot baths for his aches, and myrrh and absinthe for his rashes.

But her attempt to counsel him had not been taken as an act of kindness but as a possible indication of a demonic nature. No one had told her that every joint in his body ached, whether he moved or sat in contemplation. How could she possibly know, he wondered, of his chronic digestive problems, of the rash that covered his body under the monkish layers of linen and wool? Lioba had tried to explain the foresight granted healers by the Grace of Heaven, but Brother John grew furious at such presumption. It was not within her province to talk of medical cures, much less of gifts from their Savior.

Did she know, he demanded, that St. Benedict, in ordering his monks to care for the sick, forbade them from the study of medicine. "If I am sick, it is because of sin," Brother John had said. "Sickness has been sent to me for chastisement. It is a gift from God, to allow me to repent, to do penance for my sins before the final hour."

"But, sir," Lioba had insisted, "the Church allows the healing of the sick. The great and holy relics of the Abbey draw the sick from all over the world. Jesus Christ could raise the dead with His healing. They say that even touching the hem of His robe could return sight to the blind."

Had they not been at that moment in the presence of the Abbot, Brother John would have struck her full in the face for so blasphemous an inference. It was as if she had compared herself to the Savior of Mankind, the Anointed One.

Instead, the master of the scribes had to listen to the Abbot, an uneducated buffoon of the same ancient Roman-Gallic lineage as half the bishops of Francia, go on about Lioba's great powers: how she had often effected cures, both for the great folk of her father's court and for the local peasants, who had learned to revere and fear her. The Abbot had gone on and on about the joy she would bring the sick in the infirmary and how the cured would go forth into the world, making the Abbey as famous as any shrine of healing.

Finally, Brother John reminded him that Abbess Tetta had assigned the girl to the *scriptorium*, as Lioba had an unusually fine hand, and would bring riches to the Abbey.

"Ah, riches," the Abbot had said. "Riches are a great healer, a great healer indeed."

Lioba had often tried to rectify what she considered a terrible error. She would be far more useful among the sick than in the *scriptorium*. And to have the power to heal and not use it was as sinful as to be rich and give no charity.

But Brother John didn't believe in her powers, except those she might have gotten from enemies of the faith. Lioba tried to explain how she had so quickly discovered the problems that ailed him. It was not magic, but a simple opening of the heart. It was not demonic wisdom but God-sent knowledge. Lioba admitted that she had used this knowledge to impress him. But surely Brother John knew that many healers did the same thing. To make a quick diagnosis before a patient was to win his confidence. Patients who believed in the wisdom of their doctors, she knew, recovered more quickly. If she could glance at a beggar-woman and announce that her problem was one of the liver, or meet an aristocrat and declare him to be suffering from gout, it was not the devil who was talking through her eager lips, but her goodness. Even if her diagnosis was inaccurate, the patient felt better.

But her diagnosis was seldom wrong. If her heart was receptive and sympathetic to the pain of those around her, how could it fail to see? And if her faith was strong, how could she not help those in need of her strength?

"Do you believe in the demons and the spirits in the forests?" said Brother John, as she stood before him in the cold *scriptorium*.

"No," she said. Though she had been told a hundred times that it was brazen to stare at the monk, she met his glare with her own. If not for him, Lioba knew she could be working where she was needed, among the sick. Part of his reluctance to believe in her was his resentment of her noble status. The monk before her was probably the son of a petty landowner, but no more than that; otherwise, he would certainly be an abbot or at least a bishop's personal clerk. The interrogation he was beginning now was a waste of time, an expression of anger. She wanted to shut his noxious mouth with a kiss, drive him to his knees with the strength of her spirit.

"Do you renounce the devil and devil worship?" said Brother John.

"I renounce the devil and devil worship."

"Do you renounce the devil's work, the devil's desire, the devil's play, the devil's will?"

Lioba nearly shut her eyes, letting the words pass through her like a well-remembered hymn. She had inscribed this very interrogation at least twenty times. Hundreds of parchment copies were disseminated throughout the land of the Franks. The backward, low-class priests sent out to preach to newly converted peasants needed these words to prompt them when they questioned their savage flock.

At least it was a joy to be able to talk, to feel the muscles of her mouth and tongue and throat moving in something other than communal prayer.

"I renounce them."

"Do you renounce all idols, all blood sacrifices, all objects which pagans in their ignorance take for gods?"

"I renounce them."

"Do you believe in God, our Almighty Father?"

"Yes," she said, answering the monk and herself in the same breath. She believed, she believed in God the Father, she believed in Christ, His Son, the Savior of mankind, she believed in God, in His Trinity, in His Unity, in His Holy Church.

But Lioba believed too in her own powers, believed that no devil helped her to see past the monk's filth and stench to a cure; she believed that one couldn't copy without reading, man or woman, tool of God, or tool of the devil. She believed that she had done no wrong that day as she had sat and silently copied out the *Song of Solomon*, even if the beauty of the Biblical lovewords had swept her to the lands of pagan poems, where powerful heroes rescued crimson-lipped maidens from evil foes. She believed she had done no wrong in refusing to marry the man who had abducted her, even if her beauty had bewitched him. She believed that no one could force her to take the vows of a nun, nor even to live the rest of her life within the nunnery's cloister and the monks' *scriptorium*.

"Yes," she said. "I believe. I believe. I believe."

"You will go to the Abbess Tetta," said Brother John.

"The Abbess wants me?"

"You will not question, you will not speak unless expressly ordered to speak."

"Yes, sir," said Lioba, this time knowing that it would irk him, but no longer caring. She was leaving the *scriptorium* while daylight still painted the drabness of the Abbey with sharp forest colors of white and green and brown. It was one thing to be cold in the still of the workroom, surrounded by the crushing fatigue of endless toil. It was another to feel the wind in your face, looking up to discover the moon at the approach of evening.

"Keep your eyes on the ground, do not gawk at every servant or monk or novice, do not speak. You may go."

"To the Abbess?"

"I have told you to the Abbess! Are we to discuss this endlessly like pagan philosophers? Just go!"

"I do not know where she is," she said. An uncharacteristic reluctance had suddenly taken hold of her. She was not afraid of the Abbess, regardless of the fierce and steady gaze with which she looked out at the world. Lioba always felt a warmth and a radiance coming from the old woman, a robust healthiness that was almost as rare among the young as it was among those of the Abbess's advanced age.

"Her quarters," said Brother John. "Go to her quarters." Lioba could see that his knuckles were red about the ruler in his thick white hands. He could sense none of the dread coming from where the Abbess awaited Lioba, of course, because his heart was closed to all but rote-learned piety. That he was sick, that his body was never at peace with itself, made it all the more difficult for him to feel anything but anger.

Lioba nodded gravely at his information, lowered her gaze to the ground, pulled her shawl more closely about her neck, and turned her back to the monk. She took three steps before stopping abruptly, turning about, and saying: "Brother John, I would be very happy if you would let me fix you an herbal drink, a mixture of great antiquity."

"Silence," said Brother John.

"It will have a good taste, and be of great benefit—"

Brother John dropped his ruler to the desk in response. Before he could come after her, she walked swiftly away. But there were no angry words hurled after her. Perhaps he castigated himself for already having spoken far too much that day.

Leaving the *scriptorium*, Lioba was struck by the sound of the church's bells. They seemed unaccountably loud. At first she thought it was the shock of coming into the warmer passage, leading into the heart of the church. Though the writing room was on the church's ground floor, close to the sacristy and the visiting monk's dormitory, it was far colder; the room's windows brought in so little wintry light through their coarsely made glass, that on the bleakest of days the windows had to be opened, or the monks risked blindness.

That Lioba was not imagining the sound was verified at once by the approach of a youthful monk. He looked up at her from his meditations, boyish blue eyes blinking in fear. Unwilling to break the rule of silence, he brought the thumb and index finger of his right hand to his ear, jiggling them as if they formed a bell.

"The bells," said Lioba. "What's wrong with the bells?"

But the monk didn't wish, or was unable, to answer. He pulled back with distaste as the young woman reached out for his arm, covered though it was with the rough black-dyed wool of his habit. Once again, he used the silent code of gesticulation common to the Abbey. "Don't touch, woman," he seemed to be saying with his wide open, work-hardened hands. "Stay away, you who are impure."

Lioba didn't hate him for his thoughts, because she was long used to the practiced loathing with which the monks kept their desire stoppered. "But why are the bells so loud?" insisted Lioba.

The boyish monk brought his fingers together in the sign of the bell and "rang" it next to his ear, shaking his head as if to negate her statement. "It is not loud," he seemed to be saying. Now that she had been in his presence for more than a moment, she could better feel the stuff of his spirit: it was that of a zealot, immensely strong, but confined in too small a shell. The monk seemed to be bursting at all the seams of his flesh, so full was he of choler, so rich was his blood with youth.

All at once, he "rang" the bell-sign wildly, at the same time opening his eyes wide in fear, and nodding his head. This he followed with the sign of the cross across his broad, peasant-stock chest. Lioba wondered how often he was bled, to keep that otherworldly pallor in his cheeks.

"I don't understand," said Lioba, "Wait—"

But the monk, through communicating with her, clattered down the hall on his oversized wooden shoes. It was not till she had passed the entrance to the porter's lodge, and left the church, that she understood what was strange about the bells. It was not that they were loud; it was that they tolled at all. The sounding of the bells was a precise duty. They tolled every three hours, calling the monks to prayer eight times during the day and night. Surely, the last call to prayer had been only an hour before.

No wonder the monk was frightened. If not used as a call to the faithful to pray at the appointed time, the bells were rung only in emergency: either to summon the Abbey's soldiers to beat back an attack, or to protect the inhabitants from a sudden manifestation of devils and demons.

Lioba knew in her heart that there was no attack, as she knew that the sense of preternatural fear coming from the workers and clerics, guests and pilgrims and soldiers approaching the bells were only a reflection of the Abbess's desire to see her. She pushed her way past carpenters and masons, smiths and fullers, gardeners and cobblers and monks. Quickly, she took the path about the lodge for visiting bishops and abbots and lay princes, entering their private garden, ignoring the challenge of a novice pulling at a patch of winter herbs.

Lioba passed the low building where sacred bread and oil were prepared. She climbed the long flat steps leading past the cluster of white beeches where the larger of three monks' dormitories was situated. She shut her senses to the stench coming from the monks' latrines, and to the freshly killed carcasses of wolves waiting to be skinned behind the lodge of the hunters. Without realizing it, she had begun to run, the cold air pricking at her lungs like icy fingers. She slipped on a patch of gray ice and would have fallen if not for an elderly nun, tall and erect, who took hold of her at the elbow with a powerful hand.

"Do not be afraid, child," she said, breaking the rule of silence. The nun's Roman speech was nearly pure Latin. That and the high cheekbones and the steady look in her green eyes marked her for Lioba as one of her own; an aristocrat, immured in this lonely place. "There is no attack. The bells are rung for religious purposes."

"I am going to the Abbess Tetta," said Lioba. "She has sent for me."

"You know the way, child?"

She had never liked being called "child," particularly now that she was of marriageable age; but the woman was over fifty, and entitled to the idiosyncrasies of the old.

"Yes, Sister," said Lioba. "I will just take the short way around the place of bleeding."

"No," said the nun emphatically. "Do not take that way. And stop your running. There will be time enough for running later. Now you must be tranquil. I will take you."

"But Sister, the Abbess—"

"The Abbess has asked me to meet you, Lioba," said the nun.

This stopped all talk. The woman knew her name. The Abbess had sent for her. The Abbess had sent an older, aristocratic nun to wait for her. The bells were ringing and ringing and it was not time for prayer.

Lioba followed the tall nun's lead, lowering her eyes to the ground, placing her hands together at the waist as they walked slowly, ignoring the cold and the wind and the darkening sky. She wondered at the old woman's straight-backed strength, at the spirit of calm that clung to her frame, even at this wild moment.

The house of the Abbess was situated near the women's side of the infirmary. It rested behind a copse of barren trees, between the path leading to the nuns' dormitory and the comfortable lodging of the lay gentrywomen who visited or resided at the Abbey. Around this lodging was a great, unfamiliar commotion. An armed escort milled about the low stone gateway. They were at least a dozen men, dressed in light armor and vests of rat skin. Torches, in unnecessary profusion, had already been lit against the approach of night.

Here too, as in the crowds hurrying to the church at the sound of the bells, was fear; but somehow this fear was more rational, more directed, more certain. These men were not aimlessly crossing themselves against the coming of unknown evils; they knew of a particular evil, for they had escorted it through rough forest and wasteland to this very place.

Lioba became aware of the elderly nun's hand on her elbow, guiding her not toward the house of the Abbess, but toward this lodging, guarded by the fearful men.

"The Abbess is there," she said. "Waiting for you."

"Who has come? Why are these men guarding the way?"

"Please," said the old woman. "You must be brave, child. If it is true that God has given you the power of healing, then all shall be well."

"But who needs healing? Is that why the bells won't stop? What demons are they afraid of?"

"No demons, child. Just a woman. She is pregnant."

"I don't understand," said Lioba. "Why are all these men here? What does the Abbess want of me? What have I to do with the visit of a pregnant woman?"

"It is the pregnant woman who has need of your healing," said the nun, increasing the pressure of her strong grasp.

"But they won't let me practice healing. I work in the *scriptorium*—"

"Child," said the nun, as they stopped within a few paces of the gateway guarded by the fearful men. "The pregnant woman has asked for your help. She is your sister Monica."

"Oh, praise the Lord," said Lioba, her heart pounding.

She had no idea that Monica was with child, because no one of her family had written to her in the six months she had been at the Abbey. "I must see her then. Why did she take such a terrible journey to see me? She is not ill, is she?"

"I have not seen her, Lioba," said the old nun. "I only know what Abbess Tetta has told me. Your sister Monica is pregnant, and she swears on all that is holy that she is yet a virgin. She swears that she has never consummated her marriage to Felix."

The woman hesitated, looking into Lioba's eyes as if to measure her courage. Slowly, Lioba could feel the woman's fear break through its deceptive layer of calm. Then the older woman turned her green eyes from Lioba's own, raising them to heaven. "And she swears," said the old nun, "that through magic, the child in her womb is not hers, but yours."

Lioba waited. All this was very much, but there was more, and worse. But she didn't need the nun to tell her what she could see with her own eyes, like a vision from one of her daydreams. Emerging from the stone gateway, bending low in heavy armor that he wore with no greater effort than if it was a tunic of linen was a blond-bearded man, his cold blue eyes wild in the torchlight. The men in light armor and vests of rat skin quickly made way for him, their torches dancing about his furious face.

"Felix," she said. She spoke softly, but the name carried across the dozen paces that separated them; the warrior had stopped walking, transfixed by her stare. Lioba was as rooted to the hard ground as an ancient oak.

Suddenly, the warrior moved. He turned his head, as if it were a great weight, he shouted some commands to his men, and all of them moved from the gateway, all of them stepped away from where Lioba would pass.

"Come, child," said the old nun.

"He is not well," said Lioba, sorry for the man who had abducted her, who had abused her and ruined her name. She wanted to go to him then, as she always wanted to go to where pain ruled, so that her power and her gift could take it away. But the old nun hurried her along, taking her arm in a strong grip and walking her through the gateway to where her pregnant sister waited her confession of crimes and her healing hands.

Chapter 7

MONICA WORE a peasant's kirtle, shapeless and dull. Her hair was covered by a black veil, her hands were hidden in a muff of otter's fur, her eyes were lost in quiet fury, as if passion and anger had drained her strength to nothing.

"You are a witch," said Monica, who had always loved her. Now the hatred was clear and sure in her quiet voice. "You gave me this child, and only you can take it away."

Lioba barely heard her.

After seeing Felix, after feeling his anger, his hatred, his sickness, she was receptive to little more than the violence of her thoughts. He had wronged her, he had abducted her, and because she would not submit to his crimes, he hated her. Why did God allow such madness in the hearts of men? And why did God let the demons penetrate her spirit, again and again, so that against all reason she could feel compassion for this brutal man, compassion and kindness.

And more than this. Even as Monica spoke out her angry words, she could see Felix's image blow through her body, she could feel his clumsy caresses, the stuff of his lust, the desire that the dark spirits forced into her own body before she had been rescued by prayer and the strength of her faith.

Lioba swallowed rapidly, blinking her eyes to shut out the demon-sent thoughts. Her sister was shouting, and she needed her touch.

"She's a witch. Look how she looks at me. Look at her eyes, she's—"

"Monica," said Lioba. "Dear sister." She got to her knees,

letting Monica's terrified presence fill her spirit, not only so that she might help her, but so that her own wild thoughts would be banished by Monica's needs.

"Stay away from me," said Monica.

But Lioba was already touching her, and Monica allowed the touch, even as tears came to her red eyes. Lioba spent no time with words of greeting or blessing. Monica was indeed ill. She felt the expanse of Monica's pain, measuring it against other extremes of suffering she had felt in her rounds with the sick and the hopeless and it was a terrible pain: An unyielding pressure beat against her temples, tongues of fire slapped at her neck and back and thighs, a loathsome fullness pulled at the walls of her belly.

"Stay away from me. You're a witch, and you made me pregnant."

"But you have asked for her help," said Abbess Tetta. "That is why you have come to the Abbey."

"I don't want her to touch me. She made me pregnant. Make her stay away."

But Monica wanted her touch, no matter what words she whispered. She wanted to be eased of her pain, she wanted her marriage to Felix to evaporate into the air, she wanted the baby in her womb to disappear.

Yet Lioba could feel no life growing in her sister's womb, no baby, nothing alive but a canker.

Something black and unknown, unspeakably evil, had taken hold of her in this guise of a life-to-be. Lioba took her in her arms, and held her tight. Her sister's full belly pressed against her, pregnant with demonic fury. Monica struggled against the embrace, but Lioba could feel her sister's pain lessen, could feel a loosening of all the knots about her spine, as if the demons assaulting Monica slowly lost their strength beating back Lioba's attack.

"Let go of your sister, Lioba," said Abbess Tetta.

Lioba had been so overwhelmed by the fact of Felix's arrival, and by being in Monica's presence, that she had not noticed the austere ruler of the Abbey's women.

"I cannot," said Lioba.

Ordinarily, she would have obeyed Abbess Tetta at once, and not only because of her forbidding nature. Lioba knew that beyond the Abbess's severity was a sincere and selfless desire to do God's will. Unlike some of the monks, whose asceticism drove them to forego washing, the Abbess was scrupulously clean; but she never used hot water. Indeed, it was said by some that Tetta bathed daily in icy water, and that she never used the warming rooms of the convent, either for changing or washing or reading a book. To feel the cold was one way of identifying with the poor, one way of living the life of self-denial that led to holiness. But even though she ate no meat and drank no wine, her complexion was clear, her hair was thick, and her mouth was full of teeth at the very old age of sixty-four. Lioba knew this could only be a sign of God's favor.

Still, Lioba could barely react to the Abbess's command, much less accede to it, so strong was the force compelling her to hold Monica and assuage her pain.

"Yes," said Monica. "Let go." But already, Monica had stopped struggling. In spite of her anger, her body was telling her to accept the help flooding through her.

"Monica," said Lioba. "Let me help."

"No," said Monica. Tetta stood up from the upholstered bench on which she had sat so quietly, and for a moment did nothing more than observe. "It is your fault," said Monica. "You have made me pregnant by your sins. I will not suffer for your sins. Free me. Take this child back from me. You must free me and pay the price for what you have done."

"I will not argue," said Lioba, "only let me hold you. That is why you are here, whether you know it or not, so let me give you what God has given me."

"Don't let her talk to me, Abbess Tetta," said Monica. "She will try and convince me. She will look at me and confuse me with her evil words and convince me the way she convinced Felix, the way she convinces everyone."

"Let go, Lioba," said Abbess Tetta, placing her cold hands gently on Lioba's neck. Monica pulled free of her sister's embrace, and fell back, striking the wall. Lioba went after her, instinctively wanting to help, but the Abbess stopped her, the cold hands dropping from Lioba's neck to her right wrist with speed and strength. "Lioba," said the Abbess. "Look at me, girl. Turn away from your sister and look into my eyes."

Monica moved from the wall into the steady bright light of a lamp, burning expensive olive oil. Lioba found herself looking not at Tetta, but into the lamplight, breathing deeply, trying not to defy the Abbess and take her sister once more into her arms. Torches, sparsely distributed, provided most of the illumination for the monks and nuns in their bleak dormitories. In this room torches gave forth light that was almost incidental, over-shadowed as they were by the lights of lamps and candles. There was even light from—greatest luxury of all—flickering flames from birchwood burning in a private hearth. Neither nuns nor monks slept in heated rooms, not even allowing themselves the peasants' luxury of fire-heated stones slowly turning cold under their beds. After months of sharing the hardships of novices and servants, the olive-oil burning lamp, the rich upholstery of benches and chairs, the vivid tapestry holding back drafts from the cracked wall of the guest room seemed to Lioba the marks of a palace, not an abbey. For a moment, it seemed that Lioba could have retreated back to an earlier time, when her sister loved her, when Prince Felix was a distant illusion, when marriage was something arranged by and for adults in a world that was infi-nitely distant.

"Look at me, girl," repeated the Abbess, and as Lioba turned to her, she could feel Monica's pain returning. Now that the contact of the sisters' flesh had been broken it would grow mo-ment by moment. It was difficult for Lioba to accept the fact that Monica did not want her touch.

"My sister needs me," said Lioba.

The Abbess took firm hold of Lioba's hands. "You're so warm," said Tetta in surprise.

Lioba hesitated. She had the strength to tear herself free from the Abbess and go to Monica. But if demons were indeed at the root of hatred between sisters, she would wait for the holy Ab-bess's aid; she would wait and learn why the Abbey's bells still rang in the dark winter night.

"Yes, I am always warm when I must help," said Lioba.

"When you heal?"

"Yes, Abbess Tetta. I feel warm then even in the coldest weather. Even with snow falling on a peasant's hut, I have bro-ken out in a sweat."

"Because she is possessed," said Monica softly. "Because she is not a healer but a witch."

The Abbess kept her tight grip on Lioba's hands. "Do not

answer her. Do not look at her. Look only at me." Slowly, the warmth was draining out of Lioba's hands. "Your sister Monica has come here with an accusation that must be answered."

"It is her baby, not mine," said Monica.

"Silence," said the Abbess, turning with sharp annoyance to Monica.

"I am a virgin," said Monica. "And my sister is not. You will ask and she will tell you. Tell her, Lioba. Tell the Abbess how my husband loves you still."

A torch held by an iron cresset over Monica's head sputtered, lending a wildness to the mad accusations. Prince Felix had never loved her, of this Lioba was as certain as she was of the power she held to heal the sick. Not love, but frustration, had driven Felix to abduct her. He had been incensed at her refusal to marry him, as humiliated as if he had lost a duel to a lesser man. Felix had bedded many girls, and not only the daughters of peasants, girls too frightened to look the handsome young aristocrat in the face. There had been the daughters of great folk too, young girls and older women, widows and maidens and married women with husbands away at war. For Felix, like many of the great folk among the Franks, the Church laws against adultery were for other, lesser mortals. Many times he had paid the *morgengabe*, the "morning gift," the price of sharing the bed of a girl to whom he would give no other honors or consideration.

But in the ancient wood castle of his uncle, fortified by the broken stones of an older Roman edifice, Felix had never dared violate her person. Of this Lioba was certain. In spite of having forced herself to forget much of her ordeal, the imprisoned days and nights that seemed to last for years, the relentless hunger which coursed through his body like a sickness, she remembered every contact of his body with hers.

He had touched her of course.

Lioba would never forget the approach of his full lips, the wide-eyed wonder of his face as he drew close to kiss her.

He was beautiful.

He had abducted her, had struck her, had humiliated her; but he was so finely wrought by God's hand, so exquisite in his strength, so bright and unblemished in his passion, that in spite of all that was forbidden, she wanted him then more than anything she had ever wanted in her life.

But she had turned her back to these feelings, with violence.

She knew that they were sent by demons, as Felix himself had been sent by demons, leaving him as confused and twisted a shell of human weakness as she. The love of a man's body was sinful. Passion was meant to serve the spirit, to fire one's faith. Felix's lust was unholy, and she shut up her bodily passions and turned to God for aid.

And the Lord Jesus had protected her virtue.

He had given her strength, so that she found Felix ugly and coarse, worse than any animal. Passion turned to indifference, her warm and excited body becoming as cold and inviting as a saint's statue.

It made her no less a virgin, no less chaste, that she had allowed his brutal hands to caress her neck, that she had stilled her body as he drove teeth and tongue through her shut mouth. She could not strike at the man, for she had turned away from passion. And was not what he wanted from her body not so very different than what the sick demanded from her spirit?

Had she not, in her healing, kissed many men? Had she not, after all, lessened the pain of strangers through the touch of her healer's hands? Surely Felix was driven by evil, but he was still a creature of God, still deserving of healing.

Though he had looked at her like a bird in the teeth of his hound when his men had removed her bonds and a maidservant had pulled the straw out of her hair, something of decency had stopped him from raping her.

But Monica hadn't spoken of lust, but of love. She would have more readily forgiven Felix's attraction for her beautiful sister, if it had ended with simple physical pleasure.

"Felix never loved me," said Lioba, knowing as she spoke the words that Monica could never believe them, for she herself imagined love behind the prince's obsession.

Even if she could share her memories with her—if Monica could have seen Lioba pulled from the straw-filled trunk more dead than alive, had witnessed the kisses forced onto her dead lips, had watched her sit in numb silence, hoping to be rescued by her father—it would have only convinced Monica the more.

During her days of captivity, Felix had barely spoken with Lioba, not even attempting to apologize for his actions, or insisting that they were the result of mad passion. He had been a dark, unholy presence, the opposite of lightness and love.

Yet there was love there, a love that was unnatural and dangerous, a love that disfigured the shape of one's soul. No wonder Lioba could feel a sickness in the warrior's great frame. She had imagined a vile, omnivorous demon sitting at the very center of his young body; she had seen the future ravages that would bring him humbly back to God.

But perhaps he was not sick at all, perhaps what she had envisioned was the blackness at the center of Monica's bloated belly. Perhaps it was an illness of passion, passed from one to another, links in a chain of human misery.

For five days, while the world assumed she had become his woman, Lioba had prayed; and the Lord had accepted her prayer, sustaining her in a dreamlike state that obscured the prince's caresses behind a radiant cloud. But she wanted no revenge. She hoped for no sickness, not in her sister's belly, nor in Felix's heart. Repentance was always possible. Prayer could redeem the world.

"Monica, you must believe what I say," said Lioba. "Prince Felix never loved me at all. A man's love is always reserved for his wife. Anything else is animal lust, and the product of demons."

"You are the product of demons," said Monica. "You made him love you. And he loved you then, as he loves you now, and this is your demon's child in my womb."

"I must ask you several questions, Lioba," said the Abbess, stepping between the sisters.

"I love you, Monica," insisted Lioba. "If you would let me help you, you would feel alive and loved and full of the spirit of the Lord."

"Stop it, Lioba," said the Abbess. "Look at me. Listen. Answer with respect." Lioba took two steps away from Monica and stood up straight and tall before Abbess Tetta.

"First, are you in league with a devil, or a demon, or any spirit of any kind?"

"No, Abbess Tetta."

"Have you ever had relations with a man?"

"No, Abbess Tetta."

"Are you then a virgin?"

"Yes, Abbess Tetta." Lioba found herself smiling, not at the substance of Tetta's words, but at the spirit which prompted them. Here was a woman in search not just of truth or obedience, but of God's will. But if only they would let her go among the sick, if only Abbot and Abbess would let her raise her hands over the ill, let her pray through the night at a hundred bedsides, let her remove pain and ease suffering from all who visited the Abbey in the hopes of a cure, they would discover that she was the agent of God's will, His instrument, His little finger.

"Of course I am a virgin," said Lioba. "Do you not believe the stories of my healing? Do you think God would allow a prostitute to do His work?"

The Abbess's eyes narrowed into slits of disfavor at this display of pride. "Is the child in your sister's womb the product of magic, spell, or miracle?" she said.

"No, Abbess Tetta."

"Is the child in your sister's womb your own?"

"Abbess Tetta," said Lioba carefully. "There is no child in Monica's womb."

"No child," said Abbess Tetta, her bright spirit momentarily obscured by a cloud of irritation. "I suppose that you will agree with Monica then? This pregnancy is a miracle? Your married sister is a virgin? A child has been conceived without the agency of a man?"

"I am sorry," said Lioba. "I do not understnad how she has come to be so big in the belly."

"Do you understand that you and she both speak blasphemously? That you imagine Monica capable of a virgin birth, like that of holy Mary?"

"I do not know, Abbess Tetta. I only know that there is no child in her womb. There is nothing alive there. All I can feel there is pain."

The Abbess turned to Monica, slumped on a bench, her belly pushing through the rough kirtle.

"She has been the lover of my husband," said Monica. "He has come to her, and she through magic has given me the child that is theirs. I am a virgin. And she is a witch."

"Why do you not dispute her?" said the Abbess to Lioba. "If you have told me the truth, then what she says is a lie."

"My sister Monica is ill," said Lioba. "I can feel that as surely as I can breathe the air. She does not know what she says. I forgive her, and I shall not accuse her, no matter what she says about me."

"I know that you are a truthful girl, and will try and tell the truth. But if there is anything to your sister's accusations, you would be forced to lie by the powers of evil." The Abbess sighed, as if suddenly weary of the responsibilities of leadership and judgment.

"Both of you," she said wearily, "will have to submit to the Proof of the Cross."

For a moment, Lioba felt rebellion rise under her skin. She spoke without thinking, and her words were sharp. "My sister is unwell," she said.

"Your sister, like yourself, is in the hands of the Lord."

"But I have no dispute with her. I love her. She can say what she likes about me, and I will agree with it."

"You will agree to commit falsehood?" said the Abbess.

"She's afraid," said Monica. "God will punish her, and she knows that He is stronger than any witchcraft."

Lioba's rebelliousness was suddenly over. Tetta had meant no harm; neither did she, like so many at the Abbey, speak from ignorance or cruelty. "I do not mean that I would commit false-hood, Abbess Tetta."

"What do you mean, child?" She smiled gently at Lioba as if about to explain something very elementary, something anyone of faith should acknowledge. "If Monica tells the truth and you lie, she will have the strength of a Samson. Surely you do not dispute this?"

"No, Abbess Tetta," said Lioba, because she believed every word. How could she dispute the workings of her God? Everyone understood that ordeals and trials by combat were not tests of strength or endurance, but a way for men to glimpse God's will. When men accused one another of breaking a vow, in the absence of proof only God could know who told the truth and who lied. By agreeing to submit to an ordeal, one made a contract with God that was as inviolable as faith.

Lioba had often seen evidence of God's judgment, when no other judgment was available. At her father's court men accused of theft, adultery, incest all routinely submitted to ordeals or-dained by God's law. Men plunged hands into boiling water, knowing that the burned skin would heal swiftly if they were innocent, slowly if they were guilty. Men willingly walked barefoot across cartwheel spokes pulled out of blazing fires, believing that God would help them bear the pain to show the world their innocence.

Everyone knew tales of the timid and weak who vanquished great champions in trials by combat. Even the bravest of warriors quaked in fear before such combat if he knew himself to be fighting against the chosen of God. Lioba knew of a servant boy who had been accused of stealing; when the boy survived the ordeal of boiling water, his accuser had been punished by the law of the land: The local magistrate had ordered the perjuror's right hand to be severed.

"I will gladly submit to any ordeal," said Monica, pushing her heavy body from the bench, her exhausted eyes suddenly shining, eager to submit her complaint to the rule of God.

"Abbess Tetta," said Lioba. "I will submit, of course, and await the judgment of God. But I must know that no harm will come to Monica, if I am proved stronger. It is not her fault that she says what she does. It is part of her illness that she imagines—"

"I imagine nothing, witch," said Monica, raising both arms at once, so each was thrust out from the sides of her body like the arms of a cross. Lioba found herself staring at her sister's muff of otter's fur; a little ball of warmth, no bigger than a newborn child.

Even those few among the clergy who wondered whether God took any notice of the terrible ordeals suffered to prove guilt and innocence found it difficult to disparage the Proof of the Cross. Here was an ordeal and a test of faith crafted about the most elemental symbol of the Church. Men who under ordinary circumstances would find their extended arms shaking within minutes, would find the power—through their love of God—to enter a mystical state of being. In their faithful trance their arms would become weightless, the pain along their backs and necks would vanish, the slowly passing seconds would grow swiftly, until hours passed like minutes, until some would have punished their bodies for a day and more, every part of themselves asleep save the shoulders, glowing with a pain that had become sweet, as if it were a tribute to the Lord.

"Lioba, stand next to your sister," said the Abbess. "Raise your arms in obeisance to the Lord."

Lioba did so, shutting her eyes in the custom of the ordeal, so that she would see no temporal images, so that the only visions before her would be sent from God. The Abbess spoke to them both, her voice loud and clear and full of purpose, but already Lioba was drifting from any awareness of what was in the room.

Behind her shut eyes came a series of images: a field of wildflowers, a lengthy procession of white-clothed nuns, a profusion of lamps and candles, set up around a small and delicate gold frame, holding an ancient relic. The sound of church bells retreated, and soon faded to nothing, replaced by a plainsong murmuring.

For half a moment, she felt a flash of pain along her back; but Lioba brushed this aside, as if it were a fly testing her patience. She remembered that she had become an embodiment of the cross on which the Anointed of God was sacrificed. Lioba saw flames, and then an image of a wooden cross at its center. She could feel the warmth of the fire, and was thrilled by the fact that the wood wasn't consumed. It remained erect, perfectly formed, eager to take on any burden.

Tears filled her shut eyes, but not because of any pain. She was filled with strength, a strength whose quality was very much like that which overcame her during a healing. No wonder men had stood painlessly for so many days, crippling their arms and shoulders, when so much strength was freely dispensed by God. She felt a womanly strength too, a motherly strength such as she had seen and helped along at many birthings.

The fire about the cross gave way to a forest, thickly planted, blotting out the sun. Foliage blew away in a rush of wind. Men came to her, swinging axes, and she turned to them, feeling herself pliant, unafraid. For a brief moment, she thought she saw Felix among these woodcutters, but she rejected this image, knowing this was a test of her strength, sent by a loving God. She would love Felix, in spite of everything he had done, in spite of all he had caused her family to suffer. Even if sin ran through his blood, she would love him, as she loved her sister, as she loved the Abbess, as she loved the whole world made by God, and all men, made in His image.

And the woodcutters were no reason to fear. Lioba felt like a young tree, drawing strength from the ground in which she was planted; she felt her body grow hard and stiff as oak wood. This

was where men found their wood, where they created their cross
on which to hang the fate of the world. Eagerly, she waited for
the cut of the ax blade. She wanted to be chopped down, torn
from the earth, stripped of branches and leaves. Lioba wanted to
be nothing less than a frame for the Savior. She wanted to be firm
and sure and without passion. Lioba wanted to die, to better bear
the burden of the Lord.

But she would not die.

Blows were directed at her, harsh and powerful. Words were
hurled at her, and she was shook so much that she thought her
head would surely fall off, to be lost in the clouds. But a tree had
no head, she remembered, and men with axes didn't shout in the
voice of Abbess Tetta.

"Lioba, Lioba," she was saying. "Dear Lioba, please, it is
over. It is over, and you have told the truth."

Later she would learn that the ordeal had only lasted into the
middle of the night. But the hours had been enough to bring
Monica to her knees, the rich blood of her bloated body running
into the dirty rushes of the floor.

"It's all right," said Lioba. "It's all right now, Monica. You
were sick, but you're going to be well. I'm right with you, just
like always, I'm right with you and everything will be all right."

But Lioba, beyond the dazzling pain from her shoulders and
back, knew that all her words were lies, that nothing was the
same as always, and that everything would not be all right. As
she accompanied poor Monica, barely aware of her surroundings,
to the women's infirmary, she felt the shameful wetness in her
private parts, heard the passionate rhythm of sin beating inside
the walls of her body. Walking through the still Abbey's grounds,
all her senses were wild, open to the thrill of the cold, the taste
of frost, the rush of wind, the distant smell of bread baking for
the morrow.

"Abbess Tetta," she said. "I am not worthy of working
among the sick."

"Silence, child," said Abbess Tetta. "It is I who am not worthy, who have so long ignored your goodness, and your healing
hands. If I had any doubts, the Proof of the Cross dispels them.
The Lord favors you, and trusts you, and I shall do the same."

Lioba wanted to protest, but she did not know what to say.
Indeed, as she drew closer to the walls of the infirmary, the

sickness within drew her, the way a child draws her mother. She did not know why God had given her so much strength to heal, and so much love to succor the strength. She only knew that she had remembered her days and nights with Felix; through the ordeal of the Proof of the Cross the radiant cloud had been torn apart, revealing the truth.

Felix had taken her, and at once, and then again and again, through all the days and nights that she had been his prisoner. She was not a virgin. Lioba had been his woman, had felt his sex within her, had allowed her body to be filled with his joy.

But as the prince had taken her, Lioba had taken him. She had met his lips, his touch, his breath, his desire. Lioba had joined with his passion; and her own was wilder, newer, more sinful than that of any demon in the guise of a saint.

Chapter 8

MONICA SLEPT through Lioba's triumph. Though the Ordeal had proven her a liar before God, Monica's exhausted face had the pallid, exhilarated look of the saintly, while Lioba's eyes had the haunted glare of the damned. She wondered what prevented Prince Felix from storming into the room, his sword outstretched to avenge his wife's honor. Better than anyone, Felix must know what Lioba had done.

Blood had pushed through the heavy fabric of Monica's kirtle, leading Abbess Tetta to wonder whether God had already punished her, destroying the unwanted baby in her womb.

"But there is no baby," Lioba had insisted.

"Stay with your sister," Abbess Tetta had said. "I will reserve judgment on her perjury until she is well enough to speak."

The Abbess had left them at the entrance to the women's infirmary, separated from the dormitory for the sick by a refectory, a warming room, a room for bleeding, and a bathroom. Nonetheless, sad, desperate sounds reached them through shut doors, stone walls, still passageways: an anguished cry, torn from sleep, not in a language particular to a region, but in the universal language of suffering; the mumblings and murmurings of sleep made incomplete and useless by ceaseless pain; the urgent wheeze of tortured breathing. Here the sick were put two and three together in beds alive with vermin. It was not unheard of to wake up in the arms of one who had died during the night.

Lioba wanted to concentrate on the task at hand—the comforting and healing of her sister, but she could not stop the images of her crime from assaulting her at every turn. Felix was not only within her spirit, he was within the walls of the Abbey, dressed for murder, surrounded by his armed men. If he was sick, he was sick of love, body and spirit exhausted from too long wanting what was unattainable forever. How could she heal the pilgrims of this place, if her own nature had bewitched and traduced a prince, had betrayed her sister? No matter what Monica had said to the contrary, Lioba knew that Monica had always loved Felix, as Monica had always envied her sister. What greater burden could there be than being forced to marry a man who loved not you, but your sister? Who could doubt that whatever ailed Monica, whatever black force swelled up inside her could only be vanquished by Lioba's confession and penance? "I must clean my sister," said Lioba to the young nun assigned to help her by the Abbess.

"I do not understand," she said.

"She is filthy. I must wash her."

"But the Abbess said to put her to bed—"

"Help me take her to the warming room," said Lioba sharply, and the young nun nodded silently, gulping back a taste of fear. The Abbey was large and filled with many people, but everyone knew the story of Lioba's abduction; everyone had heard the rumors that Felix had been bewitched.

The warming room was attached to the infirmary, crowded during the winter months by the sick, shivering from fever as much as from the cold. The room was small, with benches placed along the warm walls. As they laid Monica out on a bench, the bells began to ring for the predawn service. Lioba realized that the church bells must have long ceased the ringing that had heralded the arrival of her sister to the Abbey. She wondered if the monks had been reassured that no demons were attacking them, that the bells had done their magic, and the Ordeal of the Cross had brought their proof: Monica had lied, she would be healed, and she would be punished for her lies.

She had a sudden image of the monks rising from their pallets, hurrying out of their tiny cells down the narrow passageways of the dormitory to the cold vastness of the church. There was a joy in all their movements that she could no longer fathom, and this difficulty to comprehend their faith terrified her. She told herself that her faith was intact, that her doubts were only terrors placed by dark spirits forced through her open mouth and eyes and ears. She tried to think of the monks, their sweet faces and piety, but images of their hungry male bodies, young and old, hidden behind shapeless layers of coarse clothing assaulted her; surely they dreamed of something less than divine in their lonely rooms.

She looked at the young nun, as dispassionate as a stone, and felt a deadness within her frame, a deadness that was no more holy than any corpse rotting in the ground. Was it their enforced abjuration of earthly pleasures, their genuine horror of sexual sin, which gave so many of the religious the aspect of the ill? Perhaps it was true that the dying were closer to God; and these monks and nuns, seekers of eternal life, were living life in death's shadow.

"This place is filthy," said Lioba.

"Yes," said the young nun, looking down at the rush-strewn floor. "It is where the sick come to be warm."

"It is where the sick become sicker," said Lioba, surprising herself by her continuing sharp tone. She knew that demons lurked everywhere, not only in the wild forests and swamps and heathlands outside the Abbey, but within the Abbey grounds as well. They hovered about the sick, urging them to succumb to despair, to twist about their faith to faithlessness. Demons were all about the infirmary, their baleful presence tormenting the sleep of the ill, as well as unsettling those like Lioba who were awake.

"I meant only that the sick who come here are not very clean," said the young nun, watching in astonishment as Lioba brushed her hands along the bench on which her unconscious sister lay.

"I am sorry for speaking rudely," said Lioba. "It is that I feel the filth. Not just here, but all about here. No one can be cured if she is not first clean."

"Perhaps the Abbess would not like me to contradict you, as you are a laywoman and have taken no religious vows," said the young nun. "We should not even be speaking. But what you are saying is blasphemy. Cleanliness does not cure, God cures."

Yes, of course, thought Lioba. How could she have forgotten the very concept that ruled her life?

"Praise God," said Lioba, crossing herself automatically, feeling a flush of shame rising in her cheeks. Yesterday, she would have disputed the young nun, with a strength born of certainty in her own faith.

But today she was certain about nothing.

How could she explain the proving of her "innocence"

through the Ordeal of the Cross! How could she have forgotten her complicity in Felix's crime? How could she dare administer the gift of healing, given to her by God, when she was herself not simply unworthy, but damned?

Still, Lioba felt the beckoning spirits of the ill from their squalid dormitory. They needed her touch, and they needed to be clean. This was as clear to her senses as the smell of sweat and blood in the filthy warming room.

"We will both praise God, even as we clean my sister, even as we scour this place. And you will no longer instruct me on what is and is not blasphemous. You will simply do as I tell you, you will obey."

Lioba knew this vile temper was the product of demons; the very demons who plagued her with a thousand doubts: If she had believed herself a virgin, when in fact she had accepted Felix's passion with her own, which other of her beliefs stood on shaky ground? If she had believed herself a healer, holder of a sacred talent given to her by God, what must she believe at this moment, now that she knew herself to be sinful, and possibly bewitched? If she had believed in the efficacy of the Proof of the Cross, what must she believe at this moment, after the Ordeal had sanctified her unholy oath?

The memory of passion had made a mockery of her innocence, her virginity, her faith.

"I meant no disrespect," said the young nun.

"But disrespect was there! If that was not your intention, it must have been the devil's work. And if the devil is speaking through your mouth, perhaps you should be bled. Perhaps the Abbess should restrict your diet to stale bread! Perhaps you need a flogging to rid yourself of the devil!"

"I must speak to the Abbess," said the young nun quietly, reaching without thought for the small silver cross—an important status symbol in these gold-scarce times—about her neck. "She will instruct me. If I have been wrong to address you, I shall submit to her punishment. My only wish is to do God's will."

Lioba found herself shaking her head, as if to rid herself of rude and belligerent words. She was suddenly fearful, as if standing on unsteady ground. If she could not control her words, her memories, her desires, she would no longer be part of the world of the living, but only a phantom, dressed up to fool the world.

"Forgive me," said Lioba.

"I forgive you," said the young nun without hesitation.

"I am a believer, just as you are. You had every right to speak. I am simply upset about my sister."

"Let us clean her."

As if to exhibit her good intentions, Lioba attacked the dried mud of a dozen pilgrims who had huddled on the bench on which Monica rested and bent over her sister with smiling purpose. "It is just that I would like my sister—and everyone in the infirmary—to have the chance to appeal to God for His help in a state of cleanliness."

The young nun followed Lioba's example, her frail frame and bloodless face apparently concealing a great deal of energy and zeal. But she was not through questioning the young aristocrat, as famous for her healing as for her enchantment of Felix.

"May I speak?"

"I am not your Abbess."

"I do not want to offend," said the young nun.

"Speak."

"But do you not admit that among the holiest men of the Church were those who never bathed, who wore the same clothes until they fell off their backs?"

Of course Lioba knew to whom the young nun referred: St. Paul of Thebes wore nothing but the leaves of palm trees, and for sixty years ate nothing but a daily half loaf of bread, brought to his solitary spot by a crow; St. Anthony lived more than a hundred years without changing his clothes, washing his face, or speaking to another living soul; St. Simon Stylites lived in a cistern, chained to a stone, prostrating himself before God while worms and vermin picked at his filthy flesh. These monks and a score of others, from Syria and Ireland, from Gaul and Wales and Egypt, were famed for an asceticism based on personal neglect; and this bodily filthiness led, in legend, to holiness. Lioba could not deny that these men were famous as healers, bringing sight to the blind, opening sterile wombs to the birth of children, returning the breath of life to men murdered by fate.

"It is not the dirt that made them holy," insisted Lioba. "It is not their refusal to change their clothing that gave them the strength to cure."

Lioba undressed her sister as she spoke, pulling away Monica's sticky and soiled undergarments from her large belly, her swollen breasts. There was no doubt in Lioba's heart that Monica was without child, but this made it only the more wondrous that her body had the clear marks of pregnancy. What was nearly as strange to Lioba, whose family retained a vestige of the Roman obsession with cleanliness, were the layers of filth blackening her soft and pale skin.

"You will be well," said Lioba to her sister, bringing her mouth close to Monica's parted lips, expelling with a steady rhythm the interior gusts of pain. Though Monica didn't wake, Lioba imagined that her touch gave her some comfort; the shadow of a smile appeared at the corners of her shut eyes. When they had stripped her completely, they helped her to her feet, and though Monica didn't walk, she didn't have the weight of the dead or the unconscious, but something less than this. It was a sleep like that induced by a spell; Monica was still, but Lioba was certain that she could hear and taste and feel. Wrapping a blanket about her, they moved from the warming room into the adjacent baths. Hot water had been readied for them, and clean cloths. Monica was once more laid on a bench, and wordlessly, the young nun and Lioba scrubbed at the layers of grime encrusted in her skin. The hot water did its work slowly, and because the hour was late, and the labor difficult, they fell into a scrubbing rhythm which prompted reflection.

Lioba couldn't imagine what the young nun thought of in this intimate contact with another living soul; but as she gently exposed the pink skin of Monica's belly and thighs, as she patted at the raw skin about the small of her neck, as she massaged warm water into the oily scalp, she couldn't escape the memories of another contact of hands with flesh, of rough fingers eager to be gentle, of brutal lips strangely reluctant to hurt their prey.

Felix.

In the mirror of her sister's flesh she saw her own eager mouth, her tongue reaching out to caress his chest and eyes, her long fingers extended in pleasure, framing his warrior's face. How could she have forgotten such terrible joy. How many times before had she sinned against God in this fashion? she wondered. In how many healings had she assumed the devil's guise, her kisses and strokes and scratches as experienced and sure as that of any wanton?

And he was here. Felix had come to her. As near as thirty

paces, behind a series of walls, ensconced in his armor, shaking with fear.

She forced herself to think only of healing, the blessed gift, the only contact between flesh and flesh that had worth in this sinful world. Monica was sick, she was her sister, and she must needs be pure.

It was the demons who lived in the night who drove Felix's name through her weak body, through her exhausted spirit.

She forced herself to remember the sick, one by one, retrieving memories of children with blackened limbs, of old men with rheumy coughs, of the lame, and the blind and the deaf and the dumb. One by one, their flesh appeared before her eyes, blocking out the images of Felix's proud body, made suddenly awkward by passion.

"Have you no passion?" said Lioba softly.

"What?" said the young nun, who could not hear the whispered words.

"Passion. Have you no passion?"

"I have passion for the Lord Jesus," said the young nun.

"Passion," said Lioba. "It is something that makes one sick. I have seen it. In women as well as men, in young boys and old crones. Passion is God's test. It is a trial. It can be worse than any ordeal."

Lioba was suddenly silent, shutting up her talk and concentrating on cleaning Monica. She tried to forget passion, and to think only of the sick she would live to cure. Her passion would belong to God.

But the images of the sick seemed to turn transparent as glass, even as Lioba washed Monica's body. As she peeled away the dead skin, there would be another image, not an invention or a demon-sent dream, but a memory of her time with Felix.

No matter what she had said, no matter how she had shouted, how she had protested, she had wanted him to take her; and when he had entered her body, she had responded as if the world had ceased to exist, as if God and his rules were invisible, as if nothing in the world existed for any other reason than to unite their two bodies into one union of spirit. She was a healer, and the union had been a healing, had been a blessing. Felix had been sick with passion, and now he was filled with love; she had been twisted and confused, and now she was steady and straight and full of life.

"Are you all right?" asked the quiet young nun, disturbed by Lioba's too-wild scrubbing of Monica's head.

Lioba ceased the action and nodded silently at the nun, remembering that the memory was false; she had not been full of life, but full of sin. She had performed no healing, but had submitted to lust.

"Let us dress her," said Lioba.

But Lioba made no move to cover her sister's nakedness. She was suddenly sad, seeing in the clean skin the defeat and the desertion of all her healing powers. Somehow, she had lost the gift granted her by God, lost it to a demon's temptation; standing before her sister's bloated body, filled not with life but with sickness, she had no sense of the healer's faithful power, but only the awkward helplessness of one filled with the doubts of the world.

"I must go," said Lioba, turning about in the small room, leaving the nun to deal with Monica alone.

"Where?" said the young nun, but Lioba did not even think of answering her. More urgent than any memory of passion, any terror of divine punishment for lustful sins was the need to bring back what she feared gone: her power.

As she had exchanged a passion for healing for a demon's temptation, she would thrust back this demon-sent lust and find her gift intact and glorious. She would stay at the Abbey, she promised herself. She would give up any hope of life in the outside world. She would take orders. She would be passionate in her God and thereby live to heal once again.

Hurrying through the dark cold rooms and halls, she followed the call of the sick. A child's fever brushed up against her, like the wings of a wasp caught behind closed doors; a young woman's broken limbs rattled for her attention; an old man, sightless and deaf, begged for release from the fear that was eating up his insides, like a slow-burning fire.

"I am here," she whispered, raising her hands to the dormitory, trying to fill up her faith with past triumphs, with remembered marks of God's favor. Like a lover's deathbed cry, the feverish child's pain reached out to her, more urgent and intense than any other. Surely, if God no longer wanted her to do His work, she would not be able to hear this plaintive cry, she would not be able to feel the shape and substance of the sickness of every occupant of this dark and despairing room.

A trickle of pride seeped into her frame. If the sick called to her, it was because she was special. Who could say he knew the outline of God's plan? Perhaps the very terrors that brought her to Felix's bed led also to the Abbey; perhaps Monica's trials were simply the divine means to free Lioba from the *scriptorium* and place her where she belonged, among the sick pilgrims of the infirmary.

"I am here," she repeated. "You will be well. You will all be well."

She let the child's fever draw her through the maze of beds and benches, the sputtering candles trying vainly to beat back the darkness, the paltry relics and talismans flanking empty incense burners, no longer able to contain the nocturnal stench of un-tended human suffering.

As she would help the child, he would help her. In the dark-ness, his yellow hair glowed less vividly than his fever. She would suck this excess of heat into her body, letting it break up against the walls of her heart. She would heal, and she would affirm her place in the world as one of the Lord's elect. Gently, Lioba extricated the child's limbs from those of the three children sharing his bed; none of the others called to her with as much force, as much desire to return to health. Their souls already had the indistinct outlines of corpses. But this child's soul was sharp-edged, eager for life. He had need of her help, but he would be no passive observer of miracles, no soul waiting for another's magic to bring life into dead bones. As Lioba brought his head against her breast, she felt his breath quicken, as if he wanted to breathe in her presence, filling himself with the healing she of-fered.

"Slowly," she whispered. "Come to me slowly." As he rested his cheek against hers, letting her healing hands put out the fire from behind his eyes, Lioba felt a peacefulness settle over her guilty soul.

There was passion in her heart, but it was not for Felix, or any man, but rather for all men; a passion to fulfill God's Will.

Urging her soul to join with the child's, the blessing of sleep entered her body, shutting her eyes against the horrors within and without the dormitory of the sick.

Chapter 9

A BABBLE of languages, each in conflict with the other, lifted Lioba from the rosy light of half-sleep. It was mostly the talk of peasants, Saxon and Bavarian, a harsh counterpoint to the clumsy Francique of softer folk from the south. There was little Roman speech, save the twisted Roman of a pair of Aquitanians; this was so much different from Latin that priests sent to Aquitania, Lioba remembered, had to learn the dialect and accent of the locals in order to transmit God's Latin words.

"I have good food for you, holy woman," said the blond-haired child, no longer feverish, extending a wooden bowl of milk to Lioba.

"You are well," she said to the child.

"Yes, you have made me well. I was sick, and I am well. Now I shall be famous. I have been cured by the holy woman Lioba."

"The Lord has cured you," said Lioba. "I have done the Lord's bidding, and you have helped me by your desire to be well."

The child's bowl of milk was not the only offering thrust at her as she sat on the bed. Fresh mushrooms, cooked plantains, sour wine were all extended to her by eager hands, hoping for a cure. An old man shook a metal trinket at her, which some charlatan had sold him as a repository of Saint Gregory's fingernails, and therefore capable of producing miracles. Several women clutched little bottles, which Lioba knew contained holy water, blessed by the Abbot; such little bottles were kept under every bed at her father's house, with water blessed by a bishop. These safeguards kept black demons at bay.

She got up from the bed, shrugging off the gifts and the entreaties. She wanted to find Monica and share with her what she had learned in the night's healing. Lioba had been too proud to receive the wisdom that was always about her in the healing process. She had always accepted the gratitude of patients as if she had been responsible for their cures. Indeed, pride had let her think it modest that she took such credit as the Lord's lesser partner. To Lioba, growing up under the approbation of awe-struck peasants, her sanctity seemed guaranteed by accepting thanks not in her name, but in His.

But now she would acknowledge another element in the healing process: the patient. The healer was never alone with God; the patient was not a corpse on which one wielded divine power.

Either the patient joined with the healer in the healing process, or there was no healing. Felix was not the only thing that separated Lioba from curing Monica. It was Monica's own desire to remain unwell, to keep the unholy root in her belly alive, that held her in illness' thrall.

"Please do not go," said an old peasant woman, her eyes as bright and alive as a youngster's. "You must help my man. You must give him the words."

Lioba felt the man's dead spirit even as he was pushed into her path: an old man, sick of life, tired in his bones and in his heart. It was not him, but his wife, who wanted the words, the magic. Lioba began the *Adjuratio contra malas oculorum,* speeding and slurring the words, so that the majestic Latin would have the further power of mystery and incantation. She wondered whether it was the redemptive power of Christ, or the fuzzy mythology of the great Roman warrior nation that so enraptured the pilgrims.

"*Alias nec lia nec galina,*" she said, bringing the heels of her hands against the old man's cataract-clouded eyes. "*Supra rypa maris sedebat macula, famuli tui illius sive albe, Christus spergat.*"

"Thank you, holy woman," said the old wife, her eyes shining as he led her silent, defeated husband back to his deathbed. But still Lioba could not leave the excited pilgrims. One olive-skinned woman, black-eyed and scowling, demanded of Lioba whether there was any hope for her child: There had been blood in his stool beginning a week ago, when the moon was full, and each day he grew weaker.

"There is always hope if you have faith," said Lioba, her every gesture, every syllable observed and listened to with the rapt devotion of those who wished to believe.

"But a sickness begun when the moon is full is fatal," insisted the woman. "My priest has told me the trip to this Abbey is in vain."

"A sickness which begins in the full moon means that the sickness will last a long time. But by no means does the length of an illness determine its outcome. Give me your child."

A hush descended over the pilgrims. The healer had spoken, and now she would work her miracle. Everyone in the infirmary imagined the child growing stronger even as she was passed through the close air into Lioba's hands.

So once again a body was pressed against her, this one emaciated, smelling of herbal medications. A leather amulet hung from the skinny neck, demanding the protection of some nameless, pre-Christian divinity. Even as Lioba blessed the child, those among the pilgrims versed in astrology debated the meaning of the phases of the moon in determining the seriousness of an illness. Would death come quickly or slowly if one became suddenly ill during the moon's final quarter? If one came down with a cold during the first two days of the second quarter, would the cold last longer than two days, or would it become a lingering fever? Would an arm broken during the third quarter take three months or three weeks to mend?

"Sweet child, hear my prayer," said Lioba, whispering the words into her ear, rubbing the back of her neck with a gentle circular motion.

Everyone in the infirmary hushed. This was not the prayer of a monk or a priest, but of someone from another world of holiness, a world which was—like the origins of sickness—beyond their understanding.

"May the Lord Jesus remember His creature, and take away pain," said Lioba. "May the Lord Jesus fill your soul with peace, your body with light, your bowels with tranquility. May you live to dream of green fields, and clean water, and young lambs."

There was a kiss, and the still child was lowered to the black-eyed mother's arms.

Before Lioba could move through the knot of pilgrims about

her a young man tried to kneel at her feet. He had a patch over
his eye and a disfigured nose, but still there was a sweetness
about him, a childishness in the way he desired her blessing.
Lioba took hold of his chin, bringing him to his feet, telling him
that he need pay homage to no one but the Lord.

"I am punished for terrible crimes," he said, though this was
an unnecessary confession as it was clear that some judge had
ordered his nostrils slit—usually the punishment for a second
offense for serious brigandage. The patched eye was probably a
relic of the Frankish punishment for a first offense: blinding the
left eye.

"Please forgive me for my terrible crimes," insisted the
young man.

"It is the Lord's forgiveness for which you must ask."

"You are the healer, and it is you who must forgive me if I
am to be well," he said.

Lioba could see that his insistence on her power was but a
single element in a growing wave of need directed her way. The
reformed brigand was covered with red sores, but this affliction
was no better or worse than the hundred calamities in the infirmary: Men, women and children understood little about illness
other than that it was not part of the natural order of things; to
be sick was to be other than whole, other than in harmony with
God's initial plan. Man, created in God's image, did not emerge
from the Creator's hands with broken bones, scaly skin, bleeding
gums, shaking limbs. But as God saw everything, knew everything before it happened, there must be some reason why some
of his creatures were so stricken. And what better reason than as
the result of sin, no matter how slight? Who could say what
manner of crime offended God, or when and why he felt impelled
to strike?

"Let us pray," said Lioba, standing back from the pilgrims,
raising her arms in a hieratic pose.

The pilgrims, accepting her power not as a member of the
clergy but as a representative of older, more pagan powers—
powers which still sang to them from the trees and the rocks and
the sunsets—dropped to their knees. Lioba began the *Paternoster*.
Not a single pilgrim joined in, though even those with no Latin
knew the syllables given by the Lord to the Apostles. They
wanted to hear the words from her lips, not theirs, fancying them
magical, capable of warmth and healing.

For a few moments, Lioba returned to a semblance of her old pride and power. Before she'd been banished to the Abbey, she'd often experienced such reverence from the peasantry, reverence mixed with awe; and her passionate nature thrived on such immodest glory. It was possible to forgo doubts about her abilities, questions as to her worthiness to do God's work, when so many pilgrims worshipped her as if she were a saint. The sick who traveled to this isolated Abbey were more drawn by the collection of holy relics in the church than by the hope of a physician's cure; and Lioba believed they saw her as nothing less than a living embodiment of these holy relics.

In Latin, she finished the prayer, singing out with her concern for Monica, for herself, for all God's creatures: "But save us from the Evil One."

In Roman dialect, clumsily meshed with German rhythms and words, came the response from the other side of the infirmary, beyond the quiet sea of the sick: "For thine is the kingdom and the power and the glory."

She knew the voice, had heard it whisper to her in the night, gently and insistently, a soft murmuring in a warrior's tongue.

"Forever," responded Lioba in Latin. "Forever. Amen."

"Amen," said Felix.

"I must go," she said to the pilgrims, who had become busy testing their limbs, their breathing, their sores, their pains, looking for miracles. The words of Matthew continued to rush through her mind as she approached Felix, and he took her arm in his gloveless hand: "If you forgive others the sins they have done, so your heavenly Father will forgive you. But if you do not forgive others, then the sins you have done will not be forgiven by your Father."

"You will come with me, woman," said Felix.

"Where?" said Lioba.

"Where I take you."

They left the infirmary, and walked out into the morning mist. It was cold, but the fresh air invigorated her spirits. She was able to look at him, and to keep up his angry pace.

He wore no armor, but his powerful body seemed shielded from any physical attack. The long strides, the powerful grip on her arm, the erect posture, the great shoulders and heavily muscled sword-arm seemed impervious not only to arrows, but to love or sickness of any kind. His tunic was decorated with jewels, a risky way to dress in strange parts, and the sword he wore hung from a heavily ornamental belt across his shoulder. In an age where the horse he rode was worth twenty cows, and his armor worth five horses, it seemed he was wearing the wealth of a nation on his back, in the jeweled hilt of his sword. These were not traveling clothes for a distant Abbey, but festive clothes, for a reception at court, for a celebration.

"I am sorry that your wife is sick," said Lioba.

"She is not my wife," said Felix.

There was a short row of cells to the rear of the dormitory of the sick where the infirmary's female attendants slept on pallets, waiting for the bells to call them to church or to duty. Felix had led Lioba the long way round to this place, through an herb garden and another marked with carefully prepared vegetable beds, awaiting the spring.

"You must not worry," said Lioba, letting her Latin lapse into a more colloquial Roman speech. She did not want to seem condescending. "Monica will be well. There are many instances in the literature of such illnesses. An ancient sage has explained that the womb is like an animal which must give rise to children in order to flourish. If it remains barren for too long—"

"It is your child in her womb," said Felix. "Our child."

"There is no child there. Please allow me to explain. Monica is simply ill, and she will be better. She is breathing better, and that is a good sign. According to the Roman document I tran-scribed, such conditions were rare, but they occurred. In a woman too long barren, the womb becomes angry and wild, moving about the body until it can harm the breathing process, causing much pain, and allowing the belly to fill with air and black bile."

"You know a great deal, Lioba," said Felix, turning her about so that she faced his wild eyes. "Tell me what you know about this."

And then the warrior let go his grip on her arm, placed both rough hands on her cheeks, and brought his open mouth to hers.

Lioba felt her heart leap for her throat, felt her teeth slam shut like wooden gates across a castle moat. But almost at once, like a warrior putting away his fear a moment after the battle has begun, her heart quieted, returned to its place beneath her breast; her lips opened, her teeth moved against his, her tongue, as wild and lascivious as the snake which destroyed Paradise, ran through his mouth as if in search of his soul.

A moment later, Felix let go of her cheeks, and threw back his head, breaking all contact with her. "Tell me, you who knows reading and writing. You who know why my wife is not my wife, why the baby in her belly is no baby. Tell me why that kiss gives you pleasure."

"I do not know," said Lioba, though this was as much a lie as if she had denied his statement. If she wanted his touch, if her body shivered in anticipation of his caress, if she was capable of receiving any pleasure from the sexual act, she must be possessed.

"I know," said Felix. The wind whipped his hair across his eyes, and his voice rose over the gusts blowing the mist. "I know what manner of woman I took to my bed, I know what gave you pleasure, and what you later denied. I may not read, but I am not ignorant of theology. Your sister will not sleep in my bed, and no one has yet touched her virginity. You live here among the religious, but you continue to practice the black arts. If you are not yourself a demon, you are in the demons' thrall."

He had his hand on the hilt of his sword, and for a moment, Lioba thought he would draw it, and try and cure his obsession by slaying her before his eyes.

"Felix, I am not a demon," she said. "I am a woman given the gift of healing by God. I thought you would take my gift away. I thought you would devour me, until there was nothing left of my heart, until my spirit was as dry and useless as one without faith. I am not a demon."

"Did you have pleasure when I kissed you?"

"No."

"Do you remember being with me?"

"I remember nothing. God has allowed me to forget."

"You forget nothing. And even if you forget, it would be the same again. It would always be the same, Lioba."

"I did not have pleasure with you," she said, though the lie was pulling at the cord of her throat. If it were possible to speak truly, only for a moment, without fear of the loss of heaven, without a terror of the retribution of God, she could talk of pleasure, she could admit to lust, she could pull at his hands until his body was next to hers, until he entered and joined with her spirit in a way that was more than holy, a way that would heal better than any blessing. "I renounce all demons, and I am a good daughter of the Church."

"If you are not a demon, explain why your sister is pregnant."

"She is not pregnant, she is ill. I have explained. I am helping her, as I am a healer. Do you not think the great Abbess Tetta would know me as a demon? Do you not know that I have suffered the Ordeal of the Cross?"

"I know only what she has suffered, being your sister and my wife. I know only what I have suffered, being your lover."

"St. Augustine wrote of an Incubus who visited women, leaving them with the appearance of pregnancy. But a demon has no seed. Even if a demon has entered Monica, he can not have made her pregnant. No matter what has made Monica ill and swollen, it will be relieved, it will be expelled in the name of all that is holy."

"And what of my possession? Who will expel the demon from me?"

"If you are troubled, appeal to God," said Lioba. "God will answer you if you turn to him in truth and repentance."

Once again the wind gusted forth, so powerfully that Lioba was nearly pushed into the warrior, standing still in his tightly cut Frankish court clothes.

"I have no repentance," said Felix.

He made no move to take her in his arms, but Lioba felt a rush of spirit flow from him to her, a release that took the color from his cheeks, that left him as wide-eyed and open as a child.

"If you have possessed me, so be it. If I have sinned, I will sin again. I have no repentance."

He loved her.

In the words of defiance to his God, she felt a relaxation, an unleashing of pain. This gladdened her, as any movement from sickness to health had always gladdened her; but she couldn't understand it. Lioba had always believed that faith led to health, that sickness was a visitation from the dark spirits. And who could deny that demons were what possessed men and women in sexual bonds, creating jealousy, unseemly passions that were nothing but a perversion of God's laws to populate the earth?

Felix turned about, and entered the auxiliary dormitory

where Monica had been placed, away from the crowded sickroom of poor pilgrims. Here the cells were cleaner and quieter. Men were not allowed in the cells, or in the narrow central corridor between them; but no one challenged Felix's right to see his wife in her sickness. A silent nun led them, bearing a candle; the morning light was insufficient to pass from the high windows of the cells, over the narrow slits in the shut doors to the passageway.

"I have no repentance," repeated Felix softly, his eyes turned to the back of the nun, lit by the wavering candlelight. When the nun stopped before the door to Monica's cell, Felix turned to Lioba, and let an inner surge of happiness raise the corners of his lips. The nun opened the door and entered, but Felix stopped Lioba from following with a hand on her shoulder.

"It doesn't matter," he said. "I believe in God, and I understand the penalties. I know that you have possessed me, but I can do nothing about it. I don't care what you are, who you serve. Nothing matters but that I am with you."

Lioba didn't answer. She walked past him into the cold bleak cell. The nun had extinguished the candle, and stood over Monica's sleeping form in the cold eastern light from the tiny window set just below the high ceiling. Lioba felt Monica's sickness as yet more urgent, more life-threatening than the night before. As the nun raised a wooden cross to her lips, she mumbled a Saxon prayer against the devil, words that were older than Rome, but pagan, blasphemous from the lips of any Christian.

"Leave us," said Lioba peremptorily.

The nun turned about and stared at Lioba, retaining hold of the cross she wore about her neck. She was not offended by Lioba's tone, but rather defiant of her presence. It was as if the nun had heard Felix's confession and believed as he did—that Lioba was demonic—but unlike him, she would retain her faith. Lioba's passionate nature nearly impelled her to take hold of the nun and shout in her superstitious face: Who was she, with her Saxon prayers, to question her faith?

"The poor woman," said the nun. "May Jesus Christ have mercy on her soul."

"Leave us," said Lioba, more sharply than before. She could feel the woman's anger as a reflection of inner turmoil, similar to the frustration and violence that roiled in Brother's John's innards. Even if the nun's superstitious terror was as correct as Felix's blind passion; even if some dark spirit, and not God in His Heaven, gave her the power to heal, she would take away Monica's pain.

Men were prone to error, after all. Even the Church changed its magisterial opinions with the rise and fall of famous popes, preachers learned and not-so-learned, prophets proved holy and less-than-holy. What if the notion that sickness was the result of vice was wrong?

Thousands of pilgrims dragged their sick bodies across the pathetic remnants of a once-great empire—to Saint Martin of Tours, to Seligenstadt, to Ghent, to Maestricht, to Valenciennes —to touch holy relics and receive absolution for whatever sins had caused their sickness; and what if each and every one of them chased nothing but sins never committed, sicknesses whose origin had no divine meaning at all?

"Close the door," said Lioba to Felix, who did so with violence, shutting out the nun's hatred for what she could not understand. In a moment, Lioba had pulled away Monica's linen bedclothes, revealing the swollen belly and breasts, the nipples as colored as those of any pregnant woman.

"What are you doing?" said Felix, turning his eyes from the spectacle of his naked wife.

"Come close," said Lioba, feeling herself propelled by forces greater than herself, guiding her hands, her actions, her emotions. She brought her lips to her sister's forehead, trying to breathe something of her spirit through the thin walls of flesh.

Monica stirred. She opened her lips.

"Take her," said Lioba.

Felix took a step back in the tiny cell, but Lioba reached out and grabbed the powerful man as if he had no more strength than a baby. "She is your wife, and you must take her."

"I have told you what I must do, Lioba," he said, his words slowing down of their own accord as he looked in wonder at the expanse of Monica's bewitched body. "I must submit to my feelings. You have power over me. You have won. There is no need for tests and taunts. Leave your sister and come away with me."

Lioba ignored his words, and pulled off the baldric which held Felix's sword. She wanted him to lower his head to that of his sleeping wife, but as he made no move to do that, she whispered her desire to God.

Aloud she said to Felix: "She is your wife. Put your hands on her forehead."

"I have never touched her."

"Your hands," said Lioba with impatience. As he still made no move to the woman in pain, Lioba placed his hands for him: the warrior's right hand over her eyes, the left hand over her mouth.

"It was you I wanted. The marriage is only an alliance. It means nothing," he said. But he did not move his hands from Monica's face. Though he was no healer, had no experience of the sickbed, all men can feel pain beneath their fingers, all men are capable of feeling another's need.

"She needs your love," said Lioba.

Felix started, nearly breaking his contact with Monica. But Lioba was ready for this, as she was suddenly ready for everything. There was an easy inevitability about everything that she did within the confines of the nun's cell. It was very much like memories of dreams in which she played a part. She didn't require thought or logic or feeling. Nothing needed to be weighed. Everything was preordained. She expected Felix to start, and without a word, had her hands gently at his back.

"It is your love that I want," said Felix, but the words had no more effect on her than if she had inscribed them laboriously in a dozen scrolls, indeed had heard them a thousand times before.

"Gently, Felix," she said. "You are doing God's work. You are healing the sick."

"I am not a healer—"

"Keep your hands steady. Close your eyes. Let her take what she needs from your touch," said Lioba.

Without any instruction from Lioba, Felix moved his hands from his wife's face to her swollen breasts. The intimate touch shocked him. He felt her heart race through muscle and bone to the tips of his fingers, and through them, to the very center of his body. Because his attention was so completely on the revival of his wife's bodily movements—the easing of tension along her neck, the relaxing of her jaw, the stretching of her long legs—he hardly noticed when Lioba, as if fulfilling some pagan rite, released the clasps of his tunic, removing the barrier of clothing separating man and wife.

Monica's open lips let out a gentle groan. This was not an

expression of pain, but of its release. He had an impulse to bring his lips to Monica's, but held back, confused by the conflicting passions in his heart. There was something compelling about Monica's nakedness, something more powerful than any repulsion from the sister of the woman he loved.

"I am not a healer," said Felix again. He did not know that he was responding to Monica's need, a need so powerful that it drew him past his own blind passion. "Perhaps my touch is helping her, but I do not know what to do."

Lioba was behind him, and gently she brought her hands on his bare back, she pressed her lips against his shoulder.

"You know," she said.

Felix found himself swallowing in fear and wonder. For half a moment, he wanted to turn about, to face the demon who had attached herself to his back. But he could not do this. Somehow, Lioba had united with her sister. Somehow the passion he had swallowed in her name was directed toward another.

Lioba took his right hand and moved it from Monica's breast to her soft brown pubic hair. Felix offered no resistance. He had already given up his hopes of the world-to-come in his admission of nonrepentance. Surely this was a devil's rite; but it was impossible to resist.

"She's bleeding," said Felix.

"Since yesterday."

"I don't know what to do."

"You do know," said Lioba. "You let her draw on your strength."

"You must stand next to me."

"I am here," said Lioba. "But it is you who must help your wife to live. It is you whose touch she wants. It is your regard that will give her the desire to live at all."

"But she is my wife in name only," said Felix as Lioba pressed more closely to his back, wrapping her arms about his waist, encircling him in a seductress' hold. "You are—"

"Feel," said Lioba, bringing her hands to his sex, as swollen and thwarted as Monica's breasts. Felix let out a sharp breath, his eyes seeing past Monica's body to a vision of Lioba in his bed, bent over his sex, driving his lust to frenzy. "Feel her need. You are healing her, so you must allow yourself to feel what she feels. You must join with her. She is your wife and you must join with her need and make it your own."

Monica's eyes opened, and saw only Felix.

Even if Lioba had been at his side, instead of behind his back, Monica would have seen only the vision that had prompted her sickness, that had exacerbated her jealousy, that had twisted desire into a perversion of the process of birth.

"Take her," said Lioba, not bothering to whisper, for she was as much a part of the ritual as the patient on the bed, as the object of the patient's love. She let go of the warrior's genitals, she slid her hands along his sides and into the air. "Take your wife."

Then Lioba stepped backward and out of the cell.

A tiny moment of terror followed her separation from Felix. Human passion was God's great gift, but it was fraught with dangers and confusions that could only be resolved—like obedience to God—by choosing a path and following it with faith. And now Felix must choose.

"I want you to live," said Felix, and Lioba heard the words through the shut door, though they were whispered, and knew Monica would have heard them clearly, even at death's door.

"May the Lord bless you and protect you," said Lioba, feeling them come together on their marriage bed. She had no reservations about using the Lord's name, nor would she ever again question the substance of her faith. She closed her eyes against the ecstasy on the other side of the door, against the life she had abandoned. Lioba wanted to drive herself into Felix's body at that moment, to join with him even as he would join with Monica. But she was not a demon, not capable of cleaving to a human soul, except when she was healing.

But it was Felix who healed now.

Lioba had learned the limits of her gift. Monica must enter into the spirit of the cure, and there would be no entrance for her without the desire to live.

Monica needed not only to love her healer, but to love the possibility of life. When Felix brought his mouth to hers, a hundred layers of sickness fell away. Leaning forehead and palms against the door to the cell, Lioba could feel the pain in Monica's belly ease, could feel Felix's lust pour over her sister's sickness like floodwaters over a flame.

In a week Monica would be gone from the Abbey, her belly flat, her pale skin suffused with the blush of a bride. Six months later Lioba would hear of Monica's pregnancy, this time one founded in the fact of union, and not in a fantasy born of despair. Never again would she see Felix or her sister, or the children they brought into the world. The way to the Abbey was distant and treacherous. And Lioba understood that men and women found it hard to return and look upon the face of their healer; of one who had joined with them, body and spirit, to return them to the peace which God allows all His children.

It made no difference whether she was of the devil's party or the Lord's, whether Satan gave her power, or God allowed her to heal in spite of base lusts and desires. Sickness was incomprehensible except as some disruption of what was once healthy and whole. Healing was directed at returning the body to where and when it was well, and as such, must follow tortuous paths, through evil climates, desperate memories, passions never fulfilled.

And Lioba knew she would go anywhere, risk anything, ignore any wisdom other than the impulse she felt in her heart to heal.

New York City, 1983

FIVE DAYS BEFORE, Richard had walked out of the hospital.
Elizabeth had just let him go.

She had not held the door for him, nor packed his case, nor prepared a taxi to make good his escape; but surely she knew that he was going to get out of bed and leave. She had understood from the first that he wanted no treatment; that he expected her to help him to die.

And short of holding him in her arms in his hospital bed, Dr. Elizabeth Grant had done nothing to convince him to remain. Short of understanding that her touch brought comfort to her sick lover, she had no tools, no methods, no reasons to allow him to believe that he might live.

And now he had been gone five days.

The first day, she had learned that he was not at his home, nor at the home of any friend of his that she had ever met. Neither was he registered in his own name at any hospital in the city. But when she had called his aunt in Connecticut, the woman had denied his presence with such wild indignation that Elizabeth was certain that he could be nowhere else. And so she had rented a car, had driven it out of the city, and had gone almost to the Connecticut border before turning back.

He had left no forwarding address. He had escaped. He wanted to be alone. If she were in his shoes, she might do the same thing, might demand the same privacy.

If only she could believe, she had thought, twisting and turning through the five nights and days of his absence; if only she could harness the love in her heart and let it pull her from the despair and resignation she shared with Richard.

"If only I could," she had said aloud, getting up before dawn of the sixth day since he had vanished. Once again she rented a car, rising to the challenge that had always fueled her ambition. She had voiced those same words throughout her childhood, a childhood lengthened by endless years of schooling; often she thought she would have gray hair and false teeth before she could say good-bye to spiral notebooks, library carrels, and the distant promise of summer vacation.

If only she could stomach the smells of her father's examination room, then she could learn to be a doctor and fulfilled; if only she could be the best in her high school, then she could get into the best premedical program; if only she could be the best in her college, in her medical school, in her first-year residency; if only she could be the best woman resident in surgery; if only she could be the best resident; if only she could have the largest reserves of courage, strength, dexterity, memory, self-confidence; if only she could have all these things—then she would be happy.

If only she could break through this miserable traffic and fly; if only she could make this light; if only she could pass the toll-gates; if only she could find her way to the Connecticut Turnpike.

All her life she had battered through impediments, road-blocks that had needed clearing to arrive at goals tantalizingly within reach. But beyond these goals were further roadblocks, further obstacles to overcome on the way to fulfillment. Sometimes she imagined that there would never be an end to the exams and trials, the testing of time and endurance and feeling.

And now there was a new goal, a new trial, a new impediment in the way of happiness.

She wanted Richard.

If only she could have Richard, then she would be happy.

If only she could make Richard well.

But no matter what the oncologists told her of the miracles of chemotherapy, she had seen the results of acute myelocytic leukemia before, during, and after the treatments of her colleagues. It was possible for some, doctors and laymen, to regard the invasion of their bodies as a temporary nuisance, and simply to deal with it medically and go on with one's life; it was possible for others to regard it as a fight to the death, a civil war within one's frame, and to join with the cancer specialists in a no-holds barred assault on one's own physical self.

It was more common to deny the fact of cancer, to refuse to believe in the treachery of one's own body. From denial, anger and disorientation were short steps, because one could no longer disbelieve the dizziness, the anemic fatigue, the night sweats, the pain in the joints and bones that had overnight added the weight of one hundred years. Of course, fear was officially regarded as something weak and shameful, the friend of the invading cancer and the foe of the dedicated cancer-doctors. But Elizabeth, both a doctor and the child of a parent who had fallen victim to cancer, had complete understanding of the sense of horror of the afflicted. What else was a legitimate way to feel at the knowledge of one's illness? What was more truthful than terror at confronting inside one's self the fast-growing stuff of death?

"Would you goddamnit move out of my lane?" she shouted through her windshield to first one car then another, picking up speed in the fast lane, flashing her high beams in broad daylight to let them know she was on their backs and they had better move out of the way.

Elizabeth found herself swallowing painfully, as if her glands were swollen. She wondered if her fatigue was simply the result of lack of sleep or a sophomoric identification with the symptoms of her lover. In the long days since he had put on his clothes and walked out of the hospital, not bothering to fill out a form, or draft an explanation or a farewell, she had begun to sense the smell of burning flesh—the smell of death—along every corridor of the hospital.

She knew this came from wrongheaded thinking, sentimental and full of fear.

That her father had died a protracted death from cancer was ancient history, in the speeding stream of medical advances. That the smell of his flesh after radiation therapy lingered in her nostrils throughout her first year of medical school should not logically influence her attitude toward the correct treatment for Richard in 1983. The death of her father might have led her to a surgical career, where she could cut out what was bad in the body, where she would never have to deal with the heart-rending decisions of how much to burn or poison of what was good in order to try and stem the flood of the invisible self-replicating enemy. But it should not have irretrievably damaged her capacity for hope for others so afflicted.

But Richard was not simply another patient. She loved him, and so she was able to feel his fear, empathize with his despair, understand his desire to embrace a quick death rather than face a hellish prolongation of life.

But she had to stopper this empathy. She had to forget the stench of burning flesh, the visions of hollow-eyed patients, numb and nauseous and helpless, and think of Richard's refusal to undergo treatment as an impediment that she must overcome. In spite of her feelings, she had absorbed the numbers of the oncologists: One out of three adult patients was being "cured," cured in the sense that they had survived a five-year period of remission. As much as eighty-five percent of leukemia patients who underwent chemotherapy experienced some form of remission; and even though more than half of these suffered relapses, every one of those who underwent a remission lived longer than they would have without the chemotherapy.

If only she could just wave a wand and make it go away.

But this was an impediment more difficult than could be solved by wishing, regardless of what some trendy philosophers imagined: that cancer victims had somehow created their own illness as a symptom of despair with life. No one could tell Elizabeth Grant, third-year surgical resident, that learning to laugh would cure disease, or that leukemia would respond to a diet of fruit and sitar music.

"Would you please goddamnit get out of the way," she said once again to her windshield. She flashed her high beams, she leaned on her horn, but the slow truck hogging the fast lane would not move aside. Here was an obstacle she could relish: visible, tangible, and able to be overcome.

If only she could pass this lumbering wide-bodied truck, belching exhaust fumes out rusty tailpipes directly into the ventilating system of her tailgating car.

Beyond the truck was Richard, and it was only because of the truck that she couldn't get to him, that she couldn't see him and give him comfort. For a wild moment, the truck seemed the only thing in the way of saving Richard's life. If only she could pass this truck perhaps everything would once again be clear. She would see that there was no reason why Richard couldn't be cured, why the two of them couldn't live together until they expired of peaceful old age late in the next century.

She would have to pass the big truck on the right, and at once.

"Miserable bastard," she said, stomping on the accelerator pedal of the rented Thunderbird just as the truck slowed for an approaching curve, waddling into the middle of the two northbound lanes.

She wasted a half-second leaning on her horn, nearly ramming into the rusty backside of the barn-sized truck; but as always, her reflexes prevailed, her intelligence, her capacity to solve problems under pressure overwhelming her despair, lending her performance all the marks of excellence. She jerked the wheel a quarter turn to the right, squeezing within a half foot of the guardrail before straightening the car, accelerating rather than braking in the heart of the curve so that the wheels wouldn't lock, but instead remained flat and centered on the hot asphalt.

She passed the truck, and if there had been a professor of truck-passing grading the experience, she would have gotten no less than an A, as always.

Still, the rush of adrenaline left her shaking as she flew down the deserted straightaway, pushing past eighty miles an hour on the way to Richard.

"I almost smacked into a truck," she could say. "Then I took it up close to ninety, not bad for six cylinders and four hours of sleep." Then she would twist her rigid lips into a more comfortable smile, restrain herself from asking how he felt, and take one quick plunging look into his fast-dying eyes.

"You see, darling, the only reason I am here, the only reason, is because I possess some knowledge that you do not have. This is not to say that I in any way want to interfere with your decision about how to go ahead with your—situation—I simply want to share with you what I know."

"Give it up, Lizzie," she could hear him say, spitting up a ghost of his familiar insouciance. "I like being in the dark. It gets me ready for the real thing."

The only reason she was there, she thought, bringing up the painful realization to consciousness, the only reason, was to tell him what she knew, so that she would not be at fault for holding back.

She had held back for five days. She had allowed him his chance to run without following him. But after all, even if she did not love him, she would be responsible to him as a patient. Even if she could see his point of view, she must share with him the knowledge that he did not have, even if she had to shout it into his beautiful face.

What she knew, what she was absolutely obligated to tell him was that if he did not begin chemotherapy at once, that he would die, and quickly.

But not so quickly that death would be a swift relief.

It would not be a death suitable for the silver screen. There would be no rush toward oblivion, no easy cinematic flourish. He could die in a week, or a month, but the days of that week or that month would be longer than any days he had ever known. He would die, yes, but it would not be a pleasant death, not simply slipping into sleepiness; the fatigue would be far more painful. The disease would strip away his resistance, exposing his frail human flesh to a thousand depredations. He would lie in dizzy discomfort, hallucinating about the place to which he was about to travel, a place that didn't exist except in the hopeful minds of men.

"If I were in your shoes, darling," she began again, practicing the threads of the conversation that would never take place. "If I were in your shoes I would certainly try whatever was available. That is the truth. This is not 1950, and it is not even 1980. Oncology is the fastest growing—"

"Sure," interrupted the Richard in her mind. "The cancer industry is fast growing. It's like a cancer among medical specialties. It feeds on its own ignorance, growing fatter and fatter with useless cells, crowding out anything worthwhile but the chance to die horribly, slowly, and disfigured. It certainly was nice of you to drop by, Lizzie. Next time call first, why don't you? I might be dead, and it's a long trip from Manhattan for a busy lady doctor."

She slowed down a half mile before the exit, feeling her heart race faster and faster as the speedometer registered fifty and forty and then twenty-five miles an hour. "I'm sorry to trouble you," she tried again, conjuring Richard's aunt. "I was just in the neighborhood and was hoping that Richard might like a little company."

She followed the easy curving exit from the highway onto a country road, reflecting the summer light into a fantastic series of puddles. A friendly mutt with a large head and skinny body trotted out into her path, and as she swerved out of the dog's path, she heard a bark that was nothing else than lonely. Now she was driving at less than ten miles an hour, looking for the street signs that she knew by heart, though she had only been to Richard's aunt's house twice before: Right on Elm, take Beech which goes one way, turn onto Oak which is also one way, take the left fork, red barn should be on the right, two miles to the shopping center, left turn past the parking lot, blacktop road to the end, number forty-two, which is hard to read, but the house is red brick on a block of fake colonials with aluminum siding.

Elizabeth didn't see the police car until it had drawn alongside her, and the young officer at the wheel had rolled down his window: In this Connecticut town, the police cars were air-conditioned.

"You all right, miss?"

"Yes."

"You sure? You look a little lost. And I'm packing a map or two."

"It's all right," said Elizabeth. "I'm a doctor."

"Excuse me?" said the police officer, wondering whether he should get out of his car and into the turgid heat.

"I have to see a patient," she said, turning her eyes to the glare coming through the rented car's windshield, blinking away tears.

She heard the police car's door open and close, she felt the kind eyes of the officer rest on her pale profile, she waited for him to speak. "Miss, I don't want to intrude, but if there's anything I can do?"

"I wasn't speeding, was I?"

"No."

"So I can go?"

"Of course you can go, miss. But seriously, if I can help you locate an address, or anything—"

"Thank you, Officer," said Elizabeth. "You see, it's been a long time since I've been this way. It's my boyfriend's aunt. He's at her house. Forty-two Waverly, but you can't see the sign very well. It's red brick. I think I'm going the right way." Once more she repeated the magic words: "I'm a doctor."

"You're a very pretty doctor, miss," said the police officer, not knowing any more than she why she kept mentioning her hard-earned title. For a brief moment an inappropriate smile crossed her face, remembering when she had ordered a checkbook, with the ",M.D." printed after her name. It was only after months of penning the additional comma and two capital letters on every check that she had returned to her old naked signature.

"I only meant that it's not just a personal visit," she said. She knew that if she looked the police officer full in the face his concern would lead her from a few tears to a torrent.

But he didn't press the issue. "I'm sorry that you seem to be upset. If you follow me, I'll take you to Waverly."

"Thank you."

"You're okay to drive?"

"I'm okay," said Elizabeth. He didn't put on his blinking red light, but instead lumbered along at fifteen miles an hour, signaling long before the intersections, turning about with a cheery smile to make sure that she was still there. He waited for her to ring the bell of the red brick house, and to be allowed inside by Richard's aunt before driving off, waving his hand at the shut door.

"I must see him," said Elizabeth.

The aunt looked at her with sad eyes, then put her hand on Elizabeth's shoulder. "I'll tell him," she said.

She didn't have to ask for privacy, or demand an hour of his precious time. Richard got out of the lounge chair on the screened-in porch, took hold of Elizabeth by the waist, and silently walked with her to his room at the dark, cool back of the house.

"I'm not here to ask you—" she began.

"I know," said Richard, stopping her words with the tip of his finger. "I know why you're here, darling."

When he kissed her, she was astonished at the strength of his desire. For a moment, she nearly pulled away from him, afraid that he had decided to kiss her good-bye. But she could not pull away, not when he opened her mouth with his teeth and drove his tongue inside as if he wished to follow it there with the rest of his body.

She could not keep her eyes closed, because in five days his image had diminished, the outlines of his familiar frame blurring into the terrible sameness of the dying and the dead. Even as he drove his passion against her exhausted frame, bringing his hands from her face to her breasts, she could see the color of the dead through his fading tan.

She wanted to push him away at that moment.

She wanted to step back ten paces and shout at him from across the room: "You have to try. You have to at least goddamnit try."

But she could not bring herself to push him away, when all she wanted in her heart was to hold him like this, until their bodies would freeze into mutual numbness, until there would be no thought of the future, until the only thing they would ever remember was this moment, this connection of body and spirit through the power of their love.

This was not the way he made love, not with an urgency that ignored her desire, not with an insistence that seemed to build on itself, as if afraid that going slowly would be too slow to finish.

But before she could protest, he was pulling back, letting up the pressure of his teeth, relaxing the desperate hold of his palms on her cheeks. He did not break the contact of their mouths, did not stop the gentle flow of his breath against hers. He had simply gentled the kiss, as if remembering not to count the moments, remembering instead that a moment could last a lifetime.

She could taste his tears on her cheeks, could feel the impulse to death as if he were shouting it in her face; but no sadness, no horror, no pity could stop the force of Richard's desire. "I'm so glad you're here," he whispered, and she heard the words somewhere at the back of her brain, even as he took hold of the back of her neck in his beautiful hands. "Lizzie," he said, and she fought back a flash of anger at herself, for she knew that her spirit was rising out of control of any logic, that she would soon stop thinking of where she was and who she was, and how she had come this day to talk sensibly to the man she loved.

He held her at the small of the back, pressing her body against his, he touched his lips to her eyes and mouth and chin, he brought his knee up against the inside of her thighs.

How dare you do this to me? she thought, finding herself sitting on the bed, wanting him to strip off her clothes, wanting him to pour oblivion over every misery in her mind. For a moment she tried to turn from this rising violence of passion. Elizabeth needed to think, to put words together in her mind, first for

herself, then for the man she loved. All last night she had shivered at the memory of waking up next to him, her head nestled
against his warm and inviting chest. Though his body was manly
and hard-edged, she felt as if it were of a piece with her own. She
had never been more comfortable, in or out of bed, with another
person's flesh. She liked to touch him and taste him, to feel his
hands on hers, to be enveloped in his scent. There was never a
recoiling, a pulling back, from any intimacy with him; no matter
how bleak her mood, how sudden and unexpected the touch of
his hands or lips, her feelings moved into him, never against him.
He was inviting because he was receptive; his mouth was as open
to her lips and tongue, as his spirit was sensitive to her pleasures
and pains.

"Darling," she whispered. "There is something I have to tell
you."

If he had stopped then, there would have been no words in
her mouth, only a wild hesitation, a desperate longing for a miracle in which she did not believe. But he did not stop. If his kiss
was suddenly gentler, his breath came faster, more insistently, as
if gathering his earthly energy for a final run to ecstasy. But
suddenly she understood that he had no ecstasy in sight. Richard
did not want to make love at all. "Lizzie," he said, and she knew
that he was about to tell her that it was no good, that he didn't
believe he could live, and that she didn't believe it either.

Elizabeth refused to hear this. She squeezed his body as if to
wring it of hopelessness. She clutched him so that he would
speak nothing of despair, she held him so that he would feel the
comfort that her love gave to his dying spirits.

"Richard," she whispered, not letting go of his neck, not
moving her head back more than a hairsbreadth from his dear
face. "Richard," she said again, but there were no words to explain why she held on for dear life, how she of all people could
let go of sad reason and draw hope from their love.

But better than words was the wildness in her spirit. It was
possible to shut out the world, to leave behind mortality, to find
beauty and joy. She put her hands on his chest, not in any attempt to heal his flesh, but to excite his desire. They loved each
other, and now she demanded that they share this love, that they
give to each other the best part of themselves. She could see his
eyes widen to take in the world, as if his appetite for life was

once again keen. They helped each other off with their clothes, clumsily, happily, as if this were the first time, as if they were about to be astounded by this mutual offer of intimacy. He kissed her slowly, his lips barely parted, his hands cradling her hot cheeks. Elizabeth moved beneath his powerful legs, taking hold of his excited penis, wanting to hurry their union, as if their lovemaking would lead to a solution to a problem she could only dimly remember. But Richard, overcome by happiness, refused to hurry. He would not move his lips from her face, refusing to part with her mouth and nose and jaw and teeth; even when he entered her, and she brought her legs up high against his back, he would not shut his eyes, not yield to ecstasy. He fought back her quick rhythm until it had become infinitely slow, the movement of his pelvis like a sweet rotation of the heavens. Elizabeth found herself drawn into him, as he was drawn into her; there was an entry through his open eyes directly into his dear, familiar soul. Her spirit seemed to leap from her flesh to his, her love swelled unbearably against the constraints of her mortality.

But suddenly there were no constraints.

Suddenly mortality was banished, doom dissipated under a rain of pleasure.

At the moment of orgasm, she imagined that she could feel his heart reach through his flesh for hers, that she could sense behind her shut eyes a gentle smile lift the corners of his mouth. The love that had immobilized her, the love that had left her torn between two gods—one urging an acceptance of death, the other insisting on life—had been replaced with one more passionate, more blind. There were no more choices. She simply could not accept a world without him.

"Richard," she said, wanting to be with him. "Richard, darling," she said, demanding that she would. Incredibly, a sweet madness assured her that her demand was more than childish petulance, more than a passion-born dream. There were "miracles" all the time. Not the Biblical miracles of manna from heaven or Red Sea partings, but the sudden reversals of body chemistry, the unexplained remissions, the series of misdiagnoses righted by hard, scientific work. Dr. Elizabeth Grant, who found belief only in physical symptoms and medical charts, had been overwhelmed by her heart. She would ignore statistics, and turn toward desire. Anything was possible. Men and women doomed

by the country's most prestigious clinics had gone home to live
another fifty years. There was a chance, distant and vague, but a
chance nonetheless, a chance in which she would now believe.

"Richard," she said. "I want you to know—"

But he interrupted her.

Elizabeth's wild belief had already been communicated to her
lover. He had no need of hearing her words, when the emotional
shock of her revelation rang through the walls of her body, and
from her body to his. She could not have made his decision for
him, but the sudden realization of her belief had helped his awakening will to fight immeasurably. "Lizzie. I'll tell you what I
want, and then you'll do it for me, okay?"

She watched his lips move slowly about the syllables, not
understanding why he seemed so suddenly pleased. She needed
to tell him of her own change of heart, to make him see that if
she believed, so could he. "Take me to your leader," he said.

She didn't know what this meant at first, so intent was she
on finding the words to get her own message across. She had
imagined his mind set, and did not think she would hear more
from him than the fact of his love. Richard could see that she
hadn't gotten his little joke, and to make it easier for her, he
extricated himself from her tight embrace and looked at her from
across two feet of empty space.

"Your leader, Doctor," he said. "Take me to your leader."

Later, she wondered what wild fear had made it so hard for
her to comprehend. She looked at him blankly until there, right
before her eyes, she could see past his aura of fear a determination no longer based on destruction. He was not talking about
being taken to God and suicide, but to the hospital and the beginnings of treatment.

"Do you mean that you'll come back?"

"One kiss," said Richard. "That's all it took, Doctor."

"That was more than a kiss, wise guy," she said, the adrenaline shooting through her blood as if she had once again survived a high speed pass on a too narrow road. "I'm very happy,
Richard," she added. "You're making the right decision."

They packed up a vinyl airline bag, and left the dark and cool
little room where they had made love. Driving back to Manhattan, Elizabeth was strong, and exhibited none of the terror contained in her body. She was capable of concentration, and so she

thought only of future tasks and tests, not of past failed treatments and pain and suffering. This was what she had wanted, this was the obstacle she had prayed to break through. Love had brought her to belief, and love had brought him to try and live.

"Darling," she said to Richard in the car, repeating the words for her benefit as much as for his. "I'm very happy."

She drove with precision and care, keeping the car at the speed limit, looking straight at a vision of the long road ahead.

PART THREE

England, 1724

*For the world is not to be narrowed
till it will go into the understanding
(which has been done hitherto),
but the understanding is to be expanded
and opened till it can take
in the image of the world.*

—Francis Bacon

Chapter 10

No one in the village thought it strange that the Baron, in the time of his distress, turned to young Annie, the barber's daughter.

There was no reason why the great lord should know that Annie had all her life been in love with Will Smithson, the young man he had banished to London. All that the Baron would know of Annie was what the village at large knew of her: that she was a healer, and unafraid of her calling in a time when men questioned the source of all unseen power, driven by superstition and fear to accuse women of witchcraft and men of bonding with the prince of darkness.

She had been the village healer for three years, and her reputation had spread not only to the modest homes of the tradesfolk, but to the Great House as well. The Baron's beloved was sick, and even the great doctors of London had been unable to heal her. Though Annie was barely nineteen years old, her quiet voice and pallid features had become familiar and reassuring resources of strength for the village. They had forgotten their mistrust when she had first been called upon to take her mother's place at a birthing. Though she had assisted her mother's midwifery since she had been a small child, none had believed that a maiden of sixteen had the strength of character to deal alone with the sometimes terrifying vicissitudes of childbirth.

The villagers had not known then that Annie was not simply a half-trained helpmate to a dedicated practitioner of female medicine. Like Lioba of ancient Francia, like Corinna of far more distant Epidaurus, Annie was driven to heal the pain and disease of anyone in need. This was her need as much as the need of those who were sick. It was this need that inspired her, this inchoate insistence in her heart that marked her as not just an administrant to the flesh, but a healer to the spirit.

But three years before, the healer had had to prove herself to the village. Annie was only the barber's daughter, not a midwife or a healer in her own right. She was no more than the girl who had helped her poor departed mother Margaret, midwife to the families of those whose trade and industry had lifted them from the peasant class. And though Annie believed in her own ability to heal, she knew she needed the belief of those around her, for their spirits could help or hinder the healing process.

Brought to the home where the birthing had already taken place, Annie had felt the newborn's terror beating in his tiny heart, a terror too large for his body to contain. Mouth open, the curative urge to cry had been stoppered by a crippled spirit. Quickly, she had brought her lips to his shivering chest, touching the tip of her tongue to the smooth wet skin. At once, she felt the hard black substance of fear break down, like brittle stone hit by a mallet. Even before the heart slowed its terrified racing, the infant's cries filled the hovel, washing over the rank, huddled bodies like cleansing rainwater.

But none among those present understood that a healing had taken place. All they had seen was a too-young, too well-dressed girl kiss a baby whose birth she had not assisted; and then they had heard his expected screams. Closing her eyes against the dark and the stench, ignoring the hostility of the peasant women, Annie had gentled the baby, counting fingers and toes, feeling the perfectly formed organs of sight and hearing and generation, making sure that his palate was whole, that his tongue was not tied.

"God be praised," she had said in her quiet voice. "The child is healthy."

Annie's mother, God rest her soul, would have been sorely critical of her midwifery. The women who had brought her to this filthy place mistrusted not only her inexperience, but everything about her. She was not of their class, nor was she old, nor was she authoritative. Indeed, the white-faced young midwife looked like nothing so much as a virgin, looked like all she knew of birthing and nursing was what she had been read out of some book of fairy tales. She had only been called to the birthing out of time-honored deference to her profession, and not to her own fledgling standing. The winter's shaking sickness had carried away not only Annie's mother, but nearly half the village, including the superstitious old midwife who had served the peasants with her unsanitary rites. Annie didn't even have the telltale sign of the peasant midwife, the extra-long thumbnail with which a baby's tongue-tie could be cut free.

Not having their respect, they would not let her perform the careful tasks she had learned from her mother. She was there, apparently, only to observe, and to sanction the birthing that would take place without anyone's interference.

"This will comfort her," Annie had said, but the women had pushed her away, grunting their disapproval. Everything she had brought in her birthing basket was regarded as alien, tainted by its smell of soap. They refused to let her apply hot cloths to relax the mother's genital organs; neither would they allow her to spread oil about the outlet through which the baby's head would appear in God's own time. These peasants cared nothing for cleanliness, cared less for ways to ease a pain that was given to women by God as their portion of punishment for Eve's sin.

But surely worse than her neglect of the mother's comfort and cleanliness was Annie's disregard of the cardinal rule of midwifery: to bring mother and child back together with speed.

Her own mother, of blessed memory, used to urge her through the first tasks of a birthing: the cleaning away of mucus from about the face, feeling for the birth cord in case it had turned about the baby's neck, the wrapping in flannels against the sudden cold of the world. What was most important, most urgent, vital to the health of two spirits, was to place the newborn into its mother's arms.

Everything else could wait.

There was no hurry to examine the baby, unless it needed a few slaps to get it breathing; there was no rush to cut the birth cord, no urgency to see if the baby would suck with vigor on the midwife's finger. Most infants lived, though many died; save for a few simple procedures, this was in the hands of God, not in those of the midwife. What was in the hands of the midwife was the child's body, holding its pure spirit, newly torn from its mother. This was what Annie's mother had demanded that she quickly surrender.

"Their spirits are closer than man and wife, Annie," her mother used to tell her. "Closer than a saint is to God. Closer than brothers or sisters, closer than lips joined in a kiss. You cut the birth cord later. First you bring the spirits back together. First you let the baby know it's back with the woman who gave it life."

But what if the woman who had given the baby life had also inspired its terror?

"Give her the sugar water," said Annie, nodding to the big-nosed old woman who held the filthy cup before the mother's face. This much comfort was apparently tolerated, as it was more a custom than part of any healing art. "Wait. Ease her up a bit. Don't pull. Careful, she's in pain. Just a little, so she can sip."

But no one heeded her words. Two of the peasant women pulled at the new mother as if she were a sack of grain fallen off a wagon. The big-nosed woman pressed the cup to the mother's shut lips and poured it over her chin and neck. Evil-smelling incense was swung from a censer, and a bent-over crone brought a rusty talisman close to the howling baby's eyes.

"Please, we must see that she is at ease, so that I can give her the baby," said Annie. The sugar water to slake the mother's thirst usually came later, once the baby's face had been brought against its mother's; the careful mopping of the mother's forehead, the wait for the release of the afterbirth were all usually achieved with the baby safe in its joyous and exhausted mother's arms. But Annie would not let go of the child, even as his terror grew small, even as the pulsing in the birth cord diminished. She was not only a midwife, following an ancient and intricate set of rules, but a healer, with her heart open to a thousand sources of pain. There had been terror in the child's heart, and that terror had its source in the womb, for the child's mother was a madwoman.

"You don't give her the baby, you give me the baby," said the big-nosed old woman. "She's a lunatic, and there's a full moon, in case you don't know it."

"What will you do with the child?" asked Annie.

"I'm going to eat him," said the big-nosed old woman. "I'm going to eat him raw, because raw babies is better than cooked babies."

They had laughed at her then, enjoying the spectacle of her clean clothes spotted with the blood and mucus of the madwoman's child. Perhaps they had forgotten that with her barber father's bloodletting and her mother's midwifery, she had been around the stuff of life and death since she was a child.

"When are you going to cut the cord, milady?" said another of the crones. "Or would you rather have one of us do it for you?"

"It is not time to cut the cord," said Annie, holding the child more tightly to her breast. A very fat young woman, whose spotted face she recognized from the village square, bared her breast, and came closer to Annie; even in the bad light of cheap candles she could see the filth in her hair and skin and fingernails.

"Time to eat," said the wet nurse.

"Cut the cord, silly girl," said the big-nosed woman.

The pulse in the cord had vanished, and Annie had cut through the cord swiftly, holding the baby in one arm, rather than surrender him to one of the peasants.

"If the mother is not capable of looking after the child, I can make some arrangements with the Baron," she said.

"We know all about the Baron's arrangements. The great Lord has gotten half this village with child. For all we know, he could be this one's father too."

"Do you not know who the father—"

"Give me the child," interrupted the big-nosed woman, this time taking hold of the baby with her thickly callused hands. Annie let go, and watched with sadness as the child began to scream, passed from this woman to the wet nurse, who let his wet flannels fall to the rush-strewn floor.

"The child must be covered," said Annie, looking about the hovel for something warm and clean. A young girl scurried from behind her mother's legs and picked up the baby's filthied blankets and extended these to Annie, but Annie's attention was suddenly drawn from concern at the newborn's nakedness.

The deranged mother was in pain.

This was not the ordinary pain of delivery, nor the beginning of the terrible emptiness felt by some mothers in the first moments after the birthing. The madwoman opened her eyes and mouth, and tried to scream; but like the first heart-rending attempts of her baby, she was unsuccessful. But the silent howl somehow gave her strength. She pulled herself first to an upright sitting position, then further forward, as if pulling on an invisible tow rope, until she had forced herself on to her knees.

The wet nurse had already covered the baby after her own

fashion, hiding him in the folds of her voluminous blouse; from behind this filthy shelter, the newborn was drawing sustenance and comfort. But the mother seemed oblivious to this. She drew no comfort from her infant's first suckling. Raising herself into a squat on the straw-stuffed mattress, she took hold of the birth cord that had connected her life to her child's and pulled down with an animal's unreasoned strength.

Annie thrust past the spectators and grabbed the madwoman's hands. The lunatic was strong, and fired by madness; but Annie was stronger, inspired—like a hundred and more generations of healers before her—by her need to ease the other's pain.

"No," she said in her quiet voice, but the violence with which she took charge of the madwoman and her peasant kinfolk would never be forgotten. It was from this moment that the barber's daughter began to emerge as someone of substance and fire, someone blessed by God with otherworldly strength.

Annie got onto the mattress, facing the woman, and gripped the birth cord in her own hands. She stared into the woman's wild, silently howling face, and returned her terrible hurt and hatred with kindness and love. "You are going to let go, but we must do it slowly," said Annie. "Just like with the baby, but it will hurt much less. It will be comfortable, and it will last only a few moments. Just a few moments."

"Baby," said the woman, erupting into speech.

"Lunatic thinks she got another bun in the oven," said one of the peasant women.

"Silence," said Annie, feeling the beginning of the woman's contraction. Holding the edge of her right hand over the pubic bone in the careful manner taught her by her mother, she safeguarded the womb, even as she helped guide the afterbirth out of the bloody birth canal.

There was a sudden gush of blood, running onto Annie's immaculate gown, but she noticed nothing other than the continual increasing of the woman's pain.

"Like a stuck pig," said one of the peasant women, but now the others hushed her, respecting Annie's skill and the strength of her concentration.

Even if she had not learned it from her mother's practice, she would have instinctively followed nature's hand in easing the afterbirth's delivery. Annie waited for each contraction before increasing the gentle pressure on the womb, at the same time easily pulling on the birth cord, ignoring the flow of blood that signaled nothing other than the healthy separation of the afterbirth from its nine months' home.

Ordinarily, the afterbirth's delivery came about a third to a half of an hour after the baby. The rapidity of this separation of afterbirth from womb was not unusual; what frightened Annie was the increase in pain and terror as the afterbirth was slowly delivered into her waiting hands. The pain should have reached its limit, and then quickly subsided in a euphoric relief.

"It is all right," said Annie. But the madwoman, not collapsing onto her back, but still struggling forward in her birthing crouch, did not heed the midwife's words. Her pain was wild, and growing so fast that Annie felt it in her own chest, like a monstrous weed, twisting out of the ground with unstoppable speed. But Annie could not take the woman's pain away from her. There was not a finite amount that could be washed away with a kiss or a prayer, but an unlimited torrent of pain, building on itself, growing momently more dangerous.

"Give her the stick," said one of the peasant women, urging a wet wooden rod into Annie's hand. They were afraid the madwoman would swallow her tongue, but Annie knew that the danger present was not that of an impending fit. The pain came from the heart, and unless it could be stopped would lead not to a fit but to death.

"Give me the baby," said Annie softly.

But the frightened peasant women did not obey the command. Instead, they moved back from the bed and shouted at her, as if to keep both midwife and madwoman at bay.

"Give the lunatic the stick."

"Tie her arms, she's very strong."

"Put her on her back, she'll shut up then."

Annie turned from the madwoman to the peasants, letting the bloody afterbirth slip from her hands as she repeated her demand: "Give me the baby."

"He's eating."

"You don't want to get the baby near the lunatic."

"You better tie her arms down, she's a strong one, even if she's losing blood, she's strong."

Annie was off the bed, out of the lunatic's reach, thrusting through the knots of peasant women with her bloodstained hands. Despite her small voice and gentle frame, Annie took the nursing baby off the wet nurse's breast with a wild violence. Almost at once, the infant, deprived of nourishment and warmth, began to howl.

But no one stopped Annie.

Even when it was clear that what the barber's daughter was about to do was to place the crying newborn into the arms of its lunatic mother, no one dared interfere with a purpose so strong it seemed to light the dim hovel with the thousand candles of a cathedral nave.

"They must be joined," said Annie, and now that the screaming baby had entered its mother's space, she slowly and carefully placed him against the madwoman's open mouth.

"Baby," said the madwoman, blowing the word into the child's face. Annie held the child so that it would not fall, and so that it would move with the mother as she fell back against the bloody cushions of the bed. Soon, Annie was able to let go of the child completely and to allay the peasant women's fear, explaining that mother and child had to find time to be alone together.

Once more, the peasants obeyed the young midwife. They did not understand what had taken place, whether it was a miracle that a madwoman could nurse her own child, or that a lunatic spirit could be tamed by a baby's closeness. All they knew was that the child had ceased its cries, and that the mother had turned from agony to bliss in the space of a moment. And from that time on, they had followed the dictates of the young healer without question.

But Annie had earned more than the respect of the village from this bringing together of mother and child.

There had been pain, real, powerful enough to kill, and it had been stopped by the union of loving spirits. In her three years of healing in the village, this knowledge had become the mainstay of her powers, the cornerstone of her beliefs.

When the Baron sent for her, she knew what miracle he would demand of her; but with the need to heal that fired her soul, she believed that any ill could be cured, even the black despair of madness.

Chapter 11

"**Y**OU ARE Will Smithson's cousin, are you not?''

"Yes, milord," said Annie, wondering why the question was broached. Certainly, the Baron could not know that she had never stopped loving her distant cousin, even if Will had never regarded her as anything more than a moonstruck child; even the fact of her elevated status as the village healer had not changed his opinion of her. Everything about Annie that was mysterious and serene would fall apart under Will's gentle eyes. He did not tease her with his knowledge of her love for him, but accepted it as a fact of life. Annie was not the only girl to fall under Will Smithson's spell. "His mother and my father's father's sister—"

"Of course one cannot choose one's relations in this world," interrupted the Baron.

"No, milord. Unless one believes that certain relationships, like marriage and the desire to bring children into the world, are the results of love and are not predestined—"

"You speak very loosely, my dear girl," said the Baron. "There are those in the outside world who would not take so kindly to your words of enthusiasm. It is not exactly in ancient times that London burned, or that Noncomformists murdered the King."

Though his words were perfectly articulated, his thoughts logical and direct, Annie could feel the disconnected fury behind everything he said. London had burned in the Great Fire of 1666, but surely few intelligent men of her time still blamed Nonconformists or Catholics for that disaster; the Puritan Saints were long since fallen from grace in the hearts of the English people,

but few were such staunch Anglicans as to curb talk of free will
and predestination. The last "witch" hung in England was eight
years before, in Huntington, and that was regarded by much of
the population as a black mark on their system of justice. Superstition was rife, particularly among the peasants, but Annie never
felt the need to apologize for her thoughts or her words. She
would not burn as a witch, unless God wanted this fate for her;
and she cared not at all how the world perceived the source of
her power. Annie wanted only to heal.

"I do not speak as a Noncomformist, milord," said Annie. "I
am only answering your question about relations—"

"I did not ask a question," said the Baron. "It is not polite to
presume that I have asked a question, when I was merely stating
the obvious. But perhaps it is a family trait to be presumptuous."

Surely this insult was directed at Will Smithson, and not at
Annie's father, who had lived life too quietly and plainly to have
ever given offense to one as great as the Baron. But now the
Baron had given offense, and Annie, if she so desired, could have
gotten out of the horsehair-stuffed chair and left the great lord's
presence. He had no right to bully her through his hatred for
Will. Half the village was related to poor Will Smithson, with
many, like Annie, sharing the Smithson surname.

"You have invited me to your house, milord. I hope that I
am not being presumptuous by asking you if you will tell me
why."

"Your hope is wasted, my dear girl. You are being remarkably presumptuous. When a lord invites the barber's daughter
into his home, she does not speak until spoken to, and she does
not lecture him on the rules of etiquette."

The Baron was tall and broad, with the insouciant manners
of his class. When she had first been brought in to his presence,
she had thought he was going to rise from his heavy stuffed chair;
but apparently he had thought better of extending too great a
compliment to Annie. He would ask for her help, not beg for it.
Even if serfdom was but an ancestral memory, the barber's
daughter was—like Will Smithson—still one of the people and
the Baron was their lord.

But Annie could not help but be without awe in front of any
man of flesh and bone and spirit. She spoke with the directness
that in other people would have seemed a calculated attempt at
willfulness. "I am not lecturing you, milord."

"You will stop contradicting me, girl. You will listen, and I will explain. Is that clear?"

Annie waited for a moment before answering. She did not see that the Baron was contesting what he saw as her willfulness; but she was forced into a moment's meditation by the strength of the Baron's frustration, a frustration that twisted the body into knots, that reduced the spirit to confusion and despair. Clearly, there was illlness in his body and the village healer was always responsive to another's illness.

But her delay in answering infuriated the Baron. He had expected her face to flush, and her words to stammer forth in hurried assent. But Annie remained oblivious to these petty matters. She had not come to the great house to heal any illness of his; but now she understood that he, as well as his beloved, was sick with pain.

"Answer me, girl," said the Baron. "Will you cease contradicting your betters?"

"I do not mean to contradict, milord," said Annie, feeling his spirit float her way in the still and austere room. Beyond his anger, there was a cry for help that belied every angry word, every violent motion of his confused body. "I am Will Smithson's cousin, milord," she said. "Naturally, it does me no good to hear that you hate him."

"I have never said that I hate him!" said the lord, his cheeks reddening with as much speed as if some invisible hand had slapped him with violence. But now the Baron seemed to make a tremendous effort to keep his temper in check. "I do not hold the fact of your relationship to Will Smithson against you, of course. I swear this before all that is holy." He looked at her intensely, examining the quality of her features for a clue to her heart. "Though Will Smithson is a blackguard, it is not your fault that you share his surname, and I will not withhold my trust in you on account of his crimes."

"Has my cousin committed crimes?" asked Annie. The artless sincerity further riled the Baron, used to insinuation, innuendo, sarcasm, the twisted wit of his class.

"Your cousin is a blackguard, Annie Smithson. I would have thought you heard me the first time."

"I heard you, milord. It is just that I have not heard of any crimes that he has committed. I have only heard that he was sent away."

Of course she, like everyone else in the village, suspected a good deal more than this. Will was short and slender, where the Baron was tall and broad; his speech was simple and unlearned, his manners clumsy, his expertise was with a spade in the garden and not with a sword on the battlefield. Juxtaposed to the Baron's erudition and elegance, his romantic and commandng figure, Will was nothing but the crudest of boys, barely a man in spite of his twenty-five years.

But he had the kindest eyes Annie had ever seen. Scarcely a woman in the village was not drawn to Will Smithson—not only to his eyes, but to the gentle space in his heart from which they drew their strength. Any woman could learn to love the man possessed of such gentleness, anyone who longed for love and kindness would find herself drawn to the spirit possessed by Will Smithson.

"He was not sent," said the Baron, spitting out each word with distaste. "He ran." The Baron smiled thinly, remembering something that was not altogether pleasant. Annie, already sensitive to his pain, felt the lord's hatred for Will grow into something too difficult to sustain; the hatred was too wild and irrational to take hold of, and control. It had become like a weapon not only too unwieldy to employ, but one which turned against its user.

"And he ran, because I would have killed him for his crimes."

The Baron stood up, turning his broad back to her, looking through sun-dashed windows to the avenue of horse chestnut trees connecting the manor to the gatehouse. But she felt that he gained no solace from observing the beauty about him, or imagining the chain of ancestors whose martial prowess had earned the baronial title and lands, the terraced gardens and precious plate, the furniture, rugs, tapestries, and silver, the family portraits, the books, the maps, the heirloom clocks and mugs and boxes; the weighty detritus of lives connected to his by blood was unappreciated, as taken for granted as his lordly status.

"I did not know this, milord. His mother and my father's father's sister share the same grandmother, but as she is long dead, and his father who married the bootmaker's daughter from Lincolnshire passed away nearly a year since last—"

"You will forgive me if I interrupt you," said the Baron, turning around.

"Yes, milord."

"I am not interested in studying the Smithson lineage at any great length. Neither, for that matter, am I interested in discussing your cousin. He is gone, and that is all I care to know about him. I have asked you here because you are considered something of a miracle worker. Even Parson Lockridge thinks you a saint come down from the mountaintop."

The Baron paused, regained his seat, and leaned precipitously forward, inspecting Annie as if she were one of his foot soldiers. "Were you about to say something?"

"No, milord."

"I had the distinct impression that you were about to—"

"I was simply thinking, sir," said Annie, unaware that she had just interrupted him.

"Thinking. How clever of you to be thinking. It is not something for which the weaker sex is renowned. Would you care to share your thinking—"

Once again the young girl interrupted the Baron, bubbling forth her words as if he had truly longed to hear them: "I am not a saint, no matter what anyone says, even Parson Lockridge. A saint denies himself, glorifies God by his example. But I deny myself nothing. I like to eat, I like to drink, I like to sleep late. But most of all, I like to heal. It is not something terrible I suffer. It is the greatest joy in the world."

The Baron sat up straight, folded his long-fingered hands together, and searched his excited brain for a question. Annie watched as he adjusted the red ribbon that held together his tail of blond hair.

"The greatest joy in the world?" he said finally.

"Yes, sir. Truly it is, sir. To feel one who is sick losing the badness, to feel it leave the body, and you pushing alongside, helping the sick get well. Can you imagine?"

"I do not understand what you are talking about."

"I am not very good at explaining these things. You see, milord, it is a matter of faith."

"Do you know that I have studied medicine?"

"Of course, milord."

"I believe in medicine, in surgery, not in superstition."

"I do not think it matters what we call things, as long as we can heal, milord."

The Baron picked up the scalloped flap of coat pocket and

removed his snuffbox. He lifted the tortoiseshell lid, looked inside, but did not take a pinch. Instead he shut the box, placed it on a table, and snapped at her: "Do you believe in sage?" he said.

"I am sorry, your Lordship," said Annie. "I do not understand what you are asking."

"Sage," he repeated. "Sage in mulled wine. Do you believe it has powers?"

"As an aid to the digestion," said Annie. "Of course, chamomile tea is just as good—"

"I am not talking about bellies," said the Baron sharply. "I am talking about madness."

He stood up again, his splendid clothes an outward contrast to his inner rage. In orange waistcoat, supporting a golden chain from which hung a watch half the size of Annie's fist, he could be no other than the lord of the manor. Annie had always admired the Baron's figure and carriage, the grandness of person that she believed must come from a grandness of soul.

Even without the rich brocade of his coat, the linen frills of his shirtfront, the silk stockings and silver coat buttons worth the price of four good horses, the Baron would have cast an intimidating presence. He had little need of the clothing which armored his class, separating rich from poor with a hundred distinctions too costly to duplicate. The sharp planes of his well-shaved face, the coldness of his clear blue eyes, the easy grace with which he stalked the receiving room marked him as both aristocrat and military man, one used to command and the quick obedience of his subordinates. It hardly seemed possible that young Will Smithson had ever had the temerity to stand up to him; that he could have found the strength to knock the Baron to the ground seemed altogether impossible.

"Sage is no cure for madness, milord," said Annie.

"Are you familiar with the botanical writings of Gerard?"

"No, milord."

"Gerard was a simple barber-surgeon, but he knew a thousand herbal remedies. He used sage extensively. A man who had completely lost his mind, had no memories, did not know his own name was completely cured with a cup of sage tea."

"Tea is a cure for nothing, milord. It is simply an aid. Like all medicine and surgery."

"When you cut off a diseased limb to stop the spread of

putrefaction, you are not aiding the healing process, you are killing the disease."

"And you are killing the limb too," said Annie.

"We are not talking here about war wounds," said the Baron, pulling hard on the lace-edged linen strip casually wrapped about his throat. "We are talking about insanity."

Even the artless Annie recognized that she had entered a realm that few in the village had dared imagine: She contradicted, she disagreed, she fought with the great lord. But of course, she understood what was behind the rage, what sickness urged her to fight the Baron, as she understood why he had sent for her in the first place. She nodded in slow agreement, so that her words would not offend.

"Have you given sage to the Baroness?" said Annie.

"The Baroness? Who gave you leave to mention the Baroness?" Without thinking, the Baron had moved his right hand across his waist to where the closely fitted coat parted in leather-guarded sword vents. But no man wore a sword in his own home. He looked up at Annie, the sudden violence of his anger gone as quickly as it had come. "Mary is her name."

"Yes, milord."

"She is my wife."

"Yes, milord."

"Of course I gave her sage. I have read a great deal, the great physicians, classic and modern. I am certain I have read a good deal more than any midwife."

"I have read very little, milord. My knowledge of herbs is not extensive."

"You know of my gardens. Your cousin worked in my gardens, but I never let him alone with the herb gardens. He was suited to picking out weeds, not to the careful cultivation of life-giving herbs."

"My father has often used herbs from your garden, milord," said Annie, hoping to get him away from the subject of Will.

"Your father has taken herbs from here to help stanch the flow of blood," said the Baron, quieting. "He is a good man. Competent, though I have never let him bleed Mary. Not because I do not trust him. The barber-surgeons are often better than the surgeons; and to treat a wild temper, either barber-surgeon or surgeon are superior to most physicians, trained in a thousand texts, but without the talent to bleed. But you see, I have a physician of the new breed, not a surgeon of course, but a true physician who as a special favor to me will perform bleeding. He comes from London and has quite a touch, very reassuring. Some brave physicians are actually doing minor surgery now. It is something new. Apparently one must do more than diagnose and prescribe in order to survive these days. Otherwise all the money would go to barbers and apothecaries. Do you practice bleeding?"

"No, milord."

"Of course not. You are a midwife. They bleed enough, don't they? But that's what the good Lord intended, no doubt. When he bled her she stopped crying, but only for a short time."

"Milord, may I suggest that you try to quiet your temper? You might want to take some snuff—you began to—"

"Snuff is a disgusting habit. I don't know why we do it. I am not at all sure that it is healthful to be blowing out our heads all the time. It's like the rage for coffee. People think it's a cure-all, and they drink so much they turn brown, absolutely brown."

"Please sit down, milord," said Annie, raising her hands to his flushed face. But the Baron didn't seem to hear her. He continued to pace, the square blocked heels of his red shoes beating a violent rhythm against the floorboards.

"You know they tried giving lambs' blood to lunatics? The French attempted this. It helped some of them. They were less wild. But then some died. My physician prescribed rosemary. Before the bleeding and after. Like sage, rosemary is good for the memory. But it was not her memory that was bothering her. It's that she cries. There are treatises, very learned: *Imbecilitas, consternatio, alienato, defatigatio*. These are all forms of insanity, written down, with explanations. Humoral imbalance, the love of the devil, God's punishment."

"Please, Baron," said Annie. "I want to help your wife, but I worry about her husband as well. You are very excited."

"I do not know why Mary is sick. She loved me, and I married her, and then we were cursed. I had to send her to Dr. Lewis. He understands and treats many kinds of mental illness. He has cured raving mania and St. Vitus' dance. But his treatment had no effect, and when Mary ran off, she ran to London. And so it is not my fault that she is in Bethlehem. That is where they found her, in the asylum, and if she was put in the asylum, there must have been reason. I have also tried fennel and ginger. Some have suggested that I give her the Jesuits' bark. It works wonders on the ague, but I have never felt a fever in her, even when she cries through the night.''

Annie stood up, driven by the sickness of self-loathing in the Baron's heart. The top of her fair head barely reached the splendid fabric of his cravat; her thin arms looked as frail as twigs against his broad expanse of orange waistcoat. But Annie was nothing if not strong. She took hold of the Baron's thick wrists and pulled them down to her waist; she took hold of his cleanly shaved cheeks and brought his head low, so that their eyes met; she opened her mouth and breathed her sweet spirit against his wild despair. For a moment the Baron tried to fight a wave of astonishment taking charge of his spirit. Annie could see him blink at the image before his eyes, her own image, as it turned from what was real to the fantasy for which he longed.

"Mary," he whispered, dropping to his knees on the hard wood floor. "Mary." He brought his lips to Annie's open mouth, and shut up his terror with a kiss. Annie allowed the kiss, as she allowed the Baron's caress of her neck, as she permitted his urgent hands to pull at her workingwoman's bodice, to grasp through the flimsy calico fabric at her little breasts. She felt his need to express his love, felt the debilitating effects of having lost the possession of his beloved. If her mouth and neck and breasts could be of use to heal the man's pain, then she must offer them as a substitute for his mad, runaway wife.

He was himself not yet mad, not like the lunatic whose infant she had helped bring into the world, nor like his Baroness, locked into the lunatic asylum of Bethlehem Hospital in London. But his pain was a sickness, a twisting of feelings that led to madness and worse. She did not understand why the Baroness was ill, but she knew that the Baron was being drawn by love to share her affliction.

"I will go to her, Baron," said Annie. "I will take her in my arms, and she will be made well."

Gently, she drew away from his embrace, looking at his astonished eyes, as if he had just discovered himself to be on his knees, that his wife was gone, and in her place was the barber's daughter.

"What are you doing?" he said, getting to his feet with an unaccustomed clumsiness.

"I am going to go to London," she said.

"Yes," said the Baron, the desire drained from his face. For a moment, she thought he would strike her, or turn around and leave her alone in the rich and austere room. But slowly he regained control of himself. Annie could feel the love and the hate, the desire and the violence, twist together again behind the hard core of his spirit. "She is in London," he said. "You must go and make her well."

"Yes," said Annie. The Baron was no longer looking at her as she, never before a thief, picked up the rich snuffbox he had placed on a table, and secreted it behind her mantle. The urge to steal made no sense to her, but she followed it as she recognized its source from the purest part of her spirit. For a moment, she didn't know why she had swallowed so much fear into her heart; following the dictates of her spirit to any lengths never left her afraid.

But Annie suddenly realized that it was not the theft that frightened. It was the taste of his tongue that lingered in her mouth, the touch of his hands that still stung the soft flesh of her breasts. For the taste was not sweet, and the sting was fired with anger. If he had momentarily remembered his love for Mary in his embrace of Annie, that love was unkind, selfish. Even behind his directive to go and heal the Baroness, there was something dark, forbidding; as if part of the cure must be to secure for the Baron something that his wife refused to give. "Yes, milord. I will go and she will find the healing and the comfort that she needs."

Chapter 12

Though London could be a day's journey by stage from her village, Annie had never been to the capital of seven hundred and twenty-five thousand souls, the most populous city on earth. What took a day by sleek coaches pulled by six well-fed horses, took two in the less magnificent stage wagons pulled by four skinny ones; what took two days in dry summer weather took six when the rain muddied the road into a series of impassable ditches. And that was traveling without serious mishap: The overturning of wagons and coaches on the deeply rutted roads was so common that most gentlefolk preferred to risk their necks on horseback, regardless of the journey's length. And highwaymen increased in abundance and ferocity the closer one approached the metropolis.

"You do not have to go," Annie's father had told her over and over again. "The Baron has no authority to send you where he likes." The barber explained that London was a terrible place, where hogs fed on garbage flung from tenements into slimy gutters, where rich people too lazy to walk were carried about in chairs while the crippled and the blind begged for pennies at their feet. Gentlemen carried swords because the streets swarmed with cutpurses and knaves, men who killed for a peruke, and packs of wild boys who hunted anyone for the contents of their wallets and the sport of bringing them to the ground.

But none of his arguments had persuaded Annie.

She barely knew the haughty Baroness, and to follow her to the great city, she had to turn her back on others in need. Right in the village were infants unable to sleep through the night, peasants terrified of the ague wracking their bodies with fever and pain, elderly men and women despairing through loneliness and inactivity into a walking death. The Baroness was but one of many who needed the touch of her hands, the gentle caress of her eyes, her heartfelt ministrations to spirit and flesh.

"I must go, Father," she had said, knowing full well that there was nothing logical about her choice to leave the sick of the village to find and heal a woman made mad by love. "No one is in greater need of what I can do than the Baroness," she had said, understanding for the first time that her desire to heal the Baroness was selfish, a need more specific and compelling than the general need to fulfill her calling.

The barber's daughter had a connection to Mary, a bridge between classes, between maidenhood and matrimony, between a life devoted to the spirit and one to the flesh. Annie, like most of the village, had suspected that the Baron's banishing of Will Smithson had involved the Baroness. But on the eve of her departure to London, Annie went beyond suspicion to knowledge, a knowledge that came from the same place as her healing spirit.

She understood the pull toward Mary's pain by the strength of a connection suddenly made clear: The healer and the Baroness loved the same man.

"You will never find Will in the city," her father had said, using this as his last argument to keep Annie at home. "London is not a village, where everyone knows who and what everyone and everything is. He could be the King's chamberlain or a worker on the docks, he could be in prison for debt or transported to Virginia and you'd never know. I hope that is not why you go, daughter."

"I go to find and heal the Baron's wife, as he has asked me and as I have agreed."

"The devil take all Barons," said the barber. "If they were men who worked, there would be no time for wars and no time for crazy wives." But Annie's father had done his duty in urging her to stay behind, and was not as angry as he pretended. He did not understand the nature of her healing any more than he understood the intricacies of midwifery practiced by his departed wife; it was enough to realize that her status had risen, and taken him along in her shadow. If she could cure the Baron's wife and not be burned as a witch in the process, surely God's favor would be with them all the days of their lives.

He woke with her hours before first light, urging her to drink hot tea and put jam on her black, thick-crusted bread. He walked with her to where the stage wagon would stop just before dawn, carrying her little sack and greeting the early risers on their way to the fields.

"Please take care of yourself, Father," she said, pulling him close as the two horses pulling the ancient stage wagon shocked the tranquil morning silence.

"You will only stay a few days?"

"I am not sure, Father. I have explained to you that I must be able to find her, and treat her—"

"You have the Baron's money?"

"I have a part of it," said Annie. She kissed him, and he helped her climb up onto the open wagon, handing her the little sack of clothes. "Most of it I left for you, Father. In a blue pouch, next to the cheese in the cupboard. You will find it?"

"I will find it, but why did you leave—"

"I love you, Father," said Annie swiftly.

But the driver had started the horses forward, swallowing Annie's words in a clattering of hooves. Annie fell back on her bench, against the hard wood of the wagon. She waved, and as if in a slow-moving dream, saw her father join the other villagers opening their windows, letting out their cats, taking a breath of morning air before retreating to a hundred separate tasks.

The baking of bread, like the salting of meat, the churning of butter, were familial occupations now in the process of becoming specialized. Few families still tanned their own leather or shoed their own horses, preferring this to be done by a shoemaker and a blacksmith. While most mothers continued to spin and knit and sew, there were some more adept at it than others; one could buy or barter for a wool cloak with coins or a pile of firewood. The families of the village were no longer separate little units of survival, but were on their way to becoming, like families in the great cities, interactive, interdependent. As in the cities, the homes that once teemed with a hundred occupations of daily survival were becoming special shops, with distinctive exterior markings—like the barber's pole and the cobbler's boot. Annie's father's home let in a stream of visitors for business: Hair was cut, faces shaved, ears cleaned, and teeth pulled, with her father dispensing copious free advice on everything from digestive aids to conjugal love. Here the sick gripped stout wooden sticks to facilitate their bleeding—the bloodstained poles that gave rise to the barber-shop symbol of a red-and-white striped pole.

It was this pole, long gone from her field of vision, that Annie still saw, looming over green fields and broken fences, floating in the morning mist as the clumsy wagon jolted over the rutted road into the pristine countryside. Annie was saying good-bye to the village, to her father's shop, to her father. She had left him the Baron's payment, for she knew in her heart that she would never see him or her village again.

Annie was familiar with urges to action, spiritual promptings that guided her, propelled her to heal, led her along tracks of fate so clearly marked that uncertainty and fear were strangers to her. She was following tracks now, tracks that would take her first to London, then to the Bethlehem Hospital, then to the woman she must cure and to the man both she and the Baroness loved. Past this she couldn't see, couldn't even begin to imagine; all that was certain was that she would go where she had been sent, and that she would never return to where she had come.

"Are you going to London, miss?" asked the young man sitting opposite Annie on the windswept stage wagon, breaking a silence of an hour's duration.

"Yes, sir," said Annie, turning her clear eyes from the center of his forehead to his belly, hidden under a voluminous surtout and an old blanket. The open wagon had given her only this man for company, and everything about him suggested duplicity, discomfort, disease. Bundled up against the damp, he shivered; instead of relishing the freshness of the mist, he was determined to be at odds with the weather. She had been trying, without success, to calm a nervous tic at the corner of his right eye. Sometimes she tried to ride the nervousness emanating from a patient, even an unwitting one, like this young man, channeling the badness from where it hurt until it could find an outlet from the body. But she could not locate the essence of his problem, could not find where to take hold of his sickness and make it well.

"The Norwich-London coach does ninety miles in one day," he said, his words nearly jumping to the rhythm of the tic.

"Unfortunately, we are not traveling from Norwich."

"Yes, that's good. That's funny, miss," said the young man, looking into her quiet face for a clue as to who and what she was. "I am sorry, perhaps you were not joking. It is just that we are not traveling from Norwich. Would that we were. They apprehended Mad Jack Rourke, the scourge of the Norwich-London highway. It is unfortunate that we have so few passengers in these parts. Luckily, I am armed, and not without skill."

"There are no highwaymen on this road, sir," said Annie, wondering if his tic was simply the result of fear.

"How do you know?"

"This is not a highway," said Annie.

This too was not a joke, but the nervous young man exploded into a laughter so suddenly overwhelming that the tic vanished, the nervousness running through his body blew away in a wild instant. Annie observed this, of course, but observed too that the nervousness, the tic, and the fear all slowly returned.

"There is nothing for you to worry about, miss. Highway or not, highwaymen or not, you need only trust in your traveling companion—"

"I fear nothing," said Annie.

"You fear nothing!" exploded the young man, shivering in spite of himself, looking over Annie's head to the top of the next hill. But something in Annie's expression pulled him back to earth. She was as steady as a plaster saint in a Catholic house, as clear-eyed as a witch looking through a man's eyes into the devil behind them.

"I do not pretend to know much about the way to London," she said. "But when we get past the tollgate, we will be on the highway, and then we will surely change this wagon for a coach, and we will have passengers from all over Dorset and Somerset."

"We will only change this wagon for a coach if we can afford the coach fare. There are those of us who must travel in this miserable fashion the entire way to London."

"I have never been to London," said Annie.

"You must not say such things to strangers. They will think you gullible, and easy prey. More than highwaymen break the laws of the land. I could be a thief, ready to steal your purse."

"I could be a murderess, with a dagger under my mantle," said Annie. She meant no threat, but spoke as she always did, following the logic of the moment, with no fear of the consequences.

"I envy you, miss," said the nervous young man. "Going to London the first time! The first time you see the towers, the royal barge on the Thames, the beautiful ladies in silks and satins—"

"Have you seen Bethlehem Hospital?" interrupted Annie.

"I beg your pardon. Do you mean Bedlam?"

"It is also called by that name," said Annie.

"I have been many times. I wouldn't have thought it would be your type of entertainment, miss. But perhaps there's more spirit to you than meets the eyes." He leaned forward as if to share an obscene confidence. "There's a lot to be said for the Bedlam amusements for the price you pay. It's best if you get a good keeper to show you around. Sometimes the loonies sing a good tune. If you're lucky, you get an Italian lunatic. Some of their songs! There's nothing like a pretty Italian singing a tune. But the real crowds are around the craziest ones. They calm them down with cold water, did you know that? Just pour it over them. The ones who refuse to behave get whipped. Sometimes you can't get in to see the whippings, but there are always a few keepers who will bring you up close. It's even better than watching the women get whipped at Bridewell. You can hardly see a thing at Bridewell, the crowds are so big. It's like the hangings at Tyburn. I went four times in four days, and I never saw an actual hanging, only the bodies after it was all over, and the crowd started to go home."

"You have seen them whip the lunatics?"

"It's what I'm telling you, miss. I could show you the right keepers, I could tell you who you'd have to pay—"

"Cold water, you said," said Annie. "You have seen them pour cold water over the sick?"

"They're not sick, they're crazy, miss," said the young man. "They have good doctors over there. If they were sick, they wouldn't be pouring cold water over them, they wouldn't have to be whipping them."

He did not understand her sudden silence, after her great interest in his conversation, and took it as a rebuff to his personal charms. The young man couldn't feel the damage done to Annie's heart by his cheery telling of what to him was commonplace, but to her was a horrific realization of the low estate of human souls.

In London, she knew, men were still sometimes subjected to being drawn and quartered after they had been hanged, and always to the roar of the crowds. Even in her village, Annie had heard of the much-abused servant girl who had poisoned her mistress, and been sent to her death at the stake before a mob of thousands. Hangings were so commonplace that a well-known "cure" for scrofula was often attempted by the superstitious and allowed by the authorities at Newgate: As soon as the executed were lowered from the scaffolds, mothers would grasp their still-warm hands and rub them over the scrofulous parts of their children's bodies.

It was one thing to be dimly aware of these events and practices going on in the great metropolis that was the heart of the country; it was another to feel as if being thrust directly into those events. For Annie understood that what happened at Bedlam must needs be a reflection of what occurred in the city around its grounds. It made as much sense to pour cold water over the screaming heads of the sick as to sell tickets to a torturous execution. The populace that would take out its collective anger on a prostitute sentenced to the pillory, stoning her to disfigurement or death before the end of her half-day's sentence, would not recognize what damage had been done to the spirits of those locked up behind Bedlam's walls. Their own spirits were damaged, twisted with lovelessness, with self-hatred and blood lust.

It was no wonder this young man had a nervous tic, no wonder that his body was so full of fear that it seemed to be sliding ineluctably toward disease.

Annie, the village healer, remained very still throughout the days and nights of her trip to the capital city. She changed wagons, and met new travelers. In the wagons, the passengers complained about the rich; in the coaches, they complained about the poor. She passed turnpike tollgates which had been hacked apart by rioters, upset with the cost of the toll. She learned from landowners that the dismal roads, some of which were the untouched remnants of routes built by Roman soldiers nearly two thousand years before, were being repaired by the king, so that he could consolidate all power into his hands. She learned from merchants that the landowners wanted to stifle all progress, so that the middle class could never threaten their power. She learned that the highwaymen who preyed on travelers, raping their women, cutting the throats of children, were lauded as heroes by the London poor.

Half a day from London, she felt the sickness of the city like a nightmare shaking her from sleep. She felt the bearbaiting, the drunkenness, the filth, the murderous brawls; she felt the fortunes built on the slave trade, the stench of the overcrowded jails, the diseased bodies of the city's fifty thousand prostitutes. As the stage hurried closer to the pleasure gardens of Ranelagh and Vauxhall, to the famous cathedrals and mansions, to the marble edifices of government and the pomp and glory of opera house and theater, Annie felt as powerless as a fly.

She was a healer, drawing her strength from God and the faith of her patients. Where there was a sickness in the body, all she need do was unite with the spirit in the patient's flesh, discover there the frustration, confusion, or anger that had prompted the spirit's unhappiness with its earthly frame. Surely her power was the power of love, the ability to bolster spirit with spirit, to return one's body to its natural ease with its self.

But how could she bolster the spirit of a single soul, when the spirits of seven hundred and twenty-five thousand souls were sick? How could she hope to return health to a mind and a body, when the heart of the surrounding city was rotten with disease? One could not cure a dying man by attending to a pimple on his nose. Annie had always looked to treat the whole spirit, and through this, the whole body, always taking into consideration the family which nourished or dispirited it.

But while the village was made up of families, supported by traditions, forged into bonds of custom that were seldom broken, the city was something entirely different: It was made up of taverns and masked balls, immigrants and itinerants, individuals fueled by ambition, lust, the desire for change; here rule was not by custom but by the imperfect, unjust force of law. What dispirited here was not one family, but a thousand baleful forces. What caused a spirit to be crushed was not the result of anything simple, but something as complex as the city itself.

Annie felt as if she were entering a body rampant with disease, a body that would press its ugliness through her skin, into her bones, until it could penetrate and destroy all her faith. How could she hope to cure a madwoman, when madness was what prevailed about her, when violence and depravity were the order of the day?

The coach windows had been shut up as they entered the city, clattering along a thoroughfare that seemed to be paved only in short stretches of unmatched stones. There had been no rain for more than a day, but the coach wheels threw up muddy water against the shut windows, over the scurrying figures of pedestrians, pressing against the walls of houses for protection.

"Great sight, isn't it?" said one white-wigged gentleman, laughing at the mud-splattered walkers. "Makes one feel at home again."

Annie looked through out at the filthy street, struck by the poverty and drabness. A hunchbacked old lady picked up her pace to avoid being hit by their coach; as they muddied her in passing, Annie could see that she held a baby in her arms, a baby now imbibing the hunchback's curses and hatred as mother's milk.

"There's an art to walking the streets," said another gentleman, looking up at quiet Annie as if for an opening to instruct her ignorance. The bright red color of his hose and waistcoat matched, and were in stark contrast to the grayness outside; yet he was no more healthy in his body or spirit than the hunchback or her child. "You've got to keep close to the storefronts, so you don't get splashed by the coaches, but you've got to keep an eye up for when they throw the garbage out of the top floors of the flats."

At the head of the street was a narrow causeway, slightly elevated so that pedestrians could cross without stepping into puddles of filth a foot deep. From her vantage point in the coach, Annie saw only the deformed, the downcast, and the crippled crossing the street. Sedan chairs pulled by thick-limbed men hurried into the thoroughfare, ignoring the advancing coach, peddlers bearing trays of foodstuffs, knots of pedestrians daring to impede their way.

As the sun was setting, everyone hurried to be off the dangerous streets. The law commanding a candle lantern at every tenth house applied only to moonless nights, and only from late September to the end of March. Soon it would be dark, with the only light coming from inside the shut-up houses, with criminals of every type vying for opportunities in the characteristic city fog.

Annie tried to keep her mind sharp, aware that despair was overwhelming her faith. God had not brought her here to cure an entire city, but to fulfill one mission. If that mission was doomed to failure, then it would be His will that she fail, and not because of any limit that He chose to put on her powers. God had no limits, as faith had no limits.

"Where are we?" said Annie, very quietly at first, unaware that she had as yet addressed no one in the crowded coach that day. The setting sun had been enveloped by clouds of mist, long before it could dip past the towers and spires blocking the horizon. Now a fine London rain was starting, cutting through a gray fog rising up from the gutters. But beyond the masses hurrying through the muddy streets, the barefoot children picking through the garbage, the pickpockets and prostitutes converging on the narrow footpaths, was the dim outline of stout iron bars held up in a massive wooden frame.

"Where are we?" said Annie once again, suddenly more urgent, suddenly confronted by a stillness that was yet more unsettling than the riotous violence of the city's streets.

"Just a few minutes from the inn, miss. Nothing to worry about. I think a hackney's turned over, but it's hard to say in this peasouper."

The coach had stopped, and Annie could hear the shouts of drivers and pedestrians, could imagine the horsewhip flailing through the blackness at the poor beast trying to stand on the wet paving stones.

But her attention was not long diverted.

She could see that the iron bars were added protection to gates of wood, gates that opened in an otherwise straight and tall stone wall. These gates were immense, and as her eyes grew accustomed to the dim outlines of the wall, she could make out the great stone steps leading up to the gates, and huge stone piers from which the great gates swung.

"I don't mean the inn, sir," said Annie. "Where are we now? What is this place?"

"This place?" said the gentleman with a mild smile, looking past the young girl, through her muddy window, and into what was for him the impenetrable night. "Might be Parliament, or then again, it might be the Royal Barge, and all of us are floating on the Thames."

The fog ran in bursts of darkness and light, sometimes glowing with a fierce yellow-green, sometimes lifting toward the distant lamplights of a house, sometimes twisting on its own core, growing blacker and blacker, till nothing could be seen but the fearsome specter of one's own blindness. But through the fog, past the stone steps and iron barred gates, beyond the stone walls and wide lawns, through the unknown paths to the great edifice she could feel the chains, could smell the excrement rotting in the straw, she could sense the shivering bodies and the festering welts where the whips' lashes had broken through human skin.

"I know," said the gentleman, suddenly smiling at a break in the fog, even as the coach lurched forward, making its move around the disabled hackney. "Those are the Cibber statues. Don't you know them? They're famous."

"No, sir," said Annie. "I do not know the statues."

But she could see them as well as the gentleman, hovering over the great piers of the gates, massive carvings of Portland stone. They were figures of men, nude and heavily muscled, one with an expression devoid of understanding, the other figure in chains and ready to burst forth in violence.

"*Dementia* is the one on the left. On the right is *Acute Mania*. If you would like me to explain the terms to you, I should be happy to oblige. This is the Bethlehem Hospital—Bedlam as it's called—and I come here often to watch the lunatics."

"No," said Annie. "There is no need to explain."

She had come to find Bedlam, and it was all about her. She had come to practice her healing on the inmate of an asylum, but she had discovered that the asylum was vast, a city of lunatics. Bethlehem Hospital was nothing but a centerpiece of that greater asylum, a showplace to exhibit the city's anger at her own madness, a place to pretend that only the inmates of Bedlam were sick, and that everyone else in London was well.

"There is no need to explain," repeated Annie to herself. She shut her eyes as the coach hurried on to its last stop, gathering her strength for the ordeal to come. "Doctors always like to give names to what they don't understand," she said, knowing that whatever chains held the Baroness, whether those of insanity or those of iron, she would break them with her healing, she would set her spirit free.

Chapter 13

Bedlam, constructed on London's old city moat at the edge of Moorefields, was less than a mile from the inn where Annie had spent the night. But the trip to the hospital was lengthy for the distance traveled, and Annie felt herself retreating from the ugliness of the city about her, searching her spirit the way an athlete tests his body before a contest. And like an athlete's vague malaise, Annie felt her spirit somehow strained, exhausted in a way she did not recognize. In the traffic-stalled hackney she shared with five chattering men of business she found that she could resurrect no dreams from her shallow, troubled sleep. Annie worried that she might have experienced a dream of great significance, and for lack of memory, could not be instructed by it.

She was often entertained by delightful dreams: nocturnal panoramas of wildflowers bending under the weight of a sundriven wind; memories of her mother Margaret, smiling her love at her from the land of the dead; a wistful vista of a distant garden, with a short and slender young man—Will Smithson—slowly getting to his feet from a row of vegetables and turning about to face her across a flock of sheep.

Sometimes her dreams were more than memories or whimsical wishes. There were striking visions that could be nothing but visitations from spirits, souls needing her touch through the heavy night ether. Often, she would feel a stabbing pain, accompanied by vivid colors. Violent shades of red and yellow and green would wash over happier images, and only by sending out the pure part of her own spirit, the healing center, could she break up these colors, transmuting them to whiteness and light. To have such a visitation would leave her limp and exhausted, barely able to get out of bed at first light; but there would be joy about her tired body, the sublime joy that came from giving her spirit in the service of healing.

But waking that day she had felt no joy. She could not relate the exhaustion she felt to any dream or visitation of spirits that she could remember. All she knew was that it was not the long journey to the city that had tired her, nor the poor food and close quarters, nor the threat of highwaymen. Perhaps it was nothing more complicated than the task at hand that her heart found exhausting; perhaps her memories of entering London and feeling the city's collective madness had taught her spirit the lesson of futility.

She closed her eyes and shut out the clattering of the hackney coach, the destructively ambitious talk of her fellow passengers, the crush of sedan chairs and wagons and pedestrians which conspired to prevent her from arriving at the hospital.

And then from behind her shut eyes she had a sudden vision of Will Smithson. A blessed tranquility descended over her unquiet spirit, a tranquility which did not go unnoticed by her fellow passengers.

"Are you feeling well?" asked one of the men of business, his tones more annoyed than consoling. There was no time to deal with an unwell woman on a busy morning, and surely such a beatific expression could only suggest illness.

Annie didn't respond as the hackney coach lurched forward, finding a break in the traffic. The driver announced that they were approaching the Bethlehem Hospital, but Annie kept her eyes closed. She heard the driver's words, as she heard the words of her fellow passenger; but she couldn't help but enjoy the smile on Will's imagined face.

"Miss, are you all right?" demanded the man again, this time his tone more angry than annoyed. Annie felt no necessity to respond that instant, not when she could see Will alive and well in her thoughts. At that moment she knew that the terrible city had not broken his spirit. Even if she would find him in the arms of the mad Baroness, she would know that he breathed, that his flesh was warm, that blood flowed through his healthy body.

"Palace hospital," barked the driver from his perch, as if

Annie had already created an interminable delay, a delay for which she deserved nothing less than flogging at the tail of a cart or a week in the pillory before an enraged mob. Annie could feel the unreasoning anger about her, more than she could respond to the driver's words. There was no tolerance, no allowing for another's frame of reference. In this city, everyone must walk at the same speed or be harshly judged. Annie opened her eyes to find her fellow passengers looking from her to the facade of the Bethlehem Hospital, as if she might not be a visitor, but a returning inmate.

"I get down here," said Annie unnecessarily. She hurriedly gave the driver the shilling he demanded—half the sum required to buy a piglet in her village—and looked up in awe at the entrance to Bedlam.

It was no wonder that it was called the palace hospital. What she had sensed of the great edifice the night before, she could now see in the cold London daylight. What had been imposing and sinister in the dark was now strangely beautiful; a magnificent monument to the society's madness.

"Do you require help getting down, miss?" said one of the men.

"No," said Annie, turning her eyes from the hospital to the man who had addressed her. There was so much needless urgency coming from the man, that she wanted to caution him, explain that his desire to speed along every aspect of the day was unhealthy, could lead to a disease of the spirit. "But as you are in a hurry, sir, I shall accommodate you."

She stepped down from the coach, wondering at the fearful laughter of the passengers as the driver whipped the old horses quickly forward. If she could have somehow forgotten how mad the city about her was, this laughter would have reminded her. The body was meant to live in God's shadow, to follow the course of the sun through a day measured by constructive work, heartfelt prayer, the love of family. These passengers in the hackney seemed to come from a sunless place, where their bleak lives rushed from one collision of spirit to another; there was no equanimity in their hearts, no love beyond ambition.

Though not a holiday, the bright weather had brought out more than the ordinary share of visitors. Had she been far less sensitive to the spirits about her, Annie would still have been able to sense that these visitors were not relatives and friends of those incarcerated behind the hospital's elegant walls. They seemed bent not on comforting those inside, but on personal pleasure. The enormous stone gates over which loomed the representative statues of mental illness were flanked by two smaller wicker gates. Through these entrances crushed men and women, alone and in pairs, dressed in fine silks and cheap homespun, bewigged rakes mingling with countrymen in noisy clogs, ladies with silver-embroidered coats and beaver hats rubbing against half-dressed ladies of the night. It was like a market day in her village, like a country fair, like a carnival of diseased souls.

"Would you care to take my arm, miss?" offered one young gentleman, shoving his elbow against her side with a lopsided smile.

"No, thank you," said Annie, looking directly into the man's bloodshot eyes.

"The crowd looks a little riotous today," he added, letting his eyes stray from her face to her unfashionably square décolletage. "I can see that you are not used to a riotous crowd. I can help you."

"How can you help me?"

"I can get you to see whatever you want. I know the best keepers, and they know me." With great familiarity, he took her hand and placed it firmly into the crook of his elbow. "My name is Shaxton. Daniel Shaxton. You're very pretty, and you're a country girl, is that right?"

"Will you show me the Baroness Mary Normande?" said Annie, leaving her hand where he had placed it.

"A Baroness? What have you to do with a Baroness?"

"I am here to help her," said Annie.

"Certainly you are, dear girl. I do not doubt it for a moment." Shaxton brought Annie's hand more tightly against his arm, and pulled her along into the mob at the gate. He was tall, and his bloodshot eyes were steady with violent purpose, but Annie was content to let him pull her through the crowd, as if she were a fairy child riding on the bare back of a runaway horse. "I will find you your Baroness, and you will be so grateful that you will allow me the pleasure of a single kiss."

She could feel the meanness of his spirit grate against all his phrases. He spoke of love and beauty and kisses, but Annie felt that what he wanted was not pleasure for her, but pain. As they passed through the wicker gates into a walk paved with smooth stones and surrounded by a tranquil green lawn, she felt that even the nature of love had been twisted by this time and this place. He wanted to kiss in order to destroy, he wanted to feel the touch of her skin against his in a vain attempt to prove that his body lived without the aid of his soul.

"You must give up your sword to the porter, miss," said Shaxton with his customary sarcasm. "A most unfortunate sign of the times, this rule." Like most of the men dressed in the guise of gentlemen, he wore a sword, and handed this to the tall, blue-liveried porter at the inner gates to the hospital. Annie wondered whether this was a rule designed to protect the inmates from the visitors, or the visitors from each other. "Just another example of the decline of our civilization, refusing to trust gentlemen with their weapons," said Shaxton.

"Are you and the lady entering together, sir?" asked the porter with a bow. Shaxton smiled and handed him a few pence, ignoring the sign to deposit the money directly into the poor box with one's own hands. "Thank you for your kindness, sir," said the porter, acknowledging with a wink that the money he received would go into his pocket and not for the maintenance of the inmates.

Past the porter was a vast hall, crowded with gawking visitors, with peddlers hawking nuts and candies, and as they entered, Annie found herself leaning for support against Shaxton.

"What is this place, sir?" she asked, momentarily overcome by the confusion of terror and lust that seemed to be concentrated right under the soles of her feet. ·

"An amusement park, like Ranelagh or Vauxhall," said Shaxton. "But the girls here are prettier. Much prettier. What shall I call you, pretty one?"

"My name is Annie," she said, as a blue-uniformed keeper pointed out the location of the severely disturbed inmates' gallery to the excited children of a couple from France.

"Annie," said Shaxton. "I will show you sights today, dear Annie, such as you could never see in the country."

"Drunk for a penny, drunk for a penny," said an old woman with mottled skin, her unsmiling mouth full of irregular, wolfen teeth. She exhibited her flasks of gin with somewhat more subtlety than the peddlers of cakes and pies, but was certainly no less brazen than the crimson-lipped ladies of the night searching for clients. As they penetrated more deeply into the mad space, Annie could hear the strains of harp music, muffled by the slamming of heavy doors and iron gates, disrupted by bursts of laughter and applause.

"Hurry along," said Shaxton. "You can't rely on the lunatics to repeat their tricks. There must be something good happening right now."

There were galleries to both sides, on two floors, but the most noise came from the second story on their right, and Shaxton hurried Annie up an elegant stairwell, ignoring the bust of Henry VIII, and the coat of arms of Charles II. Ostensibly, the upper stories were reserved for female inmates, the lower for male; but these rules were bent in order to accommodate the keepers, many of whom kept a special inmate as a source of sexual pleasure, to be used at their whim, like a favorite dog always at one's beck and call. Impartial observers readily acknowledged that the hospital's basement rooms—rented by the East India Company for storing large quantities of pepper—were better safeguarded than the men and women stored on the hospital's upper levels.

At the top of the stairs they came up to the harpist, herself an inmate allowed the freedom of the gallery during the day, oblivious of the jeering and laughter of the crowd about her. Annie stopped, drawn to her need, wanting to comfort her.

"We can come back to her, Annie," said Shaxton. "She's here all day, and crazy all the time."

What the crowd found crazy about her, Annie imagined, was the intensity with which she played her instrument, the passion which she gave from her spirit to the strings of the harp. She was wild-haired, of course, like a farm girl with wind-tossed hair; she wore, like any unfortunate wanderer, clothes that had seen better days. Annie wondered if the keeper guarding her as she played did so merely in order to solicit donations from lovers of mad music; or if his task was to prevent visiting rakes from tearing off the rest of the pretty harpist's clothes.

For there were other inmates allowed the freedom of the gallery, inmates who excited the visitors into frenzies of laughter or derision or a quick embrace. As Shaxton moved her past the shut doors of the cells, she could see through the barred hatches that many were empty, their occupants busy entertaining the dissipated visitors of this London landmark. Men with shaved heads, eyes shining with fever, pressed sheets of poetry into her hands in the hopes of earning a shilling. Women in various states of undress competed with professional prostitutes in offering visitors a glimpse of their thighs or breasts. Several inmates played fiddles, others attempted to walk on their hands, a few imitated the cries of animals in the hopes of earning a penny or a pat on the head.

Inmates who became too vociferous—or too boring for the visitors—were pushed back into their cells, the keepers slamming shut the heavy doors with loud finality. They were like players in a mad theater, expendable and replaceable at the whim of the audience. Eager visitors would look through the iron bars of the door-hatch to see if another patient looked interesting, and demand his or her release to the gallery crowd by the keeper.

"Why do they not leave them alone?" said Annie, but Shaxton ignored her question, so eager was he to arrive at the center of the commotion they had heard coming up the stairs. The conventional wisdom was that visitors provided needed amusement and stimulation for the otherwise abandoned patients, but Shaxton would not have bothered to dredge up this answer had he felt the need to answer Annie's question. To him, none of these people had any rights once incarcerated. If he felt no sympathy for the families of men unable to pay their debts, women and children who were forced to live in prisons far worse than Bedlam, how he could feel for men and women guilty of the God-given crime of insanity? If he cared not a whit that more than half the children born to the poor in his city died in infancy, how could he rail against unruly visitors whose charity supported the care and feeding of lunatics?

"Look, a jester, a dancing jester!" said Shaxton with a laugh, forcing Annie through the crowd around a large, vacant-eyed man, a jester's belled cap askew on his shaved skull.

"Why is he in chains?" asked Annie, watching in horror as two keepers turned the madman around and around, holding him up so that he did not trip over his manacled ankles. Along with the ringing of his jester's bells, the chains about his bare and bloodied feet clattered, as did those connecting his powerful wrists to an iron ring around his waist. But the noise of the bells and the chains could barely be heard over the laughter and the jeering of the crowd.

"He must be dangerous," said Shaxton, putting his arm about her. "But you have nothing to fear when you are with me."

"He is not dangerous," said Annie, throwing off Shaxton's arm from about her shoulders and stepping forward through the crowd, directly into the chained man's stumbling circle of shame. Without thought, she put up the palms of her hands against his chest. The inmate, momentarily abandoned by his tormenting keepers, blinked his unfocused eyes against some interior vision; he was like a blind man stopped in his tracks, halted by an unseen obstacle from the sighted world. "He is in pain," she said softly, feeling the man's need for her compassion like an unquenchable thirst.

"Come along, pretty one," said Shaxton, trying to laugh off the young woman's zeal against the sudden silence of the crowd. "You want to see your Baroness, don't you?"

"Please," said Annie sharply to Shaxton, not wishing to divert her attention from the chained man's agony, an agony that went far deeper than his silly cap of bells. Oblivious to the fury of the madman's keepers, she tried to shut out too the other calls for help all about her. Annie knew that she was once again in a situation where more than one person was in pain, more than one person was ill; better than ever before she understood that sickness was not an isolated abnormality, but a product of an entire world of events and attitudes and cycles of civilization. But if she could not give herself to every man, woman, and child in London, if she could not hope to treat every inmate in this gallery with the strength of her love, she still could not hold herself back from the wildness of this particular inmate's despair.

"Leave me," she said to Shaxton, shutting her eyes to his bruised vanity, to the hostile silence about her, as she attempted to join with the demons inside the madman's heart and expel them from his body.

"What are you doing?" said Shaxton. Instinctively, Shaxton took a step back, disassociating himself from her, from her sudden mad behavior. "I told you, he's a dangerous one."

But Annie felt no danger through the palms of her hands, but only the shocked open wound of the madman's heart. She knew that the asylum was built and maintained for humanitarian reasons; that having a place for society's insane was better than putting them in jail for crimes they did not understand, or letting them be chased to the ground by dogs for sport, or forced to beg from town to town, living with the taunts and beatings and abuse that was considered their due, as God had ordained their lunacy. She knew that doctors visited the asylum, prescribed treatments, that volunteers came forth to feed and bathe those who could not do so themselves. Surely this was an improvement over being left alone to face the random cruelties of the road.

Yet this man before her suffered, and not by any random cruelty but by the institutionalized cruelty of the hospital. Bringing her hands from his chest, she brought his grizzled face and shaved skull close to her, removing the jester's cap and letting it fall to the floor. She knew that male patients had their heads shaved for reasons of cleanliness, that they were whipped for reasons of discipline, that they were chained so that they would not attack the keepers or one another; but in this man's body she could feel a humiliation beyond being marked, chained, beaten. What she could feel was the awesome sense of being unloved, an object beyond contempt and hatred, an outcast beyond the pale of humanity itself.

"I love you," said Annie softly, whispering the words in the lunatic's ears. No one else could hear her, but it was enough for them to see her embrace, her kindness, her compassion. The disgust of the visitors was exceeded only by the hatred of the keepers; and this hatred was exceeded only by the fear inspired in the other patients, seeing in Annie's behavior something that could not be true except as a ruse.

But Annie felt nothing of the growing fury around her, for at first the crowd remained quiet, even as she stroked the madman's grizzled cheeks, even as she touched the bruises about his wrists where fetters had eaten into the skin. Her own lips lifted in a smile, feeling the gentling of the man's roiled emotions. He could not articulate what he was feeling, could not retain the image of the woman before his eyes; but he could feel the stuff of her spirit, and understand that it reached out to him, not to strike or to condemn, but to give love. A sweetness, heavy with long-dulled feelings, like a child's favorite blanket discovered again in old age, fell over his wild temper.

At that moment, the keepers pulled healer and patient apart.

Annie was strong, but she could not fight back two angry peasant boys; the madman was powerful, but he was in chains, and not ready for violence. "Please," she said, but no one was listening, because the madman had raised his voice in a terrifying cry.

Stroked, he tried to raise his chained arm to stroke her; given love, he wished to give it back with his twisted tongue. But all he could do was shake the chains that held his wrists to his waist, and spit out sounds so garbled that they sounded like the threats of an animal at bay.

"Hold him!" said Shaxton, staying away from the madman, even as he kept his distance from where the keepers held Annie in their strong hands.

But the keepers couldn't keep their hold on the chained inmate, so wild was he, so eager to fight to retain the loving embrace of the healer. He shouted at them, words that were nothing but grunts of pain; he backed away from them, baring his teeth, then moving close to Annie with quick little steps, tearing at his chains with the strength of an ape.

But the chains held, and there were too many for him to fight off, too many too eager to hurt him for the crime of bringing forth Annie's compassion. They drove their clubs into the back of his knees and he fell down heavily, tears of rage filling his wild eyes. One of the keepers holding Annie let go of her so that he could have his turn with a series of kicks, until Annie, breaking free of the man who held her, threw herself on top of the madman on the floor.

"She's crazy," said one of the keepers, not for the first time, but loud enough for all the others to agree. Whatever conspiracy had held the crowd's jeers and laughter in check was suddenly broken, as one of the keepers picked up a bucket of cold water and tossed it over Annie and the madman struggling beneath her. "Crazy she is, she's as crazy as he is!" said another keeper, letting out his tension in an explosion of head-shaking laughter. Soon, there was another bucket, and when Annie resisted getting off the madman, a kick.

The cold water shocked her system, and the kick gave her pain. But Annie remained where she was, covering the madman's bruised spirit with her love. Even if she could not save the world, even if she could not find and rescue the Baroness, even if she could not drive out the demons from this creature in her arms, she would comfort him; she would try to make him understand that even in a world gone mad there was love, there was hope, there was healing.

Chapter 14

THOUGH SHE WAS not the least bit violent, the keepers gripped Annie as if she had claws of iron, teeth of steel. They brought her to to the windowless room reserved for uncontrollably frenzied patients. But they left her in clothes, they did not beat or rape her, and after a final drenching with cold water, simply slammed the heavy door of the tiny space with a warning to be still.

But Annie was already still.

She needed peace after so much violence, she needed contemplation to understand why God had wanted her to fail in healing the madman, she needed to examine her spirit to see if it had been twisted by frustration or desire.

But though it was possible to still her body, she could find no peace, could enter no realm of contemplation; not when all about her, behind the stone walls, pacing on the other side of her cell's ceiling, were the inmates of this terrible place. It was pitch dark in her windowless room, but not dark enough to stop the images of her fellow patients chained to posts like wild animals; in her mind's eyes she could see them stripped of their clothes, forced to dig into the filthy straw covering their cell floors for shelter from glassless barred windows cut high in the bleak walls.

It was cold and damp in her own cell, a penetrating chill worsened by the icy water that saturated her clothes and hair. But how much colder it was for those unloved women, committed to the asylum by husbands tired of their faces, how much colder it was for those hidden out of sight by embarrassed parents, how much colder it was for those whose only love was given them by a cat sharing the beastly conditions of their cell.

After a day and a night of darkness, they brought her food. A doctor, distinguished by his elegant coat, felt her pulse, told her that she was ill, but that she would be made very much better if she followed the rules of Bedlam.

"If you dare to strike at a guard, he will strike back, blow for blow. If you cause a commotion, you will be whipped. If you shout, you will soon be gagged. That is how you will learn to behave." She answered the doctor not at all, seeing that his entire method of treatment was to create fear in her heart. It would do no good for her to explain that she was a healer, not a patient, and that fear engendered nothing but disease. She hoped that his own heart would open one day, before he would twist his excess of hatred directly into his spirit, before he would be more full of mad rages and diseased parts than any of his patients.

Annie allowed them to move her upstairs, to a room with a window. She slept on a pallet, and woke frequently to loud, insistent prayers from the neighboring cell, prayers which called for the salvation of the world.

She was not surprised to find that her neighbor on the other side of her cell was quieter. If she prayed at all, it was in total silence. Annie could feel the woman's resignation weighing heavily on her heart and lungs. Her breathing was irregular, as if forgetting the automatic rhythm of life. She was not looking for salvation for the world, but for an end to her personal misery, a misery that was not restricted only to this place of incarceration.

She had found the Baroness.

When the keepers threw open the doors for morning exercise, Annie caught a glimpse of her pretty face. The Baroness was caught in a sickening vise that cuts into the spirit as powerfully as a knife cuts into the body: confusion.

Annie had long recognized confusion as a source of congestion, bilious temper, headache. Confusion could take a healthy body and lead it to trip itself, to twist its vital organs into enemies of its own life force. There were many paths to take in life; Annie believed that her own perfect health was the result of following the impulses of her spirit, not pausing to consider a hundred other options, not plaguing her soul with doubts and questions as to how things might be down another path instead of the one she was taking.

But the Baroness Mary Normande was not so simply directed.

Born into a society which forbade attraction to one beneath her, she had been nevertheless attracted; fighting this attraction within the confines of her own body and spirit was unhealthy. Yielding to the force of love, she had been judged mad, and her body had accepted the judgment by sealing her lips, keeping rancor and violence and anger behind the firm walls of her flesh.

Annie had been expecting to find the Baroness, as surely as one falling downhill knows that the fall will be stopped by level ground. She knew that the task given her by the Baron was but one element in a series of tasks and events that would fit into a shape ordained by fate, and prompted by her spirit. Urges that had prompted her to steal a snuffbox, to leave behind her village, to take into her arms a madman in chains all came from the same place, were all part of an unknown, intricate design.

Out in the high-walled courtyard where the keepers marched the inmates until they had flattened the gravel beneath their feet into a circle of despair, Annie spoke with her.

"I have come for you, Baroness," she said. "Your husband has sent me, and I have come to make you well and bring you home."

The Baroness smiled at Annie, as if privy to the great joke she was attempting to play on her. But she did not answer. Her husband had put her in this place, had left her alone to be bled, to have blisters applied to her delicate skin, to be thrust into baths first too hot, then too cold, to be fed purgatives and emetics, to be denied even a single candle at dark.

"I have come to make you well," repeated Annie, this time taking hold of the Baroness's cold hands, looking for an entry to her spirit through her light gray eyes.

And then the gravel seemed to shift beneath Annie's feet. She had found an entry into the woman's spirit, but once inside, Annie was lost. For a moment, she did not understand that she had plunged into a despair that was not her own, into the wild hopelessness behind the Baroness's silence. In all the healings she had ever performed, there had been a sudden jump of consciousness, a twisting about of her own spirit to identify and absorb another's ills. But there had always been a place of welcome for her healer's spirit. Even in the incomplete healing of the chained madman, her loving nature, unable to suddenly destroy madness, was at least able to join with the man's misery, to comfort it.

But entering the Baroness's spirit, she had not merely encountered madness, but had been enveloped by it. There was no place for her to hold on to, no chance of union, no way in which she could offer comfort or solace. Whatever angels or demons drove Annie to heal, they were powerless in the abyss suddenly open before her. All Annie could do was let go. There was no healing touch being broken, nothing but the parting of skin from skin.

"You must tell me how I can help you," said Annie, knowing that the words were uselessly spent, as the Baroness had no use for her, not for any utterance of her mouth, nor any voice from her spirit.

But though the Baroness didn't answer, a tiny flash of longing showed in her eyes, a longing that was somehow familiar, somehow dear to Annie. "Please," said Annie. "If you would only tell me." She began once more to place her hands on the Baroness, but a keeper, rude and brusque, stopped her, taking hold of Annie's shoulders and pulling her away.

"Come with me," said the keeper to Annie, and Annie understood at once that the longing in the Baroness's eyes was not for the touch of a healer, but for the union with the lover denied her by the world.

"Your name is Smithson?" said the keeper sharply, as he moved Annie briskly along the paved pathway to the hospital's admitting office.

"Annie Smithson," said Annie.

"You're not crazy," said the keeper as if to accuse her of deliberately misleading him, and the entire staff of the hospital. Annie didn't respond to his statement. She was too wild with anticipation. Somehow the keeper, the hospital, the Baron, were elements of a cure that she would soon begin to see. She had no desire to debate the meaning of insanity in the midst of an asylum operated by fearful men on principles of intimidation and terror. She wondered if Shaxton might have returned to claim her, or if the Baron's long arm could have reached as far as London to vouch for his emissary.

But approaching the elaborately carved wood door of the office, Annie knew that inside was neither of these men, but one infinitely more dear; she could sense his spirit like a star shining in a bleak sea.

"Annie," said Will Smithson, turning about from where he stood respectfully before the desk of the assistant to the governor of Bedlam. He looked physically well, somehow broader and stronger than she had last seen him. She had heard rumors that he had taken a longshoreman's job, unloading the treasures from the great ships returning from the colonies. The long planned deep-water docks alongside the Thames had still not been built, and strong men unafraid of the river carried cargoes from these behemoths in lighter ships that could pull up to the shore.

But beneath his physical vigor was an exhaustion of the spirit, a profound hunger for love that was not being fulfilled. Quickly and obediently he answered the questions of the officious assistant, detailing his knowledge of Annie and her family, explaining that she was not only not deranged, but a midwife and a healer, renowned throughout his village and the countryside.

"This is not the village, young woman," said the assistant, adjusting his peruke, squinting at Annie as if she were a prize heifer brought in for a fair. "You will do well to remember that this is London, and impossible behavior leads to serious consequences."

"I will remember, milord," said Annie. He handed her the heavily inked and gold-stamped form which would allow her to gather her possessions from her cell and leave the hospital a discharged, healthy, and free woman. Will Smithson took her outside, and said nothing until he had looked toward the barred windows of the second story wing where the Baroness was locked away from him.

"Did you see her?"

"Yes." She took Will's hand, feeling his pain, and understood at once that her own love for him was something childish, unformed, compared to the force which ate at his soul. "She is well."

"You know that I love her?"

"Yes."

"The Baron knows," he said. "My cousin wrote me. He said that you were sent here to bring her back to health." Annie turned Will about so that she could look directly into his eyes, the way she had minutes before looked into those of the Baroness. She understood then what had fired Will to strike down the powerful Baron, with what force he had conquered timidity and subservience. "Do you think you can help her, Annie?"

She resisted the little-girlish impulse to ask him whether *he* thought she could help the Baroness; after all, he had never quite believed in her powers of healing, any more than he had quite believed in her infatuation for him. "Only you can help her," said Annie.

"What do you mean? I've done everything I can. I come every day." He looked away from Annie in frustration, as if she had just revealed a powerlessness equal to his own. The morning crush of visitors was beginning to move up the elegant path from the exterior to the hospital's main entrance, men and women eager to laugh at the lunacy of his beloved. "It's the Baron anyway, it's not me that's not doing. He said it to her plain. As long as she wants to leave a Baron for a peasant, she's going to be locked away in Bedlam."

"It is crazy," said Annie.

"What is crazy? We're both creatures of the Lord, aren't we? It's not insane to love beneath or above your place, it's just—"

"Listen," said Annie. "You are wrong. It is insane. In this city, in this time, in this place, if a Baroness loves her gardener, she is crazy." She understood now of what madness the Baron wished his wife to be cured. His cruelty was suddenly as apparent as the hate behind her silence.

Will Smithson became yet more agitated at her words. He had not expected such corroboration of his worst fears from Annie, the barber's daughter, to whom all things were happily possible. He did not want to believe that his beloved was mad. Even if Mary had not spoken to him, he could feel the love that still filled her heart was waiting for him, beneath the implacable silence of her rage. "She was fine, Annie. And she still is. It's just that she won't talk. And who would? In that place, with everyone laughing, and she's so high born, pushed around by those keepers."

"Will," said Annie, taking hold of his hands, and forcing him to face her so that he would feel the calm and the purpose that was her stock in trade. He did not understand that part of Mary Normande's silence was directed at him, at her own inability to throw every caution to the wind and openly declare her love for him against all the forces of English life. But Annie knew that the confusion in the Baroness's heart must be broken, that she must choose a pathway for her life, or there would never be an end to her madness. "She must leave this place with you, and the two of you must go far away. And very soon after, she will be better, she will talk, she will be free."

"What do you mean? She can't leave. They lock her up. And what can I do? She won't hardly look at me, Annie. She won't—"

"Will," she said. And then she took him in her arms, remembering how very much she loved him. Ever since she had been a little girl she had loved the way he whistled for his dogs, loved the way the wind whipped about his straight rust-colored hair, loved the gentle touch of his hand on her head. Not at all in love with her, hardly aware of her infatuation, he had never been hasty with her. There was always the extreme courtesy of his attention, as if all the cares of the world must stop until he had answered her questions, had thanked her for a cup of water in the field, had responded to her wishing him a good day.

But now Annie turned her attention to a different sort of love, one that included the Baroness, that included all the sufferers of this terrible place. She knew better now what the shape of her own fate was, and she wanted to meet it, she wanted to speed Will and his love on their way. Annie held him, so that he would feel what she felt, know that a healing was offered, was possible, was based, like all healings, on the stuff of love.

"You must take her to America, Will," she said.

"How can I—"

Still holding him in her arms, Annie brought out the Baron's stolen snuffbox from an inside pocket of her mantle. The tortoiseshell lid was ringed with gold, and the inside of the box was lined with silver. Even her urge to steal had been part of a healing. "You work on the ships?"

"Yes."

"You will find a captain who will take you and your bride to America in exchange for this rich gift."

"But Annie, how can I get her out of here, how can I get her to come with me?" She could feel the fear behind his words, the terrible doubt that his love would not be strong enough to vanquish her madness.

"She will choose to follow you," said Annie.

"But she is not allowed to leave."

"I will take her place," said Annie. There was work to be done in this hospital, suffering to be comforted, pain to be salved. She let go of Will, though the embrace brought her pleasure, though she could feel how her spirit restored his hope. The first confusion of the visitors' arrival would now be taking place. The inmates had been marched back from their exercise, to be once again pulled out of their cells for the entertainment of Bedlam's visitors. "Give this to her," she said, giving him the hospital's ornately printed release form, and taking his arm as they joined the crush of visitors going to the inmates' galleries.

"I don't understand what you want me to do," said Will, taking the release and placing it under his rough workman's jacket.

"Take her to America, Will," said Annie, taking tight hold of his arm and smiling merrily. "And leave me here to do my work."

She guided him past the peddlers of gin and cakes and sexual favors. She took him upstairs, past the mad harpist, lost in her art, past the hearty keepers swinging their sticks. She took him past the malodorous corner where frenzied patients were kept in chains, forced to take little steps in straw filthied by their own bodily wastes. Like Annie he had seen these sights before; he had seen more too, having lived among the larger cruelties of the city of which this asylum was but a smaller, purer part.

"Give him five shillings," said Annie, placing the coins in Will's hand. She could feel the fear leaving the young man as they drew closer to the shut door of the Baroness's cell. Will dropped the shillings in a keeper's outstretched hand, and asked him to let the Baroness out into the freedom of the gallery.

Annie barely heard the words between Will and the keeper, could scarcely recognize the elements of danger in the flight of a married woman and her lover from the confines of her husband's power. She was open not to words or actions, but to the interplay of powerful forces, invisible agents that roiled the unmoving air.

"We are leaving," she heard Will say to the Baroness Mary Normande. "We are going to America."

There was no kiss, no embrace between the lovers, just the momentary clasping of hands. But in that bodily contact, in that received understanding of Will's intent, Annie felt confusion fall away like dross from a core of gold.

Like the healing she had brought to a madwoman giving birth three years before, she felt the miraculous power of the union of loving spirits.

The Baroness didn't speak, but it was without the hindrance of madness that she exchanged her mantle for Annie's, that she took her lover's arm and began to walk away through the familiar crowd of visitors and lunatics. The healer didn't stop to wonder whether the hospital release form, the stolen snuffbox, Will's bravado, and the Baroness's beauty would be weapons enough to unite them in the real world. Those were physical concerns, tangible encounters with guards and boat captains and government officials.

What Annie believed was that the Baroness would take a direct, impulsive pathway that would lead her from Bedlam to a new life in America. Yielding to love, the Baroness had left confusion; leaving confusion, she had found the beginning of a return to health. Certainly no physical fate would prevent what had come together with such strength of spirit.

No law held Annie in Bedlam. Though there were many among the hospital board who believed her to be mad, there were others who were convinced that she was an angel of mercy. They let her remain, not as a patient, but as an adjunct, a helper to the keepers and doctors. Throughout her long life, at Bedlam, and in a hundred other institutions to which she was drawn by her healer's need—poorhouses, orphanages, prisons—Annie would never forget the lessons she'd learned from those made mad by the world.

No disease of mind or body existed, she believed, that was not rooted in some twisted turnings of the spirit. No madness, no infection, no fever lived without the agreement of the body that held it, without the collaboration of man and society and God.

Still, Annie knew, no illness was stronger than love.

Even in the worst of times, even in a society manufacturing disease out of its own frustrations, love could lift one to hope, could find a healing path through any obstacles, even those planted by one's own soul.

New York City, 1983

RICHARD was dying.
He had come back to the hospital, he had learned to believe in the chance of a cure, and he had begun to undergo chemotherapy. But every day his body grew weaker.

And as his body weakened, so did his spirit. He had not learned to draw strength into his body from its greatest resource, but had instead only served the disease by fueling it with anger and hopelessness. In the twisted logic of the sick, he felt betrayed by both body *and* spirit; having made the decision to return to the hospital, having expressed a belief in the healing process, having given himself up to the hands of the doctors and their accomplices, he had found only fatigue and pain.

Inescapably a student, Elizabeth tried to nurse faint hope and ease misery by immersing herself in a hundred texts, journals, notebooks.

Every day new studies appeared correlating cancer with stress and unhappiness, indicating that the rise of cancer as the chief bugbear of the modern era must be related to the rise of a modern consciousness that creates disease.

While family newspapers published the latest theories about the interaction of one's emotions with one's body, learned journals discoursed on the new discipline of "psychoneuroimmunology." Few medical authorities disregarded findings that emotions arising in the mind stimulate or suppress the white blood cells that fight disease; that the brain contained the power to unleash adrenal gland hormones and neurotransmitters that could harm or ameliorate or heal physical illness. It was no wonder that medical doctors across the country were employing hypnosis, bio-feedback, and "imaging" techniques to combat cancers that Elizabeth had always regarded as immovable foes unless ripped out of the body by surgical means.

"But that's because you're a surgeon," said Laney Spitzer, Elizabeth's only female surgical superior at the hospital, a diminutive woman with powerful hands and forearms developed through weight traning. Laney had not been able to tolerate the abuse of her fellow orthopedic residents, who took it as a matter of pride that no ordinary female had the masculine strength required to operate on shoulders, hips, and knees. So Laney had developed the strength of an Amazon, and was now much sought after when it came time to pull a reluctant hip out of a socket. "We surgeons don't conceive of things the way most doctors do now, or did in the past." She refilled Elizabeth's cognac snifter and made an expansive gesture out to the city lights beneath her "penthouse terrace"—actually, the top floor of a tenement with access to the tar-covered roof. She was prepared to get Elizabeth drunk, to show her how to tap dance, to tell her why no tragedy seen from a distance is as terrible as it looks pressed up close against your flesh.

"He's dying," said Elizabeth. "Why are we even talking about these ridiculous so-called therapies?"

"I'll tell you a secret," said Laney. "If we don't all blow up in the next war, we're going to be obsolete inside a generation. Read medical history. Surgeons were the peons of the medical world, the lowest of the low. That's because we cut through flesh and bones, just like butchers. We didn't do the hard stuff, like the witch doctors. That's because the witch doctors cured from the inside out. So we laughed at them for a century or two, but now it's going to be their turn to laugh at us. Chemotherapy is replacing cancer surgery, as well it should. And chemotherapy is going to be ancient history once this mind-body thing is clear. Hell, it's nothing new. Sir William Osler, who only invented the modern medical school, said it almost a century ago: It's more important what the patient has in his head than what he's got in his bones."

"In his chest, not his bones," snapped Elizabeth at the orthopedic surgeon. "Osler was talking about tuberculosis."

But Laney was not about to let a minor factual correction

interrupt her flow of enthusiasm. Even if she had no words that could remove Elizabeth's helpless pain in watching Richard try to endure chemotherapy, she could at least remind her that medical practice must always be about hope. She told her how Isaac Judaeus had a thousand years before exhorted all doctors to make their patients believe that they would be cured, even if the doctor had himself no idea for a treatment.

The placebo effect—or in many cases, any technically useless medication or treatment that cured the patient—had been the most effective medical aid ever devised, the major tool in the doctor's aresenal for three thousand years. Laney told her how witch doctors in the Philippines were curing patients considered hopeless by Western medicine, because the patients believed that their sickness came from a curse, and that the witch doctor had the power to remove the curse.

"Afterwards the diagnosticians come in and change the prognosis. They say that the condition reversed itself, that the white blood count increased, that the hormonal balance was restored—whatever. Even in a cancer patient, there can be spontaneous remissions that can't be explained, just obfuscated with a lot of jargon."

"Excuse me, Laney," said Elizabeth. "Are you suggesting that I put Richard on a plane to the Philippines?"

"Of course not."

"Because even if there was a witch doctor who specialized in acute leukemia, Richard would be dead before the stewardess could serve cocktails."

"I'm only saying that your attitude can't be helping—"

"Stop it, Laney. My attitude is fine. Don't give up the ship. Smile on my face at all times. Absolute certainty that remission will take place, and life will be lived. We will have grandchildren dancing at our fiftieth wedding anniversary. That's my fine and lovely attitude."

"We both know that physicians make lousy patients. Now I'm beginning to see that we make even worse lovers of patients."

"Richard is in that hospital because I let myself believe it was possible to do something to help him. And all I can do now is watch him suffer the chemo, and wait for him to die."

Laney placed one powerful hand about Elizabeth's shoulders. "Look," she said. "I'm trying to help because I would be as bad as you under these circumstances. We remember all the reasons why someone can die. All we've got is a thin layer of skin surrounding a lot of breakable bones and delicate organs. When I think of how we doctors screw up, again and again, all the useless blood that's spilled, all the ones who die without reason, like lights going out . . . That's all we live with, death every day, that's our diet, we understand futility better than anyone."

"That's right," said Elizabeth, draining her cognac snifter. "We are experts at understanding futility. What we are *not* experts at is learning to draw lessons from futility."

"What is that supposed to mean?"

"Figure it out, Dr. Spitzer. Figure out what the hell you would do if someone you loved is dying slowly, and in pain. And you a big, brave doctor. Where's the bottle?"

Laney refilled Elizabeth's glass. "Naturally," said Laney, "doctors are less capable than lay people in believing in a miracle. That does not mean that you or I should give up hope even when—"

"Cut it out, Laney," said Elizabeth. "I am full of hope. I am professionally and capably so full of hope that I could make a faith healer blush." She walked to the edge of the roof and looked east, toward the forbidding bulk of the hospital, its many wings interconnected with ugly glassed-in corridors, garishly bright against the night sky.

"Hope?" said Elizabeth, laughing, and turning about to face her friend. "I walked in on two first-year residents discussing whether it was worth hanging some blood on the patient sharing Richard's room. The guy's twenty-two, had gone blind in the last forty-eight hours, blood count had gone all the way down, internal bleeding—on the way out, he knows, we know, even the witch doctor would know. Maybe Richard doesn't know, because Richard's in his own world, listening to his own body as chemo poisons drip through his blood. But you want to know about my attitude."

"That's an extreme case," began Laney. "There are times when you have to know that it doesn't pay anymore."

"Would you for the love of God let me finish? I am trying to tell you how hopeful I am. You see I know all this hopeful stuff by heart. Isaac Judaeus, hell. My own father never told a dying

patient the truth in his life. Drove me crazy. Made him sick probably. But he thought it was part of his job to keep them in the
dark. Not because he was holier than thou. But he was an old-
fashioned doctor, just like your Philippine friends. 'If they don't
know they're going to die,' my father used to say, 'sometimes
they don't.' " Elizabeth laughed at this with a suddenness that
unnerved Laney, and reached for the cognac before her hostess
had a chance to pour.

"Come on, Lizzie, take it easy."

"I'm telling you about my attitude, Doctor," said Elizabeth,
stopping up her laughter. "You're worried about my attitude,
and I am explaining to you that my attitude—"

"You're hyperventilating."

"You're a bone-cracker, Laney. You wouldn't recognize hy-
perventilation if it fell on your head."

"Please sit, Lizzie. Please finish the story."

"I've got to go back."

"It's the middle of the night. He's sleeping."

"I need to see Richard, thank you." She banged down her
snifter next to the lone candle on Laney's low stool. This, together
with two lawn chairs, half of a defrosted pizza pie, and a nearly
empty bottle of Rémy Martin V.S.O.P. Cognac was all that
dressed the bleak roof.

"You're going to upset the nurses."

"Screw the nurses."

"Lizzie, come on, tell me what happened with the first-year
residents hanging blood."

"They weren't," said Elizabeth. "You see, that is the point.
There was blood to hang, and they were not going to do it,
because they knew it was a waste of resources."

"Please sit down," said Laney.

But Elizabeth needed to be with Richard just then. Shaking
her head, unable to find the words to finish the story, she walked
swiftly over the dark tar to the fire escape, which led not only to
the ground, but conveniently for burglars, to the roof. Elizabeth
threw her tired legs over the rusted iron bars. Laney shadowed
her, ready to steady her as she climbed back into the top floor
open window.

But Elizabeth needed no steadying. She bent low, stepped
through the tenemenet window, and extended her hand to her

friend to help her. Laney thanked her, and followed to where she was leaning bleary-eyed in front of the kitchen sink.

Elizabeth said: "I told those bastards. Hang the goddamn blood, hang the platelets, hang anything that lets that son of a bitch think you're still goddamnit trying."

"Of course you did," said Laney. She hoped that the unwanted interference from a surgical resident in an oncology ward wouldn't get Elizabeth in trouble.

"That's what I told those bastard first-year residents, and they hung the blood, they hung the platelets, and it sure taught them. It sure taught them you never give up." Elizabeth ran some cloudy tap water into a plastic cup and drank greedily. "The stuff of life," she said.

"You did the right thing," said Laney, taking the empty cup from Elizabeth's hand.

Elizabeth smiled. "The patient," she said, "died before the night was over."

"You still did the right thing," said Laney. "They must know that even with a one in a thousand chance, there's still a chance."

"A one in a thousand chance is stupid," said Elizabeth, turning her back. "Medicine doesn't support one in a thousand chances. It's too goddamned expensive. All that blood could be used elsewhere. All that health money could be spent to keep babies alive. And what about the patients? What if the patients don't want to suffer all that much? What if they don't think a one in a thousand chance is worth all that miserable pain?"

"If you can make the patient believe that he's going to be all right, you make those odds a hell of a lot better," said Laney. "That's how they healed in ancient Greece, that's how they healed with nothing but herbs in the Middle Ages."

"They didn't heal leukemia with herbs, they didn't stick IV units into Sophocles and torture him with poisons. They didn't, Laney. Sometimes it's better to just stop. To just pull the plug."

"There's no plug to pull with Richard. If you don't help him, he's going to die slowly and painfully. If you help him, he might live."

Elizabeth was near enough to the door to say the words burning in her mouth. "Not if I help him the way he wants to be helped," said Elizabeth. "You and I both know that there are other ways to die than slowly and painfully."

"Wait," said Laney. "Where are you going?"

Her face had registered no shock at Elizabeth's declaration, but as Elizabeth threw on her bloodstained white jacket over her sweaty T-shirt and grabbed the doorknob, Laney placed her hand over that of her friend. "I asked you where you were going."

Elizabeth gently pulled Laney's hand from hers and opened the front door. "You know where I'm going."

"What the hell do you think you're going to do when you get there?" said Laney.

Elizabeth took a step out into the dingy tenement hallway, but stopped short and turned her head for a parting shot. "One more thing, since you're such an authority on psychoneuroimmunology. Do you know that they've found bone cancer in dinosaur fossils? Happy-go-lucky *dinosaurs* had cancer, and you're telling me we can just wish it away, just take control of our stressful little lives and make ourselves all well? Just wish it away!"

Running down the shaky stairs to the deserted predawn street she was sorry that she had parted with so little grace, so much anger. Laney had only wanted to help. At some happier time she would have to thank her for the dinner of pizza and cognac, for the rooftop view of the city lights, and for the opportunity to talk. There was so little time for talk in her world, but only for acts and achievements. Too much introspection was weak, improper for a doctor, blasphemous for a surgeon. And Laney was not only a dear friend, but a role model, a woman who had made it into the man's world of surgery; and she had wanted very much to discuss with her what Richard wanted her to do to help him through his pain.

But in place of a discussion, she had simply blurted out the words: If Elizabeth were to help him the way he would like, his death would be neither slow nor painful.

And then she had fled.

Not because she doubted Laney's friendship, but because she was afraid that Laney would be too capable at stopping her from assisting in the crime of Richard's suicide.

"There is always hope," she could hear Laney whispering in her ear. "And you are a doctor."

But then Laney didn't love Richard, didn't feel what he felt, didn't imagine with him that all the chemotherapy, all the transfusions, all the twenty-four-hour care to prevent infection were leading inexorably to the same black place.

"I came here because I want to live, darling," Richard had said only hours before, when the summer sun had begun to set on another perfect August day. "But I don't believe that I can, Lizzie. I am very calm, and I love you very much, but what I want from you right now is to help me take my life."

"Richard," she had said, taking his hand, cold in spite of the fresh transfusion of blood. "You have only been here six days. I know they have been terrible days, but—"

"Sweetheart," he said, interrupting her with a gentle pressure from his once powerful hands. "A dog knows when he's going to die. Don't you think a human being knows?"

Elizabeth hadn't answered, had just shut her eyes against the image of her lover, so profoundly tired, so desiring of his death. Six days before, her love had given her the strength to believe in his life, but now that belief was fading against the harsh fact of his physical pain.

She had given him books to read, had rattled off the optimistic statistics, had sat with him when the oncologists had lectured about the need to fight being as important as the strength of the drugs they were pouring into his blood. He would need at least six weeks in this hospital, suffering the consequences of the treatment. The chemotherapy was devised to kill all tumor cells, but at this point, medical science had not devised a way to do this without killing normal cells as well. The normal cells, in a successful protocol of treatment, would grow back, while the tumor cells would not.

But this protocol produced no certainty of cure.

Even with the extreme toxicity of the drugs, there was only a 50 percent chance of a remission during this first phase of treatment. If a remission would occur, Richard would still by no means be home free. There was a second phase of treatment, a few weeks after the remission would begin. Usually this would require a hospital stay as well, but even if Richard would be allowed to take his treatments at home, he would be undergoing another phase of high dosage chemotherapy, and the possible concomitant side effects: nausea, loss of appetite, dehydration, hair loss, development of mouth sores. These of course only complemented the symptoms of the disease itself: fatigue, infections, bruising, bleeding; swelling of lymph nodes, liver, kidneys, and spleen.

"What are we doing this for?" he had said, and she had understood, she had stood in his shoes, she had felt his pain. Knowing what her father had suffered during his long, losing battle with cancer—albeit of a different kind, and without the benefit of the latest advances in chemotherapy—she doubted whether she herself, faced with Richard's sickness, would have had the desire to fight such formidable odds.

After all, for what was he fighting? So that he would have the opportunity to enter the third phase of chemotherapy, a maintenance diet of poisons that would allow the remisson to last for a few months, or if he was lucky, two years? And then what? More high dosage chemotherapy, more hospitalization, more fever and fatigue and pain. No matter what statistics were thrown at Richard, the oncologists couldn't deny what he already knew. No matter what treatments they tortured his body with, the vast majority of patients with his illness were dead within five years.

"I don't want to die when I can't see or hear or feel anything. The chemo is already killing my taste buds, and all I can smell is disinfectant and death." Richard smiled after he said this, as if commenting on the absurd melodrama of life itself. "I'm asking for your help, Lizzie. A friend of mine once told me that thirty Seconals and twenty codeines would take you out very well. Nobody has to know where I got them. You could get them to me, and we could say good-bye when I can still speak, when I can go still loving you and remembering that life is beautiful."

"Darling," she had said. "You came back here of your own volition, because you believed that it was possible to get well. You can still believe that, and believe that there is so much to look forward to . . ."

But he hadn't believed her words any more than she had herself. What difference did it make if twenty years before almost any diagnosis of cancer was as good as a death sentence? For Richard, the advances made in treating cancers of the breast and prostate and uterus and testis did not extend to acute myelocytic leukemia. No matter how many times he heard that innovative treatments were leading to longer survival rates for his illness, he didn't believe that any adult truly survived leukemia at all. Even if they made it through five years without a relapse, there was always the sixth year, then the seventh; there was always the chance that the drugs taken to kill the leukemic cells would a few years later lead to another form of cancer, another invasion of his body to pay him back for an earlier escape from his fate.

"He's sleeping, Dr. Grant," said the oncology nurse, bright-eyed at her station in spite of the late hour.

"I won't disturb him," said Elizabeth sweetly, not getting close enough for the nurse to smell the brandy on her breath. She was tired, and unaccustomed to drinking, but felt as sharp and aware as she always did walking a hospital corridor. At any moment she could be called upon to aid in a miracle: to cut with man-made tools into human flesh, to suture with synthetic fiber, to reshape, to remove, or modify some natural element in the body that without the innovations of science would lead inevitably to death. She must always be ready to be called; that was the pact made by every doctor of conscience: to fight back death at any cost.

She pushed open the door to his semiprivate room. The bed that had been vacated by the twenty-two-year-old boy now free of his pain had already been occupied by another denizen of the land of the sick. She wondered if this new patient would be the next to leave this room, or whether that grace would fall to Richard.

As Elizabeth's eyes grew accustomed to the imperfect dark, she could see her lover's face with greater and greater clarity. Despite the heavy blanket of drugged sleep, lines of pain stood out in his pale face.

She took a step closer, but did not touch him.

She was afraid to touch him; afraid not of the chance of waking him, but of falling victim once more to the delusion that the touch of her hands was something more than an expression of her love.

He wanted her help, he had said, with obtaining an overdose of barbiturates, a killing mixture that would take him swiftly and painlessly into a place of sleep forever. He did not, she was sure, want her turning to some fantasy about the need in his body for the touch of her hands.

Richard had lost weight in the six days of hospitalization. The IV unit led to an arm that had suffered many bruises, to a body whose fatigue couldn't be touched by a week of drugged sleep. But there was more than physical evidence of Richard's agony. The silent shout of a body in distress called to her. His skin wanted her touch, wanted to breathe in her presence through the walls of his heart.

But there was no shout, she told herself.

There was nothing to be heard in the room but the labored breathing of the sick.

Everything else was a dream.

No, she thought, forcing herself to take a step back from the bedside. She was not there to place her hands over his heart. The call she heard was self-induced, a moment of delirium, fueled as much by cognac as by despair.

I am a doctor, she reminded herself. I proceed from a knowledge of the facts. The facts are that he is not responding favorably to the first phase of chemotherapy. That he is in pain. That the chances for his survival are infinitesimal. That his own wish is to end his suffering.

What, she asked herself, could be more courageous than for her to give him what he wanted?

Thirty Seconals and twenty codeines.

A teen-ager could buy these on the street. An adult with chronic migraine or insomnia could hoard them from an unsuspecting doctor's prescription. Dr. Elizabeth Grant, with all her rights and privileges, could procure them in any of a dozen ways. And it would not be difficult to find some time for her to be alone with Richard, when the other patient was out of the room, when her fellow health professionals would give her the courtesy of a half hour with the man she loved.

For you, darling, she thought, imagining the gift of the deadly bottle. *Take thirty of these and twenty of those before retiring. Now kiss and let's say good-bye. Kiss and let's say good-bye.*

But what sort of gift was death, when life too was a gift within her grasp?

"Lizzie?" he said, and for a moment she thought she had heard her name from the same source of madness that had imagined his skin calling out for her touch as she stood near his sleeping form.

But she was not standing now.

She was sitting at the edge of his bed, and her hands were flat on his naked chest. "Richard," she said, whispering the words through a gentle smile. She blinked against the sight of him, very close to her face, and remembered that she had just kissed him, had drunkenly brought her lips to his for the briefest and saddest moment in her life. She could not remember the moment when she had stepped clumsily over to his bed, had nearly fallen on top of him, so suddenly eager was she to join her hands to his flesh. Elizabeth had no idea that she had watched his parted lips take in the dry hospital air for nearly an hour of silence. She only knew that the alcohol in her blood had given her the license to place her hands where her spirit wanted them to be.

I am not being unreasonable, she thought. *It is just that I am drunk.*

"Lizzie," he said again, this time not a question, but a statement. "You came back." He was whispering, not to save his strength, but to prevent alerting the nurses. Through the painkillers in his bloodstream he had felt her presence, had remembered the misery that he had implored her to end.

She knew what Richard was about to say, and knew too how she would have to respond. "Did you think about it?" he said. "Did you get them? The pills, darling."

Elizabeth hesitated only a moment. She hoped he would not notice the liquor on her breath, the less than subtle chicanery in her eyes. "Yes, darling," she said.

"Lizzie?" he said, bringing his head a fraction closer to her bloodshot eyes, as if to make sure that she was still the Lizzie he knew and not some caricature of his dreams, some twisted representation of the Lizzie he had demanded her to be. "Are you going to help me?" he insisted.

A slow wave of clarity had been chasing the alcoholic haze from her consciousness, the indecision from her spirit. She heard every word he uttered, and knew that everything he said with his mouth was a lie. If he looked at her so strangely, it was not that she was drunk, but that she had agreed to his demands. He wanted to live, but he was afraid to suffer. But like most sick people, no matter how he claimed to want his death, a part of him clung to the dream of life. To end his suffering would be bliss, but not more blissful than a miracle that would let him live. What he wanted was the help of her hands, but he had not enough strength of belief to ask for her touch.

All he had now was her strength. All she had now was her own spirit, slowing revealing itself in the space between imagination and darkness, between dreams and exhaustion, between life and death.

"Yes, darling," she said. "Of course I'm going to help you."

PART FOUR

United States, 1855

All that we see or seem
Is but a dream within a dream.
—*Edgar Allan Poe,*
  "A Dream Within a Dream"

Chapter 15

IN FENELLA'S DREAM, Dr. Robert Warner picked her up at the waist, held her high over his head, and ran with her along the river, through the woods that led to the Sound. He was out of his frock coat, no tie constricted this throat, and every breath he took in he exhaled with a laugh that shook the trees.

Soon he would be kissing her, soon his fine dark hair would be falling across his serious brow as he moved closer and closer to her anxious lips. Fenella would stretch her fingers through his hair, would bring her cheek against the dark shadow that grew swiftly on his freshly shaved face. This time the kiss would not be quick, not the kiss of a man concentrated on dying, nor the kiss of a man full of regrets for the life he would not have. This kiss would linger, it would last as long as their love, it would be the kiss of life, as nothing was stronger than love in conquering disease and despair and death.

"Fenella," said the doctor's mother, pulling her sharply from the daydream. She let out a puny laugh, characteristic of her imperiousness. "Hello, Fenella, that's enough. Fenella, I do believe it's entirely clean. It's immaculate, my dear. Fenella, do you hear me?"

Of course Fenella heard her.

All her life they had been asking her that question, and always when she had just begun to find the way to some place of beauty and value. Fenella looked up from the basin into which the man she loved had spit up his own blood. She had been scouring it for the better part of an hour when Mrs. Warner had discovered her. The shut-up office in the west wing of the house had once belonged to Mrs. Warner's husband, and had been used sporadically by Robert since the completion of his medical training a year before. But the consumption that had killed his father and uncle had found its way to him. In the last six months he had been too tired to see patients, or they had been too afraid of contagion to come and see him. Some days he was too tired to pick up a paintbrush and work at a watercolor; sometimes he was too listless to do anything more than sit in a chair and watch the river traffic through heavy lidded eyes.

"It's late," said Mrs. Warner. "I'm sure your mother will be expecting you."

"Thank you," said Fenella. But she did not let go of the basin in her hand and made no move to go.

"You will remember to take the food," said Mrs. Warner, trying to dismiss her., Though she disliked touching a servant, Mrs. Warner brought a single finger to Fenella's shoulder. "Come, child, I want to close up the office. We'll keep it nice and clean until he gets back from New York."

"Yes, Mrs. Warner," said Fenella. She did not know why the grand old lady disliked her, seemed to stiffen her already ramrod straight spine every time they crossed paths in the vast old riverfront house. Perhaps it was because of Fenella's Irish father: There were many in the Congregational Church who looked down their noses at Fenella, born a Catholic, and her mother, who had married one. Mrs. Warner made it a point of never speaking to Fenella or her mother at church. What she gave each of them was a barely perceptible nod accompanied by a fierce narrowing of the eyelids; as if she were warning them not to say hello. "Mrs. Warner, may I be permitted to ask if the letter from Dr. Warner contained any good news?"

"No, Fenella," said Mrs. Warner with an indignation that was completely lost on the young woman. "You may not."

"Is he no better then?" said Fenella, not understanding that Mrs. Warner had just closed the subject.

"Fenella, I have told you before that you are not to be examining the mail that arrives at this house. Mail is private communication, sent via the Post Office in strict confidence. Your job is to take the envelopes, without looking at where they come from, place them on a tray, and bring them to me in my sitting room. That is not so very difficult to understand, is it?"

"I just want to know if Dr. Robert is any better," said Fenella.

"Dr. *Warner*," she corrected. You don't understand a word I tell you, do you? It's like talking to a wall, talking to you! Just please pick up your cleaning rags, put them where they belong, take the dinner leftovers, and go home to your mother!"

Perhaps, thought Fenella, as she left the office, Mrs. Warner disliked her for another reason. After all, it was true that her handsome young son had kissed her, and not in a dream but on the back porch of this very house. Even if he had told no one of that kiss, no mother, no matter how cold and aloof, would be insensitive to the slightest emotional changes within her only child. Perhaps that was why there had been no letters for Fenella from the clinic in New York City: Mrs. Warner might have forbidden it. Maybe that was why he had begged her, the day before he left, to forget that he had ever held her in his arms. Mrs. Warner might have accused him of trifling with their Irish cleaning girl, might have told him of all her deficiencies, might have warned him with the specter of scandal. She might have threatened to cut him off from the family money that allowed him his tiny medical practice and the leisure time for his painting.

"I don't care, Mother," he might have said. "I am going to New York to recover, and then I shall return here only long enough to pick up Fenella and take her away with me forever."

But that was a dream, as everything happy was a dream to Fenella O'Hara. Because she had never been able to abide the various enmities and jealousies and hatreds all about her, she had long ago become a daydreamer, so absorbed in a self-enclosed world of fancy that some took her for a simpleton.

But she was anything but simple.

She had learned to read faster than any of the other children in the public school, adding fuel to the fire of their jealousy. She was adept at sums, had a prodigious memory, was clever at puzzles. At footraces she beat all the girls, and those few boys who dared race her. Even if some found her red hair an exotic stigma of her Irishness, none could deny that she was a beauty.

For all this she was hated.

Even without her accomplishments, she would have been hated simply for being the daughter of an Irishman, for being poor, and poorly dressed. Growing up in a village of ordinary blondes and brunettes, Fenella had felt the loathing of children

every time she had stepped outside Irishtown. She hadn't understood why she was hated and feared, by schoolmates and street
urchins, by girls jealous of her looks and boys whom she had
beaten at games. And she could not bear this hatred. She could
not stand to feel as if their loathing would penetrate her skin and
make her sick and die.

And so she had learned to keep to herself.

She became so quiet in the schoolroom that teacher and children were able to forget her early evidence of talent. She became
so distant and contemplative that they began to think her incom-
petent at all but the simplest tasks.

Fenella had always liked to be alone, content to have a corner
of the shack in which she lived, or the shady space under an old
tree, or a bit of the broken-down town pier when no ships were
riding at anchor in the Sound. These were good places for dreaming, and dreaming was her special talent.

She could dream in her sleep, and she could dream while
awake; her mother, even before her father died, would grow
furious whenever she'd catch Fenella staring blank-eyed into
space. Mrs. O'Hara knew that what her daughter was seeing was
not a part of their world of poverty and prejudice, and she would
not tolerate such blindness. She wanted Fenella to return the
insults hurled at her by other children. She wanted her daughter
to show Yankee backbone and mettle, not dreamy Irish complai-
sance.

But Fenella didn't dream simply to escape from a harsh
world. Dreaming was not only a place where she could examine
the events of the day, the shape of things tangible and bright,
mundane fantasies of power and privilege and glory. That was
ordinary dreaming, hardly a step from wakefulness. She
dreamed because her spirit pulled her inward, toward a center
that was warm and inviting, toward a place that granted fulfillment. To dream deeply was to be united with her self, her spirit,
her soul.

When Fenella made herself very still, looking at nowhere at
all until the world vanished, she coasted down a steep slope, far
from consciousness, to a place where prayer was blinded by light,
where her body seemed to float on waters both hot and cold. She
dreamed because the dream state, night and day, was as natural
as sleeping, as necessary as food and drink. She dreamed because

it made her feel not only good to herself but virtuous, as if the state was religious, as if its beauty could somehow envelop the world.

This did not stop her mother from agreeing with those who thought her lazy, fearful, odd. Mrs. O'Hara had no patience, no interest in Fenella's dreams. After Fenella's father died, any evidence of daydreaming was met with a blow. The place for solace was the Church, not the confines of one's dreams. Men and women were not good enough to make their own peace; they needed guidance, discipline, shepherding.

Once Fenella's father had told her that human nature was directed toward goodness, in the way that water was directed to flow downstream. Fenella believed this, not only because her father had left her the words in her heart, but because she believed that the state she achieved in her dreams must needs be open to everyone. As she felt her spirit as surely as she felt the bones of her fingers, she knew there must be a God from where all spirits come. So of course all things must flow toward fulfilling the spirit, and all spirits must flow toward their source, the source of all goodness, all that was inevitable.

But somehow her father, a big, gentle Irishman from County Clare, had died from a fever after unloading a ship in a driving rain. His Connecticut-born employer apparently didn't allow his goodness to flow in the direction of Irish dockworkers. Fenella had tried to bring him back to life, imagining the shape of his work-hardened hands, the gentle fuzz of his patchy auburn beard, the eyes full of childhood landscapes in a country green and wet and mild. But the dream hadn't encompassed the dead flesh, rotting in a pauper's grave; nor could it be extended to embrace Fenella's mother, already turning her love about in a reflection of her distraught spirit.

After her father's death, it seemed her mother began to share the sentiments of the urchins who pelted her with pebbles and mud. If she squirmed and shirked and hid away, it was because she was Irish trash. This was on a par with German trash, quite a few steps above free black garbage, but well below even the most ordinary native-born American. But Fenella was herself born in Connecticut. Her Celtic hair and fair skin were a legacy of her father; perhaps even her capacity to dream deeply was a gift from his ancestors.

Mrs. O'Hara was of course neither Irish nor Catholic, but a full-blooded Yankee. She would not tolerate being looked down upon by other members of the Congregational Church because her Irish husband had left her a penniless widow. It was his fault, not hers, that she lived in a shack in the Irish slum at the edge of the heavily trafficked Sound; his fault that his daughter was burdened with an Irisher's unholy name. Whatever madness had overtaken Sarah Graham and turned her into Sarah O'Hara was now banished from her spirit. Fenella's mother became probably the only anti-Catholic, anti-Irish resident of Irishtown.

Dragged on Sundays to the Congregational Church, Fenella was now attacked by the same wild boys she used to run away from on school days. Once she asked her mother why God had given her red hair. Was it so everyone would know her as Irish, and not one of their own?

Mrs. O'Hara had rapped her hands for the blasphemous question. "Who are you, Fenella O'Hara, that the Lord takes a special interest in the color of your hair? You're a fine one to be using His Name, you with your eyes closed in church, sleeping like the dead when everyone is praying."

"I pray," Fenella had said.

"You pray and I'm the Queen of England. In your dreams you pray!" said Mrs. O'Hara.

"Yes," Fenella had admitted, wanting some part of her own tranquil heart to flow into her mother's bitter loneliness. "I pray in my dreams."

But Fenella's prayers had little effect on her mother's life. Mrs. O'Hara was resigned to be miserable, and no sensitive daughter, no matter how loving, could redirect a spirit so determined to be punished by life. Refusing to admit that she had loved her husband, she forced hate down her throat; refusing to accept the fact that she missed her handsome Irishman, she twisted her spirit into fanatical knots of repression. It was no wonder that Mrs. O'Hara was always fatigued, always troubled by headache, always irritable. The town doctors scolded her for complaining, not finding any cause for her aches and pains. But Fenella knew that her mother's ills were real, as real as their source in her spirit.

Trying to ease her mother's distress, Fenella conjured dreams: Behind distant, unseeing eyes, Fenella retrieved her father, returned him to her mother's arms. Gone would be her mother's wild swings of temper, the gin-fueled ravings and beatings, the constant bemoaning of her poor physical state.

But these dreams did not cross over into the world of Irishtown.

Fanella's father remained dead, and her mother remained a bitter shrew, a ready victim for every new practitioner of medical quackery to whom she could turn for relief.

Unlike Annie Smithson of the previous century's England, or Corinna of ancient Epidaurus, Fenella was not raised in the shadow of healers, was not driven from childhood with a certain sense of the power of the spirit. Fenella was driven by whims and passions, like Lioba of Francia; but unlike that long-dead healer, she did not grow up with the sure knowledge that she had the power to heal.

She knew that Robert was ill, and that she wanted him well. She knew that she loved him and wanted him to be with her all the days of her life. But it was only in the world of dreams that Fenella believed she had power. She had not yet learned that the place of retreat within her spirit was hers to harness as a source of health and wholeness. It was only in the world of dreams that she could imagine the defeat of illness, the consummation of love.

Chapter 16

WHEN SHE CAME back out to say good-bye, his eyes grew sad, and he shook his head from side to side.

"Oh, no," he said. "Not yet. You can't be going so soon."

Dr. Robert Warner, all wrapped up in a cashmere blanket on the back porch of the house, nearly got to his feet to express his regret, but thought better of it at the last moment. He had only been back from the clinic for a few days, and already felt himself weakening under the ordinary stresses of his home, surrounded by the life he knew he was leaving bit by bit, day by day. The sun had not yet begun to set, but already the vista of cloudless sky over the river was turning a pale red, presaging the sunset's orange glow.

"Don't go," he insisted. "You haven't even finished telling me your dream."

"I'm sorry, Dr. Robert," said Fenella, remembering not to complain about his mother. Since her son had returned from New York, Mrs. Warner followed every move he made. This was not simply to cosset him, but to appropriate all his words and actions for herself, and herself alone. She had whisked Fenella away from Robert, interrupting the telling of her dream, hurrying her to polish a pair of candlesticks that had been wrapped away for the better part of two decades. "I would have liked to finish telling it to you. Not many people are interested in my dreams."

"I have a dream," he said. "Would you like to hear it?"

Fenella hesitated, then put down the tray she was about to bring back to the kitchen. Her own mother was waiting for her with more than usual excitement; tonight they were going to the

Lyceum to hear the famous mesmerist Professor Barnard. She had dreamed about him, about the flamboyance of his gestures, about the gentleness behind the wild showmanship of his words. But she had not shared this dream with Dr. Robert Warner. She knew well his feelings about mesmerists. The dream she had begun to tell him of was about a faraway cabin, high in the mountains, where Robert could breathe deeply of the fresh dry air, and have all day, every day, to paint pictures brighter than any either of them had ever seen.

"Pictures that burned," she had told him. "Like campfires. Colors that blinded. Faces that were familiar, but much too beautiful to be real. Much too beautiful." She had not told him everything in the dream, of course. It would not have been appropriate to mention that her own redheaded figure had appeared behind his shoulders as he painted, behind his head as he reclined toward a wintry sun.

"Of course I would like to hear your dream, Dr. Robert," she said politely.

"I dream," he said, "that you're going to start calling me Robert."

"Thank you. I would like that, of course. But your mother has made it very clear—"

"I kissed you. Do you remember?"

"Yes," said Fenella.

"So how can you call someone who has kissed you by anything other than his Christian name?"

"You have asked me to forget that you ever held me in your arms. That the kiss never happened." She turned her eyes from his to look up the river, where a pair of ragamuffins steered a crude raft downstream. "I believe that your mother would be happy if I left this house altogether."

"My mother does not want me to take advantage of someone she cares about," said Robert. "You must understand that I am sick, that I have a disease for which there is no real cure."

"People recover from the consumption," said Fenella.

"Not many," said Robert. "Not with my medical history."

"You will recover," said Fenella. She turned to face him, and to remove her eyes from the too-pretty play of ebbing sunlight in the flowing water. In another moment, she could find herself drifting in a dream, like a bit of deadwood caught up by the river.

There, behind the rippling lights at the horizon was a familiar place for her, a place where Robert would no longer doubt his health, where a mystical sun would bronze his skin, where magical air would blow all that was evil out of his lungs. "You must try and help yourself to get well—"

"Fenella," he interrupted, smiling over the familiar syllables of her Irish name. He had always been attracted to her beauty, to the sense of solid health behind the glowing skin and omniscient smile. Fenella had always seemed content and easy in a world discontent and wild. There was never a hint of the servile in her housekeeper's service; neither was there a suggestion of hostile superiority. She did not seem to define herself by her occupation, did not seem unhappy to be unmarried, poor, or the butt of his mother's criticism. She was untouched by most of what passed about her, as if the mundane events of cleaning and cooking could be accomplished without drawing on any of her true strength.

This was a strength that Robert was drawn to as a hungry man is drawn to a feast. He always felt better watching her sure hands accomplish some task. When her thick hair would brush against his arm when she brought him a tray, he would breathe in the delicious proximity of her fresh and vibrant face; listening to her faintly lilting voice describe the strange geography of a dream, he would find his heart racing, as if following her words up and down steep trails. But he felt obligated to forget the powerful feeling of well-being he took from the fact of her presence. His mother was right: He must not stir the affections of a servant girl, having nothing to offer her but ill health, the impossibility of a marriage, and certain misery.

"You are standing before a patient who is also a doctor," he said with considerable gravity. "I cannot pretend to have your great faith or confidence, because I know what to expect from consumption. The disease wastes the body. It most commonly occurs between the ages of eighteen and thirty-five. It runs in families. It frequently follows whooping cough."

"I do not want to hear this," said Fenella, turning back to face the river. "Such talk only helps your sickness get stronger." He answered her swiftly, but she had heard these words before, and understood them to mean only that he was full of despair.

"A sickness doesn't get stronger from talk or silence," said

Robert. "I do not pretend to know everything, but I know what I can expect after being locked in a tuberculosis clinic for three weeks. I almost died from the whooping cough when I was a teenager. I was diagnosed as consumptive when I was eighteen. Even if I didn't want to believe that diagnosis, even if I had some very healthy years in my twenties, I am now thirty-one, I know that my father and uncle both died from the consumption, and as a doctor I know what to expect. Is it any wonder that my mother doesn't want me to take advantage of you?"

"People recover from the consumption," said Fenella doggedly. She knew that he would not believe anything she would have to say on the subject, that he would see nothing happy before his eyes unless she could place him on her back as she flew into a dream of bountiful health. "You shall be one of them."

"Listen to me," he said, removing his pale hand from beneath the cashmere blanket as if he would take hold of her, but at the last moment drawing it back, as if afraid of the naked nearness of her big and capable hands. "You know about contagion?"

"Yes, Doctor."

"And germs? You of course know—"

"I know all I need to know about germs," said Fenella, as untouched by these dread words as if she were an invulnerable being, as fleshless and pure of spirit as an angel.

"Listen carefully then," said Robert. "All the current medical evidence suggests that consumption is communicable. That does not mean just to people who have a hereditary disposition for the disease. That does not just mean doctors researching with contagious germs in their laboratories. It means any contact is unsafe. Do you understand?"

"I understand that you do not want me to go. That you want me to be late, even to risk your mother's anger."

Robert began again: "I want you to understand why I have asked you to forget about the time I kissed you. To realize that my future is not in my control, and that I cannot say and do what I would like."

"Yes," said Fenella, getting on one knee next to where his head, bolstered by two pillows, was supported on the reclining chair. "I understand completely."

And then she slowly and carefully brought her lips to his, placed her warm hands over his cold cheeks, and kissed him as if everything he had said, all that was scientific and logical, had been so much dross, washed away without effort by what was illogical, ineluctable, and pure.

The kiss made her late for her mother's supper.

"I was worried about you, dear," said Mrs. O'Hara. "It's not like you to be late. I suppose it was extra work she gave you the last minute, that old witch. I suppose now that her dear son is back home, there is all kinds of extra work for you to do."

Neither Fenella nor her mother had ever gotten used to the idea that their roles had been partially reversed, with the daughter earning their daily bread, and the mother reduced to waiting for her child's return from work. After becoming a widow, Sarah O'Hara had worked as a nursemaid, laundress, factory girl. But Mrs. O'Hara, forty-two years old, was no longer a girl. The pain and stiffness of arthritis, and a general neurasthenia, left her wrapped in her shawl in a chair at the window. Fenella knew that the immaculately kept three rooms in which they lived, the freshly washed petticoats, the home-baked bread and home-fired stews, were not the products of an idle woman. But despite all evidence of her mother's energy during the long hours that Fenella was away, once she had returned home, Mrs. O'Hara preferred to do nothing but complain of her fate.

"Do you have the tickets?" asked her mother.

"Of course, Mother." Fenella exhibited them to her, and came close enough to touch her hands to her mother's warm forehead. "How do you feel?"

"I am hopeful. I am full of hope and prayer as always. Perhaps tonight my prayers will be answered."

"I hope you won't place too much hope in this mesmerist, Mother. There are some who do not believe that—"

"I am not interested in your employer's opinion, thank you," interrupted Mrs. O'Hara. "Mrs. Warner gets enough satisfaction having you work for nothing, without my having to listen to her worthless opinions."

"I asked Dr. Warner for his opinion," said Fenella. Sensing the fire start up in her mother, she quickly added: "He is very much improved, and eager for talk. And since the mesmerist is involved with medical work, I thought—"

"Where did you ask him, in your dreams? Or is the wonder worker given the run of the house now?"

"On the porch mostly. In the sun."

"So she exposes you to his presence?"

"He is out of bed, Mother. He is not so sick as all that."

"It is a dangerous disease."

"Mother, he was treating patients with his own hands and none of them—"

"That was months ago. He is just back from a clinic. There are people who want to burn those clinics, just to keep away the contagion. And you work for him. You expose yourself to that risk, for her insulting wages—"

"The wages are generous. I am not so skilled a worker that I can expect—"

"You should be married. Work only leads to more work. I could have married again after your father left us, but I waited too long. And work kills your looks, and soon you lose all chance of marriage. If I had married again, you would never have to work. I would have married a rich man. This time, I would have married a rich man with a big house, and many servants. I learned my lesson well thanks to Brian O'Hara. Not a penny did he leave me, and I had to ruin my looks just to get us enough to eat. You would have had gentlemen calling on you if I had married again, instead of washing floors for a witch and her wonder-working contagious son—"

"Mother, you should not make yourself so heated."

"I am heated, I cannot help it. It is not pleasant for me to contemplate the rest of your life as a housekeeper."

"I do not plan—"

"No, you do not," said Mrs. O'Hara. "You do not plan at all. There are gentlemen in church every Sunday nearly breaking their necks turning to get a glimpse of you."

"Mother—"

"And do you let me introduce you? No. Do you act with any ordinary civility when one comes over to the two of us to wish us well on the Sabbath? No. You are too busy dreaming. You are far too busy looking over at that half-dead consumptive's mother you work for. Just in case she might have a word for you from her dear son. Tell you if he coughed up blood in his handkerchief or in his special little porcelain bowl."

"Mother—" she began again, but stopped herself short of

fighting her mother's anger with her own sense of despair. Just minutes before, Fenella had allowed herself to be happy, to find contentment in the moment in which he had returned her kiss with a burst of hope, a tiny resurgence of the will to live. It was not in her nature to balance the hurt her mother had caused by attempting to wound her in return. Besides, in half a moment her mother would be apologizing for going too far.

"I'm sorry," said Mrs. O'Hara.

"I know."

"I worry about you is all I mean to say." Fenella had crossed the little room and placed the leftovers from the Warners' midday dinner on a side table.

"I didn't mean to be sharp with you."

"Perhaps you should come to the table now, Mother."

"It's the pain talking, not me." She got up from the chair with a potpourri of groans and grimaces. "It's moved up to my neck. All the way from the thigh in one day. It's like I've got a cross-country railroad line, running up and down, right through me." The pain seemed to travel mysteriously through her body, motivated by changes in the weather, news of advances made by the abolitionists, or favorable talk about anything or anyone in the Warner household.

"No matter what Dr. Warner said," said Fenella, "I have a good feeling about the mesmerist. I truly hope that he will be able to help you."

Her mother, though pleased to hear her contradict the young doctor, would not be pleased to know why Fenella was so sanguine about the lecture for which they would soon be leaving. In Fenella's dream of a tall man with flamboyant gestures, she had seen him quite clearly wave his hands over her mother and make her well. But her mother would reject anything Fenella received from a dream, even if it were the simplest song, the gentlest touch, the kindest word.

"Would you like a hot towel, Mother?" asked Fenella.

"No, you're tired," said Mrs. O'Hara, reaching up to her neck with a plaintive sigh, as Fenella opened the satchel of carefully wrapped food left over from the Warners' dinner. Mrs. O'Hara sat down at the table where she had long since prepared plates, knives, forks, a cold salad of potatoes and apples, and a large pitcher of water and lime juice, and watched her daughter remove cold slices of roast beef, a half loaf of bread, and a white cheddar cheese sweating in its cloth. When Fenella had finished placing it all into the plates, she came around behind her mother and touched her hands to her neck.

"I assume this is more of Mrs. Warner's charity?" said Mrs. O'Hara, before Fenella had a chance to start massaging away the pain.

"It is not charity, Mother," said Fenella, determined to keep her words even, her temper mild. She began to knead into the taut flesh beneath her fingers, and shut her eyes, letting easy breaths calm her spirit.

"Lower, my dear. I'm sorry, but your hands are altogether in the wrong place."

Fenella moved her hands imperceptibly lower, continuing to slowly work at the tight muscles in her mother's long and elegant neck. "It is not charity when Mrs. Warner and myself have a specific arrangement about any food that is left over from dinner," she said. "It is an arrangement that suits me very well, since the food is fresh and good, and I cook it myself, the same day. Why shouldn't we eat what the Warners eat?"

"Why should we eat scraps from anybody's table?" said her mother, her muscles tightening under Fenella's hands.

"It is just a different way of being paid, Mother. I could ask for more money every week, instead I prefer—"

"You should ask for more money," said her mother. Awkwardly, she turned about, so that her feverish black eyes rested on her daughter. "It is a hazard working there."

Fenella dropped her hands from her mother's neck. "We had better hurry up and eat our supper," she said.

"It's a deathly disease. If you insist on working there, you should demand greater compensation. That would be the proper way of doing things. If *those* people had any consideration."

Fenella took a bite of the cold beef, then another of her mother's salad. She drank the mixture of water and lime juice. "Aren't you going to eat, Mother?"

Mrs. O'Hara cut a piece of Mrs. Warner's cheddar cheese, and bit into it as if it were a poison she had been sentenced to consume. "I only worry as a mother worries. As she worries for her son, I worry for my daughter. The disease is contagious. They quarantine the sick, don't they?"

"He is going to be better," said Fenella. "He is not so bad, and he is going to be better."

"Why?" said her mother, taking a large bite of Mrs. Warner's beef, and continuing her question as she chewed: "Did you have a dream about it? Is he going to get well and carry you away on a white horse?" Mrs. O'Hara put down her fork. "This is what I mean about paying attention, being polite in church, not dreaming all the time. There are men who would love to marry you, but not that woman's son. You're their housekeeper and she thinks they're too good to even say hello to us on a Sunday."

Fenella asked her mother if she could cut her another slice of the heavy bread. "I baked it this morning," said Fenella.

"It's good. I taught you how, didn't I?" Her mother took a bite, chewed carefully, as if remembering and savoring the ingredients. But then she remembered another indignity that had been thrust upon her by the Warners. "At least there's a disease he's heard of. He can't do anything for it, but he's certainly heard of it. It's got a name, and it's in his books. Consumption."

"Please, Mother," said Fenella. "I would like it if we stopped speaking about this."

"I saw it coming. I told you a long time ago, to watch what you're feeling around that young man. He always had that look, like he's not long for the world."

"Please, Mother. I know you mean no harm, but it is difficult for me to stay at the table with this kind of talk."

"What kind of talk?" asked Mrs. O'Hara, biting into another hunk of beef. "What am I saying that's not true? You work for a house that's got a doctor living in it who's carrying contagious germs, and I'm telling you it's not good."

"It will be good," insisted Fenella. She had twice that day found herself drifting into dark reveries, feeling herself drawn deep into a cold place, where the air was thin, and the wind shook bleak and wintry trees. When she had waxed the oak floor of his waiting room, she imagined for a moment that she was scrubbing vainly at bloodstains, impossible to erase. When she had driven the hot iron across the back of one of his white linen shirts, she heard his voice cry out, as if the burning metal had come in contact with his bare skin. These were not omens, but dreams; and Fenella knew that her dreams were connections to her spirit, and her spirit was connected to the source that knows all things.

"It will be good when you're married and out of that place."

"Excuse me," said Fenella, getting to her feet, touching her mother's shoulders briefly so that she would know she was not angry. She needed to clear the specter of consumption running through her heart. It was not the first time that she had heard her mother refer to the too-thin, too-pale Robert as a likely fatality of the disease that had felled his own father. Fenella had always disregarded this, refusing to let the thought sit in her mind.

"Where are you going?"

"I must change," said Fenella, breaking the contact with her mother's flesh, and stepping quickly away into the next room. Mrs. O'Hara called after her, protesting that she had not finished her supper. But Fenella had suddenly found it too painful to stay close to her mother; she needed to wash her hands of their bodily contact. This was not because of her mother's constant complaints, nor because of her ill will toward her employer, nor even because of the repeated reminders that Robert was sick with a deathly and irreversible disease. It was simply the overwhelming regret of being close enough for their skins to touch, yet feel that their spirits were separated by a barrier stronger than stone or steel.

Fenella knew that no amount of kindnesses, no superior technique of massage, no eagerness on her part to greet eligible bachelors at the close of church services would do much of anything to alleviate her mother's problem. When her mother felt pain, it was the pain of a spirit wanting to be free of confusion, not a body needing a lighter touch. When her mother cried out in the night, it was not for want of suitors for Fenella, but for the love of her life that had been shattered by fate. Fenella could embrace her mother with her arms, but whatever part of her spirit rushed up to meet her mother's pain was met by a self-enclosed shell of anger and frustration.

"I don't want to keep you waiting, Mother," Fenella called out as she changed from her maid's uniform. "There will be a large crowd at the Lyceum."

"There can't be a large crowd. It only seats three hundred. A thousand is a large crowd. You don't remember that my parents lived in Boston, do you? In Boston they have lecture halls that seat two thousand, and the gaslights make it bright as day. As bright as day."

Fenella smiled at the talk of Boston, feeling the weight of her mother's woes dissipate as she spoke of things bright and large and beautiful. When Mrs. O'Hara carried on about the relations Fenella had never seen and scarcely believed to have existed, it was almost like the dreams she herself entered as simply as opening an unlocked door. Still, Fenella knew that her mother's talk of rich relations led only to attacks on her father's Irishness, whose nationality had cut her mother off from all the riches and glories of the mythical Grahams.

"There are gaslights in the Lyceum too, Mother."

"It's dark, and the candles drip, and the seats have broken slats. It's a wonder the mesmerist is coming here at all."

"Dr. Warner says they'll come anywhere there's people willing to pay," said Fenella. "He says we're wasting hard-earned money, and that we shouldn't trust anything we see with our own eyes, because it's all fake, like a play in the theater."

"He's so smart, your Dr. Warner," said Mrs. O'Hara. "He thinks everything is fake. Everything I tell him about my condition is all in my head, he says. All in my head, and I can't even move my arm half the day. He just don't know what to give me for it. Even that German barber knows more. Even the Jew peddler with the castor oil knows more. He's too grand is what your Dr. Warner is," she concluded.

"He means well, Mother," said Fenella. "He doesn't want us to be tricked is all."

"You're their housekeeper, not their nigger idiot. I won't have them looking down on you because you're Irish. Telling you the mesmerist is a fake! Has he even seen a mesmerist? No wonder he's an abolitionist. Everything in my head! He's not even thirty years old—"

"Thirty-one, Mother," corrected Fenella.

"Never had any patients! Even before he got too sick to work. And no wonder! He doesn't believe anyone is sick, until they fall down and drop dead at his feet."

There was no question of her mother falling down and dying that night. When Fenella was dressed, she found the table cleared and cleaned. Mrs. O'Hara's shawl was in place, and she took hold of Fenella's elbow not for support, but to quicken her daughter's pace.

The local newspaper had reprinted a long story from a Boston journal, detailing the fantastic cures of a European mesmerist "magnetising" Americans from all walks of life. Doctors less skeptical than young Dr. Warner had corroborated in print the evidence of their own eyes: The mesmerist had cured rheumatism, stammering, epilepsy. He had, Mrs. O'Hara had read, "magnestised" his patients, using the vital force mesmerists called "animal magnetism"—an invisible fluid present in all living things. Somehow, the mesmerist was able to transfer his animal magnetism into the body of his patients, thereby placing them into a sleeplike state, during which time a cure of their ailments was possible.

"Animal magnetism" had been the great discovery of the Austrian physician Franz Anton Mesmer—hence "mesmerists" —late in the last century, a discovery that had undergone serious modifications before reaching America. For Franz Anton Mesmer, what was important about his cures was the transfer of the invisible fluids from "magnetiser" to subject. For the mesmerists of America, what was important was the somnambulistic state: Mesmer's theories about the physical movement of unseen fluids that would restore the equilibrium of a patient's animal magnetism with an influx of the magnetiser's own renewable vital force were ignored.

Mesmerists were concerned with the action of the mind upon the body's vital principle. Even the term *mesmerist* was being abandoned by some practitioners. Some used the new term *hypnotist*, but many others preferred to refer to themselves as practitioners of "mind cure," or of the "science of life." Indeed many mesmerists who still used the old term were less interested in curing anyone than entertaining the large audiences who came to see them put their pretty assistants to sleep.

Robert had warned Fenella that mesmerists traveled with professional somnambulists, all of whom were quick to fake trances for the gullible audience. Hadn't the Lyceum already sold tickets that same year for lectures on the virtues of vapor baths, homeopathy, and phrenology? What on earth did putting someone in a state like sleeping have to do with effecting a cure? he had demanded, the violence of his condemnation out of character for a man of such gentle understanding. But of course she understood this violence: He would have liked to believe in the possibility of a cure, but could not, held in chains by a hundred books and theories.

Leaving their home, Mrs. O'Hara clutched Fenella's arm with force. She looked neither right nor left as they turned from the waterfront onto the dirt path leading out of Irishtown and its closely packed inhabitants—now more German than Irish, but still an immigrants' quarter of a xenophobic town. No one cared that Mrs. O'Hara hated the people who lived around her. In spite of what she thought, they considered Brian O'Hara's widow one of their own, another casualty of the rich Yankees who exploited them in their mills, on their ships, working their docks. Some shouted greetings to Fenella under the quickly darkening sky, but most were content to wave or nod, not wishing to intrude upon the intimacy of mother and daughter, walking arm in arm.

Fenella tried to concentrate on a hundred things about her: on the laundry blowing in the light wind, on her mother's easy breathing, on the crush of dead twigs in the dirt road beneath their feet, on the myriad colors and sounds and smells blowing at them from every shanty and shack. It was only by thus splitting her concentration that she was sometimes able to forestall a sudden entry to her private place, to a dream that would pave the ground on which she walked with nothing less than gold.

"I wonder if he will be as good as they say," said Fenella, trying to stop the steady, monotonous beating of the blood in her veins. Her mother answered her, but Fenella was already losing herself, hearing the rhythmic pulse like a drumbeat calling for a dream. She did not let herself dream deeply, so that she could see and hear everything about her; but she paid nothing much attention. Her dream state pointed her, concentrated her thoughts on her goal, and her goal was the Lyceum, where a tall man named Professor Barnard would try and put people into something like the state she was already in. She had already dreamed of this man, had already heard and rejected criticism of his profession by the man she loved. It seemed like all her steps were rehearsed, the path beneath her feet worn smooth by an experience that was already within her.

Approaching Main Street, where the tarred wood planks of the lesser street gave way to cobblestones, Mrs. O'Hara remarked that her stiff knees felt suddenly more supple, as if the very nearness of the mesmerist was already having its beneficial effect.

"Yes," said Fenella with great energy, pulling herself out of her light daydream. She wondered if her mother was not also entering some form of sleeplike state, a state when all pains, all bodily feelings were banished, and one was lighter than air. Perhaps Fenella's own short-lived trance was being experienced by many others on the way to the lecture, all so eager to be put under the mesmerist's power, that they were willingly doing half his work and more.

"Yes, I think it very likely, Mother," said Fenella. "The mesmerist must have enormous personal vitality. It would not be surprising if one felt better just coming close to him."

"It's like when you come close to Dr. Warner," said her mother. "The pain gets worse, because you know he's never going to do anything about it anyway." Mrs. O'Hara smiled, to let her lovestruck daughter know that she was only joking. "I do feel so strangely well. It's like one of your silly dreams."

Fenella would have liked to explain to Robert that what her mother was feeling now was just as real as when she felt pain a few moments earlier. Neither feeling was false, simply because he could not measure it with a medical tool. One day she hoped she could show him how very real a dream could be, real enough to relax the spirit, real enough to allow belief into a heart otherwise closed to hope.

Fenella prayed that she would learn to carry this belief from the world of dreams into the world around them. If the mesmerist could effect a cure of some terrible illness through the power of his mind, she might be able to do the same thing through the power of her dreams. She had many times dreamed of Robert's cure, with no effect on his illness. But perhaps it was Robert who needed to experience this dream. Fenella needed to show him how a dream could bring one into contact with one's own spirit; it was the spirit which needed healing more than any cleaning away of germs in the lungs.

But for Fenella to articulate her feelings about dreams to Robert would be to go far beyond the kiss with which she had shut up his dreary talk of contagion and death. She had never learned how to bring other people along to the place where she traveled, a place she could barely remember save for its warmth, its wonder, its irresistible draw. To talk to him truly of where she went in her dreams would be to open her soul with perfect candor. And such candor could not evade a love that went beyond a kiss for a man who believed himself to be dying, a love that went past her dream of a cabin shared high in the mountain air. Somehow, she dreamed, they would come together; if not as husband and wife, not as earthly lovers, then they would come together as spirits, their love more free, more pure than any fleshly marriage.

"I am glad you feel better, Mother," said Fenella.

A steady stream of villagers were making their way past the wide front porch of the sheriff's residence, past the barbershop and general store, past the law office which had once been the town's two-room schoolhouse, past the bookseller—who sold not only books and periodicals, but train and steamship tickets, and tickets to all events at the Lyceum. Though it was not yet dark, the gas lamps along Main Street were lit, casting a bright haze in dark alleys where the setting summer sun could no longer reach.

Fenella recognized half the people she saw, but exchanged greetings with no one. Her mother's piety at the Congregational Church had brought them few friends from that august congregation; half the eligible bachelors craning their necks for a better view of Fenella on Sunday did so only in the imagination of her mother. It was not simply Fenella's lowly occupation or their residence in Irishtown that made them unwelcome, but Mrs. O'-Hara's bitter demeanor. One was afraid to smile into her face, so instead they laughed at her back.

"I am very hopeful too, Mother," said Fennella. "You must know that I don't agree with everything that Dr. Warner tells me, though I respect him very much."

Even as she said the words, she could see Robert's pale face, always so absorbed in deep thinking, as he moved alongside his mother up the steps to the Lyceum. But this made no sense to her, because her dream had passed, and what she saw was what was before her ordinary senses. This was not a dream, but the doctor and Mrs. Warner close enough to call to through the subdued, excited crowd.

"Please, just a moment, Mother," said Fenella, making a show of fumbling for their tickets. She wondered how he had gathered the strength to leave the comfortable house at the edge of the river. Even if he had been helped into and out of a carriage, he was forced to walk now, forced to breathe the air turgid with an excitement that he must find deplorable. Fenella could not understand why he would go to something he had already determined to condemn, unless he had been suddenly able to feel the power that had pulled her there, that had brought her to a high point of anticipation, as if about to reach a peak from which a thousand miles of country could be seen.

As her mother didn't notice the doctor, Fenella was able to hold back a moment longer, before joining the crowd at the Lyceum door. Sitting in their twelve-and-one-half-cent seats, they might avoid Mrs. Warner and her son, sitting in judgment on poor Professor Barnard, showman and mesmerist.

But suddenly, Fenella smiled.

It was a miracle that Robert had come at all, but he had come, answering the command of some spirit, following the dictates of a fate waxing suddenly benign.

Dr. Robert Warner, Mrs. Sarah O'Hara, Fenella, and nearly three hundred others sat in their seats and waited for the mesmerist. Somehow, Fenella believed, this strange man would change the direction of all their lives.

Chapter 17

*T*HOUGH BORN and bred in the city of Boston, Professor Barnard had never taken a degree from one of that city's fine institutions of learning. He claimed to have spent a year in various European capitals—quite a feat for a man with little financial resources and no knowledge of any foreign tongue—but had somehow managed to return home with degrees, certificates of honor, and an occasionally excellent upper-class British accent.

Addressing the eager small-town audience, Professor Barnard explained that he was neither humbug nor charlatan, but a man as dedicated to the healing arts as any doctor of medicine. Many European mesmerists traveled the American lecture hall circuit—Frenchmen, Englishmen, Germans—some of whom claimed to have taken instruction at the feet of the long-departed Dr. Mesmer himself. Promises were made by these European showmen, said Professor Barnard, and wonderful tricks were exhibited. But of course, that was the European style, while he—British accent notwithstanding—was an American, and would therefore promise nothing.

"I offer you hope, I offer you a chance, I offer you the opportunity to see a somnambulist in a deep magnetic state. But I guarantee no miracles. Many of you will never be able to be magnetised. Many of you who will be able to be magnetised will not be able to be cured of what ails you. I am not a man of supernatural powers. I am simply a channel for that great force that rules the universe."

There were rings on three of the professor's fingers, and as his gesticulating hands fanned the still summer air their cheap stones reflected the gaslight with violence. Fenella, sitting twenty rows back, felt the flashes like explosions of insight. She listened intently, but her concentration was caught not by the words, but by the man's steady rhythm, his sureness of purpose, his eager- ness to share the force that ran from his fingertips in a great invisible shower over the audience. It was not long before she had stopped looking for Robert's dark head of hair somewhere in the front rows of the hall. There was a dream that she was enter- ing, and to step deeper and deeper inside she must exclude everyone and everything from her vision and her thoughts but the mesmerist on stage.

"Simply a channel," repeated Professor Barnard, and as if these words were a special cue, a very pretty young woman in a wide-sleeved white gown entered from the wings.

"That is the somnambulist," whispered Fenella's mother. But Fenella could hear nothing of what her mother said, even if she was dimly aware that she had spoken. Fenella could only concentrate on the words spoken by the mesmerist, and by the professional somnambulist who now stood in his shadow.

"My dear child," said Professor Barnard. "Please turn to the audience and tell them your name."

"My name is Grace," said the young woman, trying not to titter as she spoke. The stage lights seemed to bother her eyes, and beyond her urge to laugh was simple stage fright. Her awk- wardness and lack of solemnity contrasted both with her hieratic costume, and the mesmerist's serious tones. But Fenella knew that fear and awkwardness would be soon dispelled; she could feel the practiced sleepwalker already prepared to take flight into the dream that was always around them.

"Grace, are you presently employed?"

"Yes, sir," she said.

"And what is your employment?"

"You know, sir," she said with a laugh. "I work for you."

"And before you worked for me, did you have another job?"

"Factory girl," said Grace. "I was a factory girl in Hartford."

"But not when you first met me," said the mesmerist.

"No, not when you first met me." Grace stopped her titter- ing, and swallowed, as if gulping down a great miserable lump of the past. Fenella could sense that the girl was longing to be rid of her place on the wrong side of the dream. Grace wanted to enter the dream, to be free. "I was sick. I had the fever, and then I couldn't see."

"You were blind?"

"Yes."

"Are you blind now?"

"Of course I ain't blind, sir."

"How many fingers am I holding up?" asked the mesmerist, holding up four fingers of his left hand.

"Four." Grace, embarrassed to be asked so puerile a question, looked to those members of the audience sitting in the first row. "I ain't blind," she said. "He cured me."

Professor Barnard motioned for Grace to sit in the comfortable chair adjacent to his lectern on the stage, and smiled silently at the expectant audience. Fenella could feel the tightness about the young woman's throat, the squinting muscles about her eyes, the nervous tremors that she hid in laughter at the corners of her mouth all lift away and vanish as Grace fell into the chair.

"This young woman," said Professor Barnard, "was stricken by a disease while working at a yarn factory. She contracted a high fever and nearly died. The doctors discovered that once the fever was broken she was unable to see. They could do nothing about this condition other than to describe it."

The mesmerist smiled wickedly at this point: "Do not think it makes a girl suddenly blind happy to find out that her doctors have examined her and declared her to be blind. She already knows that. She wants to be made well, not diagnosed. Her mother brought her to one of my lectures and later, brought her to my office in Boston, where I treated her and cured her. She was blind, and when I was through with her, she could see."

The mesmerist now turned dramatically, to face the pretty young woman seated in the armchair. The audience watched him in profile as he raised his hands, and began to draw them, one after the other, across her face, not touching her, though he came as close as a few inches from her skin. Most understood that he had begun the famous mesmeric "passes," very much modified since first developed by Franz Anton Mesmer, which would lead an appropriate subject into the "magnetic state."

But the passes were but a part of the ceremony created by the mesmerist for their benefit. Everything from the look in his eyes, to the stance of his booted feet, to the quality of his voice, contributed to the vital force he projected outward. When Professor Barnard spoke, his words were virtually uninflected, a monotonous drone that gave them the quality of ancient, ancestral prayer. Grace was so willing and practiced a subject, that she seemed to Fenella already under the magnetic spell before a single pass of the magnetizer's hands had been made. But the passes had their theatrical effect on the audience; and Fenella imagined that their motion was drawing herself as well as Grace to deeper and deeper levels of trance.

"Because I cured her blindness," he said, "the doctors reversed their earlier diagnosis and decided that she had never been blind after all. Though she couldn't see when they had examined her, they decided that somehow all that had been no illness but only imagination. But I say that often illness comes from imagination, and that imagination is only another word for a disorder of the nervous system. If I cure blindness, and doctors carp and say it was no cure, I care not at all. I care only that this girl can see again.

"My friends," he continued, now moving his hands in unison across Grace's face, his index fingers pointed straight, passing from her eyes to either side of her slackening jaw. "What I am doing now is heightening Grace's innate animal magnetism, her vital force, so that it will be so concentrated that nothing else will exist for her, nothing at all."

With each pass of the mesmerist's hands, her eyes followed the tips of those fingers, as if to lose sight of them was to lose sight of life. "All her external sensibilities will be shut off," he continued in his practiced monotone, "because she will be so concentrated on the flow of my magnetism into hers. So concentrated. She will no longer hear you, even if you were to light a firecracker behind her. She will not even know that you are in this room with her. Only my words will now exist for her. She will hear and obey only what I tell her."

The mesmerist stopped the flow of his talk, and for a moment there was a heavy silence in the house. The occasional coughs and throat-clearings present during the first minutes of the lecture were replaced by a rapt mass concentration. Grace's eyes closed, and for a moment Fenella wondered if the eyes of the three hundred men and women in the hall would close as well.

"You are sleepy, are you not?"

"Yes, sir," said Grace, her words clear and quick, free of self-consciousness. Fenella could feel her free and kindred spirit like a beacon across a dark expanse of sea, like two singers singing the same song in a room filled with alien discord.

"Very sleepy?"

"Yes, sir."

"You are asleep, are you not?"

"Yes, sir," said Grace, her monotonous response not revealing the depths of her happiness at returning to the trance state. She was asleep, but she was awake too; she had power, health, imagination at her command, and only waited for the mesmerist to tell her how to employ her great strength.

Professor Barnard stopped the passes of his hands and turned to the audience, leaving Grace sitting erectly, her eyes closed, in the chair at his side.

"Stand up, Grace," said Professor Barnard, looking straight out into the audience. Next to him, the pretty young woman stood. "Open your eyes, Grace," he said, and as she did this, he added, "and find the pretty girl with the red hair in the back of the audience."

Fenella was not astonished to realize that her dream had been met halfway by that of the mesmerist. For a moment she could feel the concentration of the audience turned about to find her; she recognized her mother's wonder, and Robert's feverish intensity, as if even the mesmerist had set out to haunt him with a vision of the woman he must not have. But quickly she could shut them all out, all their confusions of love and bitterness and disbelief.

Grace opened her eyes, and turned her head slowly from one side of the audience to the other, until she had found Fenella, like a long lost sister, like a friend discovered in a dream. She raised her arm and pointed her finger, and Fenella, without being bidden, found herself getting to her feet. The audience, forgetting for a moment that it was not so very wonderful for a sighted person to be able to point out a young woman with red hair in well-lighted house, took in a collective astonished breath.

"You may sit," said the mesmerist, and both Fenella and Grace returned to their seats. But Fenella felt as if she were floating out of her seat in the back of the house, that her spirit had broken free of her flesh, drawn to the brighter fire of the magnetizer and his subject. "And now you will return to an earlier time, a time when you could not see, not the light of the morning sun, not the hand held in front of your face. You are blind, Grace, are you not?"

"Yes, sir," said the white-gowned somnambulist, and Fenella felt as if walls of darkness had slammed down about her. But she shook off this self-made illusion, and blinking against the stage lights, found herself looking in sad and powerless wonder at Grace's unseeing eyes.

"Stand up," he said, and as Grace stood, Professor Barnard drew a long dagger from a sheath concealed under his frock coat. "Tell me, Grace, what do I have in my hand?"

"I cannot see, sir."

"You cannot see what I have in my hand?" he said, moving closer to where she stood, the dagger pointed at her heart.

"I am blind, sir," said Grace.

"But you hear me well enough? You are not deaf, are you?"

"I hear you perfectly, sir," said Grace.

"Come closer," said Professor Barnard. "Come to me." As the young woman turned to the sound of the voice and took a step close to the point of the dagger's blade, a man's voice from the audience shouted a warning:

"Look out, miss!" he said, and after a moment's hesitation, a sudden explosion of laughter burst from the crowd.

But just as suddenly as the laughter had started, it stopped, as if caught up in one monstrous throat.

The somnambulist, eyes open, unseeing, was continuing her walk into the extended blade.

"Closer," repeated the mesmerist, quietly raising the dagger so that it was no longer at the level of her belly, but was instead pointed directly at her face. Fenella knew that the mesmerist would not allow his somnambulist to impale herself, as she knew that the somnambulist would continue to walk blindly in any direction she was told. That Grace could not see was clear to Fenella; just as the fact that what the mesmerist had performed in returning her to her blindness, he could perform in reverse, and return her once more to wholeness. This was more than Fenella could do, except within the confines of her dream world. But here was a dream that walked, a dream that could make true what one wished.

"Stop," said Professor Barnard, when Grace's face was six

inches from the blade. Grace stopped, her eyes level with the dagger, but seeing nothing. "What do you see?"

"Nothing, sir," she said, her voice steady and without any fear.

"What do you see, girl?" said the mesmerist sharply, bringing the knifepoint still closer to her eyes.

"Nothing, sir."

"Close your eyes, girl," said Professor Barnard, holding the dagger steady. "When you open your eyes, you will no longer be blind, you will be able to see clearly, as clearly as you have ever been able to see." Fenella held her breath as the mesmerist nodded his head once, as if to measure a moment of time. "Open your eyes," he said.

Grace opened her eyes, and Fenella felt with her the rush back to health and light. It was as if a thick shell, strong as adamant, had been cracked open with a single magical phrase. But there was no magic involved, unless what was natural to man's spirit must needs be considered magic to fight back the fear of what can never be fully known. Grace saw the threatening blade, but made no motion, expressed no other surprise than the parting of her lips to let in a breath of air. Yet a miracle had taken place, and Fenella concentrated yet more deeply, wanting the secret: She needed to know how to bring the dream past the darkness, into what was real.

"What do you see?"

"A knife, sir."

"Stand back, Grace," he said, returning the blade to his sheath. "Close your eyes. Now open them once again. How many fingers do I hold up?"

"Five, sir."

"Sit down, Grace." As his white-gowned assistant regained the armchair, he continued to address her, but turned his face to the audience, as if to stop any beginnings of skepticism on their part. "Close your eyes. You are feeling tired, aren't you?"

"Yes, sir," said Grace, almost greedy with eagerness to be driven further into the trance. Fenella let go her wondering, allowing the mesmerist's words to take her along with Grace.

"Your hands are heavy, and they are resting heavily on your legs. But your legs are heavy. And your feet are heavy. You are so heavy, that nothing could get you to stand up. All your weight is pulling you into the chair, and the chair itself is being pulled deep into the ground. Deep into the ground. Let your body sleep, even as your vital spirit rises. Let your eyes open, but only to see what I shall bid you to find. Let your body sleep, and let your spirit rise over the crowd."

Fenella found herself smiling inwardly, as if a warm bath of air had suddenly washed against her innermost parts. She had always had the ability to lose herself in a dream, even when in a crowd. But always she had held a hand onto the door that led back to awareness. There was always a crack of light she could see, even in her deepest daydreams, so that when a shout or a touch or an image called her back to the world, she would know the way back.

But now she let go completely.

She needed no one to show her the way back, because she had not entered a dream of her own device, but simply followed the path set out for her by the mesmerist; and he would take her back as surely as he had returned the gift of sight to Grace.

She had heard him tell Grace to let her spirit soar over the crowd, and from deep within her warm, immobile body, she could feel swift currents, alternately hot and cold, and with them, see bright flashes against the inside of her shut eyes. She wondered if what she was experiencing was the entry of the mesmerist's animal magnetism into her body, if it was this invisible fluid that numbed her to the world, leaving her spirit free. Fenella felt as if she could look down upon the masses of quiet heads, all turned anxiously to the stage, yet be aware at the same time of the bodies sitting about her. It was as if her spirit could fly up to the candle-bright chandeliers of the lecture hall, then down to the stage floor, close to the mesmerist's scintillating rings, then off through the roof into the clear night air.

"Let your spirit soar over the crowd," repeated the mesmerist, as if reining Fenella in from more frivolous activity. And Fenella at once found herself looking down over the massed heads, not with the simple organ of sight, but with the eyes of her spirit.

These eyes, this vantage point was as frightening as it was powerful.

Below her the vision of heads was limned with sorrow. Beyond every trivial reason for attending the mesmerist's lecture was a secret hope, and with it, hope's obverse, despair. Fenella

could sense the sicknesses that lingered, the seeds of others waiting to be born. Below her were barren wombs, crippled limbs,
stuttering lips. Mothers had come to turn about the death of a
child; children were there to let magic fill frail bodies with the
strength of life. She could feel her mother's pain, one among so
many others, demanding to be assuaged.

And then she witnessed something else, something she had
hoped never to see: Bloodred and horrible, fiery lines of destruc-
tin threatened the body of Dr. Robert Warner. A baleful force was
encroaching upon him, belittling his knowledge, his calling, with
the awful power of nature.

"Robert," she said in a soundless voice that rang against the
walls of her heart. "Robert, please." Fenella had something to
ask of him, something that would let him rid himself of all that
was bad within the shell of his body. But she couldn't think of
the words, couldn't imagine how to approach him from her seat
in the back of the audience. "Robert, you must be well. You must
not be sick. You must not." Pulled toward the man she loved,
she had begun to edge out of the far-seeing dream. She could
sense her mother's concern, feel the touch of her cold hand on
her wrist. But she could not stop and reassure her mother that
she was all right. She must try and reenter the dream, where her
spirit would soar, where she could speak to Robert simply by
opening her heart. "Robert, you must open your eyes. You must
stop imagining that you are going to die, because it is what you
imagine that will kill you."

But what Robert imagined was already made real. Fenella
felt the pressure of her mother's hand on her wrist diminish to
nothing, heard the murmuring voices of the crowd no more.
Once again she could sense her beloved's pain, she could touch
the fever behind his eyes, could suffer the congestion in his
lungs. He was sick, and growing sicker, and she must help him,
she must allow him to see that he could live.

But she did not know how to do this, her body marooned in
a back-row chair, her spirit high in the air, but without any power
except to dream. For a moment, Fenella's hard core of hope weakened with frustration. Fear entered her heart, and it seemed that
she might crash to the earth, spirit meeting body in a sudden
brutal awakening.

But then the measured sound of the mesmerist reached her

and quieted her. She found herself growing tranquil, raising her body's eyes to his head, higher than all the others, gravely turning from side to side, explaining to the crowd that Grace, in her magnetic state, would now be called upon to help the sick, even as she was once sick.

Fenella retreated from despair, holding on to her place in the dream. She would not think of Robert, but only of the magic before her. There was an answer, and she would find it if only she could be still enough to hear.

"Do not think that your illnesses are too desperate for cure, or if not cure, then at least, amelioration," said Professor Barnard. "What the doctors call fakery, or imagination, I call nervous disorder. And who in this audience," he demanded, pulling at his flamboyant red silk tie, "can possibly think himself free of nervous afflictions in this year of our Lord 1855? When else has there been so much noise and chaos, so much fanaticism in religion and politics, so much change in the way men work with their hands?"

Fenella understood that the mesmerist's words were an exhortation, a suggestive bidding to the audience to open their hearts to the possibility of belief, for without belief there can never be a cure. All about the room she could feel Professor Barnard's words wash over the sick and disappointed, the lost and the searching, like an inspiration. She felt herself battening on what she had always known, because hearing it from another soul was a corroboration, a joining together of energies.

But not everyone was prepared to be inspired. She tried to send her spirit to Robert, lower it over him like a passionate ghost. But she did not know how to do this, did not know if such a thing was possible. She was still outside of the man she loved, looking in on his anger, on his need not to believe.

In her trance, she had the sudden wondering insight that her attraction to him might have been at least in part the attraction of a child for a wounded bird. But the bird was not in her hand, neither was it allowing itself to be helped by any other. Robert had come to the lecture hall so that he could decry what he had seen on the morrow; surely his anger at the mesmerist was now the anger of a man who had been disappointed by his enemy. Expecting a silly show, he had gotten a show and something more, something undeniably spiritual. This was what he fought now, tooth and nail, refusing to allow himself the luxury of imagination.

"Our human brains were never meant to work our bodies like machines," said Professor Barnard. "Our human bodies were never meant to ride railroad trains, to work at steam engines and spinning jennies. Our nervous systems were never meant to get messages from telegraphs, to read about wars and catastrophes all over the world, to have our families split up to find land on the other side of the Continent. It is no wonder if we are out of balance, if we suffer from nervous exhaustion. Will slavery be abolished and free blacks overrun the North? Will there be a war between the states? Will Americans be outnumbered by immigrants in their own country?"

Here Professor Barnard lowered his hands and placed them over his heart. "We worry, isn't that right? We don't know where we're going, why we want to go there, and what will become of us when we get there. Whatever we have of the vital force is depleted, enervated, incomplete. That is why so many of us are sick."

Fenella could feel an urgent conflict rising not only from Robert, but from the crowd at large. A need to believe in what was said, fought an equivalent need to call it all humbug. While the sick wanted to be helped, they didn't want to be blamed for their illness; to believe that one's own worries, fears, tensions had created disease was to accept a responsibility that most members of the audience had learned to give to others.

"Grace, you will now rise and help whoever first comes forward," said Professor Barnard.

Fenella felt her heart suddenly begin to race, as if called upon to lift a great weight, or run a swift race. Suddenly, anything was possible. The world had not been destroyed by plague or smallpox, neither would tuberculosis kill forever. She knew herself to be as firmly entrenched in this dream as Grace, and therefore as responsible as she for the healing that would take place. If Dr. Robert Warner was sick, he would learn to step forward and acknowledge his fear; through her love she would help him to belief and to healing.

But it was not Robert, but Fenella's mother who was the first one to get to her feet and hurry forward.

Saying nothing to her daughter, Mrs. Sarah O'Hara reached

out both hands toward the stage, as if to pull down the healing Professor Barnard had offered.

But then Fenella heard her mother shout words that belied her intentions: "Blasphemy," she said. "Nothing but lies and blasphemy. God sickens and God heals, and only God knows why we live and die. Only God."

Fenella wanted to lift her own body out of the chair, and go swiftly forward, to take her mother's arm in hers, and to explain to the mesmerist and his somnambulist assistant that her mother meant nothing of what she said, that she wanted their help, that she believed in it, that she had already felt better upon approaching the place of the lecture.

But Fenella couldn't move the muscles of her legs, nor could she open her mouth to raise a shout. She remained entranced, disembodied, listening to her mother rave, until the burly young sheriff, seated in the Lyceum's front row, took hold of her at the foot of the stage.

"Let go of her, sir," said Professor Barnard.

"Only God!" shouted Sarah O'Hara.

"You will let her go," said the mesmerist, speaking softly, his eyes leveled on Fenella's mother. She was not surprised when the sheriff released her, nor even when she discovered that her own entranced body had stalked forward, following in her mother's path.

"Come forward, madame," said Professor Barnard, who was used to the conflicted urgings of the sick. "You will be well."

"Only God," repeated Mrs. O'Hara but this time her words were quieter, as her eyes found the steps to the raised stage from which the mesmerist addressed the crowd. Without waiting for another word from the mesmerist, Mrs. O'Hara climbed the steps, and allowed Grace to assist her gently to the armchair. Her anger had passed. Fenella, standing in the aisle near the front of the stage, could feel, for the first time in her life, her mother reaching out for the solace of a dream.

"Look at Grace, madame," said the mesmerist, and Fenella watched as the somnambulist carefully waved her hands up and down in front of her mother's shining eyes. "You are growing tired, but still you will continue to look at Grace, you will continue to keep your eyes open, even though they grow heavy. Heavy. You are sleepy, are you not?"

"Yes, sir."

"You may close your eyes. You may sleep. Sleep."

Fenella smiled, feeling a peaceful spirit descend over her mother, even as she herself drifted more deeply into trance. Grace could sense every pain, every complaint in the woman's body. Fenella imagined that she could feel whatever Grace felt. As Grace examined her mother's body, Fenella felt the sharp rush of fire before each stiff joint, before the tightness in her neck, the dull ache in the small of her back. But these ills were already diminishing. Just the touch of the somnambulist was beginning the healing of Fenella's mother.

Standing stiffly in the aisle, Fenella's shut eyes absorbed a radiant rainbow, each band of color winding like party ribbons through her shining spirit. She could imagine Grace, deep in trance, following Professor Barnard's directions: how the somnambulist touched her mother's eyelids and softly suggested that all the pain in Mrs. O'Hara's body was there, behind the shut lids; how all mother need do was blink, so that Grace could catch the sickness in the palms of her hand, and let it burn away to nothing.

"You may blink, madame," said the mesmerist, and as her mother did as she was told, Fenella felt all the colors in her heart brighten with an almost unbearable intensity. Fenella's palms shook as if from a great weight, and then a moment later this weight was replaced by a terrible burning sensation. The flesh of her palms felt as if scalded with water boiling for the wash.

"You may shut your eyes, madame," continued the mesmerist. "Your illness is gone from your body, gone to another's hands. You can feel that it has gone, can you not?"

"Yes, sir," said Mrs. O'Hara.

"You can feel that it is burning up, gone forever?"

"Yes. Yes. I can feel it burning."

"When you open your eyes, you will be awake. When you open your eyes, you will be awake, and you will be well." The mesmerist paused a moment, and commanded Mrs. O'Hara to wake. Then he asked her whether she had any pain.

"No," said Mrs. O'Hara, without hesitation. "I feel well." She moved her arms overhead, she bent her stiff elbows, she flexed her arthritic fists with wonder. "I feel very well indeed. Look, I don't feel any pain. It's a miracle."

"It is not a miracle," said Professor Barnard with a great smile. "It is simply the science of mind cure. It's nothing but the transfer of animal magnetism—"

But it was at that moment that Mrs. O'Hara, newly freed from her ills, noticed her daughter looking up at the stage.

"Fenella, what's wrong?" she interrupted, looking down in horror at the entranced face. Beyond the blissfulness in Fenella's eyes was a pain, shining through her smile like a martyr about to claim his heavenly reward. "What's wrong with her?" she demanded of the man who had just healed her. "What did you do? Did you do something to Fenella?"

"Oh, don't worry, madame," said Professor Barnard, looking at Fenella with a superior grin. Another voice came at her then, familiar and dear, but not part of the dream. She listened to the mesmerist, as someone else took hold of her. "It is not unusual for a member of the audience to be magnetized during a demonstration," said Professor Barnard, "particularly if they have good natural ability—"

But then she found herself turning to another voice, the familiar voice, the voice of the beloved for whom this trance would be a vague beginning to a new way of looking at the world. "Her hands," said Robert, "what on earth happened to her hands?" But suddenly, Fenella found herself moving forward, away from Robert's touch, up the steps to the stage, responding to the mesmerist's command. She lost even a vague awareness of the audience, of her frightened mother, of a wonder-struck Robert all crowding about her; as soon as the mesmerist gently placed the thumbs and index fingers of both hands against the interior corners of her eyes, it was as if she existed for him alone.

"Do you hear me, dear girl?" said the mesmerist.

"Yes, sir."

Moving his fingers about the orbits of her eyes, Professor Barnard slowly said, "When you wake, you will have no pain in your hands. When you wake you will have no pain, and no memory of pain, and wherever you are burnt will quickly heal." Lightly, he pressed against the edge of the bones of the eye sockets. "Wake," he said.

Fanella woke at once, opening her eyes to the concern about her. "Mother," she said. "You are well! It is a miracle!"

But no one in the audience would remember the healing of

Sarah O'Hara as the miracle of the evening. The miracle was the discovery of a new deep trance somnambulist. Fenella was so suggestible that the flesh of her palms—responding to the mesmerist's suggestion that her mother's illness was being burned in the somnambulist's hands—had been burned as surely as if held to flaming torches.

But even if the evidence of Fenella's burns had convinced Dr. Robert Warner of the reality of the magnetic state, even if her mother's aches and pains had suddenly diminished to nothing, even if she had seen that mesmerism granted her power far greater than her capacity to dream, Fenella was not convinced that her hands had been burned simply by the power of her imagination. She would go to Professor Barnard and learn from him, take a job as his assistant so that she might learn to heal even as he healed. But no one could make her believe that what her mother had suffered from was simply an overwrought imagination. As surely as her father had died, his body left to decompose in a pine coffin under six feet of earth, so had her mother's spirit twisted her body into pain and despair.

This spirt was not a metaphor, not another word for a thought without substance driven into the air. What Fenella had held in her hands had not been an illusion caught from her mother's fancy, but the hateful illness itself. This was what she had burned: not with imagination alone, but with her spirit.

Fenella was lucky enough to have discovered her calling, and no longer saw the series of steps that would make up her future as fortuitous, both out of her control and unimportant to man and God. What she would learn from the mesmerist would not simply allow her to fight the nervousness of their time, the diseases wrought by discontent and dissolution, but all disease, all illness.

And even though Dr. Robert Warner had inherited the black seeds of consumption, she would fight this illness until it too burned away to nothing in her hands.

Chapter 18

THE NEXT DAY Fenella failed to wake at sunrise. Mrs. O'Hara let her sleep until nearly eight o'clock, then brought her a strong cup of tea into which she had spooned honey and milk.

"You had better get up, Fenella," said her mother. "He will be wanting to see you." Fenella opened her eyes, wondering for a moment why her mother was waking her, as Mrs. O'Hara was usually still asleep when she hurried off to work. But this question slipped away against a more urgent occupation: trying to hang on to the dream she had slept with, a dream that confused the events of the night before with that same night's phantoms and visions.

"Mother, thank you," said Fenella, raising her head and looking at the tea as if it were a gift of diamonds. Not since she had been a small child, reluctant to face the schoolday's taunts and tribulations, had she been offered such a rich treat while still in bed.

"Come on, child, enough dreaming," said her mother, as if somehow in the night their roles had been once again reversed, and it was now Mrs. O'Hara who would see to the efficient running of their lives.

"Last night," said Fenella, "that was not only a dream."

"Of course it was not a dream," said her mother. "For once you were not dreaming. That's why he wants to see you."

Fenella stopped herself from explaining that her mother was partially right, partially wrong. If it were not for her dreaming, last night would never have happened at all. But her mother was right in thinking that the events at the Lyceum had occurred in the real world. Fenella remembered that the man she loved had held her hand in his, had seen to it that she had gotten safely home; the man she loved cared for her. Like a little child, Fenella took a sip of tea from the cup in her mother's hands.

"Who wants to see me?" she said.

"Professor Barnard," said Mrs. O'Hara. "The man who cured me last night. The man who is a true doctor."

"What time is it?" said Fenella, and when she had been told, she grew quickly upset, as Mrs. Warner expected her daily at seven o'clock.

"If the truth be told, there is a little bad feeling coming back into my knuckles," said Mrs. O'Hara. "But the night was, after all, very damp, and I have only been magnetized once. I still move a hundred times better than yesterday. I can only hope that he will take me on as a patient."

"Why does he want to see me?" said Fenella, dressing with speed for her day's work.

"There is no need to hurry," said her mother. "Professor Barnard said to let them sleep till nine o'clock. And no one is at home at the Warners'."

"What do you mean? Why is no one—"

"Drink some tea, and I will tell you. You need to fortify yourself, girl. Look at this, look what your old mother can do." With a wide smile to cover her partial discomfort, Mrs. O'Hara moved the teacup up and down, over her head, and behind her back, exhibiting the flexibility of her elbows and hands and wrists as she had for the mesmerist the night before.

"Mother, I'm happy that you feel so well, but please tell me—"

"Drink, please. No one can deny the impression you made last night, but one needs strength to be able to go up on the stage."

Fenella took hold of the moving teacup. "Why is no one at home at the Warners'?" said Fenella. "Is something wrong with Robert? Please tell me, Mother. Please tell me at once."

Even as her mother began to speak out her answer, she could feel, like a wave of sympathetic pain, the sickness rising in his wasted body. Robert had rushed to her side last night, had held her hands, had helped her out into the fresh air. He had insisted that she take the carriage waiting outside the Lyceum for himself and his mother, had put his hands on her shoulders, as if afraid she might fall down. But she had been more concerned with giving him a message of health. She was tired, she told him, but not sick; her hands had been burned, but the mesmerist had taken away the pain.

"You see, Robert," she had said in front of Mrs. Warner. "Anything is possible."

But he had not felt the truth of her words, had instead been assaulted by a thousand suspicions. He had seen an "entranced" Grace's eyelids quivering when her eyes were shut against strong gaslights; he fancied that he could even see the uncomfortable movement of her eyeballs under their shut lids when she was supposed to be in a deep trance "sleep." But even from his seat at the front of the house, he had not been able see whether the pupils of her open eyes dilated and contracted when the mesmerist had returned the somnambulist to her "blind" state; still he was certain that they had, that Grace had been no more or less blind than any trained stage actress.

And he had been angered, not convinced as she had hoped, by the evidence of Fenella's hands.

Trained as a scientist, he knew there was an explanation for what the mesmerist had done to the beautiful young woman to whom, in spite of all sense, he was so attracted. During his years of medical training at the University of Pennsylvania, he had often gone to magic shows far more convincing. The mesmerist had not driven stakes through a body, or made a lion vanish into thin air as they had in the variety theaters of Philadelphia. He was a charlatan getting credit for his inability to perform better tricks; even his evident "amazement" at Fenella's burned hands only added to his luster for the audience.

"You must go home and sleep," Robert had told her, gently helping her into the carriage. He would have liked to rush home for his medical bag and hurry to Fenella's Irishtown house, but knew that her sleep would be more important than any ointment he could apply; that he was only searching for an excuse to look down on her sleeping form, the red hair wild about the pillow.

"But you must tell me that you believe now," Fenella had insisted, and for a moment, he had not understood what she wanted from him. "Tell me that you believe anything is possible."

"Anything, Fenella," he had said, simply to help her leave the excited crowd. Now, upon awaking, Fenella could not remember if she had disbelieved him then, or if it was only during the course of her night's sleep that she realized he had been lying, that in spite of all the evidence before his eyes, his heart was still closed to the power of the spirit.

Fenella's mother repeated herself, because the words hadn't seemed to penetrate: "He took sick last night, right at the lecture. Didn't you see him spitting blood?"

"No," said Fenella, though the image was now clearly before her eyes. "He put us in his carriage." She knew that he had not yet understood that he could let go of the disease, the way one could let go of an incapacitating terror, the way one could blink away tears to clear the vision. He could have gone either way last night, chosen to see in Fenella's hands the mark of the spirit, or to hang on to the blindered logic that kept him married to his illness.

"Mrs. Warner was not very happy about giving you the carriage," said her mother. "Seeing her face was almost as good as getting magnetized. But they didn't come with us to Irishtown. There was another carriage, not their own, and they took that to get him home fast. She sent you a note this morning. Not me, you, as if I don't live here. That's how I know you don't have to hurry on down."

Fenella took it from her mother's hands. "I am taking my son to the clinic in New York on the early train. He asked me to send you this information, so as not to worry. You need not come to work today, as I shall be at my son's side." There was no salutation, and instead of a signature, she had printed in block letters: "Mrs. W." Clearly, she wanted to keep Fenella away from their trouble, away from New York, away from Robert.

But what was just as clear—if not to Robert or his mother, then to Fenella—was that Robert, even as he pushed himself blindly into an acceptance of his death-dealing disease, was reaching out for her help in the only way he knew how: by falling in love with her.

"Your hands, child," said Professor Barnard. "How do they feel this morning?"

"I am sorry to trouble you so early, sir," said Fenella, watching as he lifted a cup of coffee to his full and hungry lips; even this commonplace gesture he seemed to invest with a priestly seriousness. But it was not that early—nearly half past nine— and it was he who had asked Mrs. O'Hara to send her around to see him.

"Is there pain?" he asked.

"I would like to offer my services to you, sir," she answered, rushing out the words, nervously looking at the loudly ticking old clock on the mantel behind the mesmerist's shaggy-haired head, a head too large and imposing for his scrawny neck. Still, in the bright morning light he looked no less commanding and obsessive a figure than he had under the gaslights the night before. His blue eyes sought not her palms but her eyes for the answer to his question, even as he seemed to ignore her impulsive declaration. She wondered if he knew that she had come not to satisfy his curiosity about her abilities as a trance subject, but to take from him everything he knew.

"There is no pain, sir," said Fenella. "And the injury that came so quickly has left quickly too." She picked up her hands, palms thrust forward in front of her face, and exhibited them to the mesmerist without any sense of pride. In his eyes she saw nothing secretive nor prideful; his mastery was only in service to the mesmeric art. She knew that he would help her to learn the path to the place where she had burned away her mother's demons. It was there that she could find a way to help Robert, a way that she would take no matter what burning it would bring her, no matter what pain.

"The burn is gone," he said, the amazement plain in his sonorous voice.

"Yes." Fenella had wondered at the impermanence of the injury. If her mother's arthritic pains returned as quickly as the skin of her palms had healed, the mesmerist's cure would be worth little more than a parlor trick.

Professor Barnard touched the smooth skin with the tip of his right finger. "Grace! Grace, come out here!" he called, looking at Fenella as if he were standing before a precipice of his own design.

The mesmerist had taken a suite of rooms at the town's famous old Blue Turkey Inn, whose pre-Revolutionary War ghosts lent a note of respectability to any traveler, no matter how flam-

boyant or controversial. These rooms were not simply an expensive palliative to the rigors of travel but a necessary adjunct to
Professor Barnard's business. The magnetic cures demonstrated
in public were willingly performed in private for fees that could
only be tolerated in an itinerant wonder-worker.

But in Connecticut, wonder-workers were suspect, travelers
were watched with wary eyes, and men with rings on their
fingers were assumed to be actors or worse. In his rented
hundred-year-old sitting room, seated on a leather upholstered
brass-nailed chair, surrounded by terrible portraits in oil of the
grandparents of the inn's present owner, the Professor became
more familiar, more approachable to those townspeople in need
of his aid. Somehow the great hearth, blackened with age, the
threadbare Turkish carpets and ubiquitous antimacassars miti-
gated the effect of British accent and dandified clothes.

Grace, still chewing on some shred of her breakfast, hurried
into the room in her white gown, ready to begin her morning's
labors by being put to sleep. But she started upon seeing not a
patient, but Fenella.

"What does she want?" she said.

"Take a look at her hands, dear girl," said Professor Barnard.

Grace looked at the hands briefly, swallowing the significant
impression they made, and said: "I was blind, wasn't I?"

"Of course you were, dear girl."

"So she got a burn and it got better," she continued, as if on
trial. "I got eyes now, so I can see that. What else do you want to
show me?"

"Dear girl, you and I have never seen a burn come and go
like this."

"Maybe it was a trick, Professor," said Grace with more than
a little rancor. "It ain't exactly unknown in New England to try
and pull the wool over—"

"Grace," interrupted the mesmerist. "This young woman,
like yourself, seems to have the gift."

"What I'm saying is I got more. She ain't blind, she's perfectly healthy, just had an accident with her hands—a burn, so
what?"

Grace turned to Fenella now, as if the young woman's silence
was deliberately antagonistic. "You think it's easy, don't you?
'Sleeping beauties,' that's what they call us. They think it ain't no

work at all going under like that, day and after day, and late at night, in front of hundreds of people ready to laugh in your face first chance they get. You think it's just a joy being persecuted like you're an abolitionist. Just because you're trying to help somebody who's sick. I mean you gotta charge, don't you? Can you read a watch through your belly?"

"Sit down, Grace," said Professor Barnard, his tone leaving no room for disagreement. Perhaps it was unkind of him to think so, but when his blindfolded somnambulist "read" a watch pressed to her belly twenty minutes after a demonstration that she and everyone else knew to begin at eight o'clock, it was perhaps not remarkable that she could "see" the time—accurate to within ten or fifteen minutes.

Grace sat down across the room from where Fenella stood before the mesmerist in his chair. "I can see things sometimes," she insisted to Fenella. "In places I ain't never been. It's called clairvoyant. You never even heard of it."

"You will be silent," added the mesmerist.

"I ain't magnetized," said Grace. "So I can be allowed to be angry now, can't I? Every time some new girl shows, I got to stay backstage, and that's supposed to be fair?"

"For the last time, Grace," said Professor Barnard. "Silence."

Grace let out a great huff of air, to indicate that her silence was in no way meant to convey acceptance of any new somnam-bulist assistant. As Barnard rose and quietly asked Fenella's per-mission to place her into the magnetic state, Grace's resentment verged on a childish hatred. Though it was untrue that Professor Barnard had ever ushered her backstage for the duration of a demonstration, every time a new deep-trance girl was discovered the mesmerist showed entirely too much excitement, as if she might do something that Grace could not.

There had been that squinty-eyed girl in New Milford, Grace remembered, and the big-nosed widow-woman in Boston, not to mention the too-pretty factory girl from Maine who turned out to be a fake altogether. Well, she had shown all of them. None had lasted more than a few performances, their trances little more significant than that of any first-timer pulled from the audience and made to bark like a dog. Grace knew that the mesmerist wanted something sublime and religious, something that would prove irrefutably that animal magnetism was the most important discovery in the history of the world. If only he could explain to her what he wanted to see happen, she would be more than happy to oblige.

Fenella didn't understand Grace's animosity, any more than she had understood why children had pelted her with mud when she was growing up. Jealousy was foreign to her nature, and she knew how anger burned the spirit as surely as a knife cut the flesh. Fenella wondered how Grace—she whose spirit had soared over the crowd the night before—could not know this.

But soon, she was forced to forget about Grace, forget about the fact that Robert was sick and growing sicker in a clinic in New York, forget about everything but the finger that Professor Barnard held high above her head.

"Look up," he said in his practiced monotone. "Do not raise your head, but only your eyes. Stretch them up to meet the tip of my finger, higher, and higher still."

The way was easy.

"Sleep," he said, and as if this were the command that she had been waiting for all her life, she slept, taking hold of the waiting dream. In a moment, she could feel the wild hot and cold currents she had experienced in the lecture hall, currents that ran through a body suddenly weightless. She relished this freedom of the body, as well the freedom from being forced to choose between a myriad of tasks and concerns. Fenella had only to listen to one voice, and this voice was clear and strong and good.

The voice asked her many questions, and to all of these she answered without hesitation or fear. No, she could not read the time on the watch pressed to her belly. Yes, she remembered the position of the three hundred people in the audience of the Lyceum last night, though she didn't know all their names. No, she could not imagine the length and breadth of New York City, as she had never been there. Yes, she could feel the mesmerist's hand on her arm. No, she could no longer feel his touch, nor the prick of the pin, nor the heat of the match.

"Open your eyes, child," said the voice, "and see only my hands. My hands are moving now, and they are magnetizing you. Your vital spirit is imbued with the magnetic force. With your eyes open, you are insensible to anything but my voice in your ears and my hands moving magnetism into your spirit. Your muscles are growing rigid now. Your mind is floating free of your body. Your spirit is open to the invisible forces in the air. Your sight is now the sight of the spirit, no longer filtered by any ordinary senses. Look into this hand and feel the animal magnetism there. Feel the flowing of the fluid, directly from my spirit to yours. Now speak, when I question. Let the muscles of your mouth and lips and tongue work to answer what I ask. You feel the fluid, do you not?"

"I do," said Fenella, understanding what he meant by "fluid" to be the direction of a powerful light into her spirit, a power that could set her free of all that was stolid and earthly.

"You see my hand, do you not?"

"Yes."

There was a pause before the mesmerist could phrase the next question, and Fenella could feel the wonder behind his words, the wonder and the doubt and the fear. "What do you see?" he said.

"Green."

"Do you mean to say that you see a green fluid?"

"Light. A green light."

"You see my hand in a green light?"

"All about your hand. Through it, and about it, and made up of it. Your hand is green. Your hand is green light."

Fenella could not know how many times before Professor Barnard had magnetized highly suggestible subjects, looking for the truth of animal magnetism, searching for the substance that he knew must be able to be seen from deep within a trance. That Grace could be made blind to a source of light was wonderful surely, but her lack of seriousness, her love of theatrics, always worried the mesmerist. There was after all a sort of trance that an actor enters when before the public. And though Grace had been a factory girl and not an actress, surely her pretty face and eager pliability had let her imagine herself up on the stage boards, earning the applause of the crowd. Grace's desire to be free of her spinning jenny and on exhibit before an admiring public might be more significant to her trance than any magnetic flow. There were many times when Professor Barnard doubted the scenes she claimed to see in her clairvoyant states, wondering if they were the true products of deep trance, or simply ramblings from the cheap romances she devoured. After all, few somnambulists exhibited clairvoyance; and of those he witnessed at lectures and on stage, none had been able to convince him that they had truly reached that state.

But Grace prided herself on being a clairvoyant traveler. She parroted the mesmerist's words back to him, claiming that "direct union with animal magnetism" had given her "lucidity"—a lucidity that he himself had never experienced. He did not like to doubt Grace's word, but even if everything else she told him was completely true, he could never get himself to believe that she had reached the mystical, deepest level of the trance state. Grace had never been able to describe anything about this state when she was in it, and after it was over, she claimed that all the details left her in a violent rush. Professor Barnard felt that anyone who had actually reached the deepest trance level would at least be able to understand what it meant to see with the eyes of the spirit, what it meant to receive emanations without the intervening barriers of the ordinary senses.

And now Fenella O'Hara, magnetized by accident the night before, was already so deeply entranced today, that she seemed to see things that Grace never knew existed. He questioned her fearfully, as if to get her too close to reason would make the visions before her disappear forever.

"Fenella, do you see flesh and blood?"

"No."

"You see only light?"

"Yes."

"But you know it is my hand that you see?"

"Yes." She did not bother to explain that it was his own commands that let her see only the hand, and only through the eyes of the spirit. One value of the trance state was to let go of control, to let him have it, but already, her impatient spirit, having learned to ride fast, was chafing at this too-slow pace. Fenella wanted to go faster, further. This was no investigation into things mystical for her; she had practical need of this knowledge. She began to hear his words as encumbrances that she must get through, so that she may relieve her obligation to him, and go on, at a gallop.

"What does this green color signify?"

"Confusion," said Fenella.

"Why confusion?" said the mesmerist sharply, and waited for an answer that was not forthcoming, until he had taken hold of himself and rephrased the question. "Where is this confusion? Is it anywhere else other than in my hand?"

"It is everywhere in and about you," said Fenella.

"Look at my head," he said, as if to correct her faulty vision, turning her face so that her eyes were level with his. Perhaps his original command to see only the flow of magnetism coming from his hands was restricting the magic of her spirit. "Is there a color that you see here too?"

"Green. And other colors. Red, and orange."

"These are lights as well, not fluids?"

"Lights," said Fenella, and though she had no other bodily sensations due to the trance-induced rigidity of her muscles, she felt a sudden pressure in her ears, as if she were diving deeply into the black-bottomed waterhole behind the town's millhouse.

"Does red have a significance?" she heard the mesmerist ask, understanding his need to know, his urgency not to lose sight of a phenomenon blowing up before his eyes like a ghost on a sunny day. But she had her own urgencies, her own selfish needs, far more important than any worldly concerns of Professor Barnard. Robert's fate depended on her new knowledge; and she felt that the deeper she was entranced, the deeper would be her knowledge.

If there were indeed five levels of trance, as the mesmerist had claimed in his lecture, she had certainly approached the last, and deepest level: past the first level, of uninhibited obedience of the mesmerist's commands; past the second level, of complete insensitivity to the external world of the senses; past the third level, of a sudden rigidity of the muscles as the spirit runs free of its bodily shell; past the fourth level, where the flow of animal magnetism can be discerned in hot and cold currents.

Into the fifth level, the highest, the one most like a dream.

Here time was twisted, one's spirit roamed through space. Places never visited were suddenly emblazoned in memory, thoughts imagined on the other side of the world could be heard in one's mind. At the fifth level of trance the mesmerists claimed subjects could see emanations of colored light, feel waves of magnetic energy, could join with the universal mind and effect miraculous cures.

But these were just words imagined by men who had never traveled as far as she already had that morning. Emanations, waves, fluids, lights, energies, miracles—these were just words to clutch on to for support when the winds of the spirit blew away the confinements of ordinary reason.

"Fenella," she heard him say sharply. "Listen and answer. Does the color red signify some quality to you?" She wondered how much time had passed since his last question or whether the words she heard now had not yet been uttered, but were a prevision of a moment to come.

"Passion," she said, knowing that the word was inadequate to explain what she could see and feel. Even as she answered him and heard his further questions, she could feel other demands on her, from all about the room, flooding in from the inn, from the street outside, from the far corners of the town.

"And orange?"

"Healing."

"Is some part of me healing?"

"Either healing yourself, or ready to heal another," said Fenella, feeling as if she were the repository of a vast fund of light and warmth, of colors orange and pink and gold and white. Moment by moment she felt the needs of the outside world with greater urgency, as if she had become a fire around which too many wished to stand to warm their hands.

She knew then that she could turn inward, away from Professor Barnard's intrusions and demands, away from the distant cry of the ill. Just as she needed no one's help in entering a daydream, she knew that she could enter the trance state without the mesmerist's silly finger over her eyes, without the theatrical "passes" of his beringed fingers. She had learned the way. A simple concentration of self was the first step; and once past that door, she could go as fast as she liked, without a shepherd, going deeper and deeper, to this place of danger and beauty.

"And here, about my heart?" he was saying.

"Green."

"Are you saying that my heart is confused?"

"Yes." Fenella waited, and heard a hundred unvoiced questions now, one twisted into another, and all of them full of fear. He wanted to know if the colors she saw meant that he had doubted the effects of his cures, if he had willingly turned his eyes from chicanery in order to earn large fees, if he had allowed his vision to become clouded by greed. He wanted to know if the green she saw meant that he would die.

She could have explained that the colors she saw about him were not like simple signs in the real world; they were not simple arrows pointing to a detour, nor images painted on wood over a shop. But she could sense that he wanted simple answers, wanted to know that black signified death and white spiritual purity. And this she could not give him.

They were long past the point of mesmerist and subject. He had pushed her in a direction, and she had left him far behind. The commands and questions he issued were not all she concentrated on; the further she traveled, the less attachment he had to her spirit. For that spirit had been freed, and it reached out instinctively for the man she loved. Fenella could see both black and white fire limning an image of Robert, even as the mesmerist questioned her, and she understood the nature of this fire, understood this in a way that could not be explained to those outside the trance.

Explanations and revelations were now directed inward, were devoured whole, without translation. All the colors were but part of an entire spiritual picture, she knew, a picture that encompassed the shape and substance of a soul. But she needed to be deeper still to see that picture more clearly; and the further she traveled to clarity, the more she grew frightened of what she might see. Robert's black fire suggested death, but this death could be the completion of a cycle of wrong thinking, of spiritless living; the white fire could be the precursor of a rebirth. Or the white fire could be what was left of hope, and the black fire the sign of what was now consuming his life. One could no more explain this in a phrase than one could understand a lifetime in a glance.

"Concentrate. Answer," said the mesmerist, as if he imagined himself to still be in control of the trance. "Look at the confusion about me. Will this lead to my death?"

Fenella held herself from falling deeper. Afraid of being completely alone in the depths, she held out a spiritual hand for the mesmerist. "Often confusion is a sign of a return to health," she said, feeling his terror of illness and turning her spirit away from it. Her trance was so deep that words were superfluous, notes superimposed on a melody pure and simple. She felt that if the mesmerist's fear would subside, she could communicate directly to him, her spirit touching his, with no words needed at all. Fenella would have a mentor, a guide, instead of one more wounded soul in need of her solace. "You believe," she said, "and yet you don't believe. You have seen proof, and yet you disbelieve this proof. You want to help, yet you give first importance to the appearance of help."

"And my legs, my belly, look at me," insisted the mesmerist, feeling as if the trance he had placed her in now extended to himself. He knew that for her to see so much, she must be at the fifth level; nothing else could explain how she had penetrated to the core of his conflicted self. "Look all up and down my body and tell me if you see colors, what colors?"

"The colors are mixed, and they are changing," said Fenella, her spirit yet more vibrant, yet more radiant. She did not fully understand that her thoughts extended past the puny concerns of the mesmerist, past the excited wonderment of Grace, past the wild energies within the room. What she saw was not just within the body before her, but the pain of others closer to her heart. "Black, the color of death and destruction, becoming gray, as you are angry, and more green, as you are more ready than ever for change."

"Am I sick?" said the mesmerist, and behind his words were a thousand judgments, ready to reject or accept or modify every word she uttered. "Why did you say 'death'? What are you seeing? Tell me what you're looking at. Tell me."

"You are sick," said Fenella in words, "but I shall make you better." And then without words she told him more: to come closer, to shut his eyes, to breathe deeply of what she had to give him. He didn't understand how she could raise her arms without his command, or how he knew to step into her embrace. All he could see behind his shut eyes was a gentle glow, a rainbow of muted colors; all he could feel was a magnificent strength entering the muscles and bones of his tired flesh.

It was an embrace that he never wanted to break, though the mesmerist was barely sick, but only greedy for the healer's strength, a strength that could fill all the gaps and crevices in his confused spirit. But through his flesh, Fenella could feel the greater needs of others, reaching for her naked spirit with clawing hands. Through his flesh she could feel a fever that was not his, a pain that flew through space to sear her spirit. Fenella's mother was already retrieving the trouble she had left behind at the lecture hall; Dr. Robert Warner's fever grew worse after the early morning four-hour railroad trip to New York City; and there were others, less dear to her, but no less demanding of her spirit.

Held in the mesmerist's embrace, she felt trapped not by his arms, but by her own desire to help. This was not a dream, where all wishes remained behind upon awaking. This was no self-enclosed fantasy, but one where the self broke past all enclosures, flying blindly in pursuit of the spirit's passion.

She understood then that her passion and her love called to her, broken and twisted and full of despair. Fenella heard Robert's cry, but just as the colors of his spirit were difficult to fathom, neither was the cry of his heart clear. She could not know whether this was because he was too weak, or too distant, or because they had never expressed their love to one another past a kiss or an embrace. But now she believed that their love must be expressed, that nothing could be as strengthening as the coming together of two lovers. Fenella saw his pale face, his feverish eyes, and tried to bring that face and those eyes closer to hers, to merge her spirit with his, ignoring the confines and rules of space and time; but this effort brought her no solace, only further confusion, further distancing.

Suddenly, Robert's face was gone, and in its place was that of the mesmerist, bathed in a garish rainbow. She knew that to go farther and farther was to see with greater and greater clarity, but she had turned in fear from the terrifying, lonely descent back to the mesmerist. Fenella would not get what she needed from the mesmerist, but only from herself. Turning her spirit away from the mesmerist, turning inward, she looked for the way back to Robert.

But what if Robert was no longer there? What if the image of his face was an old one, a ghostly appearance of one already dead? What if what she had learned from the mesmerist was learned too late, and there was nothing she could do for the man she loved but stand over his grave?

Fenella hurried. She felt herself dropping fast, as if falling into a hole as deep as the earth's center. Whatever ties held her to the mesmerist were broken. She had gone very far, but found her love and terror letting her go much deeper, into a realm as close to madness as it was to truth, to a place where a vastness of knowledge threatened sanity as much as it promised revelation.

But as she went deeper and deeper into this place of power

and compulsion, she was not sure how to go back from where she had started; indeed she was afraid that she might not wish to go back at all. She tried to remember that she was in search of Robert, but a panic took hold of her. Fenella had left behind the mesmerist, like a traveler in the wilderness who has run far ahead of his guide. Even if she wished to go back, there was nobody to show her the way, nobody to let her out of this place removed from the world.

"Robert," she called, remembering his name, not knowing how he could hear this call from a place so deep within herself. "Robert, please," she said, and she felt no closer to the earth, but somehow closer to the man she loved. She sensed his need coming closer to her, and if his need was there, it meant that he lived, and if he lived, then she would not go mad in searching for his spirit. And so she took another step down, letting her love guide her, another step into the blackness, and then another and another until all she could see was the blackness over her head, and the blackness beneath her feet, and she was lost, and the pressure on her spirit was like the weight of a thousand coffins pressing her deeper and deeper into the grave. But she knew that the way back was as confused as the way forward. She knew if she took another step in either direction she'd be lost forever; she knew that if she stood still her soul would be consumed in a flash of pale white fire.

But suddenly the urgent pressure about her spirit eased. She could hear a bell tinkle, and then the swift running of the hot and cold currents about her heart lessened to a trickle and then stopped altogether. Soon she felt a soothing presence around her shut eyes, soft circles inscribed by a woman's fingertips, a breath redolent not of the spirit but of strong coffee and fresh bread.

"Easy," she heard. "You are coming to the last mile. There's a fresh cool wind now. You can feel it in your cheeks. Blowing in cool and misty from the Sound. When you open your eyes, you will be awake. Awake."

It was a woman's voice, young and sharp, but serious and caring. She heard another command, to open her eyes, and smiled inwardly, feeling free of danger, so close to the road's end. Fenella opened her eyes, and saw a fuzzy white shroud pull back and away from her face until it became the white-gowned costume of the mesmerist's assistant.

"You are awake," said Grace.

"Yes," said Fenella, feeling the blood beating in her temples, feeling the floor beneath the soles of her feet, feeling the sunlight through the heavily leaded old casement windows like stabs of mortality. She had come awake with the nagging residue of a question incorrectly answered, of a task left somehow incomplete, and for a moment she couldn't orient herself to the room, to the sight of the mesmerist collapsed on the floor, his long legs spread onto the worn carpet, staring at her as if she were a dream.

"You were there," said Grace.

"What?" said Fenella. Everything that had been so swift and intuitive within the trance was now slow and awkward. She remembered that Grace had been hostile and angry, and was now gentle and solicitous, but did not understand the circumstances that had led to that change. She turned to look at the mesmerist, but he was white-faced, too exhausted to talk. There was something that she must tell him, and at once. "You asked me a question, sir," said Fenella to a dazed Professor Barnard.

"He went too far," said Grace sharply. "He kept you going too long. He wouldn't let go of you, even when it looked like you was about to fall down." Fenella remembered that it had been she who had not been able to let go of the mesmerist, through whose body she had wanted to heal another. As Grace helped Fenella into one of the room's antique chairs, she apologized: "I'm sorry about what I said."

"What?" said Fenella. "What did you say?"

"I mean that you could be a fake or something. You're not a fake. You've got the gift. I've never seen anybody like that. Your eyes went right up inside your head, and in a second you're just gone to the world." She came over and squatted in front of Fenella's chair. "You were there, I know you were. All the way there."

"You touched my eyes."

"Touched? That ain't no touch. It's a mesmeric trick, gets you out of it anytime. I wasn't about to rely on the professor here. What did you do to him?"

"I don't know."

"You said he was sick."

"He is all right," said Fenella, answering without hesitation.

"I am all right," said the mesmerist softly, smiling at both of them.

"What was wrong with him?"

"I don't know," said Fenella. She realized that a myriad events and sensations had run through her spirit, dazzling her with their force and their speed. She remembered that she had helped the mesmerist, letting her spirit flow into his, as if she were the mesmerist and he the mesmerist's patient. "He needed to see," said Fenella.

Professor Barnard seemed to be groping for a string of words, a question that he needed to ask the more he returned from his overwhelming astonishment.

"He saw," said Grace. "'If he was looking for something all his life, he saw it today." She paused to look over at the mesmerist, then brought her pretty face next to Fenella's. "Are you going to tell me, or ain't you? You were there?"

"I was."

"Did you see it? The animal magnetism? What happened?"

"I made a mistake," said Fenella, getting out of her chair to confront the mesmerist. Slowly, the words came to her: "I'm sorry, sir. I answered incorrectly. I haven't been there, but I know it."

Professor Barnard raised his eyes and looked at her. "I couldn't speak," he said, not responding to her words, but wanting to explain how he had felt the delicious warmth of her spirit bringing him back to a sense of relaxed bliss that was already fading. "You made me feel warm."

"She was there," said Grace. "I seen it. You went under. You got pulled in, like I've never seen. I want her to magnetize me. Maybe she can make me go deeper."

"Tell me," said the mesmerist. "Animal magnetism. You saw it, you felt it. It is real, isn't it?"

But this was not the question uppermost in Fenella's mind, not the nagging statement she needed to clarify. "You asked me," she said, "if I had ever been to New York City."

"You're not listening," said Professor Barnard, struggling to his feet, forgetting his awe and his gratitude, returning the lines of command to his pale face. "I want you to listen, and to tell me what you remember."

"No," said Fenella. "You must listen to me."

"I must listen to you?" said Professor Barnard, standing over where she sat, looking down on her thick red hair and intensely serious eyes. It seemed that she had been only moments before a shy, unassuming young woman daring to look for a job. Something had been opened for her in the magnetic state, some vision had been granted her that gave her urgency and authority.

"I told you that I hadn't," said Fenella. "I hadn't ever been to New York City, but now I can remember. When I was in the trance, I was there."

"Don't worry about the answer you gave me," said the mesmerist. "Perhaps you weren't as deeply entranced at first as you were a bit later. No one can tell me that you weren't finally at the deepest level."

"I was deep. Later, when I tried to find him," said Fenella, "I was very deep." She had believed that if she could just right the error she had made while in the magnetic state, the nagging vision at the back of her mind would come into clear sight. "You must help me. There was something you wanted me to see. And when you told me to go there and see if I could bring up any images of the streets, I said that I couldn't. Now I can't remember what you asked me to see." There were tears in her eyes now, tears that the mesmerist didn't understand.

"I'm sorry, dear girl. I suppose I asked if you could see Broadway."

"Broadway," said Fenella. "A horse-drawn railroad car. Very crowded, people standing. Noisy wheels on the rails. Is that Broadway?"

The mesmerist smiled kindly, and explained that could be any big city with public transportation. "You could be remembering a trip you took as a child. Maybe Boston."

"It was New York," said Fenella with violence. "It was Broadway."

"If she says she was there," said Grace, "she was there." Now that she had shared the glory of the trance by bringing her out of it, she had cast herself as Fenella's champion, eager to boast of her talent as if it were her own.

Fenella turned from the mesmerist to the pretty somnambulist, doubting whether either of them could understand what she needed to know.

"He called for me," Fenella said, and they looked at her

without any comprehension at all. "From New York City, he called for me, from Broadway. The heat coming off the pavement, the noise of the people in the street. From New York City."

"Clairvoyant," said Grace. "A real clairvoyant."

But Fenella took no comfort in Grace's approbation. There was a state she had learned to enter, dangerous and deep, and once in that state she could work wonders. She would go to him, find the place where the sick went to die, and make him see that life could be his. But Fenella could not bring the dead back to life. And what she did not know, and what they could not tell her, was whether the cry she had heard, spirit reaching out for spirit, had come from New York City, or from the land of the dead.

Chapter 19

*I*F FENELLA had been more practical, less of a dreamer, she would have delayed her trip to New York City. There were the small matters of putting together money for a round-trip rail ticket, for food and lodgings for an indeterminate time; there were the larger matters of leaving her mother and defying Mrs. Warner. And of course there was the largest question of all: Was Dr. Robert Warner alive or dead?

But Fenella was impractical, and a dreamer.

Robert called to her, so he must be alive. Robert called to her, so he had need of her. Robert called to her, so she would go to him.

A dream could take her wherever she needed to go. All Fenella need do was turn her back to wherever she was now, and take steps, one foot after the other, until she was with him, with the man she loved.

One didn't employ logic within a dream. There was no need to examine a sequence of events, but only to follow clear emotional lines, one after the other, leaving the strictures and restraints of reasoning behind.

She barely heard the mesmerist's frenzied questions as she began to leave his sitting room: Had she forgotten her interest in working for him? Would she go on stage as a somnambulist? Was she willing to help heal the sick?

"I am going right now to heal the sick," said Fenella. "Thanks to you, sir." Before she left she asked him for a loan of twenty dollars, the spontaneous request coming out of her mouth as readily as a breath of air. Even Grace, Fenella's newfound admirer, was astonished to see the corresponding ease with which Professor Barnard was parted from his money. But like the flimsy obstacles in dreams, toppled like houses of cards, the barriers between Fenella in Connecticut and Robert in New York seemed to fall away like dead leaves from a windswept tree.

Now there was money for the four-hour rail trip. Now the mesmerist said he would go to Mrs. O'Hara and tell her where her daughter had gone. Now Grace wrapped a light cotton duster —essential protection for the railroad passenger—about Fenella's modest clothes. Now the train came, all eight cars filled with the dust and smoke of the wood-burning engine, lurching toward New York with Fenella in a cracked leather seat by a wide-open window.

Nothing upset her about the trip, for her mind was elsewhere. It was no chore to shut out the smells of burning axle grease, the sights of gentlemen in silk hats spitting tobacco juice into the aisles, the rude jokes of laboring men, their bare feet stuck out every other window for a respite from the heat. Fenella didn't suffer from the heat, for she dreamed of the cool place, the high place, where she would take Robert, away from the clinic and its useless drugs and consumptive patients stoically preparing to die. Even Robert had to admit that doctors in Germany— where one out of seven deaths were blamed on consumption— were beginning to believe that patients would have a better chance of survival in fresh, dry air than in a smoke-belching city or wet, waterfront town. But these were the beliefs of doctors, not their patients. Theories were well and good, but this did not mean that consumptives believed that new theories would have any immediate effect on their own lives.

Nearly ten years before, Robert had told her, Dr. Klencke had successfully inoculated rabbits with the disease; but other than make that doctor's reputation, what had it done for patients? What did fooling about with rabbits and postulating nature cures in the mountains have to do with the real suffering of a victim of tuberculosis? It was no wonder that Robert had run back to the clinic in New York.

But Fenella did not see why he was anxious to be in the hands of doctors who had supervised the deaths of countless tubercular patients; all they would be prepared to do was supervise his death in turn. They spoke of no cure in the clinic for consumptives. A cure seemed so unlikely that it was not considered proper to pursue it with hope. More appropriate were miserably long faces, commiserating nods, downcast eyes, while all the while fever and pulse were scrupulously monitored, blood and urine analyzed so that the sure ebbing of the life-force could be diagnosed and documented for the edification of future, healthier generations.

When Fenella spoke to Robert of hope, he contradicted her optimism with jibes at the hopes of medical researchers, as if she were a supporter of their scientific methods. Speaking with the bitterness of youth expecting to die, Robert brought up the brilliant work of Schönlein, Bodington, and Henle—all so admired among his medical school professors—asking Fenella what they had to do with letting him live. Klencke, the brilliant researcher who had inoculated rabbits with tuberculosis cells, believed that those cells acted much like cancer cells. What possible use was this theory to Robert? Brehmer recently declared that tuberculosis was curable, after cutting into corpses for three years and finding numerous cases of healed tubercular lesions. Well, Robert imagined, perhaps they'd find healed lesions in his corpse too.

But Fenella was not agitating for faith in a new medical cure, but simple faith in his own ability to survive. She wanted him to forget his medical training, turn away from the list of sorry statistics of the dead, and refuse even to give a name to what ailed him. She wanted him to believe that he could be well, and hope for recovery, and go off with her to a place where he would breathe free of pain.

Fenella knew that the slow death earlier in the year of the novelist Charlotte Brontë had effected Robert as yet another example of the "realities" of what he had to expect. Though Brontë had died during a difficult pregnancy, the cause of death was assumed by most to be tuberculosis, and therefore inevitable. Hadn't both her sisters, Anne and Emily, wasted away and died of the consumption before her? It seemed to Fenella that there was a disease within the mind of the public, a disease more powerful than tuberculosis itself.

Just as the mention of "plague" in earlier times had been enough to kill hope, a diagnosis of tuberculosis now led directly to an expectation of death. Perhaps in every time there was a particular dread name, a disease put into fearful relief by the doctors who gave this name to the world. Even when the plague killed half of Europe, Fenella thought, it did not kill the other half; perhaps the half who survived were the ones who did not know that "plague" existed. Or perhaps they chose not to embrace their fear, did not cherish their deaths as a relief from the power of the evil name.

Of course, Fenella would never get Robert to believe that tuberculosis was just a name for a set of circumstances that doctors of their time circumscribed with statistics, the way geographers drew map lines over the earth. A country did not exist except by the consent of human beings, agreeing to abide by boundaries, by place names; just as a disease was not born in the minds of man until it was named, described, and added to the tangible objects that humans must fear. Robert feared tuberculosis, because he believed in it; there was a tubercular "fate" during which one could exhibit courage, but not the courage to hope for a cure. Believing in tuberculosis was believing in the long, inevitable "decline." His courage was that of one unafraid to meet his fate with open eyes.

But Fenella wanted none of this self-pitying "courage." Her need was to get Robert out of his "decline," out of the frame of what was "inevitable," out of the clinic where dying was not the exception but the rule of the house. By the time the train had arrived at New York's Forty-second Street, where teams of horses replaced the noisy locomotive in pulling the train cars downtown, Fenella knew how to fulfill her task: She would simply pull him directly into her dream.

But first she had to get to him, to place his hands in hers, to hold his eyes with her own. She heard the conductor shout the stops at Thirty-fourth Street and Twenty-third Street, saw the masses of people crowding the sidewalks in front of tall buildings along Fourth Avenue, wondered at the speeding wagons and carts and carriages. Livestock, fresh produce, and heavy furniture seemed to be on collision courses; at every intersection peddlers, urchins, and packs of mongrel dogs tripped each other jumping into the wild traffic.

A man spoke to her, and she blinked against the image of his grinning face, red from the heat, and grinning with satisfaction at his own wit. "I'm sorry," she said, knowing that part of the dream was to listen to this man, that his words would take her to her lover. He picked up his silk hat and placed it lower still on his narrow forehead, so that it nearly covered his eyes.

"Used to be worse, miss, when there was the cattle drives," he said.

"Yes, worse," said Fenella politely, not knowing that the man referred to the time before the city finally forbade the driving of cattle herds below Thirty-fourth Street. For the last five years these drives through heavily trafficked streets to the west side slaughterhouses had been restricted to the quieter, lantern-lit nights. "Do you perhaps know the hospital?"

"The hospital?" said the silk-hatted gentleman, nearly choking on the juice from his unlit cigar. "We ain't in Nebraska, miss. We got lots of hospitals in New York. We got three just for Roman Catholics, we got one for Germans, we got St. Luke's for the Episcopalians, we got Mount Sinai for the Jews over on Lexington Avenue, far away uptown, Sixty-something Street—"

"I'm sorry, I am looking for Broadway," said Fenella, feeling the train car slow down, as the crush of pedestrians all about them on the streets grew yet more intense. The conductor announced the stop, the Canal Street station of the New York and New Haven railroad.

"Broadway's right out there, miss," said the gentleman, striking a match against the sole of his boot and lighting up his cigar. "But if you want to see Broadway, you ought to let me show it to you. I got friends in every theater and saloon. And Fifth Avenue, you ought to let me show you Fifth Avenue, you'll never want to go nowhere else again."

"No, thank you," she said, somewhere in the middle of his insinuating speech, drifting away from him as easily as if they were two soap bubbles caught in different currents of air. She left the train car without assistance, having no luggage, and no open-eyed look of panic; with her sooty duster and romantic fall of red hair, she could have been an actress en route to a week's run as Cordelia, or an heiress fleeing the ancestral estate to elope with her lover.

It was late afternoon, and hot, but at least Fenella had arrived several hours before the wild evening exodus of workers from offices and factories. A fresh breeze blew from the waterfront to her west, and keeping pace with the swift natives she found herself on lower Broadway, looking up at the great buildings for signs of Robert.

For a moment, she lost step with her dream, drifting back to reason. He was not in a hospital, but in a clinic. Not on Lexington or Fifth Avenue, but on Broadway. All she must do was stop an officer of the police, and mention the dread illness: "Consumption. I am looking for a clinic where those with consumption go. On Broadway."

"Pardon me," she said to a beautifully uniformed man, the copper buttons of his coat as magnificent as his walrus mustache. She nearly caused a collision with a woman daring to smoke a cigarette as she walked the public street, but the policeman made no protest about this indecency, and in response to Fenella's question simply shrugged his shoulders and remarked that Broadway went on for miles.

"I don't understand. It is on this street. This clinic. I must go—" But the policeman was already gone.

Fifty more people had rushed by her in both directions before Fenella realized that reason would be of no help in completing her union with Robert. She smiled suddenly, relaxing back into the sense of the dream, believing that she was near to him, closer to him with each passing moment. Continuing to walk along Broadway, her eyes were caught by a sudden flashing. She turned to see through the freshly washed windows of an elegant café, silverware caught in a slant of light; a young girl was playing with a knife and fork, while her mother read a newspaper on a wooden holder.

And behind this couple, alone at a table with a teapot and single cup, was Robert's mother, Mrs. Warner.

Fenella was not aware of the steps taking her through the café entrance, past the overbearing proprietor, through the closely placed, mostly unoccupied, tables. It seemed only a single moment from when she had turned from the departing policeman back into the fabric of her dream; it seemed but a few easy steps from the mesmerist's suite of rooms to Mrs. Warner's pallid face.

"He has no money," Mrs. Warner said, as if they were in the middle of a conversation, as if the sight of her servant in a café in the city of New York was unworthy of comment. "I have all the money, and he will have no need of any of it, and therefore you will get nothing. Do you understand what I am telling you? There is no need to believe me, you may consult a lawyer and hear the same thing. If you marry him, you will simply be a penniless widow, without a job. You would be smart if you held on to the chance of finding a husband more appropriate to your class."

"I am going to him," said Fenella, hearing the words she uttered as if she watched the scene from a little distance, as if she floated on the waves of sleep. There were more words coming at her now from Mrs. Warner, angry and accusatory, suggesting that she was a seductress, that she had taken advantage of a sick man, that Fenella and Robert had long planned to disgrace her family. If she had not already known in her heart that Robert was still alive, that he called to her, Fenella could have taken some joy from the tirade.

But the dream had already spoken to her of his life, had already promised his love. Fenella turned away from Mrs. Warner's table, gently and easily, letting the words run through her like a pale shadow of Robert's love. Robert, who had never stood up to his mother's desires, had insisted that he loved the red-haired beauty. Robert, who had told Fenella that she must forget they had ever embraced, had insisted that he would marry her because he so clearly expected to die.

But he would not die, because dying was not in the dream she was living. They were young, and at the beginning of their love, and the world promised them many years together. Fenella walked quickly now, out of the café and onto the street, on a straight-line path to Robert. She asked questions of first one gentleman, then another. The street was Broadway, the street she had imagined under the mesmerist's hands. One man knew a number and gave it to her, a gift of the dream. And when she looked at the buildings, white stones glittering in the afternoon sun, all of them had numerals over their entrances, some in gilt figures, some in black, others—like that of the clinic for consumptives—etched directly into the stone.

Fenella asked once again, though she knew quite well where she was, seeing the number before her eyes, not needing to wait for the answer from a dour man in a black suit. She barely heard him repeat Robert's name to her, looking down a neat list on a sheet of lined paper. Now she ran, and her heart pounded, and there was no urgency coming from fear, but only the urgency of love. She had never told him that she loved him, and in a moment she would be in a place where she could say this for the first time and the tenth time, and then over and again for the rest of her life. It was warm on the stairwell; but at the top of the house, on the fifth floor, a breeze blew in from the river, a wind that spoke of a distant cooler place, a place where she would take him under the protection of her dream.

But suddenly the dream stopped short.

She had entered it to answer his call, and it had swept her up, taken her into its arms, and brought her through the miles until she had reached her goal: Robert was alive.

He was there, one among the sick, and when she walked toward his bed she felt the full weight of her terror, the full load of the exhaustion she had carried since the night before. Now she would need to dream again.

Robert turned his head from the open window at the sound of her footsteps. For a giddy moment she had the sensation that while she had stopped dreaming, he had begun. But this was not the case. Robert blinked, as if she might be an apparition. She could feel the fact of his love like an embrace.

"Fenella," he said, his bloodless lips curling into a hopeful smile.

She came close to him, and touched his lips with the tips of her fingers. He brought his cold white hands to her cheeks, his eyes shining with fever. "It's me," she said.

But her presence alone could not stop the fear. Wild words ran out of his mouth: "How did you know how to find me?" he said. "I was about to write to you. How are your hands? Is the burn all right? I don't know why they let you in here. You mustn't be afraid of what I look like. They keep testing my blood, and I don't have all that much to give."

"Robert," she said, as if saying aloud his name contained the answers to every question he had asked, every fear he had raised. Just a little while ago he had been "Dr. Robert" to her; once there had been a time when he had not known that she loved him, when she could barely imagine that he would remember her name. Fenella wondered at the ease with which life can be lived, at the joy that is always accessible to the daring. She sat on the narrow bed, and brought his head against her breast.

"I want to marry you," he said.

"All right."

"It is crazy, isn't it?"

"No," said Fenella.

"I am going to die," he said. "But I realized that I want you to be my wife. That I love you." He turned his head from her eyes as he said this, but Fenella put her smooth palms on his cheeks and held his feverish gaze.

"And I love you," she said.

There was no need to contradict his assertions about death, there was only the need to take him with her into a dream, out of this place of dying. She had always known the way to the dream place in herself; but now she had learned that she could lead him with her to that same place, where his pure spirit would free his flesh of sickness and pain. Fenella tried to remember how the mesmerist had put her into the safety of the trance, what words he had used, how he had concentrated her thoughts to set her free.

"I wanted you to come," he said, and she told him that she knew, that she had heard him call quite clearly, that she had known exactly how to find him.

"How? I don't understand any of this," he said, wondering at the power of love, opening his heart to the possibility of things outside his ken. Once more she brought the tips of her fingers to his lips; then she kissed him, resting her cool forehead against his.

But then she felt the call of his spirit, pulling at her through his flesh. Suddenly, she moved greedily forward, pressing the soft flesh of her upper lip into his mouth with teeth and tongue.

Robert's body came to life at once.

The wasted flesh was suddenly taut with desire, beating with the urgent pulse of love. He breathed in her kisses, driving his love through his lips and tongue into her mouth. His weakened lungs battened on her flying spirit even as his own tried to break free. Robert's body seemed suddenly bloated with power, as if his excited penis, his wildly pumping heart, his lungs filling with Fenella's strength would burst his flimsy bedclothes.

For years he had learned that he must not want passion: that love would lead to lust, and lust would kill his sick body. But now he yielded to love, and his body glowed with strength; now he knew that he wanted her, to join spirit and flesh in a union that would make him not sicker, but whole. Fenella felt as if their kiss had brought them one wild step closer to the dream place.

Everything that she had learned from the mesmerist seemed to pale next to the fact of their love.

There was a dream that was all around them, and it could be entered together, spirit linked with spirit. There was a need to be together, and this need was potent, concentrated. She had no need of mesmeric passes of a hand wearing many rings, no need of a monotonous voice, and a flashing of jewels.

"I love you," she said again, and he repeated this phrase back to her, and she didn't know if the drawing together of their souls at that moment was something wished for or something real, if their loving union was another path to the dream place or simply an end, both peaceful and wild, in itself. But the freeing of their spirits, the lightness of their beings, allowed her to tell him that he must get up, that he must leave his bed and come away with her to a better place.

"I don't have the strength," he said, forgetting for a moment the lust that had given his body a glimpse of life and health. Already reason was calming his heartbeat, fear was settling his excitement, pain pulling back the wild inspiration of his lungs. He did not yet possess her knowledge nor her belief. Still, about the sad corners of his mouth was a doubt, a possibility made stronger by her lips breathing love into his frail frame.

"You have the strength," she said, never taking her eyes from his, never removing her hands from contact with his skin. The desire that had so shaken his frame, giving it a hint of the strength that was his to discover, had yielded to something gentler, but no less urgent. He felt himself being drawn in to her, his spirit letting go of a thousand fetters and restraints in order to make the journey to his love. Fenella did not know if it was a mutual trance that made him get off the bed and onto his feet; but she imagined that he felt what she did: That the world beyond the place where they stood—the patient in an adjacent bed, the doctor watching them from the doorway of the room, the noise from the street five stories below drifting up on the gentle wind—diminished in interest and importance, until it was no longer there, until all that existed for him was her and all that existed for her was him.

"Fenella," he said, standing before her with no confidence

that he would not fall down. The lust, the love, the feats of strength that he was exhibiting all seemed to him like bursts of wild energy from a man about to die. He wanted to get a minister, to marry her at once, to prepare for death by making her his wife forever. But Fenella would have none of it. She used no words to convince him that he would be well, but only told him to dress for the street, urged him to hurry, and watched as he slipped, bit by bit, into the dream.

"This is madness," he said, but he too felt the dreamlike rush of events, the possibility of losing the thousand objections that always stood in the way of change. They would not let him out of the clinic into the street; there was no place to go to; there was no way to get there; he did not have the strength for the journey.

But no one tried to stop them with anything more than words. A carriage took them to the train station, and there was enough money in his pocket to take them north, and then west, and then to a ferry that crossed a freshwater lake in the foothills of a mountain rising up into luminous clouds.

And he was strong enough to abide the train, though he was very afraid that he would die in the night, die before they had a chance to marry. And he was strong enough to survive the ferry, though the wind off the lake was fierce and damp, and the other passengers avoided them, fearing his cough and his bloody handkerchief.

But at the other side of the lake they found a carriage driver, sunburned and wild-haired and eager to take them wherever they wanted to go. Fenella had an image of what she wanted, a place that was like a cool gem in the summer's heat, yet full of sunshine, so quiet that birdsong would carry for miles.

The driver took them to a lodge run by his aunt; half an hour distant, at an elevation of three thousand feet, with its own two cows. Robert was not the first consumptive to try the mountain air in these parts; and every one of them, the driver exaggerated, had been cured inside of a few weeks.

Dr. Robert Warner, exhausted from the trip, slept fifteen hours a day, much of it in a long chair overlooking the lake below them. He ate three large meals a day, and at least two smaller ones. Fenella was at his side with hot chocolate, hot soup, fresh milk laced with honey every time he woke. She watched him sleep in the sun, breathing in the pristine Adirondack air. Neither knew that within a mile of this same location, within thirty years of that date, a great sanatorium for the treatment of tuberculosis would thrive. Consumptives from all walks of life would take the long journey away from stressful lives, polluted air, and poor food to come to save their own lives. There would be medical doctors in evidence, but the treatment would be much the same as Fenella's: to put weight on too-thin bodies, to give them rest, mountain air, and a belief in the possibility of their own survival.

"I am dreaming," said Robert at least once a day.

He pretended to be cross with her for one thing only: her refusal to marry him until they had come down from the mountain, until he was well and happy and ready to live his life without fear. But as the days became weeks, and the summer colder, Robert understood that the dream had become his life. In this place, he was at peace with himself. His spirit had extricated itself from fears he had created. His body now contained a spirit not wasting away to death, but growing fat with love; a spirit that would turn away from despair forever.

When he married Fenella in their hometown's Congregational Church, Robert stood tall and strong, meeting his beautiful bride's gaze with wonder at the joy and plenty before him. The summer in the mountains had brought him back to health, a health that came from deep within his spirit. He did not know that he would live to be an old man and become celebrated as the healer Fenella Warner's first great cure. But he knew that he would look at life and at his own medical practice in a new way, a way that was as old as the ancient Greeks, as honored as the oath of Hippocrates.

Illness came as much from the spirit as the body, he had learned. Indeed, the root of most disease could be found twisted about uncertainty and unhappiness. Life needed to nourish the spirit, or it would grow sick, and sicken with it its fleshly shell. Never again would he treat patients, or himself, like run-down machines, simply in need of parts or excisions. Every human being contained a spirit which needed to be understood and embraced, both by patient and healer, or there could be no true healing. And there was no sustenance, no cure for the spirit superior to love.

"I am dreaming," said Robert as he stood with her before the congregation, waiting to take their vows.

"Of course you are dreaming, darling," said Fenella. "And I am dreaming. We're both dreaming the same dream."

New York City, 1983

QUITE CLEARLY, Richard heard Elizabeth's promise to help him end his agony. Once begun, the promise became a litany, a source of joy echoing again and again against the substance of his misery. He wanted never to stop hearing the words: "Yes, darling. Of course I'm going to help you."

He tried to hold on to consciousness, but the delicate relief that now flooded his mind defeated this purpose. Exhausted—from his illness, from the poisons battling the illness, from the conjuring of a hundred and more grisly methods of suicide to escape from the illness—it was simpler to give into the soporific drugs that ran through his blood.

Elizabeth would do what he had asked her. She would take away his pain, and let him die.

He would not have to repeat his escape from the hospital—a far more difficult task now than it was less than two weeks before. He would not have to force himself off the roof of a penthouse, or run screaming into the path of a speeding train. There would be no need to slash his wrists, or go upstate to buy a shotgun, or swim out into the surf at Coney Island and try to reach the other side of the ocean. "Yes, darling," he heard her say again and again. "Of course I'm going to help you."

Stepping over the line that separates wakefulness from sleep, Richard felt infintely calmer. Her hands held his, and they were warm, sending a current of life into the dying frame of his body. For a moment, he fought this surge of vitality, this warmth that flooded his spirit. He wanted to die, not live. Soon he would be awake once again, and he would see the pills, and he would take them, five and ten at a time, gobbling them down in a ravenous self-destruction.

But quickly he stopped fighting.

For the moment, there was no pain. The woman he loved touched him, and the touch warmed his soul. For a moment death was very far away, for he still had the power of love firing his body. He had a sudden memory of how he had first seen her, a serious beauty dressed in white, reading a text as she held on to a subway strap. She didn't glance at him when he had grabbed hold of that same strap, when he had make a joke about the less than immaculate state of the train, when a short stop slammed the side of her body into his. But he had insisted on a moment of her attention. On telling her his name. On explaining that life occasionally throws out a surprise, a challenge that must be met, or it will have no surprises at all. Before they reached his Times Square stop he had dared Elizabeth into accepting a date with him, a late afternoon drink at a famous old midtown hotel.

Other memories ran through him: how she smelled with freshly washed hair; how she relished eating a just-ripe Macintosh apple and a hunk of Vermont cheddar; how she, after assisting at a failed operation had cried in his arms throughout the night; how she liked to grasp his head by holding her palms over each of his ears, then slowly kiss his eyes, one by one, until he would shut them gently and open his mouth, and meet her lips with his teeth and tongue.

She spoke to him, but he heard through an ethereal covering of sleep only the comforting syllables of her litany of help, blocks of muted sound that soon merged with the warmth of her hands into a declaration of love.

"You must get well, darling," Elizabeth whispered, not wanting to wake or disturb him, but needing to follow the dictates of her heart. Ready to let go, to accede to his wishes, to bring forth the correct mix of barbiturates and analgesic that would put him finally to rest, she now spoke silent words of healing. She had no plan of treatment, no prognosis for what would follow beyond that night. But there was no fear that he would rebel at the words, that he would imagine that she had reneged on a promise to bring him destruction; she knew that her lover could not fight back at what she had to give. Her love was too strong, his spirit too hungry.

Gently, she placed her hands at his throat, at his chest, at his shut eyes. No one besides herself and the staff at the hospital had touched Richard since he'd been brought to rest in this bed. Elizabeth could understand how the lovers and friends of cancer victims, in fearing the disease, learned to fear its victim, learned to justify to themselves why it was best to leave them alone, to desert them.

But then Richard had little family, few friendships deep enough to call upon in this time of need.

In his own hurried reading since being diagnosed as leukemic, looking for a chance to deny his disease, or blame it on something outside his control, he had often come across the five psychological touchstones of determining one's own cancer risk: whether one perceived one's childhood, occupation, and love relationship to be stable or unstable; whether or not one had plans for the future; whether or not one had experienced a recent loss.

As a frequently commissionless sculptor who had lost his parents at two years of age, in love with a doctor whom he suspected had no respect for his occupation, unable to look into the future because he had no firm footing in the present, Richard jokingly blamed his condition on this revealed willingness to self-destruct. "It's all my fault," he would say. "I've been working on my sick psychology since I was a little kid."

"It's not your fault, sweetheart," she whispered in the glow of the night-lights, as she had told him in the full light of day. She retained her hold of his cold hands, resting her eyes on his pale and weary face. *It's no one's fault,* she thought to herself. No matter what the mind-body faddists claimed about the effects of self-induced stress, there were endless examples of healthy murderers, thriving on stress and self-abuse; and their mirror images, saintly spiritualists, dead of cancer and worse, induced not by meditation, but by rotten luck.

No, she thought. There was enough blame in the world without looking for a guilty party in this tragedy. If Richard was not guilty of creating his own disease, neither must his fair-weather friends be judged wanting for their fear and dread in not being able to confront it. They were afraid to look too hard at what might be a vision of their own lives, or a taste of their own mortality. No one loved him as she did, no one wanted him so badly, and even she felt some part of herself guilty of wanting his death, of ridding the world of his pain.

How else could she explain deserting him, allowing him the luxury of fleeing the hospital, of not doing her best to track him down and bring him back until nearly an entire week had passed?

Even if she had little hope that chemotherapy would cure him, she was still a doctor, and knew that in treating cancer it is always imperative to begin as soon as it is detected. Regardless of her lack of faith in wishful thinking, she knew that she had no right to allow her own corroboration of his desperation to show. Even if she had no faith in the effect of the mind over the work-ings of the body, she knew that others did; there was always the possibility that she could have done more to help Richard through a spiritual crisis that she, in her overweening ignorance of all things outside the hospital, had chosen to ignore.

But now she had faith.

Not in chemotherapy, not in wishful thinking, not in any published body of facts or theories.

She had faith in the loving impulse that drove her to place her hands on her lover's body. This was a faith beyond thought, an action without empirical justification. She felt as if some mad-ness had taken over her, some twisting about of her understand-ing of the world; but it was a madness to which she yielded. If it was sane to offer Richard death, and madness to offer him life, she chose madness; if the modern world allowed her only a vision of death, she would turn her back to that world, and that world's knowledge.

Long ago she had learned how the revolutions wrought by science in the eighteenth century revolutionzed too the concept of the history of civilization. Mankind had always imagined that civilizations rose up, declined, and fell; that every great nation had a golden period when they could aspire to recapture what had once been held by another civilization before them. There was no true progress, with one civilization taking humankind further than it had ever gone before. Every advance was but a step forward within a cycle leading only to where man had al-ready been. Medical advances were stymied for a thousand years and more because no research, no observation was thought more correct than those enshrined in books saved from the ashes of the dead empires of the Greeks or Romans.

But all this was changed two hundred years before.

The industrial revolution brought in its wake new tools, new concepts, new ways of life. Medicine, fat with hubris from the daily gift of powerful new drugs, of antiseptic surgery, of anesthesia, decided that everything that had been learned in ten thousand years of civilization was incorrect. Cures based on prayer, on fasting and repentance, on steeping herbs in hot water or wine, on sacrifice to the gods or their demonic adversaries were either accidental or a result of the placebo effect. Medicine, like the world, had broken out of the cycles of history. Man would be healthier than any ancient Greek or Roman, would live longer, would eventually learn the secret of immortality itself.

But Elizabeth, alone with her dying lover, felt betrayed by this vision of history.

What if there was no progress, but only an inability to see that our advances were but part of another cycle, that our technology was leading only to another decline and fall? Even if enough new poisons were invented to kill cancer cells without destroying the body which housed them, who knew what new disease man would unleash on himself in its place? It was no wonder that so many people were turning to religion, when the answers of science led only to new questions—to herpes, to AIDS, to the threat of a new ice age through self-inflicted pollution, to a swift holocaust of the race through war.

Long closed to spirituality, she could not deny the illogical passion to believe that now seemed to be rising from the center of her body. Even if she were drunk, even if she were hysterical with sadness and frustration, it could not explain away the feeling of a connection to a past, of a power that she had never believed herself to possess.

"I love you," she said, not whispering the words this time, but letting them flow from the depths of the spirit she never acknowledged, through the tips of her surgeon's capable fingers. She wanted to forget knowledge at that moment, she wanted to quit remembering why she must despair, why everything she did now was doomed to failure. Rather than try to imagine how the force she felt was connected to her brain, to memories and desires inscribed in her gray matter like files on a computer disk, she tried to cease making comparisons, connections, rationalizations. To try to force her feelings into an understandable form would be to diminish them. She wanted to let herself be overwhelmed by the power she drew from her spirit, to be nothing more nor less than a conduit for its power. The lateness of the hour, the alcohol in her system, the closeness of the sick and the dying, all conspired to a giddiness that was foreign to her compulsively logical personality. All her training, all her discipline directed her to believe that Richard must die; that the correct thing was to allow him his fear-driven suicide. And so she rejected training, discipline. She took hold of a greater knowledge, not fighting it by passing it through the finite reasoning of her understanding, but taking it directly into her heart.

And she found beyond the limits of that understanding a will that could not be suppressed, a prayer that must needs be voiced.

Holding her lover's cold hands, Elizabeth felt her world turn about, felt the nagging restraints that held her rooted to a bleak and dismal reality begin to break. Never had she wanted anything so much as Richard's life, Richard's health, and she reached out and demanded it. Elizabeth felt as if the hundred thousand facts and figures in her head were being torn from the earth, flung into a void without end.

"You must get well, darling," she said, the words rushing up from her heart, unfettered by logic. "You will get well," she said in the same incantation of loving syllables that healers had used for a thousand generations of man.

She could feel the anger that had crippled his strength, that had restricted his vision until he could see nothing inside or outside himself but the necessity of death. "You will get well," she said, knowing that he could hear her gentle words, that he could feel the touch of her loving hands. After Richard had made clear his request for the deathly pills, he had begun to smile. When Elizabeth had taken his hand earlier that day, he had been so weak that it had nearly broken her heart. But he had enough strength to speak out his love, and he did, over and again, in a voice that was calm and cool and matter-of-fact. Elizabeth had been able to see right through the bravado. It was clear why he had looked at her with such love, why he had spoken so intimately in front of nurses and the orderlies, why he seemed so happy in this place that smelled of poison and death. He had wanted Elizabeth to hear the words of his love all the time now, so that she could remember it later. He had been saying good-bye, and even his eyes had smiled.

But she was offering no valediction, no loving good-bye, but a greeting, insistent and selfish and full of belief: He must get well, she believed that he would get well, she had as much need of his life as her own.

Later, he would tell Lizzie that the touch of her hands seemed to send a current through the outer shell of his body directly to the center of his life-force. It was like electricity, like a benign shock that penetrated to a part of himself that had become as distant and foreign as if it were in the body of a stranger buried beneath the sea. He felt her hold him, and give of her love, and though his eyes were shut, he could see her clearly; her dear eyes drinking in his image, her soft hair falling across his chest, her breath—in spite of her tale of smelling from cognac—as sweet as wildflowers bending in a rush of Alpine air.

"You will get well," she said, speaking the words from the purest part of her, from a place of belief that could not be shaken by the paltry knowledge of men. Like Richard, she had been pulled down to the deepest level of despair, had learned to forget hope, had imagined that his request to die was reasonable, and unlike healing, within the realm of her expertise.

But getting that close to the bottom, getting that far from the strength of her spirit, her love for him had reached out, tripped up her purpose, and left her bereft of reason, medicine, hopelessness. Her love had demanded his life, and when she brought her spirit close to his, there was a connection, there was a flash of light in the back of her shut eyes.

Dr. Elizabeth Grant shut her eyes to the IV unit, to the dawn slowly rising over the East River, to the carefully monitored world of bodily functions that was her domain. All her concentration was centered on the man she loved as she held his hands, as she pulled his spirit toward hers, away from chains of fear to the shining possibility of a miracle.

Epilogue: 1985

TWO YEARS and two months after the bone marrow sample had confirmed his leukemia, Richard walked into the place where he had suffered and endured so much pain. Here he forgot at once all the pressures attending his work—the acrylic paintings, the new multiform sculptures, the art history course he was teaching at the Institute. Here, pressure was of a different order. The hospital lobby greeted him with its familiar drama, its unnaturally filtered air. He took the elevator to the eleventh floor, requiring barely a glance to find the button on the blinking panel. His stomach began to constrict as the elevator doors opened, and his hand went automatically to his nose, as if his fingers could shut out the chemical stench that was in his memory now forever. Richard greeted three different nurses by name and hurried along the immaculate corridor. He found the number, took a final stab at freezing his smile in place, and knocked gently on the door to the ballet dancer's private room.

There was, of course, no answer, but he believed a knock added a bit of dignity to the absolute powerlessness of the patient. He found her looking toward the door as he opened it: She was beautiful, young, and evidently in terrible pain.

"Hi," he said, trying to paint himself as both sympathetic and hopeful. The corners of his mouth exaggerated the difficult smile as he tried to tear away any shreds of pity from the mask of his face. He looked at, then away from, the IV unit, the series of unread inspirational books on her nighttable, the dazzling floral displays of friends overwhelmed by her illness. "My name is Richard. I know you're not in a talking mood, but that's fine, because I'll talk enough for the two of us." He took a step closer to the territory about her bed. "You're going to love hearing what I've got to say."

The young woman opened her mouth, as if about to speak, but seemed suddenly to change her mind. Richard could feel the anger constricting her body direct itself at him. Her eyes, blue-gray and enormous, narrowed into a double-barreled baleful squint. She hated him because he stood, while she had no strength to do more than lie in bed; because his scalp was covered with short curls while her beautiful black hair, long enough to reach the small of her back, had fallen out of her head; because his windburned cheeks were red with health, while she had the pallor of the dying. But most of all she hated him because his smile excluded him from her world of pain.

"I'm not a doctor," said Richard, coming closer to the young woman, wondering what she would look like without the Yankee baseball cap covering her scalp. He could imagine her with glossy black hair tied in extravagant knots down her back as she danced in wilder and wilder circles before a thousand admirers. "I'm not a reporter, and I'm not a ballet fan."

"Leave me alone," she whispered. If he had not heard the same slurred words from so many others, he would have found them difficult to decipher. With a bravery born of practice, Richard took one of her hands in his and sat on the edge of a chair next to her bed.

"You will be cured," he said.

"Stop it," she said, making a feeble effort to remove her hand from his. But Richard held it tight.

"You will feel stronger, and the pain will be beaten, and you will not want to die. You will kill the cancer, and you will be healthy, and beautiful, and you will be alive."

"Please," she said. "I don't want it. I want to stop. I can't—"

"You can," said Richard, bringing his head so close to hers that he could feel quite clearly the cry of her spirit for love, the cry her mind refused to hear, as it refused to believe that anything was worth enduring this pain. He wished he could kiss her, that he could bring his lips to her love-starved mouth, so that she would remember what love was, so that she would find in his kiss an answer to the absent admirers and friends, too frightened of the disease to come into its presence. But he was afraid that she would misinterpret the action: In her misery, she might find a kiss a further intrusion on her powerless body, or worse, a pathetic farewell to the dying.

"You want to go on," he insisted. "You want to live, and I'm telling you that you can. What you have can be cured."

She tried to contradict, but he wouldn't allow it. He spoke the words into her exhausted face: "You have a curable disease." Like Richard before her, she had been diagnosed, given what she considered a sentence of death. All she wanted was to be allowed to embrace this sentence with speed.

"I want to die," she said. It was essential that this man, holding her hand at the behest of the hospital, understood that she wanted no further chemotherapy, no further talk. Perhaps he would report on her condition to the chief of the hospital. Perhaps if she could convince Richard of the need for her death, he would recommend that action. All she wanted was something to kill the pain, to kill it forever in one wild rush of white sleep.

"Look at me," said Richard, speaking with a sudden violence that sharpened her attention. "I have cancer. And I'm alive. And I am in the process of being cured completely." Richard could see the astonishment in her beautiful eyes, and wanted to keep her at that level of astonishment, at that place of wonder where anything would seem possible, even in the darkest moments, even when the fear of death was outweighed by the pain of staying alive.

He had told his story many times, to many victims. But each time he told the story, its words brought back his own urge to die, an urge that had seemed irresistible. Until a force greater than any he had ever known had entered him, releasing hope with the overwhelming sense of epiphany. "I wanted to die too," said Richard.

There were many volunteer jobs less taxing that he could have taken at the hospital: in the library, at admissions, in the gift shop; but what Richard had experienced must be shared with other victims. What he knew was worth any effort to bring to people on the verge of death. He had been healed not by sophisticated drug therapy alone, but by allowing love into his spirit. It had been his fight, his determination to survive that had taken him this far, but such determination had not sprung out of thin air. It had come from the touch of his lover's hands.

But Richard didn't speak to cancer patients of spiritual healing, of inexplicable flashes of light, of renewed belief in the
human soul. That would be for them to discover on their own,
when they would grow strong enough to free themselves from
anger and fear, when they would feel the purest part of themselves, the part that was not of the body, give of its strength to
their flesh. What he needed to tell them was that he had been
there, prepared to die, and that he had learned to fight back.
What he had volunteered to do was shout at those filled with
hopelessness the fact that their disease could not only be fought,
but could be beaten. What brought him back to the hospital two
and three times a month was not gratitude for his life, nor guilt
at surviving what so many others had succumbed to; it was the
chance of opening someone's heart to the love that would fuel
their spirit.

"You're not a doctor?" said the young dancer after he had
told her his story.

"Haven't you been listening to me?" said Richard. "Besides,
do I look like the kind of guy who wants to hang around sick
people all day? I'm an artist, a sculptor. I hang out downtown,
and I sleep till noon."

She smiled at him for the first time, but then the smile turned
suddenly solemn. "Did your hair fall out?"

"Sure."

"But it grew again?"

"You're looking at it, honey," he said. "It fell out and it grew
back. More than once. I wore a baseball cap too. Mets, not Yankees. But I didn't look as good as you in yours." He reassured
her about the hair, because that was the easiest thing to talk about
truly. Less simple was talking about the repeated trips to the
hospital, especially in the first year. He had spent over a hundred
days in a hospital bed, stuck with needles, fatigued and hot with
fever, waiting for the nausea to hit. Without Lizzie's touch, he
never would have survived the first weeks of remission induction. But it was his own desire to live that got him through three
depressing and debilitating weeks of consolidation therapy; that
and what he had come to believe about the untold strength of his
newly awakened spirit. Richard did not forgo drug treatment,
but his deeply felt belief that his spirit held the key to the action
of the body made this treatment bearable. He believed that his

spirit had absolutely refused to return his body to a cancerous condition; certainly this belief had eased the acute discomfort of the maintenance chemotherapy he had been undergoing for two solid years.

"How many times did it grow back?" said the young dancer.

"As many times as it fell out, of course," said Richard, running his fingers through his hair.

"I just want to know, if you could tell me," she said.

Elizabeth entered the room as he continued discoursing on the fate of his hair. He could feel her presence like an infusion of strength to his spirit; he wondered if the dancer's trammeled spirit could feel the healer's presence in the room, if it might at that moment already be straining forward for Lizzie's dear touch. The barrier surrounding the dancer's center would not stand much longer.

"It has to do with the chemo, of course. You know that. And everyone reacts differently." Richard could see her eyes lift over his head to take in the new visitor to her room.

"You," she said, a bit more circumspectly. "How did you react?"

"Every time, sweetheart," said Richard. "Every time I'd get a treatment, I'd be a skinhead. And every time it would grow back."

"Every time," said the young dancer. But she did not take happily to this fact, but instead let it pull her into the dark place. "You mean even after it grows back, it's going to fall out again. All over again!" She cried then, crying hard enough to shake the IV line, crying so hard about the hair on her head that for a few good moments she forgot about her fear and her pain. Richard was happy she hadn't asked about the pills he took every single day, or the injections he needed twice a month, or the dreaded spinal taps. She could have asked about the chances of a relapse in one year, or two years, or three years; she could have questioned the clinical definition of being a survivor simply by not having a relapse within a span of five years. She could have demanded that Richard answer whether she would ever again dance on stage before a thousand admirers.

Elizabeth came up behind Richard and put her hands on his shoulders. She knew he was tired from the effort to get through the young woman's despair; she knew too that he had come to believe the touch of her hands brought energy through his spirit into his body. Two years and two months ago he had woken in his hospital bed in her arms, her eyes puffy from tears of joy. Before he said a word, she knew that his pain had lessened, that his sleep had been deeper, that his urge to suicide had turned around in the night. Then he had spoken, and he had told her that he loved her, and that he knew somehow she had helped him through the hardest night of his life.

Elizabeth did not quite understand what, if anything, she had done. Day by day, as he grew stronger and more optimistic, he had made fanciful claims: that he had been near death until the touch of her hands had healed him; that he needed her touch and her love more than the drugs they were pouring into his veins; that he could feel the strength of her spirit as clearly as he could see her image before his eyes.

"All that matters is that you're getting better," she had said. But she knew as well as he that more than his particular dread bout with leukemia was at stake. She was a doctor, and her view of the process of healing had been logical, with a reasoned knowledge of the limits of hope. Now reason had been turned on its head. Hope seemed appropriate in places where statistical expectations promised nothing but death. Richard's getting better was a miracle that they had shared, a sublime moment in which despair had been turned about in its filthy tracks through the power of loving spirits. But such a miracle could happen again. Such a miracle suggested the possibility of a power beyond the physical world; or at least a physical power that was as yet unseen, inexplicable.

"Is she a nurse?" demanded the young dancer, focusing some of her pain on the stranger. Elizabeth was glad that she had remembered to remove her white coat and name tag. Sad experience had taught her when the authority figure of a doctor might contribute to the process of healing, and when it might do nothing but harm.

"This is Elizabeth Grant," said Richard, leaving the fact of her occupation out of the introduction. "She is my wife."

"You're married."

"Yes. We were married last year." Richard answered the question she had not yet asked. "After I'd been through remission induction and consolidation therapy. But this girl was crazy enough to want to marry me even when I had just checked in."

"Like your boyfriend," said Elizabeth.

"I don't have a boyfriend."

"He's outside."

"I don't want to see him."

"Sweetheart, of course you want to see him," said Elizabeth. Richard stood up, letting go of the young woman's hand. Elizabeth took his seat at the bedside, and brought her hands to either side of the dancer's face. She knew what ritual she was performing now; she understood that all her reassuring words were but a frame for the loving touch of her hands. "He's been waiting to see you for days."

"I don't want to . . ." said the young woman, letting the sentence trail off as she felt Elizabeth's warmth. Though she disliked being touched by strangers, there was nothing strange about Elizabeth's hands on her cheeks, but rather something familiar. The young woman concentrated, closing her eyes, as if she might remember where and when she had felt what she was feeling now.

"Sweetheart," said Elizabeth again, "you'll want to see him very soon. But there's no rush. Okay? I'll just sit with you awhile."

"Yes," said the young woman softly, not wanting this feeling to go away, not wishing to move too fast, or speak too suddenly, because somehow the pain had let go a tiny part of its hold on her body; and all she wanted, all she prayed for was that this relief would never end. "Yes, sit with me."

Elizabeth smiled, shutting her eyes like the dancer in her hands. She wondered, as she always did at this moment, what madness allowed her to believe that her presence, her touch, achieved anything more than Richard's peace of mind. He was convinced of her power, spoke with the easy assurance of the true believer. But what on earth did she believe?

"You will get well, darling," said Elizabeth softly, and she felt herself easing away, bit by bit from the doubts and fears in which she lived. There was no harm in holding a patient bereft of hope, and giving her warmth, surrounding her despair with love and human kindness. It was not as if she had given up surgery and joined a commune of faith healers. But then again, it was not as if she believed that the touch of her hands was useless.

For how could she?

The nurses knew, and Laney, her friend in orthopedics knew, and Richard's oncologist knew, and certainly a few surgeons knew.

And those patients she and Richard had helped knew.

But knew what? she thought.

Knew that Richard counseled cancer victims, and that she joined him, adding her life-affirming presence to her husband's talk? Knew that she was moved to touch these patients, to hold them gently, to spend hours alone with them so that they would be convinced of someone's care? Knew that she would be so debilitated by the intimate experience of being with a patient that she would only do so when she had no surgery scheduled the following day?

But did they know that she could feel the pull of the spirit in the young woman's flesh? Did they know that every minute spent with her hands on a patient drew her deeper and deeper into a view of the world that she had always been taught to despise? Did they know that her dreams were now filled with the grateful sounds of comforted spirits, that she slept in Richard's arms with the peace of a child?

Unless what they knew was that she was, as Richard claimed, a healer. Not a "simple" healer like Richard, who could use the fact of his own survival as a means to instill belief. Not only a healer of the flesh, as she had been trained to be, understanding the structure and function of organs, the biology of the cell, the limitations of diagnosis and treatment. Not a technician to the body, but a healer of the spirit.

"It is very natural," said Elizabeth to the young dancer, "to refuse to see your loved one at a time like this. Richard was just the same. But then he changed. He let me in. And I think it helped him."

"He doesn't want to see me," insisted the young dancer, but too quietly, too gently imploring to be taken as anything more than another cry for the love she craved. Elizabeth didn't bother to contradict her. She could feel the dancer's spirit loosen itself from despair, move slowly toward the healer's warmth, from darkness to the chance of light. Soon, the surgeon would stop wondering whether what she was feeling might be a delusion. The need to differentiate what was real from what was fancy would soon be as irrelevant as separating the material from the immaterial, the body from the soul. All Elizabeth's concerns would be pushed out by those of the spirit before her, reaching for her help with a desire overwhelming everything else in the world.

It seemed only another moment before Richard gently brushed his lips against her cheeks. "It's late," he whispered, and Elizabeth blinked against the single lamp in the dark room, and when he kissed her again, she woke more fully. Carefully, she withdrew her hands from the dancer's sleeping form, feeling the separation like a tender break in her heart. But the young woman didn't wake.

"She's better," said Richard. He spoke of no medical evidence, but only of the expression on her face, all the angry lines gentled into a semblance of peace. Before all the doubts could return to flood her consciousness, Elizabeth knew too that the young dancer was better, and infinitely so. What had been closed was now open, what had been a wish to die was now a determination to live.

"Is he still waiting?" said Elizabeth. She did not know how long she had held her hands to the dancer's flesh, but only that the sun had set, that her belly was empty, and that she felt suffused with a rare joy.

"Yes," said Richard. Quietly, he left the room, leaving Elizabeth to make her farewell to the young woman as he went off to find her boyfriend.

"You will be well," said Elizabeth. She stood now, and there were tears in her eyes, because every step she took back from the self-composed ritual removed her from the place of the spirit. "You must be well," she said, and the silent words, repeated again and again in a dull, insistent litany, were not just for the dancer.

The words were for Richard too, soon to remove his body from the maintenance chemotherapy of two years' duration, trusting his flesh to the vagaries of fate; and for her surgical patients, trusting their bodies to the onslaught of anesthesia and the cutting of her knife. The words went out from her heart to sufferers of disease everywhere, unsure of how much to trust their bodies to the magical intrusions of technology, and how much to trust to faith. "You must be well," she said a final time, catching a glimmer of the world at large, poised at a crossroads between a chance for universal peace and self-annihilation.

Richard came back, the dancer's boyfriend behind him, his eyes moving to the sweetly sleeping girl. "We'll go now," Richard whispered. The boyfriend, awed by the powerful forces in the tiny room, sat down at the bedside chair, claiming his place near the center of struggle. Elizabeth backed away. She would let the boyfriend's love take the place of her healing in the dancer's spirit.

"She will be well," said Elizabeth quietly. "You must believe that she will be well." In that moment, Elizabeth believed too; not that the dancer could be well, but that she would be well; not that love bathed the mind in a comfortable glow, but that it succored the spirit, returning tranquility and health to the body that was its earthly frame. It was her task to try and carry that moment into her life, past the fact of death, the failed operations, the damaged lives assembled before her in the hospital like a sorry twisting of humanity. It was her quest to travel back to a world of belief, without letting go of the knowledge of the present; to return to and join with an ancient line of healers, each possessed of faith and the power to bring that faith to others, without losing sight of the material world. Elizabeth didn't know if it was possible to treat both spirit and flesh, when her heart told her that fleshly ills were only reflections of spiritual distress, while her mind told her that flesh was all there was.

But when she held Richard in her arms, and felt the stuff of life beating through his skin, her love for him let her see through dark subjects, let her imagine immensities, let the vastness of the world be encompassed in her heart. He had been sick to death, and it was his spirit that she cured; his body had been out of control, and the drugs of the modern world had returned this control to him. But there would have been no cure unless he had been ready to receive it; and no frame left for the spirit unless the body had been made well with speed.

Surely there would be a time when anger and stress and war would be unknown, when calm spirits would live in bodies as clean and glowing with health as ancient sun-washed temples.

But until that time Elizabeth would remember the compromise that love showed her; that spirit and flesh must be treated together, for both existed with and for the other. Holding Richard tight, she loved him inside and out, spirit and flesh. And beyond the walls of his body she felt the love of his spirit like a flame reaching out through the night.

MAY 0 3 1986

85-29367
87 A

Gross, Joel
    Spirit in the flesh.   1986 $17

CY
BALTIMORE COUNTY
PUBLIC LIBRARY
COCKEYSVILLE AREA BRANCH

T

0525244182